She woke fro[m] ... ,
grateful for a ... f
danger. Starlig[h] ... n
was dark but f ... .
Slowly, silentl[y] ... g
up the sword ... -
foot, she went to the door and pulled it open. A black passageway faced her. The sense of danger increased; on an impulse, she called her light.

The entire passage was filled with webbing, strand after strand looped in an intricate pattern that centered on the door of Paks's room. And a black presence hung in the web, scarcely an arm's length away.

"Well, are you less eager to meet me?" The voice was strangely sweet. Paks could see no detail of the presence, could not tell shape or even size. She drew the sword. Its hilt comforted her hand.

"I am always eager to meet evil," said Paks, "with a blade."

"Silly girl, I had you in Aarenis, and in Kolobia. You are tainted with my venom; when I call, you will answer."

"No." Paks heard the squires behind her, and waved them back. "By the power of the High Lord, and the grace of Gird, I am not your creature. And by that power I command you to leave this hall."

"And where will I go, sheepfarmer's daughter? You are mortal still; you cannot be with all you love. You can save yourself: can you save them?" Paks saw her home in that instant: father, mother, brothers, sisters, and thrust the thought aside. She sensed a movement in the darkness, and braced herself.

The darkness thickened, leaped forward; Paks raised the elf-forged blade.

The Deed of Paksenarrion

Sheepfarmer's Daughter
Divided Allegiance
Oath of Gold

ELIZABETH MOON

OATH OF
GOLD

THE DEED OF
PAKSENARRION
BOOK III

BAEN

OATH OF GOLD

A Baen Books Original

Baen Publishing Enterprises
260 Fifth Avenue
New York, N.Y. 10001

First printing, January 1989

ISBN: 0-671-69798-6

Cover art by Kevin Davies

Printed in the United States of America

Distributed by
SIMON & SCHUSTER
1230 Avenue of the Americas
New York, N.Y. 10020

Oath of blood is Liart's bane
Oath of death is for the slain
Oath of stone the rockfolk swear
Oath of iron is Tir's domain
Oath of silver liars dare
Oath of gold will yet remain . . .
from the Oathsong of Mikeli

Chapter One

The village seemed faintly familiar, but most villages were much alike. Not until she came to the crossroads with its inn did she realize she had been here before. There was the paved inn court, and the wide door, and the bright sign—The Jolly Potboy—hanging over it. Her breath seemed to freeze in her chest. The crossroads was busier than she remembered; there was much bustling in and out of the inn. The windows to the common bar were wide open, and clear across the road she heard a roar of laughter she recognized. She flinched. They might recognize her, even in the clothes she wore now. She thought of the coins in her purse, and the meal she'd hoped to buy—but she could not go there, of all places, and order a meal of Jos Hebbinford. Nor was there any other place to go: she was known in Brewersbridge, and dared not beg a scrap from some housewife lest she be recognized.

Paks shook her head, fighting back tears. Once she had ridden these streets—stayed at that inn—had friends in every gathering.

"Here now, why so glum?" Paks started and looked up to see a man-at-arms in the Count's livery watching her. He smiled when she met his eyes; his face was vaguely familiar. "We can't have pretty girls down in the mouth in our town, sweetling—let me buy you a mug of ale and cheer you up."

Paks felt her heart begin to pound; fear clouded her

eyes. "No—no thank you, sir. I'm fine—I just thought of something—"

The man's eyes narrowed. "You're frightened. Is someone after you? This town's safe enough—that's my job. You look like you need some kind of help; let me know what's wrong—"

Paks tried to edge around him, toward the north road. "No—please, sir, I'm all right."

He reached out and caught her arm. "I don't think so. You remind me of something—someone. I think perhaps the captain needs to see you—unless you can account better for yourself. Do you know anyone here, anyone who can vouch for you? Where were you going to stay? Are you here for the fair?"

For an instant Paks's mind went totally blank, and then the names and faces of those she remembered—Marshal Cedfer, Hebbinford, Captain Sir Felis, Master Senneth—began to race past her eyes. But she couldn't call on them to vouch for her. They had known her as a warrior, Phelan's veteran, the fighter who cleaned out a den of robbers. She had left here to go to Fin Panir; they had expected her to return as a Marshal or knight. Even if they recognized her—and she doubted they would—they would still despise or pity her. She trembled in the man's grasp like a snared rabbit, and he was already pushing her along the north road toward the keep when another memory came to her: a memory of quiet trees and a clear pool and the dark wise face of the Kuakgan.

"I—I was going to the grove," she gasped. "To—to see the Kuakgan."

The man stopped, still gripping her arm. "Were you, now? And do you know the Kuakgan's name?"

"Master Oakhallow," said Paks.

"And you were to stay there?"

"I—I think so, sir. I had a question to ask him, that's why I came." Paks realized as she said this that it was true.

"Hmm. Well—if it's kuakgannir business—you say you were going to the grove: can you show me where it is?"

The entrance to the grove lay a hundred paces or so along the road; Paks nodded toward it.

"You know that much at least. Well, I'll just see you safely there. And remember, girl: I don't expect to see you dodging around town this evening. If I do, it's to the captain with you. And I'll have the watch keep a lookout, too." He urged her along until they came to the grove entrance, marked by white stones on the ground between two trees. "You're sure this is where you're going?"

Paks nodded. "Yes, sir—thank you." She turned away, ducking into the trees to follow the winding path picked out in white stones.

In the grove was silence. Sunlight filtered through green leaves. As before, she could hear nothing of the village, close as it was. A bird sang nearby, three rising notes, over and over. Paks stopped to listen; her trembling stilled. Something rustled in the bushes off to her left, and panic rose in her throat. When a brown rabbit hopped onto the path, she almost sobbed in relief.

She went on. Far over her head leaves rustled in a light wind, but it was quiet below. Under one tree she heard a throbbing hum, and looked up to see a haze of bees busy at the tiny yellow flowers. At last she heard the remembered chuckling of the Kuakgan's fountain, and came into the sunny glade before his dwelling. It was the same as on her first visit. The low gray bark-roofed house was shuttered and still. Nothing moved but the water, leaping and laughing in sunlight over a stone basin.

Paks stood a moment in the sunlight, watching that water. She thought of what she'd told the soldier, and how the lie had felt like truth when she told it. But there was no help for her, not this time. The Kuakgan had nothing to do with what she had lost. Kuakkganni didn't like warriors anyway. Still—she had to stay, at least until night. She could not go back to the village. Maybe she could sneak through the grove and escape to the open country beyond. Paks sighed. She was so tired of running, tired of hiding from those who'd known her. Yet she could not face them. Make an end, she thought.

She slid out of the pack straps, and dug into the pack for her pouch of coins, the reserve the Marshal-General had given her. To it she added the coppers and two silvers from her belt-pouch. A tidy pile. Enough to live on for a month, if she were frugal; enough for one good feast, otherwise. Her mouth twisted. She scooped up the whole pile and dumped it in the offering basin; the clash and ring of it was loud and discordant. She looked in her pack for anything else of value. Nothing but her winter cloak, an extra shirt, spare boot-thongs—no—there was the ring Duke Phelan had given her the day he left Fin Panir. "Send this, or bring it, if you need me," he'd said. Paks stared at it. She didn't want it found on her when she— She pushed the thought aside and tossed the ring onto the heap of coins. She looked at her pack and decided to leave that too. The Kuakgan would find someone who needed a cloak and shirt. She piled the pack on top of the money, and turned away, wondering where she could hide until nightfall. Perhaps she should start through the grove now.

Across the clearing, at one end of the gray house, the Kuakgan stood watching her, his face shadowed by the hood of his robe. Paks froze; her heart began to race. His voice came clear across the sound of the fountain, and yet it was not loud. "You wished to speak to the Kuakgan?"

Paks felt cold, but sweat trickled down her ribs. "Sir, I—I came only to make an offering."

The Kuakgan came closer. His robe, as she remembered, was dark green, patterned in shades of green and brown with the shapes of leaves and branches. "I see. Most who make offerings here wish a favor in return. Advice, a potion, a healing—and you want nothing?" His voice, too, was as she remembered, deep and resonant, full of overtones. As if, she thought suddenly, he had spent much time with elves. His eyes, now visible as he came closer, seemed to pierce her with their keen glance.

"No. No, sir, I want nothing." Paks dropped her gaze, stared at the ground, hoping he would not recognize her, would let her go.

"Is it, then, an offering of thanks? Have you received

some gift, that you share your bounty? Not share, I see, for you have given everything—even your last copper. Can you say why?"

"No, sir." Paks sensed that he had come nearer yet, to the offering basin, still watching her.

"Hmm. And yet I heard someone very like you tell a soldier that she wished to speak with me, to ask me a question. Then I find you in my grove, filling the basin with your last coin, and even your spare shirt—and you have no question." He paused. Paks watched as the shadow of his robe came closer. She shivered. "But I have questions, if you do not. Look at me!" At his command, Paks's head seemed to rise of its own accord. Her eyes filled with tears. "Mmm, yes. You came to me once before for advice, if I recall. Was my counsel so bad that you refuse it now—Paksenarrion?"

Paks could not speak for the lump in her throat; tears ran down her face. She tried to turn away, but his strong hand caught her chin and held her facing him.

"Much, I see, has happened to you since I last saw you. But I think you are not a liar, whatever you've become. So you will ask your question, Paksenarrion, and take counsel with me once again."

Paks fought the tightness in her throat and managed to speak. "Sir, I—I can't. There's nothing you can do—just let me go—"

"Nothing I can do? Best let me judge of that, child. As for going—where would you go, without money or pack?"

"Anywhere. East, or south to the hills . . . it doesn't matter—"

"There's enough dead bones in those hills already. No, you won't go until you've told me what your trouble is. Come now."

Paks found herself walking behind the Kuakgan to his house, her mind numb. She saw without amazement the door open before he reached it; he ducked slightly to clear the low lintel. Paks ducked too, and stepped down onto the cool earthen floor of a large, long room. Across from her, windows opened on the grove which came almost to the Kuakgan's house. The ceiling beams were hung with bunches of pungent herbs. At the far end of the room gaped a vast fireplace, its hearth swept and empty. Under the windows were two tables, one covered with scrolls, and the other bare, with a bench near it.

"Come," said the Kuakgan. "Sit here and have something to drink."

Paks sank onto the bench and watched as he poured her a mug of clear liquid from an earthenware jug. She sipped. It was water, but the water had a spicy tang.

"Mint leaves," he said. "And a half-stick of cinnamon. Here—" He reached down a round cheese from a net hanging overhead. He sliced off a good-sized hunk. "Eat something before we talk."

Paks was sure she could not eat, but the creamy cheese eased past her tight throat and settled her stomach. She finished the cheese and the second mug of water he poured her. By then he had sliced a half-loaf of dark bread and put it in front of her. She took a slice; it was nutty and rich.

Master Oakhallow sat at the end of the table, his hood pushed back, eating a slice of bread spread with cheese. Paks glanced at him: the same brown weather-beaten face, heavy dark eyebrows, thick hair tied off his face with a twisted cord the color of bark. He was gazing out the window beside him, frowning slightly. She followed his gaze. A black and white spotted bird clung to the trunk of the nearest tree; as she watched, it began to hammer on the bark. The strokes were loud and quick, almost like a drum rattle. Paks wondered why its head didn't split. She'd never seen anything like it, though she had heard that sound before without knowing its source. Bark chips flew from the tree.

"It's a woodpecker," he said, answering her thought. "It seeks out insects under the bark, and eats them. A forest without woodpeckers would be eaten by the little ones devouring the trees."

Paks felt her muscles unclenching, one by one. "Is it—are there more than one kind?"

The Kuakgan smiled. "Oh, yes. Most of them are speckled and spotted, but some are brown and white or gray and white, instead of black and white. There are little ones and big ones—bigger than this—and many of them have bright color at the head. This one has a yellow stripe, but it's hard to see so far away."

"How can they pound the tree like that without hurting themselves?"

He shrugged. "They are made for it; it is their nature. Creatures are not harmed by following their natures. How else can horses run over rocky ground on those tiny hooves? Tiny for their weight, I mean." He reached to the jug and poured another mug of water for Paks, and one for himself.

Paks took another slice of bread. "I heard a bird when I came in; it sang three notes—" she tried to whistle them.

"Yes, I know the one. A shy bird. You'll never see it; it's brown on top, and speckled gray and brown below. It eats gnats and flies, and its eggs are green patterned with brown."

"I thought most birds—except the hawks and carrion-crows—ate seeds."

"Some do. Most sparrows are seed-eaters. There's one bird that eats the nuts out of pine cones. Watch, now—" He took a slice of bread and crumbled it on the broad windowsill, then took a slender wooden cylinder from his robe and blew into it. A soft trill of notes came out. Paks saw the flickering of wings between the trees, and five birds landed on the sill. She sat still. Three of the birds were alike, green with yellow breasts. One was brown, and one was fire-orange with black wings. Their tiny eyes glittered as they pecked the crumbs and watched her. When the bread was gone, the Kuakgan moved his hand and the birds flew away.

Paks breathed again. "They're so beautiful. I never saw anything so beautiful—that orange and black one—"

"So. You will admit that you haven't seen everything in this world you were so eager to leave?"

She hunched her shoulders, silent. She heard a gusty sigh, then the scrape of his stool as he rose.

"Stay here," he said, "until I return."

She did not look up, but heard his feet on the floor as he crossed the room, and the soft thud of the door as he closed it behind him. She thought briefly of going out the window, but the grove was thick and dark there as the sun lowered. The spotted bird was gone, the hammering coming now from a distance. She put down the rest of her slice of bread, her appetite gone. The room darkened. She wondered if he would be gone all night; she looked around but saw no place to sleep but the floor. From the grove came a strange cry, and she shivered, remembering the rumor that the Kuakgan walked at night as a great bear.

She did not hear the door open, but he was suddenly in the room with her. "Come help me bring in some wood," he said, and she got up and went out to find a pile of deadwood by the door. The last sunglow flared to the west. They broke the wood into lengths and brought it in. He lit candles and placed them in sconces along the walls, then laid a fire in the fireplace, but did not light it. He went out again and came back with a bundle that turned out to be a hot kettle wrapped in cloth. Inside, a few coals kept several pannikins warm. As he unwrapped the cloth, a delicious smell of onions and mushrooms and meat gravy rose from the kettle. Paks found her mouth watering, and swallowed.

"Hebbinford's best stew," he said, setting the dishes out on the tables. "And you were always one for fried mushrooms, weren't you? Sit down, go on—don't let it get cold. You're too thin, you know."

"I'm not hungry," said Paks miserably.

"Nonsense. I saw your look when you smelled those mushrooms. Your body's got sense, if you haven't."

Paks took a bite of mushrooms: succulent, hot, flavored with onions and meat. Before she realized what she was doing, she saw that the mushrooms were gone, and so was the stew. She was polishing the bowl with another slice of the dark bread. Her belly gurgled its contentment; she could not remember when she'd eaten so much. Not for a long time, not since—she looked up. Master Oakhallow was watching her.

"Dessert," he said firmly. "Plum tart or apple?"

"Apple," said Paks, and he pushed the tart across. She bit into the flaky crust; sweet apple juice ran down her chin. When the tart was gone, the Kuakgan was still eating his. Paks cleaned her chin with a corner of the cloth that had been around the kettle. She found herself holding another slice of bread, and ate that. She felt full and a little sleepy. He finished his tart and looked at her.

"That's better," he said. "Now. You'll want to wash up a bit, and use the jacks, I expect. Let me show you—" He touched a panel beside the fireplace, and it slid aside to reveal a narrow passage. On one side was a door, through which Paks caught a glimpse of a bunk. On the other, a door opened on three steps down to a stone-flagged room with a channel along one side. Paks heard the gurgle of moving water, and the candlelight sparkled on its surface. "Cold water only," said Master Oakhallow. "There's the soaproot, and a towel—" He lit other candles in the chamber as he spoke. "If you're tired of those clothes, you can wear this robe." He pointed to a brown robe hanging from a peg. "Now, I'll be out for awhile. When you're through go on back to the other room. Whatever you do, don't go outside the house. Is that clear?"

"Yes, sir," said Paks. "I won't."

"Good." He turned and went back up the stairs; Paks saw the light of his candle dwindle down the passage.

The little room was chilly and damp, but smelled clean and earthy. Paks started to wash her hands, gingerly, but the cold water merely tingled instead of biting. She splashed it on her face, started to dry it, then glanced warily at the door. Surely he was really gone. She went up the steps and looked. Nothing. She came back down and looked at the water for a moment, then grunted and stripped off her clothes: she felt caked in dirt and sweat. She wet the soaproot and scrubbed herself, then stood in the channel and scooped water over her soapy body. By the time she was through, she was shivering, but vigorous towelling warmed her again. She looked at her clothes and wished she had not put her spare shirt in the offering basin. Her clothes were as dirty as she had been. She looked at the brown robe, then took it off the peg. It was soft and warm. When she came from the jacks, she looked at her clothes again. She wondered if she could wash them in the channel, but decided against it: she needed hot water and a pot. She shook them hard, brushed them with her hand, and folded them into a bundle. She slipped her bare feet back into her worn boots and went up the steps, down the passage, and into the main room.

The Kuakgan had lit more candles before he left, and the room had a warm glow. He had drawn shutters across the windows; she was glad of that. She sat down at the table to wait, wondering how long he would be. She thought of where she'd expected to be this night—alone in the hills, perhaps to see no dawn—and shivered, looking around her quickly. This was pleasant: the soft robe on her shoulders, the good meal. Why didn't I ever—? I could have bought mushrooms at least once— She pushed these thoughts away. She wondered where the Kuakgan was, and if he'd bought the meal with her offering. And most of all—what was he going to do? She thought she should be afraid, but she wasn't.

She eased into sleep without knowing it, leaning on the table; she never knew when he came in. When she woke again, she was wrapped in a green blanket and lying on the floor against the wall. The windows were unshuttered and sunlight struck the tree trunks outside. She felt completely relaxed and wide awake at the same time. Her stomach rumbled. She was just unwrapping the blanket when the door opened, letting in a shaft of sunlight.

"Time for breakfast," said the Kuakgan as he came in. He carried a dripping honeycomb over a bowl. Paks felt her mouth water. She climbed out of the blanket, folded it, and came to the table where he was laying out cheese, bread, and the honeycomb. "You won't have had this honey before," he said. "It's yellowwood honey, an early spring honey, and they never make much of it." He glanced at her and smiled. "You slept well."

Paks found herself smiling in return. "Yes . . . yes, sir, I did." She sat down.

"Here," he said, pouring from the jug. "It's goat's milk. Put some honey in your mug with it."

Paks broke off a piece of comb and floated it in the milk. He sliced the cheese and pushed some towards her. She sipped the milk; it was delicious. The honey had a tang to it as well as sweetness. The Kuakgan dripped some on his cheese; Paks did the same, and had soon eaten half a cheese, each slice dripping honey. Bees flew in the window and settled on the remains of the comb.

"No, little sisters," said the Kuakgan. "We have need of this." He hummed briefly, and the bees flew away. Paks stared at him; he smiled.

"Do you really talk to bees?" she asked.

"Not talk, exactly. It's more like singing; they're a musical folk. They dance, too; did you know that?" Paks shook her head, wondering if he was teasing. "It's quite true; I'll show you someday."

"Can you speak with all the animals? Those birds yesterday, and bees—"

"It's a Kuakgan's craft to learn the nature of all creatures: trees and grass as well as birds, beasts, and bees. When you know what something is—what its nature is, how it fits into the web of life—you can then begin to speak its language. It's a slow craft; living things are various, and each one is different."

"Some mages speak to animals," said Paks.

The Kuakgan snorted. "Mages! That's different. That's like the ring you had. A mage, now, wants power for himself. If he speaks to an animal, it's for his own purposes. Kuakkganni—we learn their languages because we love them: the creatures. Love them as they are, and for what they were made. When I speak to the owl that nests in that ash—" he nodded to the window, "it is not to make use of him, but to greet him. Of course, I must admit we do get some power from it. We can ask them things; we know their nature. But we are the ones who serve all created things without wanting to change them. That's why the Marshal in the grange is never quite sure I'm good enough to be an ally."

Paks watched him, feeling that she should be able to find some other meaning in what he said, something that would apply to her. She could not think of anything. She wondered when he would start to question her.

He sat back from the table and looked at her. "Well, now. Your clothes are drying on the bushes out there, but they'd be clammy yet. You'll be more comfortable outside in something other than that robe, I daresay." He rose and went to a chest near the wall. "This will fit close enough." He held out homespun trousers with a drawstring waist, and a linen shirt. "Come outside when you're ready; I want to show you something." He went out the door and shut it behind him.

Paks looked at the clothes. They were creased as if they'd been in the chest a long time. She fingered the cloth, looking nervously at the windows. She looked for the passage beside the fireplace, but the panel was closed, and she couldn't find the touchlock. At last she sat on the floor beside the table, breathing fast, and changed from the robe to the pants and shirt. She put on her belt over the shirt and looked for her dagger; it was on the table.

When she pushed on the door, it opened silently. Outside, the sunny glade seemed empty, until she saw the Kuakgan standing motionless by the end of the stone-marked path. He gestured to her, and she walked across the glade.

"You must stay near me," he said. "The grove is not safe for wanderers; experienced pathfinders cannot be sure of its ways. If we are separated, be still. I will find you. Nothing will harm you as long as you are still, or with me. It may be that I have to leave you suddenly . . . I hope not, but it might happen. Just stay where I left you. You will find enough beauty to watch until I come back." He began to move through the trees, as silent as a current of air; Paks followed closely. From time to time he stopped, and touched a tree or herb lightly, but he said nothing, and Paks was silent as well. As the morning warmed, more birds sang around them, and the rich scents of leafmold and growing things rose from the ground. Paks found herself breathing slowly, deeply. She had no idea where they were in the grove, but it didn't matter. She began to look with more attention to the trees and bushes they walked past. The Kuakgan touched a tree trunk: Paks saw a tiny lichen, bright as flame, glowing against dark furrowed bark. She saw for herself a clump of tiny mushrooms, capped in shiny red—a strawberry in flower—a fern-frond uncurling out of dry leaves. She realized that the Kuakgan was standing still, watching her. When she met his eyes, he nodded.

Chapter Two

So passed the rest of that day, with the warm spring sun and the silence unknotting the muscles of back and neck that had been tight so long. They came on a tiny trickle of clear water, and drank; for awhile in the early afternoon they sat near a mound of stone, and Paks fell asleep. When she woke, the Kuakgan was gone, but before she had stretched more than twice, she saw him coming through the trees. From time to time her mind would reach for the memory of yesterday's pain, but she could not touch it: it was as if a pane of heavy glass lay between that reality and this. She could not think what she might do next, or where to go, and at last she quit trying.

They came back to the Kuakgan's house in the last of the sunlight. Paks took her clothes, now dry, from the bushes, and folded them in her arms. She felt pleasantly tired, and slightly hungry. The Kuakgan smiled.

"Sit here in the warmth, while I bring supper," he said. "Or will you come with me?"

Paks thought of the inn, and the misery returned full strength. This time she felt the tension knotting her brow and hunching her shoulders, and tried to stand upright. But before she could frame an answer, the Kuakgan shook his head.

"No. Not yet. Stay. As I feared, it will take more than one day of healing." And he was gone, across the glade and along the path to the village.

She sat trembling, hating herself for the fear that had

slammed back into her mind. She could not even go to an inn—even here, where she had had friends, and no enemies. She stared at her hands, broad and scarred with the years of war. If she could not hold a sword or bow, what could she do? Not stay forever with the Kuakgan, that wouldn't do. Her hand felt for her belt pouch, and she remembered that she'd put it in the offering basin. Everything was gone; everything from those years had gone as if it had never been. Warriors can't keep much, but that little they prize; the loss of the last of her treasures to the kuaknom still hurt: Saben's little red horse, Canna's medallion. Now she had not even the Duke's ring left (the third ring, she thought ruefully, that he's given me and I've lost somehow).

As before, she wasn't sure how long the Kuakgan had been gone when he returned. He was simply there, in the evening dimness, carrying another kettle. She forced herself up as he came toward her. He nodded, and they went into the house together. This time she helped unpack the kettle, and made no protest at eating. He had brought slices of roast mutton swimming in gravy, redroots mashed with butter, and mushrooms. Again. She looked up, to say something about the cost, met his eyes, and thought better of it. She ate steadily, enjoying the food more than she expected to, but fearing the questions he would surely ask after supper.

But he said nothing, as long as she ate, and when she finished, and stacked her pans for return, he seemed to be staring through the opposite wall. His own dishes were empty; she reached for them, wiped them, and put them in the kettle. He looked at her suddenly, and smiled briefly.

"You're wondering when I will start to question you."

Paks looked down, then forced herself to meet his eyes. "Yes."

"I had thought tonight. But I changed my mind." A long silence. Paks looked away, around the room, back to his face. It was unreadable.

"Why?" she asked finally.

He sighed, and shook his head. "I'm not sure how—or how much—to tell you. Healing is a Kuakkganni craft, as you know." Paks nodded. "Well, then, one part of the healing craft is knowing when. When to act, and when to wait. In the case of humans, one must also know when to ask, and when to keep silent. You are not ready to speak of it, whatever it is."

Paks moved restlessly. "You—I would have thought you'd have heard something. . . ."

"Hmmm." It became as resonant as his comments to the bees. Paks looked at his face again. "I hear many things. Most of them false, as far as talk goes. Brewersbridge is a little out of the way for reliable news." He looked at her squarely. "And whatever I might have heard, what is important is you, yourself. Just as you, yourself, will heal when you are ready."

Paks looked away. She could feel the tears stinging her eyes again.

"There. You are not ready, yet. Don't worry; it will come. Let your body gain strength for a few days. You are already better, though you don't feel it."

"But I couldn't go—" her voice broke, and she covered her face with her hands.

"But that will pass. That will pass." She felt a wave of warmth and peace roll over her mind, and the pain eased again.

But several nights later, the dream returned. Once more she was fighting for her life far underground, tormented by thirst and hunger and the pain of her wounds. She smelled the rank stench of the green torches, and felt the blows of knife and whip that striped her sides. She gasped for breath, choked, scrabbled at the fingers knotted in her throat—and woke to find the Kuakgan beside her, holding her hands in his.

Soft candlelight lit the room. She stared wildly for a moment, lost in the dream, trembling with the effort of the fight.

"Be still," he said softly. "Don't try to talk. Do you know me yet?"

After a minute or two she nodded. Her tongue felt too big for her mouth, and she worked it around. "Master Oakhallow." Her voice sounded odd.

"Yes. You are safe. Lie still, now; I'll get you something to drink."

The mint-flavored water cleaned remembered horrors out of her mouth. She tried to sit up, but the Kuakgan pushed her down gently. A tremor shook her body; as she tried to fight it off, the pain of those wounds returned, sapping her strength.

"You still have pain?" he asked.

Paks nodded.

"How long ago were those wounds dealt?"

She tried to count back. Her mind blurred, then steadied. "From—it would have been last summer. Late in the summer."

"So long?" His eyebrows rose. "Hmm. What magic bound them?"

Paks shook her head. "I don't know. The paladin and Marshal both tried healing. It helped, but the—the kuaknom had done something to them—"

"Kuaknom! What were you doing with them?"

Paks looked down, shivering. "They captured me. In Kolobia."

"So. I don't wonder that you have grave difficulties. And they dealt these wounds that pain you now?"

"Not . . . exactly. It—" As the memory swept over her, Paks could not speak. She shook her head, violently. The Kuakgan caught it, and held her still.

"No more, then, tonight. Sleep." He answered the fear in her eyes before she could say it. "You won't dream again. That I can still, and you will rest as you did the first night, and wake at peace. Sleep." She fell into his voice, into the silence beyond it, and slept.

In the morning she woke rested, as he had promised. Still the shame of her breakdown was on her, and she came to the breakfast table silently and did not smile.

"You will not have those dreams again," he said quietly,

as she ate. "When I release your dreams again, those will be healed. This much I promise. I have waited as long as I could for your body's healing, Paksenarrion; it is now time to begin on the mind. Whatever ill you have suffered has clearly injured both."

She nodded, silent and intent on her bread.

"I will need to see these wounds you spoke of." He reached for her arm. Paks froze an instant, then stretched her hand out. He pushed up her sleeve. The red-purple welts were still swollen. "You have more of these?"

"Yes."

"Many?"

"Yes." Despite herself, she was shivering again.

"And they are all over a half-year old?" Paks nodded. "Powerful magic, then, and dangerous. Have they faded at all? How long did it take for them to heal this far?"

"They . . . fade sometimes," Paks said softly. "For a week or so, as if they were healing. Then they swell and redden again. At first—I don't know how long it was. I think only a day or so, but I lost track of time."

"I see. Have any true elves seen this?"

"Yes. One that came with us. He thought they had used something like the true elves use to speed and slow the growth of plants."

"Ah. It might be so, indeed. Perverted, as they would have it—to heal quickly partway and then stay so. But why that far?"

Paks fought a desire to roll into a ball like a hedgehog. It was harder to speak than she had expected; that was hard enough. "So—so I could fight."

"Fight?" The Kuakgan paused. When she said nothing, he went on. "You said they did not deal these wounds themselves. They wanted you able to fight, but hindered. And now you cannot fight. Was that their doing, too?"

"No." She could not say more. She heard the Kuakgan's sigh.

"I need to try something on one of the wounds. This will probably hurt." He took her arm, and held it lightly. Paks paid no attention. She felt the fingers of his other hand running along the scars. After a moment she felt a trickle of cold in one, then heat in another. The feelings ebbed. She glanced at his face; it was closed and remote. A savage ache ran up her arm from the wrist, and was gone instantly. A pain as sharp as the original blow brought a gasp from her; she glanced at her arm; the scar was darker than ever. Then it passed, and the Kuakgan's eyes came to focus on her again.

"The true elf was correct in his surmise. These will heal no better without intervention. Did he try?"

"He said he had not the skill. He had known one who had, but—"

"I see. Paksenarrion, this will take time and patience. It will not be easy for you; it is a matter of purifying the wounds of the poison they used. If you can bear the pain a short while longer, you should be strong enough in body for the healing. Can you?"

Paks forced a smile. "After these months? Of course."

His faced relaxed briefly. "Good. And now we must come to the other—it's not for this pain that you were ready to throw away your life. What else did they do to you?"

"Do I have to—? Now?"

"I think so. Healing those—getting that poison out—will take strength from us both. I must know what else is wrong, what reserves you have, before I start that." He started to gather up the remains of breakfast, though, as if it were any other morning. Paks sat where she was, unspeaking. After brushing crumbs onto the windowsill for the birds, he turned back to her. "It might be easier outside. Sunlight cleanses more than dirty linen. Come walk with me."

They had wandered an hour in the grove before Paks began to speak, starting with her first days in the training barracks at Fin Panir, and the sun was high overhead when she came to the kuaknomi lair. Even in the bright sunlight (for they had come again to the glade) she felt the darkness and the foulness of that place. Her words came short, and halted, but the Kuakgan did not prompt her.

The fountain's chuckling filled the silence until she spoke again.

"I could not say his name," she said finally. "I couldn't call on Gird. I tried, at first. I remember that. But after awhile . . . I couldn't say it. And I had to fight: whenever I woke again, they were there, and I had to fight." She told what she could remember of the battles in the arena, of her horror at seeing the great bloated spider that devoured those she defeated. "After awhile, I don't remember more. They said—those who came and found me—that I was wearing enchanted armor, and wore Achrya's symbol around my neck."

"Who found you?"

"Others in the expedition: Amberion, Marshal Lord Fallis, those. I don't remember that at all. They told me that after a day I was awake and talking to them clearly, but the next I remember is walking along a trail in another canyon, and finding the way to Luap's stronghold."

"So it was real—you found it?"

"Oh yes, it's real. A great citadel, deep in the rock, full of all kinds of magic." In her mind's eye the dark lairs were replaced by that soaring red rock arch between the outpost and the main stronghold. "We'd hardly be back to Fin Panir by now had it not had magic. That's how we came."

"Magic, then, but no healing?"

Paks stopped short. "No. Not for me, anyway." She went on to tell him what had happened when she returned to Fin Panir. How the Marshal-General had said she was deeply tainted with kuaknomi evil, and how she had come at last to agree. She shivered as she spoke, and the Kuakgan interrupted.

"Let's go back for supper. It's late." Already the sun was far behind the trees. When they came to the house, Paks feared to stay alone, and could not say it. But instead of leaving her, the Kuakgan came in and brought out bread and cheese. They ate in silence, and he seemed abstracted. After supper, for the first time, he lit a fire on the large hearth, and they sat before it.

"Now go on," he said. "But don't hurry yourself. What did your Marshal-General propose to do? Why did she think Gird had not protected you?"

"She didn't say why," said Paks, answering the last question first. "But I think they believe I was too new a Girdsman, and too vulnerable as a paladin candidate. They'd said we were more open to evil, in our training. She said that fighting under iynisin command had opened a passage for their evil into my mind. It could be taken out, but—" Paks broke off, steadied her voice, and went on, staring into the flames. "She said the evil was so close to the—to what made me a fighter, that to destroy it might destroy that too."

"And what did she say that was?"

"My courage." She barely breathed the words, but the pain in them rang through the room.

The Kuakgan hummed briefly. Paks sat rigid as a pike staff, waiting for his reaction. He reached a poker to the fire, and stirred it. Another pause, while sparks snapped up the chimney. "And now you are not a fighter. You think that is why?"

"I know it. Sir." Paks sat hunched, looking now at her hands locked in her lap.

"Because you know fear? Did you never fear before? I thought you were afraid of me, the first time I saw you. You were afraid of Master Zinthys's truth spell—you said so."

"Before, I could always face it. I could still fight. And usually I wasn't afraid. Very."

"And now you can't." His voice expressed nothing she could take hold of, neither approval nor disapproval.

"That's right. As soon as I could get out of bed again, afterwards, I tried. But my own armor frightened me. Weapons, noise, the look on their faces, all of it. It was some little time before I could walk well, and I was clumsy with things at first. The Marshal-General had said that might happen, so when I picked up my sword and it felt strange, I wasn't upset. At first. But then—" she shook her head, remembering her first attempt at arms practice. "It was just drill," she said slowly. "They knew I'd been hurt; they wouldn't have injured me. But I couldn't face them. When that blade came toward me, I froze. They told me later that I fainted. It didn't even touch me. The next day it was worse. I started shaking before I got into the practice ring. I couldn't even ride. You know how I loved horses—" she looked up, and the Kuakgan nodded. "My own horse—the black I got here—I couldn't mount him. Could not. He sensed my fear, and fretted, and all I could think of was the size of his feet. They all thought it would help somehow, so they lifted me onto a gentle little palfrey. I sat there stiff, and shaking, and as soon as she broke into a trot I fell off."

"And so you left them. Or did they throw you out?"

Paks shook her head. "No. They were generous. The Marshal-General offered to have me stay there, or train me to any trade I wished. But you know, sir, that Gird is a fighter's saint. How can they understand? It's not right, and Girdsmen know it. And the Duke—" Her voice broke again.

"Was he there?"

Paks fought for control. "Yes. He came when he—when they told him I—what they might do. He said he would take me then, as a captain or whatever. But—I knew—they were right. Something was wrong. It had to be done. I still think so. And he was there after, when we knew it had gone badly. He gave me—"

"That ring you left in the basin." Paks nodded. The Kuakgan sighed. "Your Duke is a remarkable man. He has no love for the Girdsmen in general, and the Marshal-General in particular. He must think a lot of you."

"Not now," said Paks miserably.

"He gave you the ring afterwards, did he not? After he knew what had happened? Don't underestimate your Duke, Paksenarrion." He stirred the fire again. "I saw him once, long ago. I wondered then what sort of man he would be. I have heard of him, of course, in the years since, but only what anyone might hear. For the most part."

"Why does he dislike the Girdsmen so?" asked Paks.

The Kuakgan shook his head. "That's not my story to tell. I have it only by hearsay, and may have it wrong. Perhaps he will tell you someday."

"I . . . don't think so."

"Because you think you'll never go back? Nonsense. In courtesy you must see him again, and ease his concern."

"But—"

"You must. Whether you draw sword for him again or not, Paksenarrion, you cannot leave him wondering whether you are alive or dead. Not tonight, no, nor tomorrow—but you must go. And when you go, you will agree with me on that."

Paks said nothing. She could not imagine going to the Duke's hold with her fear still unconquered. Unless she regained her courage, and could fight, she could not face the Duke and her old companions.

"One thing more, tonight, and then you will sleep. What was it like, when you first thought your courage gone? How did you know it?"

Paks thought how to describe it. "When I first trained, with the Duke," she began, "I could feel something—an eagerness—in the drill. When Siger—the armsmaster—threatened with his blade, I felt it rising in me. Excitement, eagerness—I don't know how to say it, but I wanted to fight, wanted to—to strike, to take chances. When he hit me, the pain was just pain, like falling. Nothing to be afraid of, or worried about. And after that, in the battles—I was scared, the first year, but even then that feeling was inside, to draw on. As soon as the fight started, it seemed to lift me up and carry me along. It never failed me. Even in the worst times, when we were ambushed, or when Macenion and I faced the old elf lord, I might think that I was likely to be killed, but it didn't affect my fighting. Unless, perhaps, I fought all the better for it. That's how we all were; those that feared wounds or death left the Company. That danger was our life. Some, indeed, loved the fighting so much that they were kept from constant brawling only by the rules. I had had one trouble with brawling; I didn't want more. I liked my fights for a reason." Paks stopped again; she was breathing faster, and her mouth was dry. The Kuakgan rose and brought the jug of water. They each had a mug of it, then she went on.

"At Fin Panir it was like a dream. Everything I'd ever thought about, when I was a girl: the knights, the paladins, the songs and music, training every day with warriors known all over the Eight Kingdoms. There were none of the—the things that bothered me, in the south. We would fight only against true evil. And I met real elves, and dwarves. I could learn any weapon, learn as much as I could. They said I did well; they wanted me to join the Fellowship of Gird, they asked me to become a paladin-candidate. For me, for all that I'd dreamed of, that was—" She stopped, poured another mug of water, and took a sip. "I never dared dream so high, before. It came like a burst of light. All the strange things that had happened in Aarenis seemed to make sense. Of course, I agreed. I felt I was coming to my true home, the heart of my life."

"And now?"

"It was the happiest time of my life." Paks drank the rest of her water. "It will seem silly to you, Master Oakhallow, I don't doubt. A sheepfarmer's daughter with silly daydreams of wielding a magic sword against monsters, a runaway girl joining the mercenaries, still holding that dream somewhere inside. I couldn't make them understand, in Fin Panir; maybe it's so silly it doesn't matter. But I had tried to learn my craft of fighting well enough to be of use, and there, where all were dedicated to honor and war—there I was happy indeed."

"I don't think it was silly," said the Kuakgan. "Such a dream is most difficult to fulfill, but it is not silly. But tell me, now, what it was that changed, after the Marshal-General did whatever she did."

"It was gone, that's all. That feeling or whatever that came when I was fighting. It was gone, and left emptiness—as if the ground suddenly disappeared under one foot, and left me with nothing to stand on. I had no skill and no courage to cover the lack. I thought at first it would come back; I kept trying. After awhile I could move better, and control my sword, but as soon as I tried to fence with someone the emptiness seemed to spread and spread until all was gone. Sometimes I fainted, as I said, and sometimes—once I ran away, and once or twice just stood, unable to do anything. Now when I try to face something, when something frightens me, I have nothing inside to do it with."

"So you left Fin Panir and—did you plan to come here?"

"No! Never! I wandered along the roads, looking for work. I thought I could do unskilled work, at least: farm labor, and that. But so many things frightened me—things that frighten no one but a little child—" She wondered whether to tell him about the trader's caravan, the robbers at the inn, and decided not to. What difference did it make, after all? "I wandered, mostly. I didn't know this was Brewersbridge until I came to the inn. I would have fled, but a guard thought I was acting strangely and wanted to take me to the keep."

"Wouldn't Marshal Cedfer have vouched for you? You said the Marshal-General promised safe-conduct in all the granges of Gird."

"I suppose he would have, sir, but I couldn't ask him. I asked, once, in Fintha—they don't understand. If I had lost an arm or leg, something they could see, they might. But as it is—cowardice—they think of that as shameful weakness, or punishment for great evil. With soldiers it's even simpler. Cowardice is cowardice, and nothing else. I suppose they're right, sir, but I can't—" Her voice broke, and tears burst from her eyes. "I can't—live with that—with their scorn. The Marshal knew me before—he'd say I wasn't a criminal—but he'd despise—"

"Enough. I know the Marshal better than that. He is fair, if sometimes narrow-minded. And you are not being fair to yourself. But it is late, and you need rest. We will talk more of this tomorrow. Don't fear to sleep; your dreams are withheld for the present."

Paks thought she could not face the morning, but when she woke, she felt more at peace than she had for a long time. She awaited the Kuakgan's questions. But he said nothing during breakfast, and afterwards called her to walk with him in the grove as usual. The first hour or so passed in silence. As always, Paks found something new to look at every few paces. She had never lived near a forest before, and it had not occurred to her how full a forest could be. Finally he turned to her, and spoke.

"Sit down, child, and we'll talk some." Paks sat against the trunk of a tree, and he stretched on the ground nearby. "You are stronger of body than when you came, Paksenarrion; are you aware of it?"

"Yes, sir." Paks felt herself flushing. "I've been eating too much."

"No, not too much. You were far too thin; you need more weight even now. But the day you came, you could not have endured what you did yesternight without collapse."

"But that was my mind—"

He made a disgusted noise. "Paksenarrion, your body and mind are as close as the snail-shell and the snail. If you poke holes in the snail-shell, will the snail live?"

"No, but—"

"By the Tree, you must be better, to argue with me!" He chuckled a moment, then turned serious again. "You did not say, when I first saw you, how you planned to die—if you'd thought about it—but it was clear that you were near death for some reason. Some trouble I could see at a glance: your thinness, your weakness. Some seemed clear, more was certain. I began with what was easily cured; good food and rest heal many wounds of body and mind both. Then you were frightened even by that rabbit on the path as you came in. Is that true now?"

"No . . . not here, with you. I don't know what it would be like outside." Paks tried to imagine it, tried to see herself walking down a street somewhere. The panic fear she had felt before did not return. "I can think of being somewhere else, at least."

"Very well. Your body is beginning to heal, and with it the mind heals also."

"But I thought you said the wounds would need more?"

"Yes. They will. But that will sap your strength again, for a little, and I wanted to build it first. It is a delicate thing, Paksenarrion, to choose the best time. First to gain your trust, so that even the pain I must cause you will not awake the panic. Then to let food and rest do what they may with the parts of your body that were not wounded, so that the strength there offsets— Do you understand any of this?"

"Not really. I would think if the food and rest could heal—"

"It should heal all? Ordinarily it might. But the kuaknomi have difficult magic, and their poisons outlast normal human lifespans. The poison takes the strength from you, and will, until we get it out. And until your body is clean of it, your mind shares the poison."

"Oh."

"And you fear what I might do to heal you," he added shrewdly.

"Yes. Sir, I—I went through that once. They were saying it was in my mind, but the same thing. Evil. Something to be ripped out. And now you—"

"Hmmm. Yes. But I can show you what I will do. Look at that scar on your arm—the one that hurt you so that night." Paks shoved up her sleeve and looked. It had been redder the following morning, but now had faded to a dull pink. When she prodded it with a finger, it held no underlying soreness.

"Is it truly healing?" she asked.

"Yes. In a few weeks it should be pale as your old scars. I could not use quicker methods, after what they had done."

"But the others?"

"You remember the pain of that one? It was almost like the original wound, wasn't it?" Paks nodded. "And you have many others. To work on them all at once will be very painful for you. I could force you into a sleep, but then we are faced with the trouble in your mind. If you still wish to die, you could go then, while I was busy with your wounds. I cannot care for both, alone. I would prefer to have your cooperation, mind and body, before I begin." He seemed to look past her, over her head, into some distance. "I might have called on another Kuakgan for aid, or on the elves—or even Marshal Cedfer—but until I knew where your trouble lay, and from what cause, I had no right to do so."

"But you can heal the wounds," said Paks, confidently.

"Yes."

"Will that heal the—the other? Is that what caused it, truly?"

"I don't know. I think you were already weakened so by the wounds, by the poison in them, that even without the Marshal-General's intervention your mind would have been affected in time. Without probing deeply into it, I am not sure what she did. But anything that would remove a deep-seated evil would be likely to affect other things; evil spreads like ink in water, staining everything it touches. Your body was damaged again, by that: you said when you woke from her treatment you could not walk at first. What I hope is that thorough healing of the body will allow your mind to heal, too. Whether what you have lost will regenerate or not, I cannot tell. But you are already better, in both, and that gives me hope."

Paks stared at the ground before her. "I'm still scared. Not the pain, so much—that comes anyway—but the other."

"I know. I can treat one at a time, but that will take months. And I must warn you that the poison itself will resist, given time for it. The last ones will be much harder to cure than the first. Yet to do this, without your free consent, is likely to widen the rift in your mind. It is for this that I waited, hoping that you would be able to trust me."

"How long would it take?"

"All at once? A day of preparation for me; you would have to keep quiet within doors, and let me meditate. I have most of the materials I need; I could gather the rest today. Then a day or two for the healing itself: I cannot tell, until I have seen and tested each wound, exactly how long. You would be very weak for the first day afterwards, but your strength would come quickly."

"And I would sleep through it?"

"The healing itself, yes. I would recommend it. Even if you were willing to endure all the pain awake, your reaction could break my attention to the healing."

"I wish—" she began, and then stopped. She took a deep breath and went on. "I wish it could be done, and over, and I didn't have to decide."

His voice was gentle. "No. It is not the way of the Kuakkganni to force a good on someone if there is time for choice. Each creature has its own way to travel; we learn much of them, but we do not change the way. And for humans, the way involves choice."

"You forced me to eat, that first day."

"Then there was no time. I had to buy that time, to find out what was wrong. Now you are beginning to heal, and I judge you well enough to make a choice for yourself. I will give you advice, and have, but you are free to follow it or not, as you are free to take what time you need for the decision."

Paks had taken a twig from the ground, and was digging little holes in the dirt at her feet. She made a row of them, then another row. For a moment she saw them as positions in a formation, then scraped the twig across the design.

"You think I should let you do it now?"

"I think you should ask yourself if you can trust me. I think you should ask yourself if you can trust your own mind to hold on until your body has a chance to heal. If when you are well again you still wish to waste your bones on the hills, I've no doubt some orc or wolf will be glad to assist."

"I don't, now," she said very softly.

"Good."

"I think—I know I want to be well again. If it can happen. If what is wrong is that poison, then—I must let you do it. Whatever it is."

For the rest of the afternoon, they gathered herbs and

other materials from the grove. Most of it was unfamiliar to Paks; the Kuakgan explained little, merely pointing out the plants to take. That evening he went to the inn for food, after telling her to stay inside. When he came back, one of the potboys from the inn was with him; Paks heard his voice outside. The Kuakgan had him leave his burden on the step, and when he had left, called Paks outside to carry it in.

"We'll need food for several days," he explained. "You must eat well tomorrow, while I meditate, and I must eat something during the healing." He unpacked loaves of bread, a small ham, sliced mutton in pans, eggs, and other rich foods.

It seemed to Paks that the next day lasted forever. She had become used to wandering outside; she was restless in the house. The Kuakgan had left the hidden panel open, and she spent some time taking a bath and washing her hair, but that left hours of idleness. She forgot to eat at noon. Sometime in the afternoon her belly reminded her, and she ate several slices of ham, then some cheese. As the daylight faded outside, she wondered if the Kuakgan would appear for supper. The door to his private room had been closed all day; she dared not knock. But she felt it would be discourteous to eat without him.

The last light had disappeared, and she had lit candles in the main room, when he came to the door of the passage. Without a word, he nodded to her, and went to close the shutters. Paks started to speak, but he forestalled her with a fluent gesture of one hand. He laid a fire on the hearth and lit it. Paks stood, wondering what to do. He pointed to the ham, and then to her. When she offered him a slice, he shook his head, but sat at the table to watch her eat. Her appetite had vanished; the ham lay in her stomach like a huge stone, and her mouth was dry. She looked over at him; he was watching her, his dark eyes warm. That gaze soothed her, and she was able to eat a bit more, and drink a mug of water. At last he reached and touched her hand, and gestured toward her pallet against the wall. She looked toward it, and at once the panic she thought had gone rose in her mind like a fountain, bursting her control. She choked on the breath in her throat, shut her eyes on the tears that came unbidden, and sat with her hands clamped on the table. He said nothing. Time passed. At last she could breathe, could see again her white-knuckled hands, could unclench those hands finger by finger. She did not try to meet his eyes again, but forced her stiff unwilling body to rise from the table and cross the room.

His hands on the sides of her head were dry and cool, impersonal as the bark of a tree. She lay with her eyes shut, rigid and waiting. When the first touch of power came, it was nothing like she expected. It seemed more a memory of recent mornings, of spring itself, of gold sunlight filtering through young leaves. She felt no pain, only peace and quietness, and let herself drift into that light like a leaf in the fountain. She did not know when the dream of light faded.

Return from that beauty and peace was more difficult. A call she could not answer, struggle, confusion, the return of fear. She woke with no knowledge of time or place—for a few moments, she thought she was back in the Duke's Company, trying to reach the Duke after the Siniava's attack on Dwarfwatch. "The Duke," she managed to say. "Saben—" Then she remembered enough to know that Saben was dead, and the Duke far away. The Kuakgan's face was strange to her, and only slowly did she come to know where she was.

"You wandered a long way," he said at last. His face was lined and drawn. "A long way indeed. I was not sure you would return." He reached for her wrist, and felt her pulse. "Much stronger. How do you feel?"

"I—just weak, I think. I don't want to move."

"No wonder. You need not, for a time." He sighed, then stretched. "I wonder that your Marshal-General did not see how bad those were. It may be they've gotten worse. But, Paksenarrion, you were almost beyond my healing powers. One of the wounds still had a bit of the weapon in it—a stone blade of some sort—and that one I had to open completely." He reached for a jug and poured out a mug of liquid. "You must try to drink all of this." He raised her shoulders and held the mug to her lips. Paks sipped slowly, and finally drained it completely. She was desperately tired. Later she could never remember if that first waking had been in daylight or night.

She slept, and woke again, and slept. Finally she woke to firelight, hungry for the first time, and able to move a little by herself. The Kuakgan was beside her, as always. When she stirred, and spoke to him by name, he smiled.

"You are certainly better. Hungry? I should hope so. Let me help you to the jacks first."

She wavered when she stood, dizzy and weak, but by the time they had gone down the passage and the stairs, she could support herself along the wall to the jacks. She came back alone, and slowly, still touching the wall. She tried to think, but had no idea how much time had passed. In the meantime, the Kuakgan had set food on the table: stew and bread. She half-fell onto the bench, and propped herself on the table. But she ate the last bite of her food, and was able to walk more steadily back to her pallet.

The next morning she woke normally, no more weak than if she had worked too hard the day before, or fought too long. Her mind seemed curiously empty of all feelings, but her body obeyed her, if a little sluggishly.

Chapter Three

"You will not regain your full strength for some time," Master Oakhallow said, as he sat with her at breakfast. "But we need to consider your other problem now." He paused for a long swallow of sweetened goat's milk. "If you still have one. Can you tell?"

Paks shook her head. "I don't feel much at all right now. When I think of fighting, it's very far away."

"Hmm. Maybe that's for the best. Perhaps you will be able to think more clearly." He cut another slice of bread, and bit into it. Paks swallowed her own milk. She was discovering that nothing hurt; she had not known how that constant pain had weighed on her. For a little while she did not care whether she could fight or not; it was pleasant enough to sit eating breakfast without pain. She felt the Kuakgan's gaze and raised her eyes to meet it. His face relaxed as he watched her. "At least the poison's out. Your face shows it. Well—are you ready?"

"For what, sir?"

"To talk about courage."

Paks felt herself tensing, and tried to relax. "Yes."

"Very well. It seems to me that two mistakes have clouded your mind. First is the notion that having as little courage as an ordinary person is somehow shameful, that you must have more than your share. That's nothing but pride, Paksenarrion. So it is you felt you couldn't live with the meager amount of courage most folk have: it was too shameful. And that's ridiculous. Here you are, young, strong, whole-bodied now, with wit enough—with gifts above average—and you feel you cannot go on without still more bounty of the gods."

Paks blushed. Put that way . . .

"Paksenarrion, I want you to think of those common folk awhile. They live their lives out, day by day, in danger of fever, robbers, fire, storm, wolves, thieves, assassins, evil creatures and powers—and war. They most of them have neither weapons nor skill at arms, nor any way to get them. You've lived among them, this past winter: you know, you *feel*, how helpless is a farmwife against an armed man, or a craftsman against a band of thieves. You are right, they are afraid—full of fear from moment to moment, as full of fear as you have been. And yet they go on. They plow the fields and tend flocks, Paksenarrion, and weave cloth for you to wear, and make pots, and cheese, and beer, and boots, and wagons: everything we use, these frightened people make. You think you don't want to be like them. But you *must* be like them, first. You must have their courage before you get more."

"But—sir, you said they had none."

"No. I said they were frightened. Here's the second mistake. Courage is not something you have, like a sum of money, more or less in a pouch—it cannot be lost, like money spilling out. Courage is inherent in all creatures; it is the quality that keeps them alive, because they endure. It is courage, Paksenarrion, that splits the acorn and sends the rootlet down into soil to search for sustenance. You can damage the creature, yes, and it may die of it, but as long as it lives and endures, each living part has as much courage as it can hold."

Paks felt confused. "That seems strange to me—"

"Yes, because you've been a warrior among warriors. You think of courage as an eagerness for danger, isn't that so?"

"I suppose so. At least being able to go on, and fight, and not be mastered by fear."

"Right. But the essence is the going on. A liking for excitement and danger is like a taste for walnuts or mushrooms or the color yellow. Most people have a little—you may have noticed how small children like to scare themselves climbing trees and such—but the gift varies in amount. It adds to the warrior's ability by masking fear. But it's not essential, Paksenarrion, even to a warrior. The going on, the enduring, is. Even for the mightiest warrior, a danger may be so great, a foe so overwhelming, that the excitement, the enjoyment, is gone. What then? Is a warrior to quit and abandon those who depend on his courage because it isn't fun?" Paks shook her head. "No, and put that way it's obvious. You may remember such times yourself. It's true that one who had no delight in facing and overcoming danger would not likely choose to be a warrior, except in great need. But consider your own patron Gird. According to legend, he was no fighter until need—his own and his neighbors'—drove him to it. Suppose he never enjoyed battle, but did his best anyway: does that make him unworthy of veneration?"

"No, sir. But if what you say is so, will I always be like this? And can I fight again?"

Master Oakhallow gave her a long considering look. "And how do you define *this*? Do you feel yourself the same as when you came here?"

Paks thought a moment. "No. I don't. I feel I can go on, but I still wish I were the way I used to be."

"It was more pleasant, doubtless, to feel no fear and be admired."

Paks ducked her head. "Yes, sir, but—I could do things. Help—"

"I know. You did many good things. But if we consider whether you will stay as you are now, we must consider what you are now, and what you wish to be. We must see clearly. We must have done with daydreams, and see whether this sapling—" he touched her arm"—be oak, holly, ash or cherry. We can grow no cherries on an oak, nor acorns on a holly. And however your life goes, Paksenarrion, it cannot return to past times: you will never be just as you were. What has hurt you will leave scars. But as a tree that is hacked and torn, if it lives, will be the same tree—will be an oak if an oak it was before—so you are still Paksenarrion. All your past is within you, good and bad alike."

"I can't feel that, any more. All that happened before Kolobia . . . I can't reach it."

"That we will change. It's there, and it is you. Come, you are strong enough to walk today; the sun will do you good."

As they wandered the grove's quiet trails, he led her to talk about her life, bit by bit. She found herself remembering little things from her childhood: watching her father help a lamb at birth, rubbing it dry, carrying her younger brother on her shoulders from the fields to the house, listening for wolves' wild singing on winter nights when they ventured near the barns. It seemed that she was there again—where she could never go—clinging to the hames on the shaggy pony as her father plowed their one good field, or catching her fingers in the loom as her mother wove the striped blankets they slept under. Seen so, her father was not the wrathful figure of those last days at home, but a strong, loving man who made a hard land prosper for his family.

"He cared for me," she admitted at last, staring into the fire that night. "I thought he hated me, but he wanted me to be safe. That's why—"

The Kuakgan nodded. "He saw danger ahead for you as a fighter. Any father would. To think of his child—his daughter—exposed to sword and spear, wounded, dying among strangers—"

"Yes. I didn't think of it like that. I wanted danger."

"And danger you had. No, don't flinch. You'd have made a very bad pig-farmer's wife, wanting to be a warrior. Even now, you'd make a bad pig-farmer's wife."

"Not for the same reason."

"No. But your pig-farmer—what was his name?—is better off with whoever he has."

Paks had not thought of Fersin Amboisson in years. She had never wondered whom he married instead. Now his pleasant, rugged face came back to her. He had looked, but for being a redhead, like Saben.

"I hope he found somebody good," she said soberly.

"The world's full of good wives," said Master Oakhallow, and turned to something else.

Day by day the talk covered more and more of the years. Her first days in the Duke's Company, her friends there, the trouble with Korryn and Stephi (which seemed to interest the Kuakgan far more than Paks could understand—he kept asking her more and more details of that day—things that seemed to have nothing to do with the incident itself).

And as she talked, her life seemed to gain solidity—to become real again. She felt connected once more to the eager, adventurous girl tagging after older brothers and cousins, to the determined young woman running away from home, to the young soldier fighting beside trusted companions in the Duke's company. This, it seemed, was her real self—bold, self-willed, impetuous, hot-tempered, intensely loyal once trust was given. She began to see how these same traits could be strengths or weaknesses in different circumstances. Trust given the Duke would lead to one thing; given to Macenion, to a far different outcome.

"I never thought, before," she said, as they sat one day in a sunny spot, "I never thought that I should choose. I thought others were either good or bad, and nothing in between. Vik warned me about that, once, with Barranyi, but I didn't understand. It's still me, isn't it? I have to decide who is worthy of trust, and even then I have to decide each time whether something is right or wrong."

The Kuakgan nodded. "It's hardest for fighters, Paksenarrion. Fighters must learn to obey, and often must obey without question: there's no time. That's why many of us—the Kuakkganni, I mean, now—will have nothing to do with fighters. So many cannot do both, cannot give loyalty and yet retain their own choice of right and wrong. They follow chaos, whether they know it or not. For one like you, who has chosen, or been chosen for, a part in the greater battle, it is always necessary to think as well as fight."

Paks nodded. "I see. And I didn't, did I? I did what I was told, and assumed that those I followed were right. If I liked them, I assumed they were good, and forgot about it." She paused, thinking back. "Even when I did worry—when I wanted the Duke to kill Siniava quickly—I couldn't think about it afterwards."

"Yes. You pushed it out of your mind and went back to being a plain soldier. You were challenged again and again, Paksenarrion, to go beyond that, and think for yourself: those incidents with Gird's symbol you told me about, but—"

"I refused. I went back. I see." Paks sighed, and stretched suddenly, reaching toward the trees with her locked fists. "Hunh. I thought I'd never refused a challenge, but I didn't even see it. Was that cowardice, too?"

"Have we defined cowardice? Why did you refuse? If you refused simply because you were certain that you should be a follower, that's one thing. But if you were afraid to risk choosing, risk being wrong—"

"Then it was. Then while I thought—while everyone else thought—I was brave, maybe I—"

"Maybe you were afraid of something, like everyone else. Don't be ridiculous, child! You're not perfect; no one is. What we're trying to do is find out what you are, and what you can be, and that does not include wallowing in guilt."

Paks stared at him, startled out of her gloom. "But I thought you were saying—"

"I was saying that you consistently refused to make some choices. That is something you need to recognize, not something to worry about in the past, where you can't change it. If you want to, you can decide to accept that challenge from now on."

"I can?"

"Certainly. I'm not speaking, now, of returning to soldiering. As a fighter, you're tempted to see all challenges in physical terms. But you can certainly decide that you, yourself, will consider and act on what you see as right and wrong. Whatever that may be."

Paks thought about that in silence. When she turned her head to speak, the Kuakgan was gone. She thought about it some more as she waited for him to return.

When he came, he was accompanied by another, clearly of elven blood. Paks scrambled to her feet awkwardly; she had seen no one but the Kuakgan all this time.

"This is Paksenarrion," he said to the elf. "She was gravely wounded by the dark cousins—" The elf murmured something softly, and the Kuakgan frowned. "You know the truth, Haleron; they are no myth. Paksenarrion, this is Haleron, an elf from Lyonya. He tells me that the rangers in the southern hills there are looking for new members. I think that would suit you; the outdoor work would restore your strength, and they will hire you on my recommendation."

Paks was so surprised that she could not speak. The elf frowned at her, and turned to the Kuakgan.

"We have no need of the weak," he said in elven. "Let her find another place to regain her strength. And is she not the one I heard of, from Fin Panir, who—"

Paks felt a wave of anger, the first in months. "May it please you, sir," she said in her best elven, "but I would not have you think me an eavesdropper later."

He stared at her. "My pardon, lady, for the discourtesy. I didn't know you were learned in our language."

"She knows more than that," said the Kuakgan. "And I assure you that she is quite strong enough for your woods work." He and the elf stared at each other; Paks could feel the battle of wills. The elf seemed to glow with his intensity; the Kuakgan grew more and more solid, like a tree. At last the elf shook his head.

"The power of the Kuakkganni is from the roots of the world." It sounded like a quote. The elf turned to Paks. "Lady, the rangers are in need of aid. If indeed you seek such employment, and have the skills of warfare, we would be glad to have your assistance."

Paks looked at the Kuakgan. His face was closed; she

felt shut out of his warmth into darkness. She thought of the things he'd said, and sighed. If he turned her out . . .

"I would be glad to aid the true elves," she said carefully, "In any good enterprise." She shot a quick glance at the Kuakgan; his eyes were alight, though his face showed no expression.

The elf nodded. "Very well. I leave at dusk—unless you require more rest—if you are weak—?"

Paks felt fine. "No. I'd like to eat first."

"Of course. And pack your things, no doubt."

"I have none." She thought of her pack, cloak, and clothes, but did not even glance toward the Kuakgan. The elf raised his eyebrows. She stared back at him in silence.

"And where, Master Oakhallow, shall we eat?" the elf asked.

"Oh, at the inn, I think." He was watching Paks; she could feel the weight of his eyes. She swallowed, and braced herself for that ordeal.

But, in fact, it was no ordeal. No one seemed to notice her on the street, though several people glanced sideways at the elf. At The Jolly Potboy, the elf and the Kuakgan argued briefly and quietly over who would pay, and the elf finally won. She kept her eyes on the table at first, concentrating on the good food, but finally looked around.

The inn was not crowded, as it would be later, but she saw one or two familiar faces. Mal leaned on the wall, as usual, with a tankard at his elbow. Hebbinford's mother, in the corner, knitted on another scarf. Sevri darted through on her way outside; she had grown two fingers, at least, since Paks had seen her. But no one seemed to recognize Paks, and she relaxed. She listened to the talk, the clatter of dishes—so loud, after the Kuakgan's grove—but it didn't frighten her as it had. She almost wished someone would call her by name. Almost. The Kuakgan ordered tarts for dessert. The elf leaned back in his seat, and glanced around the room. Paks watched him covertly. He was a half head taller than she, with dark hair and sea-green eyes. The leather tunic he wore over shirt and trousers had dark wear-marks at shoulder and waist: Paks decided these were from sword-belt and bow. He caught her looking at him and smiled.

"May I ask, lady, where you learned our language?"

"I was honored with the instruction of a true elf from the southern mountains." If he knew she came from Fin Panir, he would know that already.

"You speak it well for a human. Most are too hasty to take time for it."

"Paksenarrion, though a human warrior, knows the folly of haste," said the Kuakgan. Paks looked at him, and he smiled at her, lifting his mug of ale.

"That is a wonder," said the elf. "Are the younger races finally learning patience of the elder?" He was watching the Kuakgan.

"From experience," said the Kuakgan. "Where all who know it learned it. Surely elves have not forgotten their own early days?"

"Alas, no. However remote, the memory remains." He turned to Paks. "I beg pardon again, lady, for any discourtesy."

"I took no offense," said Paks carefully. She wondered if the Kuakgan and the elf were old enemies. Surely the Kuakgan wouldn't send her to someone evil. She thought of their last conversation and wondered.

As they came out of the inn, the sun dropped behind the high hills to the southwest. A group of soldiers from the keep was coming down the north road toward the crossing; despite herself, Paks shivered.

"Are you cold?" asked the elf.

"No. Just a thought." She looked at the Kuakgan. He smiled.

"If you come this way again, Paksenarrion, you will be welcome in the grove."

"I thank you, sir. I—" But he was already moving away, nodding to the approaching soldiers, waving to a child in a doorway.

"We'd best be going," said the elf quietly. "I mean no discourtesy, but we have far to go, and if you have been unwell you may find it difficult to travel at my pace."

Paks tore her gaze away from the Kuakgan. She had not thought to part so soon. "I—yes, that's fine. I'm ready."

"You have nothing to take with you? Nothing at all?"

"No. What I have, I'm wearing."

"Hmmph. Those boots won't last the trip."

Paks looked at her feet. "I've worn worse for longer."

The elf laughed, that silvery sound she remembered so well. "Very well, then. Come along; we go this way first."

She started a pace behind him, then caught up. They were walking east out of Brewersbridge, on the road she had come in on a year and a half before. The Kuakgan's grove was on her left, dark and alarming in the evening light. On the right were cottages: she tried to remember who the people were. The woman in the second one had knitted socks for her, socks that had lasted until this last winter.

Past the last plowed field, with the young grain like green plush, the elf turned aside from the road.

"This way is the shortest for us, and we will meet no other travellers. Follow in my footsteps, and they will guide your way."

Paks did not like that instruction, but she did not want to start an argument, either. She wanted to think about the Kuakgan, and what he had done, and why. She dropped behind the elf as he started across a sheep pasture. The sky was still pale, and she could see her way well enough. As the evening haze darkened, though, she saw that the elf's footsteps were marked in a pale glow. When she stepped there, she found a firm flat foothold.

By dawn she was heavily tired, stumbling even as she followed his tracks. She had no idea how far they had come, or which direction: she had not been able to check that by the stars and see his steps at the same time. But she had smelled woods, then grassland, then woods again.

"We will rest here awhile," the elf was saying.

Paks looked around. They were in open woodland; clumps of trees left irregular meadows between. The elf had found a spreading oak near a brook, and was spreading his cloak on the ground. Paks stretched her arms overhead and arched her back. Those casual strolls around the grove had not prepared her for such a long march. Her legs ached, and she knew they would be stiff after a rest.

"Here," he said. "Lie down and sleep for awhile. I will watch."

Paks looked to see if he mocked her, but his smile was almost friendly. "You have walked as far," she said.

"I have my own way of resting. If you know elves, you know we rarely sleep soundly. And you are recovering, the Kuakgan said, from serious wounds. Go on, now, and sleep. We have a long way to go."

Paks stretched out on the cloak after removing her boots. Her feet were hot and swollen; she took her socks off and rubbed the soreness out of her calves and feet. When she looked up, the elf was looking at her scars.

"Were those truly given by the dark cousins?" he asked.

"Not by them," said Paks. "At their command, by orcs." The elf tensed, frowning, and looked away.

"We had heard that they dealt with the thriband, but I had never believed it. I would think even iynisin would call them enemy."

Paks shook her head, surprised that she was able to talk about it without distress. "Where I was, the kuaknom—iynisin, I mean—commanded orcs as their servants and common warriors. When I was captured, in a night raid on our camp, the iynisin made their orcs and other captives fight with me. Unarmed. I mean, I was unarmed, at first."

The elf looked at her with a strange expression. "You fought unarmed against the thriband?"

"At first. Then they gave me the weapon of one I killed, to fight the next battle with. Only then there were more of them. And the next—"

"How many times?" he interrupted. "How many battles did you fight?"

"I don't know. I can't remember that. If you count by scars, it must have been many."

"And you lived." The elf sat down abruptly, and met her gaze. "I would not have thought any human could live through their captivity, and such injuries, and still be sane. Perhaps I should admit I have more to learn of humans. Who cleansed the poison from your wounds?"

"The Kuakgan. Others had tried healing spells, but though that eased the pain for awhile, the wounds never fully healed. He knew another way."

"Hmm. Well, take your rest. I think you will do well enough in Lyonya."

Paks lay for a few minutes watching the leaves overhead take shape and color as the dawnlight brightened, then she slept. When she woke, it was warm afternoon, and sunlight had slanted under the tree to strike her face. The elf had disappeared. She looked around, shrugged, and made her way to the brook to drink and wash her face and feet. She felt stiff and unwieldly, but after stretching and drinking again she could think of the night's march without dismay. When she came up from the brook, the elf was standing under the tree, watching the way they had come.

"Trouble?" asked Paks. She could see nothing but trees and grass, and the flicker of wings as a bird passed from tree to tree.

"No. I merely look to see. It is beautiful here, where no building mars the shapes. We will not be disturbed on this journey. I have—I don't think you will understand this—I have cast a glamour on us. No mortal eye could see us, although other elves might."

"Oh." Paks looked around for some revealing sign—flickering light, or something odd. But everything looked normal.

"Are you hungry? We should leave in a few hours. It's easier to blur our passage when we cast no sharp shadows."

Paks was hungry indeed; her stomach seemed to be clenched to her backbone. She nodded, and the elf rummaged in the small pack he wore. He pulled out a flat packet and unwrapped it.

"It's our waybread. Try it."

Paks took a piece; it looked much like the flat hard bread the Duke's Company carried on long marches. She bit into it, expecting that toughness, and her teeth clashed:

this bread was crisp and light. It tasted like nothing else she had eaten, but was good. One piece filled her, and she could feel its virtue in her body.

That night they crossed into Lyonya. The trees loomed taller as they went on, and by dawn they were walking through deep forest, following a narrow trail through heavy undergrowth. When they stopped, the elf pointed out berries she could eat. "It's a good time for travellers in the forest," the elf said. "From now until late summer it would be hard to starve in the deepest wood, did you know one plant from another."

"I know little of forests," said Paks. "Where I grew up we had few trees. They called the town Three Firs because it had them."

"Ah, yes, the northwest marches. I was near Three Firs once, but that was long ago for you. I had been to the Kingsforest, far west of there, and coming back found an incursion of thriband—orcs as you call them. The farmers there had fought them off, but with heavy losses."

"There were orcs in my grandfather's time. Or maybe it was my great-grandfather."

"And no war since, that I've heard of. What made you think of becoming a soldier?"

"Oh—tales and songs, I suppose. I had a cousin who ran away and joined a mercenary company. When he came home and told us all about it, I knew I had to go."

"And did you like it?"

Paks found herself grinning. "Yes. Even as a recruit, though we none of us liked some of the work. But the day I first held a sword—I can remember the joy of it. Of course there were things, later—I didn't like the wars in the south—"

"Were you in the campaign against Siniava?" Paks nodded. The elf sighed. "Bitter trouble returned to a bitter land. When we lived in the south—"

"Elves lived there?" Paks remembered being told that elves lived only in the north.

"Long ago, yes. Some of the southern humans think that

the humans from Aare drove us out. They have their dates wrong; we had left long before."

Paks wanted to ask why, but didn't. After they had walked another long while, and the sun was well up, he went on.

"Elves are not always wise, or always good. We made mistakes there, in Aarenis as you call it, and brought great evil into the land. Many were killed, and the rest fled." He began to sing in a form of elvish that Paks could not follow, long rhythmic lines that expressed doom and sorrow. At last the music changed, and lightened, and he finished with a phrase Paks had heard Ardhiel sing. "It is time to rest again," he said quietly after that. "You have said nothing, but your feet have lost their rhythm." They had come without Paks noticing it to a little clearing in the undergrowth; a spring gurgled out of the rocks to one side.

"Tell me about Lyonya," said Paks after drinking deeply from the cold spring. "All I know of it is that Aliam Halveric has a steading in it somewhere. And the King is half-elven, isn't he?"

His voice shifted again to the rhythms of song and legend, his eyes fixed on something far away. "In days long past the elves moved north, long before humans came to Aarenis, when the towers of Aare still overlooked the deserts of the south. All was forest from the mountains to the Honnorgat, and beyond, to the edge of the great seas of grass, the land of horses. In Dzordanya the forest goes all the way north to the Cold Lands, where nothing grows but moss on the ground. We settled the forests between the mountains and the great river, rarely venturing north of it. The forest was different, over there, alien to us." He paused, looked at her, and looked away. "Are you by any chance that Paksenarrion who was involved with the elfane taig?"

"Yes."

"Mmm. You may know that elves do not live, for the most part, in buildings of stone. We have ceremonial places. That—where you were—was one such, a very great one. It centered a whole region of elves; the elfane taig was both powerful and beautiful. But old trouble out of Aarenis came there, and the most powerful of our mages could only delay it long enough for the rest to escape. He paid the price for that delay with the centuries of his enslavement."

"That was the one we saw? The same?"

The elf nodded. "Yes. He risked that, to save the rest, but he could not save himself. We have no worse to fear than such slavery. A human can always hope for death; you will not live even a hundred years, but for an elf to endure the touch of that filth forever—" He stopped abruptly and stood up, facing away from her.

Paks could not think of anything to say. She had finished her piece of the waybread, and she went to the spring for another drink of water. When she returned, the elf had seated himself again, and seemed calmer. "Do we travel again tonight?" she asked.

"No. We will meet the rangers here, at this spring. If you are not ready to sleep, I could tell you more of Lyonya—"

Paks nodded, and he spread his cloak and reclined on it.

"I told you how the elves came here," he began. "The land was not empty even before. The rockfolk, both dwarf and gnome, quarried the mountains and hills. Orcs harried the forests, in great tribes; we drove them out, foot by foot. Other, smaller people lived here; they all vanished, quite soon, and we never knew them. For long we had the forest to ourselves, and for long we planted and shaped the growing of it, flower and tree and moss. Then men came." He stopped, frowning, and paused long before going on. "The first to come was a shipload of Seafolk, fleeing enemies up the broad Honnorgat. They cut a clearing on the shore, and planted their grain. We watched from afar. A colony began along the coast, where Bannerlith is now, and another across the river's mouth. More ships came. We held council, and decided to meet with them."

"What happened?"

"They were hasty men, used to war. I think they thought they could drive us all away. But one sea-captain's son, and his crew, befriended an elf trapped by wolves along the shore, and as one note suggests a harmony, one honorable deed suggests the possibility of friendship. After awhile those who wanted to live with us settled on the south shore, and the rest took the north. Elves are not much welcome in Pargun and Kostandan. Then men began coming from the south. These were different, and they moved into Fintha and Tsaia. When we met them, they had friendly words, not blows, for us. Many of them had met elves in the mountains west of the south marches. Here, in Lyonya itself, we made pacts with the humans, and agreed on lands and forests. We had begun to intermarry, very slowly, and when Lyonya grew to become a kingdom, elven blood ran in the royal family, though little enough in the present king."

"And it's now shared by elves and men?"

"Yes—as much as immortal and mortal can share anything. Those that will meet us here are both elven and human—most of mixed blood."

"Aren't you one of them?"

"I?" He laughed softly. "No. I wander too much. Master Oakhallow knew of the need, and used me for a messenger and guide. He is, as all the Kuakkganni are, one to make use of any chance that comes."

"Don't you like him?"

"Like him? What has that to do? The Kuakkganni are alien to elves, though they know us as well as any, and we are alien to them. They took our place with the First Tree; some of us have never forgiven that, and none of us have forgotten it. I neither like nor dislike a Kuakgan. I respect him."

Paks stretched her legs, then her arms. She was glad they would not have to travel that night.

"You had best sleep," the elf said. "I will watch."

Chapter Four

Paks did not see the rangers before they stepped into the clearing; their soft green and tawny cloaks and tunics, patterned in muted shades of the same colors, hid them well in the woods. Haleron greeted them.

"Here I am back, friends, from Tsaia, with a recruit for you for the summer. This is Paksenarrion, a proven warrior."

"Greetings to you, lady," said the tallest of the rangers. "Do you know our tongue?"

"Yes, by the kindness of Ardhiel of the Kierin Vale," replied Paks, as formally as she could. He nodded to her, with a brief smile, and turned back to Haleron.

"We thank you, Haleron, for your help, though we had hoped for more than one."

Haleron frowned, and shot a quick glance at Paks. She had the feeling he wished she didn't speak the language. She started to speak, but could think of nothing to say. The tall one noticed her discomfort, and gave her another smile.

"It is not that we think you are unable, Paksenarrion, but we lost so many to the fever that were you a demigod you might find more than you could do. May I ask what experience you have had? Haleron's word is enough for your character, but each sword has its own virtue."

Paks had expected some such question; she hoped her hesitation would be laid to the unfamiliar language. "Sir—"

"My pardon!" he interrupted. "You have not had the courtesy of our names yet. I am Giron, of mixed elf and human parentage, as are most of us. And these are Phaer, Clevis, Ansuli, and Tamar." The others nodded to Paks, and she nodded back. "Now, if you will?"

The pause had restored her calm. "Yes, sir. I was in Duke Phelan's Company for three campaign seasons, as an infantry soldier. Then—for a few months—on my own—" She was reluctant to bring up the elfane taig.

Haleron was not. "Do not be modest, Paksenarrion. Giron, she freed our brother and the elfane taig—you know that tale."

"Indeed! You are that Paksenarrion, then. I had heard that you went from that to the Girdsmen at Fin Panir."

Paks nodded. "I did. I trained with them for half a year, and then rode with the expedition to Kolobia."

"And was Luap's stronghold found?" Giron seemed genuinely interested.

"Yes." Paks felt her throat tighten; she did not want to tell these strangers all that had happened. Again Haleron broke into the conversation.

"Paksenarrion was staying with the Kuakgan of Brewersbridge when I came there. She had recovered from old wounds under his healing; he recommended her to me."

"Ah." Giron looked hard at Paks. "You left the Girdsmen, then. Why?" From his tone and look, she thought he must have heard something, and wondered which tale it had been, and whether false or true.

"I could not fight, for a long time. They—I—thought I might never be able to again. So I left."

"The Kuakgan healed what the Girdsmen could not?" Paks nodded. "Mmm. You have left a lot unsaid, Paksenarrion. Can you fight now? We need no ailing rangers; we have enough of those."

"I think so, sir."

"We have come from Brewersbridge as fast as I would have cared to come alone," said Haleron.

"That may be, but—" He shook his head, and smiled ruefully. "We need help, yet I must not accept someone who cannot serve our need. People change, as swords weaken and break. I judge that you do not fully trust yourself; how then can I trust you?"

"The Kuakgan—" murmured Haleron softly.

"The Kuakgan! You yourself have no love for the Kuakkganni; shall I let an old man in a distant grove choose my sword-companion? Whose blood will run to the tree-roots if he is wrong? Not his, I daresay!"

For an instant everyone was still as Giron's anger roiled the glade; the sun seemed to fade slightly. Paks wished desperately for the leap of anger she knew she would have felt a year ago—for the courage to confront him and demand a chance. It did not come. She was aware of the others staring at her, aware of their scorn, only barely withheld. She could almost see herself through their eyes: rumpled, dirty, threadbare clothes, boots worn thin, no weapons at all. Not much of a warrior, to look at. Suddenly she found it almost funny. How was it that *nothing* of her past had stuck to her—that nothing remained of the armor and weapons she had used, nothing of the skills she had learned?

She found herself smiling at Giron. "Sir, while each warrior wishes to choose a weapon for his hand, it is foolish to choose one by looks alone. The blade with 'I am a champion' inscribed down the rib may be a piece of fancy-work done for a prince's court. Gird himself found that a length of hearth-wood could fell a knight, were it applied to his skull. Perhaps all that's left to me is to be a rough club: but if you have the skill to use the skills I have left, that would be better than no one at all. However, please yourself. I can walk back to Brewersbridge, even without Haleron's guidance."

The others were smiling now; Tamar, the only other woman, grinned widely. Giron shook his head again, but relaxed. "I see you have wit enough, at least. And you are brave, if you would walk back alone. How would you eat?"

Paks grinned. "Well, sir—if I could not forage something, I must go hungry, but that's nothing new."

"Hmmph. Can you use a longbow?"

"I have used one. I would not claim to be an expert in it."

"You were a swordfighter, I heard."

"Yes."

"How long since you last fought?"

"Something more than half a year."

"Tamar, lend her your blade; it's the lightest we have here." Tamar came forward, and drew her sword for Paks to take. She offered it over her wrist, in the elven way.

Paks felt her heart pounding. Could she? She wrapped her hand around the hilt, and sent a mental cry to Gird: Protector of warriors, help me now, or never. After so long, the sword felt strange as she hefted it. She turned her hand minutely, and felt it settle into her palm. There. At least she would not drop it. She heard the soft ringing of steel as Giron drew his own blade. When she looked up, he was eyeing her.

"I would see your skill, before deciding," he said. "I will not speak of rumor, but I must know what you are." He took a step forward. For an instant, Paks was sure she would bolt. Her vision wavered, and her breath stuck in her throat. She clamped her hand on the sword, and tried to think of Gird. The Kuakgan's voice came instead: courage is going on. She nodded abruptly, and came to meet Giron.

With the clash of the blades her mind seemed to clear a little. Her arm moved of itself, countering his first slow strokes. She could tell they were slow, could tell that he intended to probe no more than he had to. He moved a little faster. She watched the play of his wrist, remembering slowly what it meant. If this, then that. The elbow bent *so* allows the angle here—she met each stroke squarely. It felt as if she were learning all over again: she had to think about almost every move. More came back to her; she tried a thrust past his guard. Blocked: but he looked surprised. So was she. Her body moved less stiffly, the sword began to feel natural in her hand again. He circled; she turned to meet him. Her feet shifted without her thought. Again he circled, and speeded his attack. She was frightened now, but pushed the panic down, and blocked each thrust with a grunt of effort. Only think of the strokes, she told herself. Only that. Her left foot came down on a stone, and she lost her rhythm momentarily. His blade raked her arm, leaving a narrow line of blood. She caught his next thrust on her blade and blocked it. He stepped back.

"Enough." He looked at her with new respect. "You need practice, but you have plenty of skill to draw on. We use the sword little; bows are more use in the woods. But you are welcome to stay with us."

Paks heard, but did not answer at once. She felt dizzy with relief: she had not dropped the sword, had not run away, had not fainted. The slash on her arm stung, but did not bother her; it was not pain she had feared.

"Are you all right?" he asked. She looked up.

"Oh yes. Well enough. It has been a long time, that's all." She looked for Tamar, and held out the sword. "I thank you for the use of it; it's a fine blade, indeed."

"A family weapon," said Tamar, smiling. "It was my aunt's before me, and her mother's before that." Paks thought of old Kanas's sword that hung over her father's mantel. "Here—" she took out of her pouch a little jar and a roll of cloth. "Clean that scratch and put some of this on it." Paks thanked her and rolled up her torn sleeve to wipe the blood away.

"You have scars enough," commented Giron. Paks nodded without speaking, and spread ointment from the jar along the line of the cut. "You'll need more clothes, too," he said. "We should make the nearest karrest by nightfall; plenty of stores there. You haven't asked what pay you'll get."

Paks looked up, then handed the jar back to Tamar. "No. I haven't. Whatever I earn, I expect."

He laughed, for the first time a natural laugh. "Well enough. It won't be as much as it might, since we must outfit you with clothes and weapons. But the crown of Lyonya has its honor."

* * *

Within a week, Paks felt at home with the rangers, almost as comfortable as with the Duke's Company. She wore their green and russet with leaves and crown woven into the pattern, and she was getting the same calluses on her fingers from the great blackwood bow she'd been given. So far she had seen no fighting; she had wandered the woods with the same small band, uncertain just what they were doing or where they were.

"I still don't understand," she said one day as they were stretched in the sun resting. "Are we guarding a border, or hunting robbers, or what?"

"Lyonya is not like other kingdoms," said Giron. Paks had heard that so many times that she was tired of it; it wasn't the explanation he seemed to think it.

"I know that, but—"

"Impatience!" Tamar laughed gently at her. "You are all human, aren't you?"

"All but my name. Go on."

"In Lyonya, we have not only the borders to worry about—the clear borders—but the taig of the forest itself. You met the elfane taig, in the valley, and that was but one taig. Each place has its own, some greater and some lesser. Here the forest is unbroken enough to have a taig—I should rather say, to be a taig."

"Does it have a name?"

"If it does, I am not the one to know it. The taig of a forest would not speak to me, not directly. It is too mighty for that. Even the Kuakgannir would not claim to speak to a taig so vast."

"I still don't know just what a taig is."

They all laughed, but it was friendly laughter. "No. And I don't know how to explain it. If you live long enough, Paksenarrion, perhaps this understanding will come to you. But you can feel a taig, as you know, even when it does not speak to you: you felt the lure of Ereisbrit." Ereisbrit, they had told her, was the name of a tiny waterfall only two spans high, that poured itself into a moss-edged slash of blue-gray rock. When she first saw it, she had stood frozen in delighted awe.

"Yes. I remember that."

"We are to feel the taig of the forest, and tell the King if anything goes amiss in it. We can wander far, listening and feeling for anything wrong. As for robbers, there are few in Lyonya, and the lords have their own guards to hunt them. They may ask our help, and if we have time we give it. Borders—yes, we guard those. But surely you are aware that we have more than mortal borders here." He looked at Paks sharply. She glanced around the sunny glade where they lay.

"I'm not sure—"

"Lyonya is human and elven. Elves are immortal. Does that tell you nothing?"

Paks thought hard. Haleron had said something about elven magic, about other levels. "Magical borders?" she guessed finally.

He grunted. "Magical—yes. Elves—the true elves, not we mixbreeds—are not wholly in the world humans know. In the elven kingdoms, the borders are so other that unescorted humans never pass them: never know they are there. Here, in a mixed kingdom, we have both kinds of borders. We rangers worry less about the obvious ones. With loyal lords holding close to Tsaia—and Tsaia itself an ally, for the most part—we need not look for armies of that sort. Brigands—if we see them, we deal with them, but the lords of steadings rarely need help. To the south, though, in the high mountains, are remnants of old troubles: these sometimes come down and try to invade. And through both borders. Thus the thriband—what you call orcs, or urchii—and sometimes far worse."

"Like that—whatever it was that held the elf lord?"

He nodded. "That and others. Some are very subtle. Not all evil desires immediate dominion. The foul weaver of webs—I will not name her—" he glanced at Paks. She shuddered and nodded vigorously. She did not want to hear that name aloud. "Her minions have tried our borders again and again. They insinuate themselves—hiding, perhaps, or feigning to be merchants or farm folk. For years they will bide without action, weaving slow coils of evil about them, plotting in many ways. A little gossip, a little rooting of secrets they can sell. No ordinary guard can detect them. But we are to sense, in the taig of forest and field, that slight unease. The fern knows when it has been trodden by a cruel foot; the sly levets—"

"Levets?" Paks had never heard the word.

"Swift running, long but low. Hunters of mice and such. Dark bright eyes, sharp claws and many teeth. Farmers call them bad, for they will take eggs, and the large ones even hens on the nest. But like all such little creatures they are not truly good or bad but only levets. The levets, though, are much prized by the web-worshippers, and their bodies may be used in evil rites. Also they can be spelled, and forced to serve as messengers. This we can detect, by their behavior and that of their prey."

"I see. But if you have that ability because of your elven blood, how can I help? Except to fight, if that is necessary."

"You do feel the taig," said Tamar quickly. "We saw that at once. And you had contact with the elfane taig before."

"Besides," said Giron, "the Kuakgan of Brewersbridge sent you. He would not send someone wholly blind to the taig."

"You didn't accept—"

"I didn't accept his judgment of your ability to fight, Paksenarrion. I had listened to rumors, to my shame. But I knew you would be able to sense evil in the taig."

A few days later, threading along another forest trail between Tamar and Phaer, Paks felt a strange pressure in her head. She stumbled, suddenly dizzy; Phaer caught her arm before she fell. Tamar whirled, alert.

"What happened?" Phaer looked closely at her face. Paks could feel the sweat springing cold on her neck.

"I—don't know. Something inside—in my head. It all whirled—" She knew she wasn't making sense. Her stomach roiled. Pressure crushed her chest; she fought for breath. Out of her past came the image of Siniava's ambush in the forest, the day of the storm. "Danger—" she managed to gasp.

"Where?" Giron, now, stood before her. Paks felt, rather than saw, his concern. She leaned against Phaer, unable to speak, sick and shaking with fear and the unbearable touch of some evil. She heard Giron say "Stay with her, Phaer. The rest of you—"

She was huddled on the ground; beneath her nose the soil had a faint sour tang. At last she managed to draw a full breath, then another. Whatever it was had not disappeared—she could still feel that loathsome pressure—but it seemed to be concentrating elsewhere. Paks pushed herself up on hands and knees. Above her, Phaer's voice: "Are you better?"

She nodded. She didn't trust her voice. Slowly, feeling at every moment that she might fall into separate pieces, she sat back on her heels, managed to rise to her feet. Deliberately she took the great bow from her shoulder, and braced her leg to string it. With the bow strung, she pulled an arrow from her quiver, checked the fletching, then took another, to hold as she had been taught. She looked around. The others had disappeared into the trees; only Phaer was visible, standing beside her now, his own bow strung and ready.

"Can you speak? Are you spelled?" She knew instantly that one of his arrows would be for her, if she were.

"No." Her voice surprised her; clear and low, it held none of the unease she felt. "No, it's looking elsewhere. It is very close, but I can't tell where—too close."

Phaer nodded. "After you fell, we all could feel something wrong. Did it attack you, or—"

Paks shook her head. "I don't think it did. Somehow I must be sensitive to it—whatever it is—as night creatures are to a flash of light."

"It is rare for a human to be more sensitive to anything than an elf or part-elf." Phaer sounded faintly affronted. "Do you have a god, perhaps, enlightening your mind?"

Paks did not want to discuss it. The sense of wrong and danger was as strong as ever, though it didn't center on her. Now that the sickness was past, she tried to feel her way toward its location. She turned her head from side to side, eyes half shut. A slight tingle, there. She could see nothing openly. Phaer was watching her, still alert.

"I think—that way—" Paks nodded to the uphill side of the trail.

"I still don't feel any direction." He looked worried. "Perhaps we should wait until Giron comes."

"No. If we move, we have a chance of surprising it, whatever it is. If we wait here—" Paks took a cautious step off the trail. The tingle intensified: a sort of mental itch. She shivered, and moved on. She looked at each tree and stone as the rangers had taught her: she knew the names, now, of nearly all the trees and herbs. When she glanced back at Phaer, he was following in her tracks, his bow already drawn.

A fir, another fir, a spruce. A massive stone ledge, high enough to break the forest roof and let in more light, lay just uphill. Paks went forward, one slow step after another. She felt a wave of vileness roll down from above.

"Now I can tell," murmured Phaer from behind her. "Don't move, Paks; I'll call—"

But the ledge itself heaved and shuddered, lifting in stinking coils. Without thought, Paks flipped her first arrow into position, drew, and saw it fly across that short sunlit space to shatter on rock-hard scales. She had the second arrow already nocked to the string.

"Daskdraudigs!" yelled Phaer. This meant nothing to Paks. The menace, too large to conceive, reared above them, tree tall, and yet the ledge still shifted, as if the stone itself were moulting into a serpent. Paks breathed a quick prayer to Gird, and loosed her second arrow at the underside of a lifted coil. It seemed to catch between two scales, but did not penetrate. She hardly noticed. Great waves of hatred and disgust rolled over her mind. She struggled to keep her eyes fixed on the thing, tried to fumble another arrow out of her quiver. Suddenly something slammed into her back and knocked her flat. "Daskdraudigs, I told you!" Phaer growled in her ear. "Stay down, human; this is elf work." Through the noise in her head she yet managed to hear the other rangers: Giron shouting in elvish; Tamar's higher voice rising like a stormwind's howl. She turned her head where she lay and saw Phaer fitting an arrow to his bowstring.

"Why can't I—"

"Special arrow. You don't have these." Paks noticed now that the fletching looked like stone; the arrowhead certainly was a single piece of chipped crystal. Phaer stood, drawing the bow. Above them more and more coils had risen, and the front of the creature was moving downslope to their left. He stepped forward, looking along the monster's length (she could not tell for what purpose), then shot quickly and threw himself down.

The arrow flew true, and sank into the monster's scales as if they were cheese. As Paks watched, that coil seemed to stiffen, to return to the stone she had first seen. Already Phaer had pulled out another of the special arrows. This time he aimed for the next coil ahead of his first target. Again his aim was true. But the unbound coils of the monster's trailing end whipped and writhed, rolling down upon them. Before Paks could leap up to run, the trees they sheltered in were crushed, broken off like straws. Coils as heavy and hard as stone rolled over them.

Chapter Five

Paks was aware of something cold and hard touching her skin before she could think what had happened. It was dark. She began to shiver from the cold. A pungent, resinous odor prickled her nose. When she tried to rub it, she found she couldn't move her arms. Sudden panic soured her mouth: dark, cold, trapped. She tried to squirm free. Now she could feel pressure along most of her body. Nothing moved. She heaved frantically, heedless of roughness that scraped her. She stirred only dust that clogged her nose and made her sneeze. The sneeze stirred more dust; she sneezed again.

A ghost of reason returned: if she was free enough to sneeze, she was not being crushed utterly. She tried to think. Her head hurt. Her arms—she tried to feel, to wiggle her fingers. One was cramped under her; she worked those fingers back and forth. The other moved only slightly as she tried it. It felt as if it were under a sack of meal—something heavy, but yielding. When she tried to lift her head from the dust, it bumped something hard above her: bumped on the very place that hurt so. Paks muttered a Company curse at that, and let her head back down. Her legs—she tried again, without success, to move them. They were trapped under the same heavy weight as the rest of her body. She rested her cheek on the dust beneath it and wandered back into sleep.

When she heard the voices, she thought at first she was dreaming. Silvery elven voices, much like Ardhiel's, wove an intricate pattern of sound. She lay, blinking in the darkness, and listened. After a moment, she realized that the darkness was no longer complete. She could see, dimly, a gnarled root a few inches from her nose. Remembering the hard barrier above her head, she turned cautiously to the side, and tried to look up. Tiny flickers of dim light seeped through whatever held her down. The voices kept talking or singing. It might not be a dream. She listened.

"—somewhere about here, if I heard the call rightly. Mother of Trees! The daskdraudigs must have fallen on them."

"So it must. Look how the trees are torn."

"But the firs would try to hold—"

"No tree could hold against that." Paks suddenly recognized a voice she knew. Giron. Rangers. A dim memory began to return.

"They must be dead." A woman's voice. Tamar? Yes, that was the name.

"I fear so." Giron again. "I fear so, indeed. Yet we must search as we can. I would not leave their bones under these foul stones."

"If we can move them." Another man. Clevis, or Ansuli—Paks could not think which. He sounded weary, or injured; his voice had no depth to it.

"Not you, Ansuli. You but watch, while Tamar and I search and move."

It occurred to Paks, as slowly as in a dream, that she should say something. She tried to call, and as in dreams could make no sound: her mouth was dry and caked with dust. She tried again, and emitted a faint croak. She could hear the bootsteps on nearby stone; that sounded louder than her attempt. Once again—a louder croak, but no human sound. Then the dust caught her nose again and she sneezed. Boots scraped on rock.

"Phaer! Are you alive? Paksenarrion?" The sounds came nearer.

Paks tried again. "Ennh! 'Ere. Down here." It was not loud, but the rangers' hearing was keen.

She heard a scraping and swishing sound very close; more light scattered down from above. "Under this tree?" asked Giron, overhead somewhere. "Who is there?"

"Paks," she managed. "Down here."

"Where's Phaer? Is he alive?"

"I don't know." But as she said it, she realized what the "sack of meal" weighing down her right arm must be. She tried to sense, from that arm, whether he breathed, but could not; the arm was numb. "I—think he's under this too."

"Can you move, Paksenarrion?" That was Tamar, now also overhead.

"No—not much. I can turn my head." She tried to unfold the arm cramped under her, without success.

"Wait, then, and don't fear. We'll free you."

"What is it that's holding me down?" There was a brief silence, then:

"Don't worry about it. We'll free you. It will take some time."

In fact, it seemed to take forever. The sky was darkening again when Tamar was able to clamber down cautiously and touch Paks, passing a flask of water to her lips. Then she planted one foot in front of Paks's nose and went back to work. By the sound of saw and knife, Paks knew that much of the weight and pressure came from a tree—or many trees. Gradually a wider space cleared before her. She could look down her body now, and see Tamar trimming limbs away from her hips. Directly above was the main trunk of the tree; she still could not raise her head more than an inch or so from the dust. She worked her left arm out from under her body. It felt heavy and lifeless; she could not unclench her fist. She turned her head carefully to look the other way.

Phaer's face was as close to her as a lover's. Cold and pale, stern, and clearly dead. Paks froze, horrified. She had not known he was so close—and being so close, how had he been killed while she was safe? She crooked her neck to look over her right shoulder. Phaer lay on her arm; tree limbs laced across him, and on the limbs a tumble of great boulders that ran back up the slope to the base of the ledge she had seen. Paks tried again to pull her arm free, but she couldn't move it.

"Tamar!"

"We're working, Paks. We can't hurry; the tree could turn and crush you completely."

"I know. But I can turn a little, and I saw Phaer—"

"We know." Giron's voice came from the other side of the rock pile. "Tamar was able to see past you."

"But he—" Paks found her eyes full of tears suddenly.

"He died well. He shot the daskin arrows, didn't he?"

"Daskin? Those with the crystal?"

"Yes."

"Yes—he did. They both went in. But then the tail end whipped over—"

"I know." Giron sighed; he was close enough for her to hear it. "Yet we must call ourselves lucky, Paksenarrion, to lose only two to a daskdraudigs. We might all have been killed, and the foul thing loose to desecrate the very rock. I honor your perception; none of us sensed it before you did, and none of us could find it. That is its skill, to spread its essence through the very stone so that it cannot be found."

"Paksenarrion," said Tamar, now back at her head. "Can you tell how much of your body is trapped under Phaer's?"

"No—at least my right arm—maybe a leg—"

"We cannot hurry this, but you are weakening. Here—drink this, and let me feed you."

Tamar sat in the space she had made, and held the flask to Paks's lips. She drained it slowly; she could not take more than small sips. Tamar massaged her left arm, and slowly sensation came back, first as prickling, then as a fiery wave. Paks flexed her fingers, wincing at the pain, but was able to take a bit of waybread from Tamar and get it into her own mouth. Meanwhile, Tamar had taken off her own cloak, and she spread it along as much of Paks's body as she could reach. "Don't lost heart," she said. "We will certainly free you, and Phaer's body."

"What *is* a daskdraudigs?" asked Paks. "Phaer kept yelling that, and I didn't know."

"Hmmmm—" It was almost as long as the Kuakgan's hum. Finally Tamar said, "If you truly don't know, I would rather not speak of it here. Time enough when we are far from this place, and at peace."

"But it's dead—isn't it?"

"Do you sense any life in it?"

Paks shivered; she didn't want to feel for that foulness again. But nothing stirred in her mind—no warnings, and no revulsion. "No," she said finally.

"Good. Then we needn't worry, for now." Tamar stood, after laying her hand lightly on Paks's brow. "Trust us, and lie still. Be ready to answer us when the load begins to lift. We do not wish to cause you more injury."

But darkness rose from among the trees of the forest as they worked. The stones in the pile were large and heavy, and awkward to lift or move. Twice they shifted suddenly under Giron's feet. He and Tamar both came near being crushed by the stones they tried to move. Ansuli came and tried to help; Paks heard the pain in his grunts of effort. Finally Giron stopped them.

"We cannot work this pile in the dark; we could all be crippled by a misstep here. We must make a light, or use other means, or—Tamar, do you think Paksenarrion can last the night?"

Hearing that question, Paks wanted to cry out. She could not—could *not*—stay under that tree, motionless, another night. She clenched her jaw. She could not make them do anything: if they decided to leave her there, there she would stay.

"Giron, she has withstood more than I would expect of any human. But another night, in this cold—with no way to ease her limbs—no. We must keep working somehow."

"We agreed we would not use the elfane hier before her—"

"She is one of us now. We owe that to our own."

"I think so too," said Ansuli. "She has seen the elfane taig, she has been in the hands of the daskdusky cousins—

and were we not told that the Lord Ardhiel blew that elfhorn, of which it is said that the High Prince of the Lord's Inner Court will hear the call, and bring aid. She has seen as much elfane hier as many elves, already."

Paks tried to make sense of this. The elfane taig she knew—but what was the elfane hier? The blowing of the elfhorn—she could never forget that, and the beauty of the winged steed that bore an unearthly warrior. Before she could think further, she saw a soft white light, as if all the stars' lights were mingled together in one place. She could not see where it came from; it seemed to spread, like sunlight in mist, without shadows.

"Have you the strength for the lifting?" asked Ansuli.

"More than you," said Giron. "Maintain the light, if you would. Tamar?"

"I am ready."

Again Paks heard the rasp and scrape of stone on stone, then distant thuds as stones were dropped. She could not see, past Phaer's shoulder, the size of the pile remaining. Cold edged into her, from the ground and the stones she touched. She tried to stay calm, and save her strength; at last she slept, exhausted.

Sharp pain woke her. Her right arm, her back, her legs: all were afire. Someone was pulling at her, dragging her, and she had no skin left— She opened her mouth to scream, and saw Tamar's face before her.

"Paksenarrion. Be still. You are free. You feel the blood returning, that's all. By some miracle of the gods, you have not even a single broken bone."

Paks could not have told that from the feel. Everything ached, stabbed, throbbed. She tried to take a deep breath, and found herself coughing convulsively. Tamar held her, offered a flask of water. Paks managed to swallow some between coughs, and the spasms eased. Gradually the pains settled down to recognizable bruises and scrapes. Cramped muscles relaxed, fibre by fibre. She looked around. Giron had kindled a small fire; she could feel the warmth along one side. She did not know where they were. She could see a lump of blankets beyond the fire: Ansuli, resting at last.

"Phaer's body is laid straight in the forest," said Tamar, as if answering a question. "Tomorrow we will lay the boughs upon him; for tonight, Giron has set a warding spell to guard. Clevis, who was killed when the forward end of the monster came upon us, has been laid straight as well. You and Ansuli will mend, though you will be weak some days, I expect." She moved her arms out from under Paks's head. "I'll get you something hot from the fire; you're still chilled."

The hot drink began to ease the rest of Paks's pains. She tried to move her feet, and felt them drag slowly against the ground. Her right arm still seemed numb and unresponsive. Tamar began to move it for her, bending and straightening the elbow and wrist. At last the feeling seeped back. She had been able to move all her limbs on her own, and was thinking of sleep again, when she noticed the first lifting of dawnlight in the sky. Giron, who had been standing guard outside the firelight, came back to cook a hot meal. Tamar went for water. Ansuli rolled partway over, groaned, and pushed himself up on one elbow.

"How is she?"

"I'm fine," said Paks. She still felt heavy and stiff, but knew that would pass.

"Well," said Giron, looking from Ansuli to Paks and back, "if she's not fine, she's better than we would have expected." He stirred the cookpot again. "Tamar says you don't know what that was. Is that so, Paksenarrion?"

"Yes, I had never heard the name."

"Daskdraudigs. Rockterror. Some call it rockserpent, though it is not a serpent. It has only a similar form, being long with a writhing body and coils. Some say, too, that the dasksinyi, the dwarves, breed such creatures to guard their treasure vaults. I think that is a lie: dwarves and elves seldom agree, but dwarves are not evil. Most of them, anyway. As you saw, it seems rock until it is aroused: most often a ledge, but sometimes in the form of ruined walls or buildings." Paks thought of all the ruins she and

Macenions had ventured near—what if one had been such a creature? "Even when it rouses," Giron went on, "it has the strength and weight of rock. Ordinary weapons blunt or break against its scales. The daskin arrows, dwarfwrought, will pierce its substance and fix the stone in place. Their virtue passes but slowly along its length, though—so the daskdraudigs has time to avenge itself. And worse, in after times it can renew itself and regain its mobility."

"But why did it attack my mind?"

"I know not, Paksenarrion, why you were so sensitive to it. The revulsion you felt is what all who can sense the taig feel, when they come within range. The creature terrifies and confuses. Those who cannot sense a taig may wander near enough to be consumed. We do not understand why a creature of stone would desire kyth-blood, but so it seems. Certainly it is an evil thing, and the gods of light designed the races of the kyth for good. Perhaps that is enough."

Hot food restored a sense of solidity, but Paksenarrion was still stiff and weak. She looked along her arms; dark bruises mottled them, and she was sure the rest of her body looked as bad. Ansuli had been hit by flying stones; he had a couple of broken ribs and a bad gash on his leg. Tamar had only a scrape across her forehead—from the tree limbs, she explained—and Giron limped slightly from a bruised foot. They all rested around the fire after breakfast. Then Giron sighed and stood.

"We must see to the bodies of our friends," he said. "Ansuli, can you walk if I help you?"

"For that, of course." Ansuli pushed himself up, grunting with the effort, and Giron steadied him.

"Paksenarrion, I doubt you can stand—but if you would try, Tamar will help." Paks felt as stiff as stone herself, but with Tamar's aid she was able to stand at last. She tried to take a step and nearly fell. Giron shook his head. "You can't go so far. Lie down again—"

"No." Paks shook her head, waking the pain in her skull. "I don't want to stay here alone—"

Giron raised his brows. "You would face a daskdraudigs

and fear this peaceful site? But perhaps you sense something again?"

"No. I meant—Phaer was with me. He—we—we fell together, and if he had not pushed me ahead, I too—"

"Ah. You wish to join us in honoring him."

"Yes. With Tamar's help, I can walk." She took another step to prove this, and stayed upright, though with difficulty.

"Very well. We will go slowly." They had spent the night, Paks saw, on the edge of the band of trees splintered and torn by the falling daskdraudigs. She wondered again how she had escaped being crushed by either tree or stone. Giron led them downslope, back to the trail they had been on and beyond. In a small glade surrounded by silver poplars, Phaer and Clevis were laid side by side, their bows beside them.

"Stay here and watch," said Giron, "while Tamar and I seek the sacred boughs." Paks and Ansuli sank down, one on either side of the clearing, to watch and wait. For some time they said nothing. Sunlight glittered on the leaves of the silver poplars; Paks smelled the rich mold of leaves decaying under them. She looked at the fallen leaves: each one a delicate tracery of veins, each one different. Her eyes kept straying to the two bodies laid bare in the sun; she glanced quickly away each time. It seemed indecent to leave the faces uncovered—she had heard the elves' ways were different, but had not seen them. In the sun that poured into the clearing as if into a well, the elven bone structure of brow and jaw seemed more alien than when they were alive. Paks shivered. She was sure Ansuli wondered how she had survived, when an old comrade, a half-elf, had been killed. She was sure he was watching her. She looked across and met his gaze.

"You have no elven blood; you do not understand our way?"

"I—we bury our dead—"

"And wonder why we leave ours prey to the winds and animals?" Paks nodded. "You humans fear harm, do you not, to the spirits of the dead from harm done even to their dry bones? Yes? Elves, and those of the part-elven who adopt elven ways, need have no such fear. Humans are of the earth, and like all earth-beings share in the taigin." Paks stared at him; she had never heard anyone speak of men and the taigin together. He smiled, and nodded. "Yes, indeed. Some of you are more—are granted more by the high gods—but all humans are to their bodies as the taig to its place. But elves, when they are killed, have no longer any relation to the bodies they used, and harm or injury done the body cannot affect them. An elf may be possessed, but only while alive. Death frees elves from all enchantments. Thus we return the bodies to the earth, which nourished them, without care except for the mourners. It is for ourselves that we lay straight, and bring the sacred boughs."

Paks nodded, but still had trouble looking at the bodies. Ansuli went on. "You surely lost comrades before, when you fought with the Halveric's friend?"

"Yes. But—" She looked at Ansuli, trying to think how to say it. "But if Phaer—"

"Be at rest, human. Some god gave you the gift to sense evil, and to trace it. Phaer placed two daskin arrows in a daskdraudigs, by what you said, and that's enough to make a song for him. He did what he could, and the fir tree moved as its heartwood willed, and by these acts your gift was not wasted. Would you quarrel with the gods' gifts?"

"No. But—"

He laughed shortly, as if his ribs hurt him. "But humans would quarrel with anything. No, I'm not angry. Paksenarrion, do you think we regret that you lived? We mourn our friends, yes, but you did not kill Phaer or Clevis." Paks said nothing. She still felt an outsider, the only one who had no elven blood. And she had not fought the daskdraudigs. Ansuli coughed a little. "I was wondering about this gift of yours," he said then. "How long have you had it?"

"Please?"

"The gift to sense evil. How long have you had this? All your life?"

"I don't know," said Paks. "In Fin Panir they said that

paladins could sense good and evil—that it was a gift given by Gird when they were chosen and trained. They had some magics, as well, so that we candidates could feel what it was like, but—"

"I don't mean humans in general. I mean you."

"Oh. Not—not long. Not before yesterday—" but as she spoke, Paks thought of some things that had happened in the Duke's Company. She told Ansuli of them, but finished: "But that must have been Canna's medallion, not my own gift, for the Marshal-General said that the gift was found only in paladins of Gird—"

"She denied the power to paladins of Camwyn and Falk?" His voice was scornful.

"No, but—"

"However wise and powerful your Marshal-General of Gird, Paksenarrion, she is not as old or wise or powerful as the gods themselves. Nor as old as elves. Did you know that there are elves in the Ladysforest who knew Gird—knew him as Ardhiel knew you?"

"No—" Paks had not thought before of the implications of elven longevity. She looked curiously at Ansuli. "Did you?"

"I? No. I am not so old, being of the half-blood only. But I have spoken to one who knew him. Your Marshal-General—and I grant her all respect—did not. She is not one to bind or loose the gods' gifts. I think she would say that herself, did you ask her. In her time, perhaps, in Fin Panir, the gods give the gift to sense evil to those chosen from among paladin candidates. But in old times and other places, the gods have done otherwise—as they have with you. Your friend's medallion might focus the power for one unknowing and unskilled in its use, as you were, but the gift was yours."

Paks felt a strange rush of emotions she could not define—she felt like crying and laughing all at once. And deep within, the certainty of that gift rooted and grew. Still she protested: "But—the way I am now—?"

"Ah, you will speak of it, eh? Giron is not the only one who had heard rumors. Yet you mastered the sickness, did you not? Arrows are missing from your quiver; I suspect you, too, shot at the daskdraudigs—"

"The arrows broke," whispered Paks, staring at the ground.

"So would any but daskin arrows, on such a beast. Get you better weapons next time, warrior; it was not your skill that failed." He laughed again, softly. "I wonder what other gifts you have hidden, that you have not seen or used. Are you a lightbringer or a healer? Can you call water from rocks, or set the wind in a ship's sails?"

"I—no, I am no such—I can't be such. It would mean—"

"It would mean you had some great work to do, which the gods gave you aid for. It would mean you should learn your gifts, and use them, and waste no words denying what is clear to—" he broke off as they heard Giron and Tamar returning, singing softly one of the evening songs.

Giron led the way into the clearing, not pausing in his song as he moved to help Ansuli stand. Tamar helped Paks to her feet, and together they moved to the center of the clearing and laid the boughs of holly, cedar, rowan, and fireoak on the bodies. Paks followed the pattern Tamar set, not knowing then or for many years why they were laid as they were.

When they were done, Tamar helped Paks back to their camp, and she slept the rest of that day and night. The next morning she was able to rise by herself, though still sore and stiff. Ansuli lay heavily asleep, his narrow face flushed with fever. When Paks had eaten breakfast, Giron and Tamar came to sit near her.

"Can you heal?" asked Giron, as calmly as if he asked whether she could eat mutton. She answered as calmly.

"I tried to, once, using a medallion of Gird belonging to a friend. I don't know whether it worked—"

"Wound or sickness?"

"An arrow wound."

"And did it heal?"

"Yes, but not at once. It might have been—we found surgeon's salve, and used that as well."

"Did it leave a scar?"

"My—my friend died, a few days later." Paks looked down. "I don't know if it worked or not."

"Hmm. I see. And you never tried again?" She shook her head. "Why not?"

Paks shrugged. "It never seemed right—necessary. We had surgeons—a mage—"

"Healing gifts require careful teaching," murmured Tamar. "Or so I have been told. Without instruction, you might never know—"

"We must see, then. You have experienced such healing at the hands of others, haven't you?"

"Yes." Paks thought of the paladin in Aarenis, and of Amberion in Fin Panir. And of the Kuakgan, so different and yet alike.

"Then you must try." When she looked at him, surprised despite his earlier words, he smiled. "You must try sometime, Paksenarrion, and you might as well begin here. Ansuli has painful injuries, as have you yourself. Try to heal them, and see what happens."

"But—" She looked at Tamar, who merely smiled.

"We shall tell no tales of it," said Giron. "If you have no such gift, it is no shame to you; few do. If you come to be a paladin later, it will no doubt be added to you. But here and now you may try, with no prying eyes to see: no god *we* worship would despise an attempt to heal. And if you succeed, you will know something you need to know, and Ansuli will be able to take the trail again."

"But I have not called on Gird these several months," said Paks in a whisper. "It seems greedy to ask now—"

"And whence his power? You told us he served the High Lord. Call on him, if you will."

Paks shivered. She feared to have such power, yet she feared to know herself without it. She looked up and met Giron's eyes. "I will try." Giron picked her up, and laid her next to Ansuli. This close, Paks could feel the heat of his fever. She rested her hand on his side, where she thought the ribs might be broken. She did not know what to expect.

At first nothing happened. Paks did not know what to

do, and her thoughts were too busy to concentrate on Gird or the High Lord. She found them wandering back to the Kuakgan, to the Duke, to Saben and Canna. Had she really healed Canna with the High Lord's power? She tried to remember what she had done: she had held the medallion—but now she had no medallion. She looked at Ansuli's face, flushed with fever. She knew nothing of fevers, but that they followed some wounds. We're short of men, she thought, and wondered that Giron had said nothing of it. They had needed her, and more, and now two were dead and another sick. She tried to imagine her way into Ansuli's wound, past the dusky bruises.

All at once the bruise beneath her hand began to fade. She heard Giron's indrawn breath, and tried to ignore it. She could feel nothing, in hand or arm, to guide her, to tell her what was occurring . . . only the fading stain. She looked quickly at Ansuli's face. Sweat beaded his forehead. Under her hand his breath came longer and easier. Paks felt sweat cold on her own neck. She did not know what she had done, or when to stop. She remembered the Kuakgan talking about healing—his kind of healing—and feared to do more. What if she hurt something? She pulled back her hand.

Chapter Six

Dressed in the russet and green of Lyonya's rangers, Paks moved through the open woodland toward the border almost as quietly as the elves. They had given her the long black bow she'd used all summer, and offered a sword if she would stay with them until Midwinter's Feast, but Paks felt she must return to the Duke as quickly as she could.

Now she was near Brewersbridge again. I know this town better than my own, she thought ruefully. I can scarcely remember where in Three Firs the baker was. Ahead she could see the dark mass of the Kuakgan's grove. She turned toward the road: she would not risk that grove despite her new woods learning.

A caravan clogged the way; she had seen its dust rising over the trees without thinking about it. It was headed east, into Lyonya. As she came across the fields, she saw the guards watching her. So close to Brewersbridge they would think her a shepherd or messenger, not a brigand. She neared the road.

"Ho, there! Seen any trouble toward the border?" That was a guard in chain-mail, with his cross-bow cocked, seated on the lead wagon.

"No—but I've not been on the road. Headed for Chaya, or the forest way to Prealith?"

He scowled. "Chaya, if it matters to you."

"I can't help you then. I was in the southern forest three days ago; it's quiet there."

"You're a ranger?" He was clearly suspicious. Paks turned up the flap of her tunic to show the badge. His face relaxed. "Huh. Don't see Lyonyan rangers this far into Tsaia, usually. You don't—pardon me—look elven."

"I'm not." Paks grinned. "I hired on for the summer. If you see a band near the spring they call Kiessillin, you might mention me—tell them I was safe in Brewersbridge."

"Tell them who—a long lass with yellow hair?"

"Paksenarrion," she called, as the wagon rolled on. He looked startled, but subsided.

She had not been in Brewersbridge in the summer. At the Jolly Potboy, the stableyard was crammed with horses and mules; five wagons blocked the way outside. Paks threaded her way between the crowds of people. She heard Hebbinford turning a party away as she passed the door. Down the north road came another group of wagons; these were ox-drawn, and the drovers looked as heavy as their beasts. At last she understood how the town had grown so big. Clearly she could not find room at the inn; the fallow fields near town were full of campsites already. Probably every spare room had its tenant. That left Gird's Grange or the Kuakgan. She must speak to Marshal Cedfer, certainly, but—she turned up the north road to the entrance of the grove.

A party of soldiers hailed her. "You! Ranger!"

After the first twinge of fear, she could stand and talk to them. "Yes?"

"What are you doing in Tsaia? Is the border secure?"

"As far as I know. I've left the rangers; I'm headed north."

"North? Where? And who are you?" None of the group looked familiar.

"To Duke Phelan's stronghold; I'm Paksenarrion Dorthansdotter—"

"Oh!" said one sharply. "You're the Paksenarrion who—?"

"Quiet, Kevil!" A heavy-set man with red hair peered at her. "Paksenarrion, eh? Known to anyone here?"

"Yes." Paks was surprised herself at how calm she felt.

"Marshal Cedfer knows me, and Master Oakhallow. I daresay Master Hebbinford will remember me."

"Well, then." He sucked his teeth. "D'you know our commander?"

"Sir Felis?" He nodded, and Paks went on. "I knew Sir Felis, yes."

"Hmph. We've had a bit of trouble lately—have to watch strangers—"

Paks looked at the crowded streets and grinned at him. "Keeps you busy, does it?"

He did not grin in return. "Aye, it keeps us busy. It's not funny, neither. I'd heard you were a swordfighter, not an archer."

"The rangers use bows," said Paks. "I spent the summer with them."

"Ah. Well, where are you staying?"

"I don't know yet. The inn's packed. I wanted to see Master Oakhallow—"

"Thought you were a Gird's paladin or some such," said one of the other soldiers, with an edge to his voice.

"No," said Paks quietly. "I am a Girdsman, but not a paladin."

"Quiet," said the red-haired man again. "You've been here before, from what I hear—if you are the same Paksenarrion. But we've had trouble, you see—we don't want more—"

"I don't intend—"

"That's all I mean. If you stay with the Gird's Marshal, or the Kuakgan, or some friend, well, that's fine. Or if not, come out to the keep, and I daresay Sir Felis will speak for you. Only I'm supposed to keep order—"

"I understand," said Paks. He nodded abruptly and led the group away. Paks could hear them talking, and the redhead shushing them, before they had gone ten yards.

As she came to the grove entrance, she suddenly wondered how many times she would come there. It seemed for a moment that she was constantly entering and leaving the grove. She shook her head and went on. As suddenly as always, the noise of the street dropped away, leaving only the sound of leaves and wind and small creatures rustling in the growth. This time she knew the different trees, knew the names and flowers and berries of the little plants that fringed the path, knew the names of the birds that flitted overhead. She knew enough to be surprised that incense cedar and yellowwood grew side by side, that a strawberry was still in flower.

Again, that empty glade with the fountain murmuring in its midst. Paks had been thinking what she might put in the basin. When it came to it, she laid a seed she had found, from a tall flowering tree she had not seen anywhere but in one part of Lyonya. No one appeared; she stood beside the fountain, listening to the water, for some time. Was the Kuakgan gone? She had never imagined the grove without him. What kind of trouble had the local soldiers so upset? Her feet hurt; she folded her legs and sat beside the lower pool to wait.

Then he was there, not three yards away, smiling at her. Paks started to stand, but he motioned her back down.

"So," he said. "You carry a bow now. You are well?"

"Yes." Paks felt she could say that much honestly. Not as she was, but well.

"Good. You look better. Where are you bound?"

"To Duke Phelan's. I felt it was time."

He nodded soberly. "It is, and more than time. Did you fight, Paksenarrion?"

"Yes. I didn't—I couldn't feel the same. But I can fight. Well enough, though I can't tell if it's as well. The rangers have different training."

"True. But you are a warrior again? In your mind as well?"

She hesitated. In her own mind a warrior longed for war—but she knew what he meant. "Yes—yes, I think so."

"Did you want to stay here a night or so?"

"I thought to stay at the inn, but it's full. If I could, sir—"

"Certainly. I told you when you left you were welcome

to return. Besides—" he stopped suddenly and turned to something else. "Have you eaten?"

"No, sir. Not since morning."

"That's not what I taught you." His voice was severe, but she caught the undertone of laughter. "What did I say about food?"

Paks grinned, suddenly unafraid. "Well, sir, the rangers fed me well enough—as you can see—and I just didn't stop at noon. I wanted to get here well before dark—"

"We'll eat at the inn, if that's agreeable." He stood, and she clambered up. "You might want to leave your bow here; the local militia have become nervous of weapons—"

"I noticed. What about the Girdsmen?"

"They don't bother the Marshal, of course. The others—well, they don't carry weapons much, anyway. It's the rumors, mostly—that Lyonya is in trouble, that the king is dying—" He led the way to his house. "There's a fear of invasion, from Lyonya—stupid, really, since if they've got trouble, they'll be fighting at home. But our count worries." Paks followed him indoors, and stood her bow in the corner of the front room, laying her quiver of arrows carefully beside it. "Did you want to wash?"

"Yes. Thank you." Paks had bathed in a creek that morning, but morning was many dusty hours back. When she came from the bathing room, she felt almost rested. The Kuakgan was looking at her bow.

"Blackwood," he commented. "I'm surprised they sold you one of these."

"They didn't," said Paks. "It was a gift."

He raised his eyebrows. "Indeed. You did well, then, in Lyonya."

"I tried to." Paks finished tying up the end of her braid. "Now that you've mentioned food—"

He smiled, and they left the house for the inn.

Hebbinford knew her at once. "Paks! I never thought—I mean, I'm glad to see you again." His eyes were shrewd. "You've heard about not wearing weapons, or armor, I see—"

"Yes, thank you."

"I'm sorry we're full—I haven't a room, not even a loft—"

"No matter. I have a place."

Hebbinford looked at the Kuakgan, and back at Paks. "I'm glad indeed to see you. You will eat here?"

"If you have enough room for that," said the Kuakgan. "And enough food. Paks tells me she is truly hungry—"

"And you know my appetite," said Paks, grinning. Hebbinford waved them in.

"Of course. Of course. Fried mushrooms—I don't forget. I'll call Sevri, too—she's asked many times—" he moved away.

"You have many friends," said the Kuakgan. "Only a village innkeeper, perhaps, but—"

"Hebbinford?" Paks looked at him. "You know better than to call him *only* a village innkeeper."

"Good. You might like to know that Sevri has defended you—to the extent of a black eye or so—when the subject of your—uhm—problems came up."

"I'm sorry she got into fights for that."

"Loyalty isn't trivial, even if the insult was."

"Paks!" It could only be Mal, whose delighted bellow would carry across any intervening noise. "Paks! You're back! Where's your big sword? Where's that black horse of yours?"

The Kuakgan's eyes were dancing with mischief. Paks sighed and braced herself for Mal's hug.

"I can't carry a sword here—remember?"

"Oh, that. Well, it shouldn't apply to you, Paks. Talk to the Marshal, or Sir Felis, and—"

"I've been in Lyonya," said Paks, heading him off. "I've been using a longbow."

"You?" Mal looked at her critically. "My brother Con used a bow."

"You said so before, so I thought I'd try it."

"I still like an axe." Mal had settled at their table, and the serving girls were already bringing a pot of ale. "I told you before, Paks, an axe is better than any of 'em. It'll break a sword, and a mace, and—"

"Yes. I tried an axe myself."

"You did? Where? Isn't it better?"

"Not for me," said Paks. "I nearly cut my own leg off."

"Well, it's not for some," conceded Mal. "My brother Con, that uses the bow, he says that. But if I had to have a sword, and then I was out working in the forest, and I was chopping a tree, and something came along—then I'd have to drop the axe, and find the sword. I say, give me an axe." He took a long pull at his mug of ale, and refilled it from the pot. "Listen, Paks, is it true what I heard?"

Paks felt her stomach lurch. "Is what true?"

"Some man came along and said you got in trouble in Fin Panir—stole something from the Hall—and the Girdsmen threw you out and that's why you aren't a paladin. That's not so, is it?"

"No," said Paks with relief. "That's not so."

"I didn't think so." Mal settled back in his seat, and glared around the room. "He came saying that, and I said it was a lie, and he laughed at me." He looked sideways at her to catch her reaction, then looked at the Kuakgan. Paks said nothing. "So I broke his arms for him," Mal went on, with relish. "Liar like that. Thinks we don't know anything down here, being a little town. You wouldn't steal nothing, I told him, and if you had you wouldn't get caught. I remember you sneaking around in those tunnels, quiet as a vole."

Paks shook her head. She wanted to laugh, but she didn't want to start any more questions, either.

"Is that the fellow that complained to Sir Felis?" asked the Kuakgan. "I remember some sort of trouble."

"Oh, aye. Said I'd attacked him for no reason. Wanted me up to the Count's court. Couldn't have gone, anyway. I had all those trees to trim up for the new work on the town hall. Anyway, he told Sir Felis what I did—and I told Sir Felis what he'd said—and Sir Felis told me to go home, and sent him away."

"I heard he told you to go home and stay there and not break any more arms." The Kuakgan's voice was quiet.

"Oh . . . he might have. Something like that. But you know, sir, I don't go breaking arms for no good reason. Not like some. But a liar like that. And Paks. Well, even if it was true, he shouldn't be saying it. Not around here, anywhere, where folks know her." Mal stared at the table top. "No, the one who got mad was the Marshal. You'd think I was a yeoman, the way he gets after me. I said the man was a liar, and he said even so, and I said he needed more than his arms broke, and he said—"

"I said, Mal, that if anyone needed to defend Paksenarrion's name, it would be the Fellowship of Gird." The Marshal stood beside the table, his eyes challenging.

"And I said you hadn't broke his arms yet, and I was glad to." Mal sat back and grinned, the wide gap-toothed grin that Paks remembered so well, then pushed himself to his feet and wandered away.

"Paksenarrion. I'm pleased to see you again." The Marshal's unasked question: what are you doing with the Kuakgan? hung between them.

"And I you, Marshal Cedfer," said Paks. "Will you eat with us? I have just arrived in town."

"So I heard from Sergeant Cannis. I'll sit with you; it's a drill night." He paused, then asked. "Will you be coming to drill?"

"Not tonight, I think, Marshal." Paks did not elaborate.

"Ah. You've journeyed long today, I imagine." He looked at her, then around the room. "You've found our busiest season this time. You're—" he looked sharply at the Kuakgan. "There's a place for you at the grange, any time," he said formally. "Even without any notice from the Marshal-General—"

"Marshal, I thank you. I will be traveling on tomorrow; I'm heading north, to the Duke's stronghold. And tonight—"

"You're staying in the grove." He sighed. "Perhaps it's best. But I hope you will come by the grange before you leave. We still count you in our fellowship—here in Brewersbridge, perhaps, more than elsewhere."

Paks was moved. She had still feared Marshal Cedfer's reaction. "Sir, I will do so. I have been with the rangers in Lyonya this summer—"

His face lightened. "Indeed! Very good. And did you—" he stopped, and she wondered if he had been about to ask about fighting. "I mean," he amended, "if it's not breaching some vow of your service, I wondered how things stand in Lyonya. You may have heard rumors here—"

"Yes." Paks was glad the conversation had gone this way. "I cannot say much, since I spent my time in the southern forest. But my companions were concerned about some threat to the realm as a whole. They even mentioned trouble coming from Tsaia."

"Tsaia! From us? Surely not. These kingdoms have been at peace for generations. We have no designs—"

"Nor they, I assure you," said Paks. "They mentioned only rumor, as you have had here. They didn't understand it, but feared the work of—" she paused and looked around the busy room. "Achrya," she said softly.

The Marshal's face tightened, and the Kuakgan frowned.

"That one," said the Marshal. "*Her*. Well, it might be so. That was her agent near here. Yes, and her doing with the other moneychanger, as I recall. Well. If she's active again . . ."

"Is she ever inactive?" asked the Kuakgan. "And would anything please her better than trouble between friends?"

"You're right," said the Marshal. "Gird's cudgel, this will be a mess if that happens." He looked at Paks. "Well, if you've been with the rangers, I expect you've learned some archery."

"Yes." Paks wondered if he would ask her to demonstrate, but he shook his head, and got up.

"I have drill, as I said, and must get ready. If you change your mind, Paksenarrion, you'll be welcome." He waved as he went out.

The Kuakgan raised his mug in salute. "I told you once the Marshal would surprise you. You have come far, Paksenarrion, since last spring."

"Yes." She looked into her own mug, drained it, and refilled it.

"Yes, but? Not all the way, eh?" She did not answer, but shook her head briefly. "Does it bother you so much, now?" he went on.

"No. Not really. I wish for it, but I can do without it." She traced a design on the table with one finger. "I wonder, though, what would happen in serious trouble—"

"You don't consider a daskdraudigs serious?"

Paks looked up, startled. "You knew about that?"

"Mother of Trees, did you think I'd send you off like that and not pay attention? Yes, I know about it. I know you didn't kill it yourself, and I know you did face danger steadily." He paused to drain his own mug. "Ah . . . here comes the food." Neither of them spoke while a serving girl laid the trays on their table: roast meat, gravy, mushrooms, bread, and cheese. A dish of onions, and one of redroots, and one of stewed pears. Finally she left, taking the empty jug and promising to bring another. "I know you didn't panic, Paksenarrion, when you might have. And they tell me you were able to sense the daskdraudigs before anyone else."

"Yes." Paks was piling meat on a slab of bread. "I was still frightened, you know. But I kept thinking of what you'd said, and then what I'd been taught of fighting—this arm here, and that step there—and I was able to keep on." She bit into the food. "I threw up afterwards," she said around a mouthful of bread and meat. "The first time, at least."

"Yes. But you were able to keep on. Good." They ate in silence awhile. Paks was just about to say something when Sevri came to the table. She had grown even more over the summer.

"Paks? Dad says you aren't staying with us—I could've found room—you could've slept with me."

"Sevri. Are you tired of everyone saying how you've grown? Are you still working mostly in the stable?"

"No, and yes. I do some in the inn, too, but I like the stable work better." She had the same friendly smile as before. "Are you all right, Paks? You look different without your sword."

"I'm fine. When did they start telling everyone not to wear a sword?"

"Over the summer. It's helped a little, with the caravaners. We've had fewer fights." She glanced at the Kuakgan. "I'm sorry, Master Oakhallow, that I didn't greet you—"

"No matter."

"Do you still have the black horse, Paks? Or did you get another?"

"I'm traveling on foot right now," said Paks carefully. "I left Socks in Fin Panir—they said they'd keep him until I came for him."

She could see the thoughts passing through Sevri's eyes, but Sevri finally said, "I hope he's all right. I remember how scared I was of him at first, and by the time you left I could feed him from my hand." She looked at Paks's clothes curiously. "Are you a ranger now? Or shouldn't I ask?"

"I spent the summer as a ranger. Now I'm going to see Duke Phelan." Paks tried to think of something comforting to say, and couldn't. Sevri sat in silence a moment, and then got up.

"I'd better get back to work. We're feeding one of the caravans, too, and they'll be sending in for it any minute." She started away, then turned back for a moment. "I'm glad you're here, Paks. I hope you come back."

"Sevri's talked of joining the grange," said Master Oakhallow. "She's said she would like to be like you."

Paks shivered. "She shouldn't. She's too—"

"She's tougher than you think. She'd make a good fighter—in some ways like you—though I think she shouldn't plan to make her living at it. But if trouble comes here—she could fight, I think, and well."

Though it was nearly dark when they left the inn, the streets were just as crowded. Paks felt sleepy and full: the meal she'd eaten, on top of the long day's march, had her longing for a bed—any bed. But the Kuakgan, when they came to his house, laid a fire and lit it. He seemed wide awake and ready for a long talk.

"The seed you brought me is indeed rare," he said. "I have no arissa in the grove, and I am glad to have the chance to sprout one. Did you see it in bloom?"

"Yes." Paks yawned. "Like—like great lights, high in the forest. Not the sort of flowers most trees have."

"Tell me something of the forest you traveled." Paks wanted to sleep; she yawned again, but began to talk of her summer's work, remembering as best she could the trees, flowers, vines, birds, and animals. The Kuakgan interrupted now and then with questions. Then he asked about the daskdraudigs.

"It felt—bad. Sick." Paks felt itchy talking about it. "I felt it, inside my head—I fell down, at first."

"And then?"

"And then I could tell which direction. Not very well." She described the search for the daskdraudigs, and the fight when it was found. She was wide awake again. The Kuakgan sat crosslegged in front of the fire, staring into it as she talked. When she was done, he turned to her.

"Paksenarrion, do you have yet any hope of being made a paladin?"

Paks stopped short. "I—haven't thought of it." That was not quite true, for the rangers had prodded her to acknowledge and use her gifts. She could not quite believe their hints; she could not wholly disbelieve, when she looked at Ansuli, obviously healed and free of pain. She thought of it then, thought of the dream she had had, of the pain when it died. Had it died? Once, yes, and then it had sprouted again, as a dead seed revives in spring. But was it the same dream, or another?

"You said you considered yourself once more a warrior. A warrior for what, or with whom?"

"I." She stopped. "I have to say? Yes. A warrior for—for good."

"Still that."

"Yes."

"Which means a paladin, to you? Or a knight of Gird, or Falk, or Camwyn or some such?"

"It means—just what I said. To fight, but only for what I think is good."

"What *you* think is good? Not at the direction of others?"

Paks thought hard. "Well—no. Not really. Not any more. But if the gods—if I knew that the gods said—"

"Ah. But no man or woman."

"No." As she said it, she felt herself cut off from all the warriors she'd known—for she was forswearing allegiance to any lord, any captain, any king, even. Could she consider herself in the Fellowship of Gird, if she would not take the orders of the Marshal-General? She shivered a little. Did she mean it? Yes.

He sat back, as if satisfied, and turned again to the fire. "Did the elves tell you, Paksenarrion, of the origin of paladins?"

"No, sir." Hints, yes, but nothing clearer for her questions; she had finally quit asking.

"Hmmmm. Once the gods themselves chose paladins, chose them from among those mortals who desired good and would risk all danger to gain it. The gifts which all expect paladins to have were given by the gods, some to one, and some to another, as they grew into their powers. The heroes whose cults have grown up over the world—some of them now called saints—were chosen and aided the same way. Or so it is said. But after awhile, the cults themselves began to choose candidates, and prepare them, and—so it is said—began to intervene between the gods and the paladins. Although, once chosen, the paladins were supposed to take their direction from the saints or gods—" Paks thought of Amberion. Had Gird truly told him to take her to Kolobia? Or the Marshal-General?

"I'm not attacking the Girdsmen," the Kuakgan said slowly. "Though it must sound like it. The Fellowship of Gird has done much for these kingdoms, and the fighters it trains have at least some care for the helpless. But what was once a grace bestowed freely by the gods—flowers wild in the field and woods—has become a custom controlled by the clerics: flowers planted in safe pots along a path. The flowers have their virtue, either place, but—" He stopped and looked at her.

"It may be, Paksenarrion, that once in a while the gods decide to do things *their* way once more. If you are, as you declare, no longer depending on man or woman for your guidance of good and evil—and yet you have, as you've shown, some of the gifts found in paladins—" She wondered how he knew that, but if they'd told him about the daskdraudigs . . .

Paks ducked her head. "I—don't know. I don't know how I would know."

"There's that. A paladin unbound to some knightly order or cult is rare these days. And a Kuakgan is hardly one to know much of these things." Paks found that hard to believe, at least of this Kuakgan. "When you were here last," he went on, "you left everything you came with in the basin. Willingly, at that time."

"Yes." Paks did not like to think of that mood, even now.

"Hmmm. But you gave a gift you had no right to give."

"Sir?"

"This." He held out to her the Duke's ring, the foxhead graved on the black stone. "This was not yours to give, Paksenarrion, and I cannot accept it."

Paks stared at it a moment, then at him. "But, sir—"

"Take it. You are going to him; you can take it back." He held it until she reached out, then dropped it in her hand. "Put it on." Paks slipped it onto a finger. She had not expected to see that ring again. She turned it with her thumb until the seal was inside, invisible, the way she had worn it before.

"You have been well enough to fight," the Kuakgan went on. "You seem to be wholly well in body, and you are well enough in mind to sense evil and good—a gift that cannot work when the mind is clouded. Do you still desire that joy of fighting you had before, or can you see it as a danger—as a temptation to fight without cause?"

"Sir, I have had enough experience to know what comes

of fighting for the joy of it alone. It is not that. But I still wish I could feel the joy when it's needed. Or perhaps I should not say needed, since I can do without it, but—I heard a woodworker, sir, say how much he liked the feel of his plane slipping along the grain of the wood, and the smell of the shavings. My father liked being out with his sheep—I can remember him standing on the moor, drawing in great breaths of that wind and smiling. Isn't that natural, in a craftsman, to enjoy his work as well? And I wish for that, to enjoy it sometimes. To pick up a sword with pleasure in its balance, not always overcoming fear of it."

"Is the fear any less?"

"I think so. Or else I am getting used to it."

"Yet you haven't asked me, Paksenarrion, if I have any healing magic to restore this to you."

"No, sir. You have done much for me already, and—I thought—if you wished to do more you would say so."

"Yes. I don't know. What I can do has been done." Paks felt the certainty of this, and braced herself to carry her fear forever. "But," he went on, "there may be more you can do. You have spent a summer with elves and part-elves and the powers of the forest. I think you have spent it well—not thinking only of fighting, but learning, as you could, of the natural world. I cannot promise success—but if you have the courage to try a desperate chance, it may return your joy in your craft."

"I will try," said Paks at once.

"I have not told you what it is."

She shook her head. "No matter. I will try."

"Very well." He stood up and moved to the woodbox. "I have saved these from the spring; they'll be dry by now." He began to stack short lengths of wood by the fireside. "This is heart'oak—to look at, much like any red oak. The elves call it fireoak. And here are two lengths of blackwood—don't worry, not long enough for a bow, even for a child. I wouldn't burn bowwood. And—let me think. Yellowwood, shall it be, or rowan? What do you remember best, Paksenarrion, about your visit here this spring?"

She tried to think; the bees that had come in to the honeycomb came to mind. "Bees," she said. "You sang them away."

"From yellowwood honey. Very well." He pushed most of the existing fire to one side of the wide hearth, and quickly piled the sticks he'd selected in its place. Then he lit them with a brand from the fire. Paks flinched: flames roared up from the tiny pile as if it had oil on it. They were bright, brighter than the yellow flames on the other wood. The room came alive in that dancing light. "It won't last long," said the Kuakgan, turning to her. "You must name your gods, to yourself, at least, and place your hands in that flame. The heartwood of fireoak, for courage, and blackwood for resilience and endurance, and yellowwood for steadfast loyalty to good. Quickly!"

Paks could not move for an instant—the magical flames were too bright and hot. She could feel the sweat break out on her face, feel the clenching of her stomach, the roiling wave of fear about to sweep over her. She spread her hands in front of her and leaned to the fire.

The flames leaped up joyously to engulf her. She would have jerked back, but it seemed too late—the fire was too big. If I'm going to burn, she thought, I might as well do it all. She had forgotten to ask what would happen—if the flames would really burn—if they would kill her—and it was too late. Gird, she called silently, Gird, protector of the helpless. And it seemed to her that a stocky powerful man held his hand between her and the flames. And her memory brought her another vision, and other names: The High Lord—and the first man stepped back, and trumpets blew a fanfare, and in the fire itself a cup of pure silver, mirroring the fire. —Take it— said a voice, and she reached into the flames to find herself holding a cool cup full of icy liquid. —Drink— said the voice, and she drank. Flames roared around her, hot and cold together—she could feel them running along her arms and legs. A wild wind shook the flames, drums thundered in her feet: she thought of horses, of Saben, of the Windsteed, father of many foals. She rode the flames, leaping into darkness, into nowhere, and then across endless fields of flowers, and the flowers at last wrapping the flames in coolness, in sweet scents and breaths of mint and cinnamon and spring water. Alyanya, she thought at the end. The Lady of Peace—strange patron for a warrior. And kind laughter followed, and the touch of healing from the Lady's herbs. Then she thought of them all together, or tried to, and the flames rose again like petals of crystal, many-colored, closing her off from that vision as the Hall's colored windows from the sky. Higher they rose, and higher, and she walked through them, wondering, until she saw in the distance an end.

And recovered herself sitting on the cold hearth of the Kuakgan's house, with every bit of wood consumed to ash. The Kuakgan sat beside her, as she could feel, in the darkness. She drew a long breath.

"Paksenarrion?" He must have heard the breath, and been waiting for it. She had never heard him sound so tentative.

"Yes." It was hard to speak. It was hard to think. She was not at all sure what had happened, or how long it had been.

He sighed, deeply. "I was beginning to worry. I feared you might be lost, when you did not return at once."

"I—don't know where I was."

"I do not propose to suggest where you were. How are you?"

Paks tried to feel herself out. "Well—not burned up—"

The Kuakgan laughed. "And not burned witless, either. That's something, I suppose. Let me get a light—"

Without thinking, Paks lifted her hand: light blossomed on her fingertip.

"Mother of Trees!" The Kuakgan sounded amazed. "Is that what happened?"

Paks herself stared at the light in confusion. "I don't know what I did! I don't know—what is it?"

"It's light—it's a light spell. Some paladins can do that—haven't you seen it?"

When she thought of it, Paksenarrion remembered the paladins making light. "Yes, but then—"

"Then what? Oh, I see. Well, as I half-suspected, you are a paladin outside the law, so to speak. Human law, that is."

"But it can't—I mean I can't—and anyway, how do I do it? Or stop it?" She was still staring at the light; she was afraid to look away or move her hand.

"Just a moment." The Kuakgan rose and took a candle from the mantle, and touched it to her hand. Nothing happened. "Ah."

"What?"

"It's true spell-light, not witchlight. Witchlight lights candles, but not spell-light." She could hear him rasping with his flint and steel. The candle flared, a yellow glow pale beside her hand. "Now you don't need it. Ask for darkness."

"Ask who?" Paks felt stupid.

"Who did you name? Who were you with? You're a paladin, remember, not a mage: you don't command, you ask."

—Please— thought Paks, still in confusion. The light vanished. A bubble of laughter ran through her mind. "But do you mean it?" she asked the Kuakgan, turning to watch him as he lit more candles. "Do you mean I really *am* a paladin, after all that's—" her voice broke.

"I am no expert on paladins," he said again. "But something certainly happened. I know you aren't a Kuakgan. We both know you aren't a Marshal of Gird. You aren't a wizard. Or an elf. That leaves few explanations for your gifts and abilities. Paladin is the name that fits best."

"But I was—" she didn't want to say it, but knew he would understand.

"Hmmm. I used to wonder how the paladins of Gird could be considered protectors of the helpless when they had never been helpless. Rather like asking the hawk to feel empathy for the grouse, or the wolf for the sheep. Even if a tamed wolf makes a good sheepdog, he will never understand how the sheep feel. You, Paksenarrion: you are most fortunate. For having been, as you thought, a coward, and helpless to fight—you know what that is like. You know what bitterness that feeling breeds—you know in your own heart what kind of evil it brings. And so you are most fit to fight it where it occurs. Or so I believe."

Paks was still shaken. She stared at the finger that had held light. She wanted to argue that it could not be true—she had been too badly hurt—she had too much to overcome. But far inside she felt a tremulous power, a ripple of laughter and joy, that she had not felt before. It was much like the joy she remembered, yet greater, as the light of her finger was greater than candlelight.

Chapter Seven

The road north from Vérella was vaguely familiar, even after three years. Paks stayed most nights in village inns; the fall nights were cold. She made good speed during the days, but did not hurry.

As she came over the last hill before Duke's East, a cold thin rain began to sift down through the trees, dulling the brilliance of their changing leaves. Paks grinned to herself: so much for her imagination. She'd hoped to arrive at Kolya's looking fairly respectable. She unslung her bow, and put the bowstring in her belt pouch to keep it dry. At least she wouldn't have to stay on the road if it got muddy, as she had in the Company. She pulled the hood of her cloak well over her face and trudged on. It grew colder. She had to blink the rain off her eyelashes every few minutes. At least it was downhill. The rain came down harder. The slope levelled out, and Paks began to look for the village ahead. There. There on the right was the stone cottage with apple trees around it, Kolya's place, and there ahead was the bridge, with the mill upstream.

Paks looked at her muddy boots and wet cloak, and decided to go on to the inn. Kolya wasn't expecting her—might not recognize her—Paks turned away from the gate and went on. Under the bridge the water ran rough and brown. They must have had rain up in the hills, she thought. The stones of the bridge were bluer than she remembered.

Although it was still daylight, few people were in the

street. Light glowed behind curtained windows. Paks turned left out of the market square, toward the inn. It loomed ahead, and she hurried toward it, thinking of warm fires and a hot meal. The inn door was closed tight against the wind and rain, but swung easily when she pushed it. Paks slipped through and closed it behind her. The common room was bright with lamps and the fire on the hearth. Her wet cloak steamed. She blinked the rain out of her eyes as she pushed back her hood.

"Well, traveller, may I help you?" The wiry innkeeper looked just as he had the year she left. Then she had been an awed recruit, wondering if she would ever go there casually, as the veterans did.

"Yes," said Paks. "I'd like a meal and a bath—"

"A room for tonight, as well?"

"I'm not sure." Paks shrugged out of her pack and cloak.

"It's late to be starting out again in this weather—" he stopped suddenly, and Paks saw he was looking at the black signet ring on her right hand. He looked up, frowning. "You're one of the Duke's—?"

Paks nodded. "I was with the Company. The Duke gave me this, the last time I saw him, and said to come if—when I had—finished something."

The innkeeper's eyes were shrewd. "I see. And you were planning to make his stronghold by tonight, eh?"

"No. Actually, I planned to visit a friend here in town first. Kolya Ministiera."

"Kolya! A friend of yours—might I ask your name?"

"Of course. Paksenarrion." She could not interpret the look on his face, and did not care to try. They would all have heard some story or other. She busied herself with the fastening of her pack. "I was in Arcolin's cohort."

"Yes. I've—heard somewhat—" He looked hard at her a moment. When he spoke again, his voice was brisker. "Well, then. Food and a bath—which would you first?"

"Bath," said Paks. "I've clean clothes in here, but I'm mud to the knees. And do you have anyone I could send with a message to Kolya?"

"My grandson will go. Do you wish writing materials?"

"No. Just ask him to tell her that I'm here, and would be glad to see her again."

"Very well. Come this way, and I'll arrange your bath."

A short time later, Paksenarrion was scrubbing the trail grime off with a linen towel, hot water, and the scrap end of scented soap she'd bought in Verella. When she was done, she poured the rest of the hot water over herself, then dried in front of the little fire in the bathing chamber. She'd hung her clean clothes near the fire to take the chill from them. They felt soft and warm when she put them on. She counted the coins in her purse and decided that she could afford a good dinner. When she came back down the passage to the common room, she felt ready to face anyone. The big room was empty, but for a serving girl. Paks chose a table near the fire, leaning her bow against the wall. The girl came to her at once.

"Master said would you want a private room to eat in?"

"No," said Paks. "This will be fine. What do you have?"

"Roast mutton or beef, redroots, white cheese or yellow, mushrooms with gravy, barley pudding, meat pasties, pies—"

"Enough," said Paks, laughing. "Let's see—how about roast mutton and gravy, barley, mushrooms, and—do you have soup?"

The girl nodded. "We always have soup. If you're cold, I can bring mulled cider, too."

"Good. I'd like that." The girl left the room, and Paks pushed the bench closer to the wall so that she could lean against it. She stretched out her legs to the fire. The fire murmured to itself, occasionally snapping a retort to some hissed comment. She could hear the rain fingering the shutters, and the red curtains on the windows moved uneasily, but by the fire she was warm and felt no draft. She wondered what Kolya would say to her message. What had Kolya heard? Her eyes sagged shut, and she slipped a bit on the wall. She jerked awake and yawned. This was no time to go to sleep. She ought to be thinking what to say to Kolya, and to the Duke.

The door opened, letting in a gust of cold wet air and a

tall figure in a long wet cloak. Paks thought at first it might be Kolya, but as the woman came into the light, Paks saw that she was younger, and certainly had both arms. A man came in behind her. The woman threw back the hood of her cloak to reveal red-gold hair, stylishly dressed. Under her cloak she wore a simply cut gown of dark green velvet, and when she drew off her gloves, she wore rings on both hands. Her companion, who seemed vaguely familiar to Paks, wore black tunic and trousers, and tall riding boots. Paks wondered who they were—they belonged in some city like Verella, not up here. Before she thought about it, she had turned the Duke's ring round on her finger so that only the band was visible. The serving girl had appeared as the door closed, and led the pair at once down a passage toward the interior of the inn. They must be known, then, thought Paks. She felt uneasy as they crossed the common room to the passage, but they did not seem to look at her.

"Here you are," said the innkeeper, breaking into her thoughts. The platter of food was steaming, and smelled good. "And Councillor Ministiera sent you a message—she's in a meeting right now, but would be pleased to have you stay with her. She'll come here when she's through with the meeting." Paks thought that Kolya's invitation impressed him. "This room is often crowded from suppertime on, and noisy—if you'd prefer a quieter place to wait, I have several rooms." Paks thought about it, and decided she would rather not see Stammel just yet.

"Yes—thank you. I think I will. But I'll finish supper first—no need to move this." She gestured at the platter and bowls. He smiled and left her. The mutton was tender and tasty; the soup warmed her to the toes. By the time she had finished, several townsmen had come in and ordered meals, staring at her curiously. She signalled the serving girl, and asked directions to the jacks and the private rooms.

"Right along here," said the girl. "And master said you were to have this room—" she pointed to a door, "when you were ready." Paks opened the door to find a pleasant little room with a fire already burning on the small hearth.

Three chairs and a small round table furnished it, with a bench along one wall. The girl lighted the candles that stood in sconces on either side of the mantel. "Will you be wanting something from the kitchen?"

"No, not now. Probably when Kolya comes." Paks tried to compute the probable cost of the meal, bath, and private room. But she wouldn't be paying for a room tonight, and she had enough.

When she came back from the jacks, she settled into one of the chairs by the fire, and took her bow across her knees. She inspected it as she'd been taught, and rubbed it lightly with oil until it gleamed. She took the bowstring from her pouch and slipped it on, then bent the bow to string it. It was as supple and responsive as ever in her hands. She unstrung it and set it against the wall.

Her hand was on her dagger, and then she was standing, staring at the door. She shook her head and sat down. Silly. Here, of all places, alone in a room in the Duke's realm, there could be no menace for her. She turned his ring again, looking at the seal in the black stone. It must be simple nervousness—fear of what Kolya had heard, or what she might say. Paks found her dagger in her hand, unsheathed. She stared at the blade, and felt the edge with her thumb. Sharp enough, and smooth. She slid it back in its sheath and stood again, pacing the length of the little room.

At the far end, away from the fire, she could just hear the murmur of other voices. It could not be coming from the common room, she recalled—it must be from another private room on this passage. She stared at the wall, her sense of something wrong growing, then turned back to the fire. She pulled her chair to face it, and found she could not turn her back on the far wall. She could not seem to sit still; her earlier sleepiness was gone. Nothing like this had happened on the journey north, and she was still fighting with herself, a little angry, when a knock came on her own door.

"Yes?" The door opened, and the innkeeper glanced in.

"Councillor Ministiera," he said, and stepped aside.

Kolya appeared in the door as Paks stood up. The gray streak in her hair had widened, but otherwise she seemed the same. Her strong dark face was split with a broad grin.

"Paks! You brought more rain with you." She gave Paks a long, considering look.

"Come on in. Don't you want some ale? Or cider?"

"Ale," said Kolya. "I get all the apples I want at home." She entered and sat in one of the chairs, while Paks spoke to the innkeeper about ale. She cocked her head up at Paks. "You will stay with me tonight, won't you?" Paks nodded. "Good. You're looking well. The Duke will be pleased to see you. We heard several things—" She paused, and gave Paks another long look.

But Paks had been ready for this reaction. She smiled. "No doubt. There have been several things to hear. I have a message for you, Kolya, from Master Oakhallow—" She turned and rummaged in her pack until she found the scroll in its oilskin wrapping, and the little oiled pouch that she had never opened.

"Thank you." Kolya started to speak, but paused as the innkeeper brought their ale and left. "He sends me seeds and cuttings—did you know he helped me start my orchard, after I lost the arm?"

"No." Paks was surprised; she knew only that Kolya was kuakgannir. She had not known even that, until the Kuakgan gave her his message to take.

"Yes. He knew me, before I joined the Company."

"Are you from Brewersbridge?"

"No." Kolya did not explain. She was looking at the scroll, which she'd unwrapped. She looked up. "Well, I see that some of the tales we've heard cannot be true."

"Ummm." Paks poured the ale into both mugs. "I don't know what you've heard, Kolya. Some things are true that I wish were not. But now—"

"Now you're a warrior again—aren't you?" Kolya picked up one mug and sipped. "As the Duke said you would have been without the Girdsmen's interference."

"I am a warrior, yes." Paks wondered how much to tell her, and how soon. Seeing Kolya again, she realized how much older the other woman was, how young she might appear. "What happened was not the fault of the Girdsmen," she began.

Kolya snorted. "The Duke thinks so. You're not going to tell me you—" she stopped, obviously looking for a tactful way to say it.

"I am telling you that they did what they knew how to do. The Kuakgan knew more—of some things."

"Are you kuakgannir now?"

"No." Paks did not know how to explain.

"Still of Gird's fellowship?"

"No—well, in a way—it's difficult to explain—"

"But how do you feel, now? You can fight again?"

"Yes. I feel fine. I spent the summer with the rangers in Lyonya; we saw some fighting there."

"You're not wearing a sword," said Kolya.

"No, that's true. I used a borrowed one there; I haven't the money to buy my own. But they said they'd keep my arms in Fin Panir. Even if they haven't, I expect they'd give me a sword when they got over the shock."

"Shock?"

"Well—they didn't expect me to recover like this."

"Oh. But the Duke said they gave you money . . . what happened?"

"It's a long tale—the short end is it's gone."

Kolya nodded. "When are you going back to Fin Panir?"

"I don't know." Paks felt the uneasy restlessness she'd struggled with before Kolya came. "I wanted to come here first; to see you, to thank the Duke for all his help. I thought perhaps I could do something for him—I don't know."

Kolya drained her mug. "You could join the Company again, if that's what you want. I know he'd take you. Or are you still set on being a paladin?"

Paks shifted the mug in her hands. "I have no choice, Kolya—or you could say I've already made it." She finished her ale, and set the mug down. "I—don't want to talk about it here. Can we go?"

Kolya stared at her in surprise. "Paks, it's safe here. Piter's the Duke's man as much as I am. He tells no tales."

Paks stood up. "I don't doubt you, or him, but something—Kolya, I cannot explain this here and now, but I must not ignore these warnings." She stepped to the door, opened it, and glanced into the passage. Nothing. "I'll go pay the reckoning."

"I'll come." Kolya stood, and Paks collected her bow and pack. She slipped the bowstring off the bow again and rolled it in her pouch. Then she led the way down the passage to the common room.

It was noisy and crowded there now, and it took a moment to catch the innkeeper's eye. He came to them, and greeted Kolya, then asked Paks what more she needed.

"Just the reckoning," said Paks. "Your hospitality has been more than generous."

He looked at her, then at Kolya. "There's—there's naught to pay, this time."

Paks turned to Kolya, whose face was blank. "What? You can't mean that, sir. I've had a fine meal, good cider and ale, bath, a private room—"

The innkeeper looked stubborn. "No. You carry the Duke's seal. One time for each of the Company—I've been a soldier; I know what need is."

Paks felt herself blushing. "Sir, I thank you. But another time, I might have need. This time I have the means to pay."

"You aren't carrying a sword. No, if you come back someday, with all your gear, and want to pay, that's fine. But not a copper will I take this night, and that's final." He glared at her.

"Well—my thanks, then. And I hope to enjoy your brew many a cold evening." Paks and Kolya went out into the cold windy night. The rain had stopped, though the wind smelled wet. They said nothing for some distance, but as they turned into the market square, Paks asked, "What was that about?"

"What?"

"Not paying. Does he really give a free meal to each of

the Duke's men? I wouldn't think he could make a living that way."

"Paks—no, wait until we reach the house." In a few minutes they had crossed the bridge, and neared Kolya's gate. Kolya led the way up the flagged walk to the cottage, and pushed open the heavy door. Inside, the front room was dimly lit by a fire on the hearth. Kolya poked a splinter into the fire until the end flared, and lit candles in sconces around the room.

"If you need to dry anything, here's a rack," she said, pulling a wooden frame from one corner. Paks dug into her pack for her wet clothes, and spread them on it, glancing around the room. It was both kitchen and living room, with cooking hooks in the fireplace, a dresser holding plates, mugs, and two blue glasses, a net of cheeses, one of onions, and a ham hanging from beams, a sturdy table and several chairs near the fireplace. The other end of the room held a desk and stool, and more chairs around a striped rug on the floor. Under the front windows was a long bench covered with bright weavings. Kolya disappeared through a door beside the fireplace, and returned with a deep bowl of apples and a small one of nuts.

"You may be tired of apples, but these look good," said Paks.

"They are. This is the first year I've gotten much from these two trees. The green and red striped ones are from Lyonya: Master Oakhallow sent the seedlings years ago. The dark ones are a new strain, according to the traders—at least it was new when I bought some. These trees are—oh—about nine years old by now. What I sent you, in the south, were Royalgarths—what they grow in the king's groves in Pargun. They travel well, and are sweet, but these are better—thinner skinned." It was clear that Kolya was glad to talk of something harmless. Paks fell in with this.

"How many kinds of apples do you grow?"

"As many as I can acquire. Apples do better if you mix varieties, and some tend to skip years in bearing. Right now I've got seven that are bearing well: these two, the

Royalgarths, the Westnuts from Fintha, Big Ciders and Little Ciders, and Westland Greens. I've got two kinds that just started bearing this year, but not heavily: another summer apple, but yellow instead of green, and a big red and yellow stripe that does well in the markets south of here. And the pears have come in since you left. Over twenty bushels of pears this year."

Paks had taken a bite out of the green and red apple. Juice flooded her mouth. "This one is good," she said. Kolya had cracked two nuts against each other in her strong hand; she began picking the meats out of the broken bits of shell.

"Yes. Paks—you are welcome to stay here; I hope you do. But—what did you come here for? Was it just to thank the Duke for his help?"

Paks took another bite of apple. "I'm not sure I can tell you. I don't know how much you know of what actually happened to me—"

"The Duke told us—the Council—some of it. Nothing to blame you for—"

"He didn't know all." Paks could feel Kolya's look as if it were a hand on her face.

"He said it was the Marshal-General's fault," said Kolya. "He's never blamed you for it—"

"It was not her fault. Not in the way he means. Did he tell you about Kolobia? What happened there?"

"Not really." Kolya shifted uneasily. "Something about capture, and evil powers."

"Yes." Paks struggled for calmness. Surely she should be able to tell this tale calmly by now. "I was taken by the kuaknomi, who serve Achrya." Kolya nodded, eyes intent on her bowl of nuts. "They offered the chance to fight—to fight for a chance at escape. Or that's what I thought they offered. The fighting was against orcs, for the most part, in a sort of arena they had underground."

"Most part? How many times—?"

"I don't know." Paks set the apple down carefully, as if it were alive. "I don't remember. Many times, to judge by the marks they left. At the end, I was forced into charmed armor—"

"Mother of Trees!" said Kolya, staring now. She had brought up her hand in the warding sign. Then she looked at her hand, and shook her head. "Sorry. Go on."

Paks took another apple out of the bowl, and looked it over. "In the fighting great evil entered my mind. It grew beyond my control. This is what the Marshal-General saw, in Fin Panir. She was not the only one to see it, Kolya. Even I, when they—" she stopped to take a long breath. "Anyway. They saw but one possible cure. And the Marshal-General, two paladins, and an elf tried to cut that evil from within. Which they did."

"And left you, the Duke said, as crippled as if they'd cut off your legs."

Paks shook her head. "Not so. You—forgive me, Kolya, but you have truly lost an arm. Nothing, now, will make it grow back. I had my limbs—legs and arms both—but not the use of them for awhile."

"And within? The Duke said they did more damage within, that they had ripped the very heart out of your self, the courage—"

"So I thought, and they thought, but the Kuakgan showed me that this was not so."

"Are you certain?" Kolya peered closely at her. "We had heard that you were to be a paladin yourself—and here you are without money enough, you say, to buy a sword—"

"Do riches make a paladin? Or do I look so scared, to you?" Paks smiled at her.

"Well—no. You don't. But you wouldn't be scared of me, anyway."

"I would have been. I was. Kolya, I cannot hide this—I was, for those months, as craven as you can imagine. I don't know what the Duke told you: but he saw me unable to lift a sword even in practice. He saw me afraid to mount a horse—even a gentle one. He saw me—a veteran of his Company—faint in terror because an armsmaster came toward me with his sword raised."

"You'd been hurt—"

Paks snorted. "You know better than that. Kolya, I have been where very few soldiers ever come—to the fear and helplessness that the common folk have. And I've come back from that, with help. Why I'm here—well, that's a long tale. Tell me, would you think me crazy if I told you—" she faltered, and Kolya looked at her curiously.

"What?"

"Kolya, things have happened to me—since I was first in the Company—which seemed strange to me. In Aarenis—especially the third year—others noticed, too—" It was remarkably hard to say, flat out, that she thought she was a paladin.

"Stammel said something to me." Kolya cracked another pair of nuts. "He said it had to do with a Gird's medallion you'd been given by a friend—you could sense things the others couldn't, he said."

"Yes. That was part of it. That was why I thought they were right, when they said I could be a paladin."

"They weren't?"

"Well—yes. In a way." Paks found that she was sweating. "The fact is—I—do have some gifts. They are somewhat like those paladins have, but I never finished the training and took vows. Master Oakhallow thinks they were given directly by the gods. And if so—" she stopped again.

"If so, then you are a paladin of sorts, is that what you mean?" Kolya glanced sideways at her. "A remarkable claim. Not that I doubt your word—" she went on quickly. "It's only that—I never heard of such a thing. When I think of a paladin, I think of those I saw, when I was in the Company. They were not as you are now."

"I know." Paks leaned forward, elbows on knees. "And I trained with them: I know what you're remembering. Shining mail, on a shining horse, so bright that anyone would follow. I don't claim to be that sort of paladin yet, Kolya. I do say that something—and I believe it to be the High Lord, or Gird his servant—has called me here for a purpose. I sensed, in the inn, some evil thing—and felt in myself the answering call: this is what I came for. I cannot see how this will harm the Duke or his realm, unless he has turned to evil, past all belief."

"Will you tell him this openly?"

Paks shook her head. "No. As you say, I don't look like a paladin. I have no clear message for him. I can but be here, and ready to serve his need, when it comes. I think it will be soon."

Kolya stirred in her chair. "I cannot believe you lie. Master Oakhallow bids me trust you—I have reason to trust him. And what I know of your past—by the Tree, Paks, I wish I understood."

"So do I," said Paks.

"And you are not a Girdsman?" asked Kolya again.

"I cannot say. I am not—I cannot be, any longer—under the command of the Marshal-General. But I swore to follow Gird's way of service: that oath I would not break."

"The Duke will not be pleased with that."

"Can you tell me what he has against the Girdsmen, Kolya? I know it is something more than happened to me, but I don't know what. Master Oakhallow wouldn't say."

"What do you know about the Duke's lady?"

"Not much. Only that he was married, and she died ten or twelve years ago. He blames the Girdsmen, somehow. Did you know her?"

"Yes. We were in the Company at the same time. Before she married the Duke." Kolya sighed, and stared at the fire. "Paks, we don't speak of her much—he doesn't like it—but I think you should know the story. It might help you understand.

"Her name was Tammarrion Mistiannyi; we all called her Tamar. She was a fighter, one of the very best. Tall, strong, and—" Kolya shot Paks a glance. "Much like you, though her eyes were bluer. She had the same way of moving. She was a Girdsman when she came—most of the Company were, in those days. She tried to convert me, but gently. The whole Company liked her. She was always cheerful, didn't quarrel, worked hard, and—by all the gods, to have her beside you in a fight! She had a temper, and that's when it showed. Her eyes would go very blue, and she'd laugh just a little, and I never knew anyone to lay a blade on her. Not by the time I came, though she had scars to show.

"The Duke was only a few years older than the rest of us. I think any of the men would have bedded her gladly, but she didn't care about it, or about women, either. But the Duke— He fought with the ranks back then: the Company was just the one cohort, a few over a hundred, and they fought side by side often. And he married her, at the end of my first campaign season." Kolya shifted in her chair again, and picked up one of the striped apples.

"Things were very different then. The Company so small, and the stronghold more than half earth walls and wooden huts. Tamar never played the lady with us, but worked as hard as ever, the Duke's other self. Together they planned the buildings there, and in the villages, and together they went over the contracts for each season. Not so much in Aarenis, then—the Duke had to garrison the stronghold by the terms of his grant. Those were good years. I'm no Girdsman, but it was a good Company then, and the contracts meant fighting where you had no doubts. They had a Marshal living in the stronghold. He pestered those of us who weren't Girdsmen, but we liked it anyway. You could trust your companions, and do your work without worrying about what kind of work, if you understand what I mean." Paks, remembering the last campaign in Aarenis, understood very well, and nodded.

"Well, then," Kolya went on, "when the children were born—"

"Children? I never knew the Duke had children."

"It's not mentioned. They died with her. The elder was a girl, maybe eight when she died—she would have been about your age had she lived. The boy was just three. When they were born, the Duke wanted Tamar to go somewhere safer, but she never would. Of course she didn't fight for awhile each time, but I remember her riding and working out when she was this big—" Kolya gestured to indicate advanced pregnancy. "And as soon as she could get back in armor, she was training again. She began to stay here, with part of the Company, when he took contracts far away, but she was no fine lady sitting at a loom.

"Then one year the Marshal-General—not this one, the one before—wanted the Duke to take the entire Company to some war in Aarenis. It had been cleared with the court of Tsaia. The Duke wanted to leave a force with Tamar, or have her come, but she wanted him to take them all, for the glory of Gird. She said the children were too young for a southern campaign, and she'd be fine with the Tsaian militia that were supposed to come for the summer. She said a member of the Duke's household should be on his land, in case something happened to the king. We all knew, by their way with us, that they were fighting—and we knew they were both high-tempered, not that they didn't—" Kolya faltered a moment. "They were as close, Paks, as any man and wife I've ever seen, close as comrades and lovers both. But if anything, she was bolder. Certainly where Gird was concerned. She finally convinced him to take both cohorts. He started south, leaving her with the children and perhaps ten men-at-arms until the militia came. And the craftsmen, of course, and the steward and servants, and the Marshal. He was no mean fighter himself. Not that it did any good." Kolya got up and moved restlessly around the room for a moment. "Do you want anything to drink?"

Paks was not thirsty, but thought it would ease Kolya to stop for awhile. "Water—that ale was strong."

"Yes. Just a minute." She disappeared to the back again, and returned with a jug. She took two mugs from the dresser and poured into them. "Here."

"Thanks." Paks took a swallow, and shifted in her chair. She wondered if she should say something. Finally Kolya settled back in her seat, after poking the fire up.

"Nobody knows what happened. We think she went out for a ride with the children—maybe hunting. The steward and the Marshall were with her, and a couple of soldiers to help with the children's ponies. They didn't come back at lunch. No one worried, then. After all—five warriors, all mounted—and there hadn't been any trouble for over a year. But they didn't come back by dark. She would have sent a messenger if they'd intended to stay out.

"The sergeant started searching an hour or so before full dark, and didn't find anything. He took torches, and dogs, and they tried to trail through the night, but something got the dogs off scent, and they didn't find anything until the next day. Back up on the moors, north of the stronghold, they found the first body. That was the old steward: he'd been shot full of arrows, and slashed with a knife or sword. Then they found the rest of them. They must have tried to take Tamar alive, because there was a stack of bodies around her and the children. Young Estil had tried to fight, too—she'd already been training with a little practice sword, and Tamar let her carry a dagger. It was bloody to the hilts. She had fallen across her little brother. We don't think they bothered the children's bodies, but Tamar and the Marshall had been stripped and hacked at. Their armor and weapons were still there, in a heap."

Paks had felt her eyes fill as Kolya talked. She could see in her mind the five adults, desperately trying to protect the children, and the little girl—she thought of herself at eight, wrestling with her brothers—defending the boy with her dagger.

"What were they, Kolya, that attacked? Pargunese? Orcs?"

"Orcs and half-orcs, by the bodies. We found twelve dead, and blood-trails of others. Two more bodies, about a mile away."

"Were you here, then?"

"Yes. Estil, the girl, liked to play with me. Tamar had asked me to stay, until the militia came. That day I had gone into the mill—we had no village here, but the mill had been built—to bring back a load of flour. When I got back, in the afternoon, the sergeant was just getting worried. We never knew why they had gone north—of all directions, the most dangerous—or why such a large party of orcs was out in the daylight. Something must have drawn them, but we never could find out what.

"Well, we brought the bodies back, and sent a courier to the Duke. All of us were terrified. You've seen him, when he's really angry—not something you want aimed at you. And then we felt we should have done something—anything—to prevent it. I must have cried every day for a week; I think everyone did. Then the Duke came. Just about what we'd expected: I thought the very ground would smoke where he stepped on it. He asked each of us, of course, where we'd been, and why we hadn't been with her, but it was all very straightforward. When we had talked to him, he said nothing to condemn us. But all that anger went toward the Girdsmen: he blamed the Marshal-General, for taking him away with all his troops and for Tamar's encouragement. It was very difficult. He went storming off to Fin Panir, and Verella. We were afraid he might disband the Company, but he didn't.

"He did start enlarging it, though, and took a contract in Aarenis every year. He wouldn't have a Marshal around, though he never interfered with Girdsmen, and still recruited them. He began to hire mages for healing. He wasn't as choosy with recruits—not taking riffraff, exactly, but not as careful as they had been. In most things he himself didn't change. Had I still both arms, I'd fight for him, and gladly. He is as brave as ever, as fair and just a leader. But—I heard some things about that last year in Aarenis, Paks, that would never have happened if Tamar had been alive. He wouldn't have wanted to do them."

Paks thought of the death of Siniava, and stared at the fire a long time after Kolya stopped speaking. Finally she looked over to see that Kolya's eyes were closed and tears glistened on her cheeks. "Thank you for telling me. It must be hard to speak of, to one who never knew her—"

"But you are so like her!" Kolya interrupted in a hoarse whisper. "When you joined the Company, Stammel saw it at once. He told me, when I came as a witness that time. When you were well, I could see it myself. And he told me what you did, in Aarenis—when you stopped the Duke. Paks, it must have been like hearing Tamar's voice from the Afterworld—that's what Stammel said. No one else could have stopped him like that. I think that's why the Duke was so furious when the message came from Fin Panir about you. It was like having it happen all over again—"

"But he never said anything—"

"No. Of course not. You're his daughter's age, after all. He wouldn't tell you. But what did he say when he gave you his ring?"

"That if I ever needed or wanted his help, to bring or send it."

"That's what I thought. When he came back, he told us—his officers, the Councils of Duke's East and West—that if you showed up, or the ring showed up, we were to do anything to help you. Anything. Without question. Spend our last copper, if we had to, or kill if you were in danger, and he would make it good. Whatever. That's why Piter wouldn't take your money. He'd give any Duke's man a meal once, but tonight was the ring, and what the Duke said."

Paks blushed. "But Kolya, I'm all right now. I don't need—"

"He couldn't be sure. You aren't carrying a sword. The Duke said you might look like anything: beggar, thief, slave, common laborer, guard—but unless you showed up mounted, in full armor, we were to assume that you needed our help. And that you'd not admit you needed it." Kolya paused, and sighed. "You are going out there after what I've told you?"

"Yes. Tomorrow, unless you have a reason to wait."

"No. Go on. It will bother him that you don't have a sword."

"You said he would hire me—perhaps I'll earn one from him."

"Oh, he'll have you. He's had fever in the stronghold this year."

"Where did he campaign this season?"

"He didn't tell you? No, I suppose he wouldn't. About the time you left the Company, he heard from the Regency Council in Verella. They'd found out that he had taken the whole garrison south, and they were furious."

Paks was confused, and must have shown it, because Kolya explained.

"He holds this steading under a grant from the crown of Tsaia. He's supposed to strengthen the stronghold—which he's done—and maintain a garrison against any invader. It was a Tsaian outpost before he got it, you see. Anyway, he always had at least fifty fighters here, usually more. But that last year in Aarenis, he pulled everyone out: active or retired, anyone who could swing a sword. So they claimed—the Regents—that he'd broken his oath to the crown, and they would have forfeited the grant. Only no one else wanted to come up and fight the orcs, and cross our Duke in the process.

"Arcolin heard part of it—the Duke said his oath to his men came first, and that he'd had no reason to expect trouble. It was the only time in twenty years he'd failed in the slightest part of his oath to the crown. Then before they could forbid him to go south again, he said he was staying in the north. He'd gotten profit enough, and was short of men. So that winter—winter before last—he routed out the orcs nearby, and recruited some, and that summer recruited some more. He had to get rid of many who'd joined in the south. By this spring he was nearly up to strength. He sent one cohort east to Pargun to man border forts, but he stayed here."

"So he's been here over a year."

"Yes, except for those weeks with you in Fin Panir. It's the longest he's been here since Tamar was killed."

"How is he?"

Kolya looked away. "Oh—well, I suppose. He's kept busy. He hasn't been sick; he trains all the time."

"But what—?"

"I don't know what. That trouble with the Regency Council—with the Marshal-General—and I daresay he worries about an heir. We've wondered if he thinks of marrying again." She rolled the apple around the table under her hand. "There's nothing I can name—only the sense of great anger underneath. We worry—the veterans, the old ones—what will happen when he—if he—"

Paks nodded. "I felt some of that anger, the last season in Aarenis—and when he came to Fin Panir. But he won't do anything bad, Kolya, I'm sure of it."

"You! And I have known him how many years? No, I'm sorry. You may know more than I, indeed."

Chapter Eight

In the morning, a weak sun struggled through low scudding clouds. Paks came over the rise south of the stronghold, and saw its massive walls. She noticed a group drilling to the west and wondered if it was recruits, or regulars. As she came nearer, she could see no changes in the stronghold itself. The Duke's colors swirled in the wind. The main gates were open, as usual in daylight. Paks kept up her steady pace. Her stomach began to clench. Would the gate guards know her? Who would be in the courtyard?

She thought of her first march toward these gates, and how she'd blushed as Stammel marched them in. It was odd to be so nervous still, after all that had happened. Her thumb felt for the Duke's signet, turning it on her finger.

"Ho there! Traveller!" She looked up to see sentries on the wall. She halted. A man appeared in the gate opening. "Come forward and speak for yourself. What's your business here?"

Paks walked forward. She didn't recognize the dark bearded face. "I'm Paksenarrion Dorthansdotter," she said. "I was a member of this Company. I would like an audience with the Duke."

He scowled; Paks decided that he was quite young—perhaps just beyond recruit. "With Duke Phelan? What makes you think you—*who* did you say you were? With this Company?"

"Paksenarrion Dorthansdotter. I was a member of Arcolin's cohort for three years."

His eyes widened. "Paksenarrion—yes—" His glance fell to her hands, and she held out the signet. "Of course. Come with me; the Duke is in council, but I'll send word in at once. Have you eaten?"

"Yes, thank you." She followed him through the gates into the familiar courtyard with the mess hall and infirmary beyond. Someone led a tall horse across the courtyard. Armed men and women in familiar uniforms walked briskly about on their errands. She tried not to gape, and followed her guide to the Duke's Gate. But they ran into Stammel almost at once.

"Paks! By Tir, I'd hardly hoped it was really you!" He grabbed her in a hard hug. "You're coming back to us, I hope."

Paks found herself grinning widely. "I must see the Duke—"

"Of course. Of course. But stay, Paks—don't be going back to Fin Panir—"

"Not for awhile, anyway." She pulled away; the young sentry was watching wide-eyed. Stammel grinned at the boy.

"Go on, then—take her in. You won't find another the Duke would rather see." And to Paks, "I'll see you when you come out." She turned to follow the sentry. She could see unasked questions hanging on his tongue. They were halfway across the courtyard when she heard other voices she knew.

"It looks like—"

"By the gods, it is Paks! Paks! Gods blast it—" Paks turned to find Arñe and Vik almost on her. She was buried for an instant in sound and arms; tears rushed from her eyes.

"I knew you'd come. I knew it." Arñe, who rarely got excited, was laughing and crying together. "No matter what they said, I knew—"

More people crowded around. "Wait until Barra hears—" she heard someone say. Volya and Jenits, her old recruits, joined Arñe in another hug. Paks had not expected this, had not realized how much she missed these particular people. She held up her hands, finally, as the questions and comments rained on her. They quieted, as if she were an officer.

"I—I must see the Duke," she said. "First, and then—"

"You'll be back," said Arñe. "You will, won't you?"

"For awhile, yes. It depends on the Duke."

"He'll have you. He always would." Arñe threw back her head and laughed for a moment. "Ah—what a time we'll have. You beginners—you don't know what you've missed. Just wait."

"Arñe—" Paks began, embarrassed.

"Never mind," said Arñe. "Go on. See the Duke. Then we'll hunt orcs together. You haven't forgotten how, I'll wager."

Paks shook her head, and followed the now-bemused sentry through the Duke's Gate.

She had never been in this part of the stronghold before. The inner court was separated from the main one by the back walls of the mess hall, infirmary and one barracks. The other sides were composed of the Duke's own quarters (where the cohort captains also lived, as well as the Duke's servants), the armory, and the storehouses. In the center of the small courtyard was a well, with a stone bench around it, and a small tree growing out of the pavement nearby. The Duke's residence took up the north and west sides.

At the door another sentry took over from the first one. This was another that Paks did not recognize. But as he started to lead her into the hall, Arcolin came down a passage and spoke to her.

"Paks! Is it really you? The Duke will be pleased—"

"Yes, Captain." Paks found herself reverting, in her mind, to the Company private she had been.

"You look well—are you?"

"Yes. Very well."

"Good. Follow me—" He led the way upstairs and

along a passage on the north wing. "The Duke's in his office—you haven't been up here before, have you?"

"No, sir."

"It's the third door on the right." But he led her all the way. The door was open; Paks could see, as they neared it, a large room full of light from windows that opened on the court. He stepped in; Paks paused on the threshold.

"My lord, it is Paksenarrion." Paks could see the Duke, sitting at a desk littered with papers. His head came up; the face had hardly changed, but for looking tired. He looked for her, and his grim expression eased as he met her eyes.

"Come in, Paks. Or do you use your full name, now?"

"Thank you, my lord. Either will do." She stepped into the room, and Arcolin went out quietly. The Duke looked her over.

"You look better than the last time I saw you."

"Yes, my lord. I am."

"Come, sit down." He gestured to a chair near the desk and she took it. "You wear no sword," he said. "Have things stayed, then, as they were?"

"No, my lord. I spent the summer in Lyonya, with the rangers. They use bows, mostly. I hadn't money enough for a sword."

"With the rangers?" His face seemed to come alive, then freeze. "Then you could—" He stopped, and she knew what he would not ask.

"My lord, I can fight again, and did. I came to thank you for your help—and for your trust." As she spoke, he stood, and came to her. He stopped a few feet away and looked her up and down.

"It is repaid by seeing you whole again. What can I do for you—besides give you a sword?"

"My lord, I didn't come to beg a sword of you, but a place. If you have need of another soldier, I have need of work."

"You aren't going back to Fin Panir, then?" He looked pleased.

"If I do, I'd like to have my own weapons," said Paks.

"Ha!" He grinned suddenly. "You are better. But I promised you a captaincy, remember."

Paks laughed. "My lord, you are generous beyond measure. But to be honest, I don't think I can stay with the Company forever."

"What then? Fin Panir and the Girdsmen, or what?"

"I'm not sure. But I will stay six months with you—perhaps more—if you'll have me. Not as a captain, though. It would not be fitting for me to take high rank from you; there are those here who have earned it."

"None more than you." The Duke glanced down. "No. I see what you mean. And of course I'll be glad to have you. We've had too much fever this past summer. Let's see. Suppose you go back in Arcolin's cohort. Veteran's pay: that should get you a sword by next spring, without question. You are still thinking of paladin, aren't you?" He looked at her shrewdly. Paks nodded. He asked no more about it but went on. "Then you'll need experience leading—but we've plenty of trouble with orcs: you can take squads this winter. And another thing—"

"Yes?"

"Most paladins are drawn from the knightly orders. They've had the chance to learn manners of court and hall. From what I saw last year, you aren't really easy with that yet. True?"

Paks blushed. "Yes, my lord. I've tried to learn—"

"And done well for a sheepfarmer's daughter. I didn't start in a palace either, Paks; now I can dine with kings without worrying about my elbows. That's something we can teach you, too, if you're willing." He paused briefly, scanning her face. "It won't cause trouble with your companions in the Company; it's going to be obvious that you are not an ordinary soldier. If you agree, you'll spend some of your free time in my library, learning history and other things, and with me and the captains discussing politics and strategy. Well?"

Paks was stunned by the offer. "My lord, I—yes. I would like that. I know very little."

"Very well, then: take this order to the quartermaster,

and this to Arcolin, and get yourself settled in. Arcolin will arrange your schedule. I want you to dine with us as often as you can, whenever it doesn't interfere with your duties."

"Yes, my lord."

An hour later, Paksenarrion was dressed once more in the maroon tunic of Phelan's Company, and had a sword at her side. Her legs felt cold and exposed again; she knew they looked chalk-white next to the others'. Armsmaster Siger, after an admiring look at her longbow, asked for a demonstration.

"Not now, Siger," said Stammel. "We've still got to get her on the rolls."

"This afternoon, then," said Siger. "Fine bow: I hope you've learned to shoot to equal it. And I want to see what fancy strokes they taught you in Fin Panir."

Paks laughed. "Nothing for a short sword, and I haven't handled a blade that much lately. But when I've practiced—"

"Good. Good. I know they teach knight's work, but I always like a new trick."

Before lunch, Paks had a longer interview with Arcolin. He urged her to accept a corporal's position, both because he was short one, and because then she would have more time and opportunity for the extra study the Duke recommended. Paks agreed, wondering meanwhile if her old friends would resent the promotion. They had been glad to see her, but how would they react to all that had happened, and to her being placed over them? She said nothing of this to Arcolin, who was telling her that she already had a reputation with the newer ones—by his tone, a good reputation.

Through the noon meal, Paks talked with Stammel and Devlin about her new duties and the changes in routine from what she remembered. With all three senior cohorts and the recruits in the stronghold together, there were many changes. Then Stammel called the cohort out for weapons practice, and they went to the field together. Siger was already there with her bow, and had set up the targets.

"Now let me see," he said eagerly. Paks strung the bow

and chose an arrow. The wind had dropped a little, but she knew her first shaft might miss. She bent the bow smoothly, and released it. She was lucky: Siger grinned delightedly. "Do it again," he said. She placed three more arrows in a pattern one hand could cover, as fast as she could draw the bow. She heard murmurs from those watching. "May I try?" asked Siger.

"Of course," she said. "It is sized for me, though."

"De, it's a strong pull." Siger eased it back from the half-draw. "You're right, it's very long for someone my height. I'll leave it to you. But let's see your bladework."

"Certainly." Paks unstrung her bow and started toward the targets to retrieve the arrows.

"Don't bother," said Siger. "Ho! Sim! Go fetch those arrows." A lanky youth in recruit brown jogged toward the targets. "Put your bow over here—" he nodded to a bowrack.

Paks set her bow in the rack and returned to the area Siger had cleared for them. He was ready, sword in hand. "Do you want a banda?" he asked.

"Against you? Always." Paks spotted the pile of bandas and shrugged her way into one. She noticed Arcolin standing behind a double row of onlookers. Siger noticed them.

"By Tir, will you stand around like cows at a fence row? You want to see Paks fight? You'll be facing her yourselves, soon enough. Get on, now, to your own drill, or I'll sore the ribs of the lot of you. Go on!" The others drew away reluctantly, and began grouping for their own drill. Paks felt a tingle of apprehension. It had been long indeed since she used a short sword, or had drilled as Siger would drill. She drew the sword and stepped forward.

With Siger's first stroke, it all came back. The first stirring of joy she had felt that last night with the Kuakgan woke and surged up her sword arm. She felt she was hardly touching the ground. They stayed with the drill briefly, as Siger increased the pace. Then he shifted to more difficult maneuvers. Paks found that her skill—her instincts—her delight were all there. Siger got no touches on her for some time. Then with a clever twist he turned her blade and tapped her sharply on the arm. He danced back, grinning.

"I'd almost thought you beyond me, girl." Paks could hear effort in his voice. Was Siger—Siger the tireless—getting tired? She wondered if it were a trick, and pressed her attack carefully.

"You should be beyond me," she said cheerfully. "You started first."

"Ah, but—" he grinned again as he narrowly countered one of her strokes. "But I'm older, now, and slow—" This with a lightning thrust that Paks took on the banda. "You're lucky you wore that," he commented.

"A shield would help, too," said Paks. "Old, indeed. Slow as an adder's tongue, you are." She tried the trick she'd used on him once in Aarenis, but he remembered the counter.

"Your old friend Vik has kept me in practice for that one," he said. Paks tried another, and this time slipped past his guard to rap his shoulder. "Aah!" he cried. "Well enough. Well enough. Let's see what you recall of formation work—we're not all knights, here." He stepped back and lowered his sword. Paks looked around. Despite their attempts to look busy, it was obvious that most of the cohort had been watching.

For some days, Paks was busy and happy, relaxing into the familiar old friendships of her years in the Company. Her duties as corporal kept her scurrying from place to place, and she had forgotten a surprising amount of the formation drills. And in every spare minute, her old friends clustered around asking questions and telling tales. Clearly they did not mind her promotion—in fact, seemed surprised that she was only a corporal. She herself had more questions than tales. She learned that Peska, junior captain to Dorrin in Aarenis that last year, had left the Company as soon as they came north. Instead of hiring another captain, his senior squire had taken over as junior captain: first Jori, whom Paks remembered from Aarenis, and now Selfer. Jori had gone for training with the Knights of Falk.

Kessim, who had been little more than a boy when Paks knew him, was now the Duke's only squire.

Paks thought about that arrangement and frowned. "That still leaves two cohorts without a backup captain—or the recruits without one."

"Valichi's back with recruits," said Kefer. "You're right, really. Four captains for three cohorts, and Pont is seconding Cracolnya again. But we're staying together, and in one place—we don't really need the others—"

"Gods grant they don't get the fever, any of them. You know, Kef, it would be difficult if Arcolin or Dorrin got sick. Or took an orc arrow." Stammel yawned; it was late.

"But the Duke's never had trouble with fever," she said one morning. "And here, in the north—"

"I know." Vik nodded. "It is odd. The surgeons think it may be that with so many of us—though we clean out the jacks twice a season now—"

"It's not only that," put in Stammel. "We're seeing a lot more trade, now—more people coming in from Verella and such. They might be bringing it."

"Hmm." Paks thought back to the lectures in Fin Panir on fortifications and water supplies. Surely nothing was wrong in the design—but she thought she'd look for herself.

"Besides, we may be getting something from all the orcs around." Devlin reached across her for another hunk of bread. "Tir knows there's enough of them, the filthy beasts."

"Where are they coming from?"

"Out of the very stone, for all we can tell." Stammel frowned. "You won't know about this, Paks, but off to the northeast of here is a mess of caves and passages that were full of orcs when the Duke took this grant. The Lairs, it was called, and that's where the trouble started. Thing is, it'd take five Companies the size of this one to find and clear all the caves. And they've been striking west of here—we wonder if they have another complex of caves somewhere west."

"What have you done?"

"Everything the captains can think of. Random patrols? Fine, but some of them are out three days without spotting an orc, and others run into bunches too big to tangle with. Pursuit of each band spotted? The last ones we tried that with took off straight north up onto the moors and kept going. Setting ambushes in likely spots? Again, sometimes a patrol's out for days without any orcs, and another time it's nearly wiped out. Perimeter control? We haven't enough for that, if we're going to hold the two villages, the stronghold, and protect the road at all."

Paks couldn't think of anything else herself.

"So far, they're under control—despite some losses, the crops are still going in and being harvested, and the villages haven't been burned. But they're keeping us busy, day after day. We can't tell exactly what they're after, either. Sometimes it seems they're just asking for a fight. They haven't tried a full-scale assault on the stronghold or the villages—of course that would be stupid of them."

"What I think—" Stammel stopped, and looked around. Most of the others had left, and he glared at Vik until the redhead shrugged and went out. That left Devlin, Paks, and Stammel at that table. "What I think," Stammel began again in a quiet voice, "is the Duke's not keeping his mind on it. That sister of Venner's—"

"I don't believe he'll marry her," said Devlin. "I can't—"

Stammel shook his head. "He's thinking of heirs, now. At his age, if he's to sire his own, it's time he was at it. I don't like her any more than you do, Dev, but she's the only woman around who—"

"I don't understand," said Paks. "You say the Duke is planning to marry? I thought Kolya said he never would, after—" She stopped before saying the name.

"That's what I would have said. But these past two years, staying up here—he's started thinking, you see, what will happen when he's old. I know he's thought of naming one of the Halveric sons his heir. But that might not sit well with the court, they being Lyonyan. He's not one to take a young wife, not now. And this sister of Venner's—she's handsome enough, and knows her way with men—"

"She's a widow," put in Devlin. "So it's said. She came up here to get Venner's help with the estate."

"What does she look like?" asked Paks. "Does she ever come out of his courtyard?"

"She's—well, as I said, handsome. Reddish hair. She rides out with Venner every now and then—"

"Goes to the Red Fox with him," added Devlin. "Piter's told me that. They take a private room and have dinner."

Paks thought back to the woman and man she'd seen the first night. She could not imagine the Duke marrying someone like that.

"It's not our business," said Stammel, but he sounded unconvinced. "If the Duke wants her—"

"It's more whether she wants him. Any woman like that would: he's rich, well-known, with large landholdings—"

"I still can't believe it," said Paks.

"Well, we can hope. I only wish he'd either do it or not, and pay more attention to these orcs. I can't believe they're causing all this trouble after years of peace without something else going on."

"If we had a paladin here—" began Devlin, then looked quickly at Paks and flushed. "Sorry, Paks. I didn't think—"

She shook her head. "That's all right." She wasn't ready to claim or demonstrate her gifts. "You're thinking of being able to find a source of evil?"

"Yes. I agree with Stammel that something must have stirred the tribes. What if it's a cover for something else? You had to do with greater evils in Kolobia—what if something like that is out there?"

Her first encounter with the orc problem was typical. A young boy came to the stronghold, out of breath and crying, to report an attack on his family's farm near Duke's West. Paks led two mounted squads, hardly considering whether anyone might resent her command. As she'd been told, the orcs scattered and ran as soon as they saw the soldiers. They were hard to hit from horseback, and easily distanced footsoldiers, loping over the uneven ground as smoothly as hounds. Paks finally called her squads in, before they were too far apart, and returned to the farm to help clean up the mess.

As the days passed, she had similar encounters, all inconclusive. What, she wondered to herself, was a paladin supposed to do in a situation like this? It wasn't that the soldiers were unwilling to fight, or were badly commanded. She could think of nothing to do that had not been tried. She knew that Stammel, at least, expected more of her, some miraculous intervention that would solve the mystery of the orcs' interest in the Duke's lands that year, and eliminate them. She prodded her mind, trying to force the vague feeling she assumed came from the gods into something more direct and definite. If she was supposed to be there, why? For what purpose? What sort of danger or evil should she be looking for? But all she found inside was the certainty that she should be where she was, doing what she was doing. And that seemed to accomplish nothing.

Chapter Nine

Paks had hardly seen the Duke in the days since her first interview. Now, preparing to enter the Duke's Court, she had time to wonder what she would find. Would it be like dinner with the Marshal-General? Or the candidates' hall in Fin Panir? She found she had no idea what the Duke and his captains did: what they wore, what they ate, how they talked. Did he have a minstrel? And it seemed even stranger to be coming to his table in her uniform—she shook that feeling away. Simple nervousness, no doubt.

At the door, the sentry nodded. She knew him: a veteran in Cracolnya's cohort. She had another attack of nervousness inside the hall, as she wondered which way to turn.

"Paks? Over here." Dorrin beckoned from the left, a wide passage. Paks turned that way, and came into an oblong room with a large table in the center. "We eat here, and it's also a conference room." Now that Paks knew what to look for, the emblem of Falk that Dorrin wore was plain to see: the tiny ruby glittered in the lamplight. "You're early," Dorrin went on. "Cracolnya's still out on a patrol. Pont won't be here tonight. Arcolin's upstairs with the Duke, and Val's settling the recruits." She looked closely at Paks. "How do you like being back?"

"Very much, Captain." Paks had never had much to do with Dorrin. She was next in seniority after Arcolin; Paks wondered if she had known Tamar. She looked around the room. The table was already set: plates and the two-pronged forks she'd learned to use in Fin Panir were laid before each chair. Goblets of pale blue swirled glass—tall flagons to match—squat mugs for the ale that would follow the meal. Loaves of bread were already on the table, too, as were dishes of salt and the condiments the Duke had grown used to in Aarenis. On one wall were weapons: a gilded battleax (Paks wondered at that—she had never seen the Duke use one), a slender sword with a green jewel in the hilt, two curved blades with inlaid runes in blue sea-stone on the broad blades, and a notched black blade that made Paks shudder to look at it.

"You should know who else may be at dinner with us. The Duke's surgeons sometimes—you may remember Visanior and Simmitt. Master Vetrifuge, the mage, would be with us, but he's visiting another mage down near Vérella for a few weeks. Kessim, of course. And the Duke's steward: did you know Venneristimon when you were here before?"

"No, Captain."

"Not surprising. He has nothing to do with the recruits. Well, he sits with us, many times. His sister, too, has been visiting here: she's a widow, and he's helping her with her estates. So it's been explained." By a slight chill in her last phrase, Paks guessed that Dorrin didn't like the steward's sister. She wondered if anyone did, remembering Stammel and Devlin.

"Paks. Good, you're here." Arcolin and Valichi came in together. Paks realized suddenly that none of the captains were wearing swords. Arcolin must have noticed her quick look at each hip. "We don't wear swords in the hall," he said quietly. "The Duke sometimes has visitors he would not wish armed at his table."

"But you—" began Paks.

"They cannot object if we do not wear them."

"I see."

"We have nothing to fear from each other," he went on. Paks felt a sudden surge of unease, as if the floor dipped slightly. She almost shook her head to clear it, then looked around. At the door, the Duke stood beside a red-haired woman in a blue gown. She had her hand on his arm, and her body seemed to lean toward him. Paks recognized her at once: the woman she had seen in the inn the first night she returned. Behind them was the slight form of Kessim, the Duke's squire on duty. Arcolin murmured, "That's Venner's sister—Lady Arvys Terrostin."

The Duke led the lady in. She smiled and spoke to all the captains, and to Paks when she was introduced.

"Paksenarrion? What an unusual name, my dear. Kieri has told me so much about you—I could be jealous, if I had any right to be—" She extended a soft hand, and Paks took it, aware of her own rough palm. More than that, she was shaken with revulsion. She fought to conceal it. However much she disliked this woman, she was the Duke's guest. But Dorrin turned the conversation, speaking to Paks.

"Is it a family name, Paks? I remember wondering about that—"

"My great-aunt was named Paksenarrion. I don't know for whom, but I was named for her." Paks wiped her hand on her tunic; she felt dirty.

"Ah. And I was named for my father's grandmother. It was supposed to honor her, but when I turned soldier the family was furious and changed her name in the family records." Dorrin smiled. "They sent me the one letter, to be sure I knew it, and that's all I've ever heard." Paks had never thought of any of the captains starting out.

"Eh, my lord—sorry I'm late—" Cracolnya, in the doorway, unwrapped his swordbelt and tossed it at a servant in the passage outside.

"What did you find?" asked the Duke.

"What we've found so far." Cracolnya stumped over to the table, obviously stiff from the saddle, and poured himself a glass of wine. His mail jingled faintly as he moved. He drank the wine down. "They made for the Lairs again—a band of forty or so. We killed fifteen, and wounded a few, but we couldn't catch them before they went underground."

"I'm sure you tried very hard," put in Lady Arvys. For

the barest instant everyone looked at her. Then they all moved to find a seat at the table.

"We're not formal," said Valichi, the recruit captain. "Not unless we have visitors from outside. Just find a place somewhere—" Paks waited until the others had sorted themselves, and took a seat at the far end of the table from the Duke. She noted that Lady Arvys sat on the Duke's left, and Master Simmitt, one of the dark-robed surgeons, was on his right. Cracolnya, Valichi, and Visanior, the other surgeon, took the left side of the table, while Arcolin, Dorrin, and the Duke's steward (who entered at the last minute) took the right side. Kessim sat beside Paks. Servants brought in platters of food, and the meal began. Paks ate quietly, sharply aware of something wrong, but unable to locate it. She remembered feeling like this in the inn; she wondered if it was the red-haired woman. She looked at the faces, trying to pick out the woman's escort that night. Around her the talk was of orcs and their raids.

"After so many quiet years, I simply can't understand it." Valichi gestured with his wine glass. "I must have missed something, staying up here with recruits—somehow I let them build up—but I swear to you, my lord, we had no trouble. No trouble at all."

"I believe you." The Duke's eyes were hooded. "I can only imagine that they are moved by some power—" he paused as Lady Arvys's hand rested lightly on his arm for a moment. She murmured something low into his ear. His face relaxed into a smile, and he shook his head. "Well," he said in a milder tone, "we need not mar our meal with such talk. Tir knows we've covered the same ground before. Has anyone a lighter tale, to sweeten the evening?" Paks saw the others' eyes shift sideways from face to face. She herself had never imagined the Duke being deflected from a serious concern by anyone, let alone someone like Arvys. Meanwhile Simmitt had began talking of rumors from Lyonya: the king's illness, and turmoil among the heirs. The lady listened eagerly.

"Did you hear anything about Lord Penninalt?" she asked, when Simmitt paused.

"No, lady, not then. Did you know him?"

"Yes, indeed. A fine man. My late husband held his lands from Lord Penninalt, and we went every year to the Firsting Feast." She turned to the Duke. "He is not so tall as you, my lord, or as famous in battle, but a brave man nonetheless."

"You need not flatter me," said the Duke, but he seemed not displeased.

Paks shivered. She looked up to find Venneristimon, diagonally across the table, staring at her.

"Are you quite well, Paks?" he asked. His tone was gentle and concerned, but it rasped on her like a file on bare flesh.

"Yes," she said shortly. Something moved behind his eyes, and he passed a flagon of a different wine down the table.

"Here—try this. Perhaps it will help." Now the others were looking at her, curious. Paks poured the wine—white this time—into her glass. She didn't want it, but did not want to make a fuss, either.

"I'm fine," she said. She passed the flagon back, and speared another sliver of roast mutton. She drenched it in gravy, and stuffed it quickly in her mouth. The others turned back to their own plates. When she glanced up again, Venner was still watching her, sideways. His mouth stiffened when she met his eyes. She felt her heart begin to pound; her skin tingled. The lady and Simmitt talked on, idle gossip of court society and politics. Paks looked back at her plate. She had nearly cleaned it, and the dishes on the table were almost empty. She reached for the last redroots on the platter.

"Still hungry, Paks?" The lady's voice, though warm and friendly, had the same effect on Paks as Venner's. "I suppose you work so much harder—"

Paks felt her face go hot. She had not realized the others were through. Her stomach clenched, but Val was answering.

"All soldiers learn to eat when they can, lady." She glanced over to find him cutting himself another slice of mutton. "Paks is not one to talk when she has nothing to say."

"I didn't mean to upset you," said the lady, smiling down the table. "Paks, do say you forgive me. . . ."

Paks mouth was dry as dust. She took a deliberate sip of the white wine, and said, "It's not for me to forgive, lady; you meant no offense." The wine seemed to go straight to her head; her vision blurred. As if she looked through smoke, she peered up the table and met Lady Arvys's eyes. They changed from green to flat black as she looked. Paks felt the jolt in her head; she looked toward Venner as if someone pulled her head on a string. He was watching her, lips folded under at the corners, like someone satisfied but wary. Her sense of wrong seemed to grab her whole body and shake it. Half-stupefied by the wine (how could one swallow be so strong?) she looked from one face to the other. Of course. *Venner* had been her escort. Even so, what was happening?

She might have sat there longer, but Venner spoke. "Ah . . . do you find the wine too strong for you, Paks? Are you still feeling ill?"

A flicker of anger touched her, and with it a warning. The anger, too, was wrong. It felt alien, as if it came from someone else. She reached deep inside for her own sense of self, and found not only that but a call for guidance. Her tongue felt clumsy, but she formed the words: "In the High Lord's name—"

Venner's face contracted; black malice leaped from his eyes. At once the hall was plunged into darkness. Stinking lamp smoke flavored a cold wind that scoured the room. Without thought Paks asked for light, and found herself lined with glowing brilliance. She leaped up, looking for Venner. She could hear the scrape of chairs on the floor, the exclamations of the others—and a curse from Venner's sister. The Duke gasped; she knew without looking that he'd been wounded somehow. At Venner's end of the table, nothing could be seen but a whirl of darkness.

"You fool," said his voice out of that darkness. "You merely make yourself a target." Something struck at her, a force like a thrown javelin. She staggered a little, but the light repelled it. She looked at the captains: they sat sprawled in their chairs, eyes glittering in the spell-light, but unmoving. "They won't help you," Venner went on. "They can't. And you are unarmed, but I—" She saw the darkness move to the wall, saw it engulf the terrible notched blade she'd seen there. "While *she* takes care of the Duke, I will kill you with this—as I killed before—and again no one will know. When I let these captains free, it will seem that you went wild—as Stephi did before you—and killed the Duke, while I tried to save his life."

Paks was already moving, clearing herself of the chair. She had picked up a bronze platter—the largest thing on the table—and looked now to the walls for a weapon of her own. She was nearly too late. Venner had taken more than the notched sword: out of the darkness the battleaxe whirled at her. She flung out the platter, and it folded around the axe, slowing it and spoiling the blow. She had her dagger in hand now—far too short against an unseen opponent. The ragged edge of Venner's sword caught the dagger and nearly took it out of her hand. She jumped back.

"You can't escape," his voice said, out of the blackness. "You—"

Paks saw a glow on one wall and leaped for it. The notched blade clattered against the wall just behind her. But she had a sword in her hand—the sword with the green stone. Its blade glowed blue as she took it. Before she could turn, Venner struck again. She felt the black sword open a gash along her side; she tucked and rolled away, and came up ready to fight.

Now she could sense, within the darkness, a core—more like the skeleton of a man than a man entire. One thin arm held the dark blade; the other held a dagger almost half as long. Paks thrust at the dark blade. Her own sword rang along it. Venner countered, stabbing with the dagger. Paks swept it aside, and attacked vigorously, beating him back and back.

"You can't see me!" screamed Venner. "You can't—"

But she could. Dark within dark, his shape grew clearer

as they fought. Suddenly the dark was gone, as if Venner had dropped a black cloak. Paks stared, uncertain. He had disappeared; she could see the wall and floor where he should be. A blade came out of nowhere to strike her arm; she felt rather than saw the flicker of movement and managed to counter it. Now she sensed him as a troubling thickness in the air, a nearly transparent glimmer, barely visible in her own brilliant spell-light. She kept after him. The sword she held seemed to move almost of its own will, weightless and perfectly balanced in her hand. Venner retreated again, toward the head of the table. Paks followed. She had not expected the Duke's steward to be much of a swordsman—she hadn't thought of it at all—but he was skillful.

Venner swept the table suddenly with his left arm, sent food and dishes flying between them. Paks slipped on a greasy hunk of mutton. Venner stabbed wildly with the sword. She rolled aside and let the thrust pass. Her sword caught him in the ribs; she heard a rasping gurgle, and he was visible, hand held against his side. Paks lunged at him. He dropped the sword, and dodged. While she was still off balance, he grappled with her, trying to rake her with the dagger. She could see the brown stain along it, surely poison.

"You stinking kellich!" he snarled. "You Girdish slut! You'll die the same as she did, and Achrya will revel in this hall—"

Paks could not use her sword in close; she dropped it and dug her strong fingers into his wrist. Red froth bubbled from his mouth as they wrestled on the floor. He was surprisingly strong.

"Arvys!" he cried suddenly. "Arvys! Help me!" Paks heard noise around the room—chairs and boots scraping on the stone, voices—but she was too busy to listen. Venner had both hands on the dagger hilt, and she had to use both hands to hold it off. "Achrya," he said viciously, glaring at Paks. "You found before you could not stand against her. She will bind you in burning webs forever, you Gird's dog—"

"By the High Lord," said Paks suddenly, "neither you nor Achrya will prosper here, Venner. His is the power, and Gird gave the blessing—"

"You will *die*," repeated Venner. "All in this hall—and she will reward me, as she did before—" But he was weakening, and Paks managed to force him back. She could feel the sinews in his wrist slackening. She closed her own fingers tighter, and all at once his hand sagged open, releasing the dagger. It clattered on the floor. Paks kicked it far aside, and shifted one hand from Venner's left wrist to her own dagger, dropped nearby.

"Now," she said, "we will hear more of this—"

"I spit at you, Gird's dog. I laugh—" But he was choking, and he sagged heavily under her hands.

"Paks! Hold!" Arcolin's voice. She held her dagger to Venner's throat, and waited. "What's—"

"The Duke!" Master Simmitt, this time. "By the gods—"

"He's dead—or dying—" Arvys's voice was savage. "And Achrya will have his soul—and *yours*—" she broke off in a scream.

"Not yet," said Cracolnya. "Don't you know you can't knife a man in mail?" Paks's attention was diverted for an instant. Venner surged up against her hold; without thinking she slammed her hand down. Her dagger ripped his throat, and he died.

She scrambled up to see what else had happened. Shadows fled before her spell-light. Simmitt leaned over the Duke, who was slumped in his seat. On the other side, Cracolnya held Arvys, her arms twisted behind her.

"Light," snapped the surgeon. "Come here, Paks, if that's you making a light." She came around the table. She saw Dorrin working with flint and steel to relight the lamps. The Duke's face was gray; a slow pulse beat in his neck. He seemed to gasp for breath. Visanior too had reached the Duke's seat; the two surgeons maneuvered him from the chair to the tabletop. Simmitt slit his tunic and spread it. There on the left side was a narrow wound—Paks glanced at Arvys and saw the sheath of a small dagger dangling from her wrist.

"That's close—" commented Visanior.

"Poison, or in the heart?" Simmitt bent close to listen to the Duke's heart.

"Poison, and close to it." Visanior turned away. "I've a few drops of potion in my quarters—"

"Too late," hissed Arvys. "You won't save him—or yourselves. Nothing you've got will touch that—and your precious Duke, as you call him, will never take his rightful seat—" Cracolnya tightened his hold, and she gasped.

Paks reached out to touch the Duke's shoulder.

"Get back, Paks—you're no surgeon, and I don't have time—"

"Let her." Dorrin brought a lamp near, its light golden next to the white spell-light. "She alone saw Venner's nature; she alone could free herself to fight him. Perhaps—" She looked at Paks, her own hand going to the tiny Falkian symbol at her throat. "Perhaps you learned more than we knew, is that so?"

Paks felt a pressure in her head, and could not answer. She only knew she had to touch the Duke—had to call what powers she could name. As she laid her hand on his shoulder, the spell-light dimmed except along that arm. She closed her eyes against it: she had no time to study what was happening.

Touching the Duke was like laying her hand on the skin of running water: she felt a faint resistance, a surface tension, and a strong sense of moving power underneath. Without realizing it, she brought her other hand to his other shoulder. She felt within herself the same moving power that she sensed in the Duke, although in her it ran swifter, lighter. She tried to bring the two powers together.

At first it seemed that the surface between them thickened, resisting. The Duke's rhythm slowed and cooled, as if some moving liquid stiffened into stone. But her plea to the High Lord and Gird brought a vision of movement, of sinking through the surface as a hand sinks in water. She let herself drift deeper. In that thicker substance, that cooling stream, she loosed her one fiery essence, the flames that had danced deep within since the night of the Kuakgan's magic fire.

Slowly the Duke responded. Whatever the flow might be, it flowed more swiftly—it moved lightly on its way, with returning joy. Paks followed the flow, to find a source of stagnation—some evil essence. She felt herself touch it, and it dissolved, running away, overtaken by her flame, and then gone. With that, the Duke's body swung back to its own balance. She felt the restored health, and the rejection, at the same instant, and pulled herself back into her own body just ahead of it.

His eyes were open. Blank for a moment, then fully aware: startled and intent all at once. Paks stepped back, shaken by her gift. Simmitt stared at her. They all did. The room's light was golden from lamps; her spell-light had disappeared.

"What—?" The Duke had his head up now, raking the room with his glance. His hand lay over his ribs, where the dagger had gone in.

"My lord, it was Venner—"

"This so-called lady—"

"Paks was the only one who could—"

"Quiet." Arcolin's voice cut through them, and brought order. "Cracolnya, Valichi—guard her: nothing else. My lord Duke, it seems your steward was a traitor of some sort. Paks has killed him. The rest of us were somehow spellbound, unable to move, though we heard enough. Kessim is dead. And that—" he paused and glared at Arvys.

"She stabbed me," said the Duke calmly. "I remember that. Some kind of argument, and then darkness, and then I felt a blade in my side." He sat up on the edge of the table, and looked down at the blood that streaked his skin and clothes. "Heh. No mark now. Who had the healing potion so handy?" He looked at Visanior and Simmitt.

"Not us, my lord. Paksenarrion."

"You heal, as well as fight?" The Duke looked at Paks. She met his eyes.

"With the High Lord's permission, my lord, I have been able to. Sometimes."

He looked at Arvys, and his face hardened. "You," he said, and stopped. "You—will you say why? You were willing, you said, to share my name—why kill, then?"

She said nothing until Cracolnya shifted behind her, then gasped. "You—petty, base-born lout! Duke, you call yourself—that's not the title you *should* bear. I was willing to share your name, as long as it served my Lady's purpose. But you'd have had a blade in your heart someday, as you still shall."

He raised an eyebrow. "Your Lady? And who is that? Is the Queen that angry with me?"

She laughed, a harsh, forced laughter. "Queen! What do you know of queens, who call a mortal human queen? When you see her webs around you, and feel her poison, who has enmeshed those far higher than humans, then you will know a queen. I speak of the webmistress Achrya, whose power no man can withstand."

"And yet I live, and you are captive. Was Venneristimon also her agent?"

"Why should I answer you?"

"Because your mistress is far away, and I am here. You may wish an easy death, though you would deal a hard one."

"Kill as you please," she answered. "Whatever you do, my lady will avenge me, and him, and give you endless torment."

"I doubt that." The Duke looked among the litter of things swept to the floor and picked up a small narrow-bladed dagger, hardly as long as his hand. "This is yours, is it not? Would you wish to taste your own brew?"

"As you will." She seemed to droop in Cracolnya's arms; Paks and the others stared, surprised at her. Then Paks gasped as her face changed, shifting from the fair-skinned soft curves she had shown to something older and more perilous. Their cries warned Cracolnya, who gripped more tightly as she shriveled in his hold, her red-gold hair turning gray and her rounded limbs wiry and gnarled. She struggled; Valichi moved to help Cracolnya. Paks hunted on the floor for the sword she had dropped, and scooped it up. By the time the transformation was complete, and Cracolnya held a wizened muscular hag instead of an attractive young widow, she had the tip of that sword at the hag's throat.

"Here's something you will like less well," said Paks. "An elf-blade."

"You farmbred brat!" Her voice, as a hag, chilled the blood. "You saved your precious Duke, eh? Did you? And you will take him to his appointed end, I daresay. Do you think he'll thank you for that? When he dies in the bed *you* make for him?" Her head turned, and more than one in the room flinched from her vicious eyes. "Tell her, Duke Phelan, how you come by your name. Tell her what happened to the last yellow-haired girl to hold that sword." Her voice shrilled higher. "Or shall I? Shall I tell her how the thriband knew where your wife and children would ride that day? And who suggested that trail, where the wildflowers bloomed? He is safe from your wrath, mighty Duke, but your children will never return." She laughed, a hideous laugh. "You, Duke Kieri Phelan—no, let us use it all—Kieri *Artfiel* Phelan—you harbored that woodworm and trusted it as your pet. Your wife it was who suggested he be assistant to the steward—and then—"

Paks pushed the blade gently on the hag's skin. "Be still. You have nothing worth listening to."

"Have I not? You are eager to kill, little peasant girl. Little runaway daughter of a sheep herder—how many times have you run away? Do you guess that I can tell them? The Duke doesn't know the worst, does he? The men in Seameadow? The time you ran from the sheepdog—not even a wolf—in Arnbow?" She stopped, and wheezed a moment. Then: "I know many things that you would be better knowing—and him, too—before he trusts you—" and she stopped and clamped her lips together.

"Ward of Falk," murmured Dorrin, behind them. "Against an evil tongue."

"In the High Lord's name," said Paks. The hag's eyes glittered but she said nothing.

The Duke had come near, and stood looking from one to another. "When one stabs, and another heals," he said, "I know which to trust."

"You! You are no true duke, and she will take you to your end, if you are unfortunate enough not to meet another."

"I'll chance that. Paks, you had scruples before about such things: how should she be killed?"

Paks did not look away from the point of her blade. "Quickly, my lord, as may be."

"I'll save you the trouble," gasped the hag, and she lunged forward, managing to scrape her arm on the dagger the Duke still held. Almost at once she sagged.

"I don't believe it," said Cracolnya. "Paks—or Val—finish her."

Paks ran the sword quickly into her chest, feeling between the ribs for her heart. The limp form in Cracolnya's hold shuddered again, this time shifting from that of a hag to no human shape at all: a great belly swelling below, bursting out of the blue gown Suliya had worn, the upper body falling in to become a hard casing that extended suddenly into more legs. Cracolnya lurched back, loosing his hold. The thing was free, hampered only slightly by the remnants of clothes. The head—no longer human at all—turned a row of emerald eyes on Paks; fangs dripped. Paks alone was able to move; she hardly saw what was happening before her arm went up and a long stroke took off that terrible head. The body twitched; gouts of sticky fluid spurted from the barely-formed spinnerets on the belly, but did not reach anyone.

"Gods above," muttered Cracolnya. "What is *that*? A spider demon?"

"A high servant of Achrya," said Paks, watching the body on the floor. "They have that power, to change to her form at will."

"Is *that* what you faced in Kolobia?" asked Arcolin. "Tir's gut, I couldn't—" he stopped, choking.

The Duke himself was white. "Paksenarrion, again—you have gone far beyond our thanks—" He shook himself like a wet dog, and looked around the room. "Captains, we must know what all this means, but for now we must be sure where we are. If I understood any of that—if any of it can be believed—this stronghold is in danger, even with them dead. We'll double the watch. Arcolin, you have been here since we built the place: take some of the older veterans, who know it as well, and start looking for—" he stopped, and rubbed his hand through his hair. "I don't know what, but anything out of ordinary. Dorrin, are there any of the soldiers from Aarenis that still worry you?"

Dorrin thought a moment. "Not in my cohort, my lord. That Kerin fellow, in Arcolin's—"

"Arcolin, turn him out." Arcolin nodded. "Any more, Dorrin?"

"No, my lord."

"See to it, then. About the house servants—"

"And why haven't they come in?" Valichi looked around, worried.

"I don't know. Venner hired them; I don't know if they are innocent or his agents. Bring in a squad—no, two—and we'll go through this end as well. Paks—" he looked at her again, and his eyes dropped to the sword in her hand. "By the—you've got *her* sword!"

"My lord?" Paks looked at the sword in her hand.

"Tammarrion's—my—my wife's—"

"I'm sorry," said Paks. "I didn't know—it was the only one I could reach—"

He shook his head. "You used it well. I do not regret that. But no one has wielded it since she—" He took a long breath and went on. "Paks, you and Val stay with me here—you surgeons, as well. We'll do what we can for Kessim. Cracolnya, take a look in the passage—if we must fight our way out—"

Cracolnya stepped to the door, opened it slightly, and looked out. "Nothing this way, my lord. Let me call the sentry from the door."

"I think not. He's better where he is. Paks—" Arcolin and the Duke leaned over Kessim's slumped form; he had been struck by the battleaxe when Paks deflected the blow from herself. His skull had been crumpled by the blow, and he was clearly dead. The Duke looked up. "Damn and blast that witch! This lad had no chance at all. A fine squire, and would have made a fine man, but for this."

Paks felt a surge of guilt—if she had not thrown that blow aside—she had never thought of Kessim sitting there unable to move—but the Duke forestalled her before she could speak.

"If you hadn't, Paks, we'd all be dead. I certainly would, and you, and I can't imagine the rest would be let to live long. Don't think of blaming yourself. Now—"

"My lord, let me check the kitchen entrance." Paks had moved to the other door in the room, from which the servants had brought in the food. She opened the door and looked. This passage was narrower than the front one. She could smell cooked food and smoke from the left; the passage was empty. She shut the door again, and pulled a chair against it. "No one in sight," she reported.

"Good," said the Duke. "Let's arm ourselves, captains, and get started. Paks, keep that blade for now—until the Company is roused."

The senior cohort captains left, Cracolnya returning in a few minutes with the Duke's sword and mail. "I told the sentry we'd had a small problem with the steward," he said. "He'll stop any servants from leaving by that door, at least. He heard nothing, by the way. Perhaps Venner's magic kept any of that from getting out, as well as kept us still. Dorrin's squads will be here shortly. What shall we do with the bodies?"

The Duke, struggling into his mail shirt, did not reply until he had settled his sword belt to his satisfaction. "If I knew certainly that Venner was human, I would know—as it is, I don't know whether to burn, bury, or dismember it. Do you, Paks?"

"No, my lord. The shape-changing servants must be beheaded, for they can shift the location of the heart with the change of shape. But Venner—I believe this body is dead, but I don't know what powers he may still have." She felt within for any warning, and found nothing but distaste. "I feel nothing wrong, my lord, as I felt before—"

"Before?" The Duke's eyebrows went up. "When? Before dinner—no. Not yet. When we're secure, then we'll talk about it. Safe or not, I don't want this mess in my dining hall—we'll take them out—clear outside the stronghold, and just in case we'll behead Venner's corpse as well. Kessim can lie in the other hall, until morning. We'll hold his service tomorrow, and display the others to the troops, so they'll know what's happened." Then a commotion at the door—Dorrin with two squads, eyes wide but disciplined.

"Gather the servants," the Duke told her. "Don't tell them what happened, and don't hurt them—they may well be innocent—but guard them well."

Chapter Ten

By the start of the third watch that night, the stronghold was in a very different mood. The servants Venner had hired over the years were huddled in one of the third floor storage rooms, guarded by Dorrin's soldiers. They were clearly confused and frightened. Paks, on the pretext of bringing Dorrin messages from the Duke, had wandered among them. None triggered her warnings of evil, and the Duke now believed them to be innocent. But he was taking no chances, and they remained under guard for the next day and a half. Kessim's shrouded body lay in state in one of the reception rooms, with an honor guard from all three cohorts.

Arcolin and the oldest veterans prowled the stronghold, looking for any signs of hidden weakness. Some they had already found, in the Duke's quarters. "I didn't build it this way," muttered an old carpenter, as he pried a board loose in the back of a closet in the Duke's sleeping room. "Look—you can see where these boards are newer, and stained dark. 'Tis easy to open this—like a door—and come through or listen. It'd take a week to do such a job. Who? Not me, is all I say. But that Venner, now, he'd bring folks up from Verella—my wife saw them, time and again, on the road, but we thought it was your will, my lord—" In the Duke's study, again, a hidden panel swung out giving access to the next room, where files had been stored.

On the walls, the doubled watch peered through the

night. They knew from their sergeants' faces that this was no night to gossip when they met at the corners or ask questions at the change of watch. Many had seen the blanket-wrapped bundles carried out the watch-gate: they didn't know who, but they knew trouble had already come.

The Duke seemed to be everywhere, with Paks at his side. He walked the walls himself, midway of the second watch, and strolled through each of the barracks. In the infirmary, he paused by each bed, until the sick had seen and recognized him. He paused to speak to sentries and guards at each post. Gradually the Company settled into watchfulness. The Duke was alive, and obviously well, and very obviously in command. Some of them looked sideways at Paks and wondered why she carried a longsword, but they did not ask.

Midway of the third watch, Arcolin had found nothing amiss in the front court. "It will take days to search everything, my lord," he reported. "But Siger and I think we've covered the most obvious places for trouble. I'd expect a passage outside, for instance, but there isn't one. We thought of the jacks pit, but the gratings are still locked in. But in here—"

"Yes." The Duke looked tired; he sat heavily in the chair in his study. "We've found so many things already. Mostly ways of spying on me, or on you captains. I daresay we've hardly said a word, these last years, that he did not know. I think I know now how the Regency Council found out about that last campaign in Aarenis."

"Did you—could you hear what he said as he and Paks fought?"

"No. After the dagger, I heard and saw nothing."

"He did more than that, Kieri. He—"

"Later. I suspect more. But for now—*did* he have a way outside, and are we going to be attacked? And when?"

"More when than if, I think. Has Dorrin checked the lower levels?"

"Not yet. There's so much up here—"

"Did he ask permission for any construction, and changes, in the past year or so?"

"I don't—gods above, Jandelir, he did! The new wine cellar—remember?" Arcolin nodded. "He said he wanted to enlarge, if we were all staying here—and I told him to stay within the walls, but—"

"Let's go." Arcolin stood, and stretched his arms. "Tir's gut, I'm tired. Why that rascal couldn't have started this after I'd had a good night's sleep—"

The Duke was no longer sure which cellar had been extended. He, Paks, Arcolin, and a squad from Dorrin's cohort began the search at the kitchen stairs. A passage ran north, the length of the building. Doors opened off it at intervals. But they found nothing in any of the outside rooms, and no signs of new construction.

"Would one of the servants know?" asked Paks.

"They might." The Duke rubbed his eyes. "Tir's gut, but I'm tired. It must be near dawn. Let's go up and see."

The cooks knew at once which cellar was meant. "Sir, it's the third on the right, the last on that side before the corner. He said 'twas to give room, so's not to run into the well, there in the court. Can you tell us, sir, what's wrong? Is Venner angry with us? We done nothing, sir, I swear it—"

"It's all right. The third on the right?"

"Yes, sir, it—" But they went back out, into a cold dawn, and crossed the courtyard again.

"An inside cellar," said Arcolin. "What was he up to?"

"No good," said the Duke shortly. His shoulders were hunched against the cold. The sentries—four, now—at the door, saluted smartly. One of Dorrin's squad, following, stumbled on the steps. The Duke frowned. Dorrin waited inside.

"My lord, I brought food from the Company kitchens."

"I don't need—" He stopped abruptly, and looked at the others. "Maybe I do, indeed. Thank you. I'd forgotten I have the cooks locked up."

Sometime during the night, Dorrin had cleared away the mess in the dining hall. A steaming pitcher of sib and a kettle of porridge centered the big table. Bowls and mugs were stacked to one side. Paks sat with the others, unconcerned about order and seniority. After a bowl of porridge and several mugs of sib, she felt more awake. The Duke's face was less pinched. Dorrin had had a fresh squad ready inside, and sent the first one off to breakfast with the rest of the Company.

"Well, now," said the Duke, over his third mug of sib. "We'll see about that cellar, and then—barring immediate trouble—we'll get some sleep."

"Agreed." Arcolin stretched and yawned. "Is Pont back, Dorrin?"

"Yes. I sent him on to sleep when he came; he's up again and ready to take the day watches. Nothing's happened outside. Oh yes—my lord, I took the liberty of sending word to the villages—"

"I should have thought of that. Good for you."

"As of this morning, nothing's happened there, either. The Councils will meet with you at your convenience; they've alerted all the veterans. Piter has a list of all the travellers in the Red Fox, and they won't be going anywhere today."

"Oh?"

"Something's happened to their horses—or their wagons—and it seems a thief went through last night and stole left shoes."

The Duke laughed, and the others joined in. "That Piter! It's a good thing he's on my side." He pushed his chair back. "Let's get to that cellar, then, and hope to find nothing we need worry about until after rest."

The cellar door in question yielded to none of the keys on the ring. Dorrin had searched Venner's quarters, and had found another ring in a hollow carved into his bedpost. She handed it over. These keys were thinner and newer than the others. One of them slipped into the lock and turned it.

Inside, it looked like any wine cellar: rows of racks with slender green bottles on one side, and barrels, raised off the floor on chocks, on the other. The new extension, clearly visible, made it almost twice as large as before. Along the far wall were more racks for bottles: most of these were empty. They prowled around the cellar, tapping on walls. All seemed solid. Paks stayed near the Duke. It seemed to her that the room could have held many more racks if they had been arranged differently. Racks and barrels both sat well out from the walls. She asked the Duke about it.

"I don't know—" he said, looking surprised. "I suppose—perhaps the air is supposed to move around them—or it's easier to clean."

It was very clean, as if it had been swept recently. Paks bent to look under the racks. Surely there would be dust underneath—they couldn't move all the racks and barrels every time. She saw something dark and heavy. It didn't look like dust. She swiped at it with her hand, and teased it out into view. A dried lump of clay—the same sort of clay that clung to their boots in the field.

"What's that?" asked Dorrin behind her.

"I don't know—clay, I think. But why under there?" As she said it, she thought of mud from boots, falling off, being swept under—

"Hunh. Not exactly like our clay. Grayer."

"Well, it's dry—"

"Even so." Dorrin flattened herself on the floor and looked under the rack. "Is that—can you see that different colored stone, there?"

Paks lay down and looked. One of the square paving blocks that floored the cellar looked a shade darker than the others, but it was under the rack, after all. She reached out to touch it. It was stone. Dorrin had gotten up. The Duke leaned over to look.

"We'll move this rack," he said. Paks and the others laid hands on it and shoved it aside. The stone in question was slightly darker gray. The space between it and the stones around it was filled tightly with earth.

"It can't be a door," said Arcolin. "Look how the crack's filled."

"The others aren't." Dorrin pointed. Between other stones a broom had swept out some of the earth, leaving little grooves. But on this one, the dirt looked unnaturally smooth, filling the crack to the brim. Dorrin drew her dagger and picked at it. It came out in long sections, exactly like dried mud. Beneath that surface of mud the crack was clean and empty.

They all stared at it a moment. "Let's use sense," the Duke said finally. "Without knowing what, who, and how many, we're fools to open that now. Can we block it for a day?"

"We can guard it, certainly. As for blocking it, that depends on what's coming through. But if it's a mage of some kind, the guards could be overcome."

"Two sets," the Duke said. "Clear this room to the walls, and post some inside and some in the passage out there. I don't want to open this until I have some idea what's going on."

While the room was being cleared, and guards set, the Duke went to his quarters for sleep, and ordered the others to do likewise. Paks had thought she would not sleep at all, but she was hardly in her bunk before sleep took her, dreamless and deep.

Stammel woke her in the afternoon; heavy clouds darkened the day, and lamps had been lit already. Paks yawned and shook her head to clear it. Stammel looked around the empty barracks before speaking again.

"The story is that you healed the Duke." He paused, and Paks tried to think how to say what she must say. He went on. "You remember, we talked once, a long time ago, about you maybe being a paladin someday. I never forgot what you said about Canna, that time. I suppose you did heal her. And then the Duke came back—he never said anything to us, but we heard you'd had some trouble in Fin Panir." He stopped again, and looked away, then back at her. "I want you to know that I never did believe all I heard. The Duke, now—I've been in his Company since I left home, and never found a better man to follow. When you left, I had my doubts—but if this is what you came back to do, well—it's good enough." His face relaxed slightly. "But you could have told me, I think, what you could do. We could save the pay of a surgeon, at least."

Paks shook her head, smiling. "I'm still finding out what I can do."

"You mean you didn't know you could heal? What about that other? Glowing light and all?"

"Who told that? No, I knew some of it. It's come slowly. But I still don't know what I can do until I try. That's the second time I've made light; the first time it scared me half to death."

"I suppose it would." Stammel sounded thoughtful. "Was that in Kolobia?"

"No. A month or so ago, in Brewersbridge. With a Kuakgan."

"Kolya's friend?"

"Yes. Anyway, last night—when the darkness came, from Venner, I just—asked for light, I suppose."

"And the healing. You'd healed before—Canna—"

"And one other, in Lyonya. A ranger. But I'm still learning. The elves said healing was a hard art to learn. It isn't power alone, like light, but knowledge, as well. The Duke's wound was a simple stab . . . I'd be afraid to try something like a broken bone."

"Well—we're all glad you did it. I don't suppose you'll be here long, now—?"

Paks shrugged. "Why not? I don't have any plan to leave. Nothing's called me."

"You had a call to come here, though, didn't you?" She nodded. "I thought so. I thought it was more than bringing the Duke back his ring. Well, then. Are you a paladin, Paks? Gird's paladin?"

She had been waiting for this. "I'm not sure what I am. I have some gifts paladins have. I am a Girdsman. But Gird himself followed the High Lord, and I have had a—" She could not think how to describe her experience at the Kuakgan's that last night. Vision? Miracle? She stopped, paused, and started again. "I have had a call, which I feel bound to follow. It brought me here, with a feeling that the Duke needed me. I will stay until it takes me somewhere else. The Kuakgan and the elves told me that the gods used to call paladins directly. Perhaps I am one, but it's not what I expected."

"A long way from Three Firs," said Stammel soberly. "You were—" he shook his head. "You were such a *young* recruit. I could see the dream in your eyes: songs, magic swords, flying horses, I daresay—and yet so practical, too. And the Company wasn't what you expected either, was it?"

Paks laughed. "No. Cleaning, repairing walls, mending uniforms—we all hated that at first."

"But you stuck it out. And now you've saved the Duke's life—again. I don't forget what happened in Aarenis. Well, I've talked long enough. Too long, it may be. The Duke wants you in conference before dinner tonight."

The Duke looked much better; rested and alert, he leaned over the maps spread on the table. The captains were all there but Cracolnya, who had the watch. As Paks came in, they looked up. The Duke smiled and waved her over to the table.

"We're trying to remember, Paks, the details of something that happened when I first took over this stronghold. You've never been to the Lairs, I think. When I first came, we drove the orcs out of there—we hoped for good—and explored some of their tunneling. Unhealthy sport: we lost several men to cave-ins, and I finally forbade any more of it. But Jandelir thinks he remembers one tunnel that led off southwest—toward us—"

"I'm sure of it," said Arcolin. "I remember because it was straighter than the rest, and wider. It wasn't all that long—" he pointed out the spot on the map. "Couldn't have come past here. You know that swampy area where the springs are? It ended there, in a cave-in. Those stupid orcs had tried to burrow mud. We thought they'd intended to get close enough for a surprise attack. Those old rubble walls weren't worth much—"

"The first stronghold," Dorrin put in. "Built by someone from Vérella."

"But now we wonder if that tunnel's been repaired and brought on in," said the Duke. "If it ends, for instance, in that wine cellar—"

"They'll have a surprise," said Dorrin grimly.

"Bad place to fight," said Pont. "Cramped. The way orcs fight, we'll have to count on losing some." He paused for a sip of water. "Better than fighting in their tunnel, though. If they have polearms, that'd be suicide."

"Surely we can trap them." Dorrin rested both elbows on the table. "If we clear the room, we can have archers ready to pop the first ones through. That hole isn't big enough to let more than two out at once."

"If we knew what they're planning—" began Arcolin. The Duke interrupted.

"Exactly. Paksenarrion, you have more experience in this than we have. You recognized the lady as an agent of Achrya, and you have dealt with her agents and clerics before. What can we expect?"

For an instant, as they all watched her, Paks could say nothing. She was the youngest there, the lowest rank—how could she advise them?

"My lord, I am not sure what you already know—"

"Don't worry about that. Start at the beginning."

"Well, then—Achrya, the webmistress, is not high in the citadels of evil, according to my teachers in Fin Panir, but she involves herself directly with men and elves, and is therefore more familiar. She delights in intricate plots, and ensnares men to evil deeds by slow sorceries of years. Where Liart—the Master of Torments—prefers direct assault and torture, Achrya spins web within web, and likes the struggles of the victim as much as the final meal, so they say." Paks paused for a breath. She hated speaking directly of Achrya or Liart either one. "She hates the elves most, it is said, because they see clearly, and her arts cannot fool them—and Girdsmen and Falkians, because they will not compromise with evil for any immediate good. Her plots cannot prosper in peaceful, well-kept lands, so she is always brewing plots and treacheries. Just so might a normal spider encourage clutter in a house, to make its web-spinning easier, if it could keep the housewife from sweeping."

"But what of that shape-changing?"

"I'm coming to that. Some of her clerics have the power to change shape, both from one human form to another, and from human form to that of her icon: the appearance of a giant spider. I saw that in Kolobia, and heard of it at Fin Panir."

"Are all her clerics human, then? I thought you had seen kuaknom in Kolobia—"

"Yes, that's true. The elves that turned from the High Lord—some say when the first of the Kuakkganni sang to the First Tree—worship her."

"But what will she do here?" asked Dorrin. "Will she know her cleric's been killed? And Venner?"

"It depends. I don't know how her clerics contact her. I was taught that Achrya, unlike more powerful deities, does not know all that occurs by her own powers. She depends on her agents for information. If that's true, and Venner and his sister were her only agents here, then she might not. But she might know when her cleric was killed—I can't say. What she will do, when she finds out, depends on what resources she has near here. The orcs, yes—but even for her they are undisciplined and careless fighters. And we still don't know *why* she influenced Venner here—at least I don't. How long had he been steward?"

"Since the old steward was killed—at the same time as Tammarrion," said the Duke. "He had been injured, as a recruit, and became assistant steward. He was so for several years, as I recall, and then after the massacre—well, he knew the job."

"From what he said last night," said Arcolin, "that was his doing as well."

The Duke nodded, his face grim. "I expect so. I wonder if he was her agent from the beginning."

"Surely not. The Marshal wouldn't have missed that."

The Duke looked at Paks, a clear question. She answered. "No, my lord, he wouldn't have missed it if Venner had been committed to her then. But Achrya gains adherents in subtle ways. At first he may not have realized what he was doing—"

The Duke flushed. "Arranging a massacre? How could he not?"

"I didn't mean that, my lord. Earlier. We don't know—perhaps he had cheated someone, or told a minor lie: I have heard that she makes much of that. Or he may have been told lies, about you, that justified him to himself, in the beginning. By the time he realized whose service he had joined, it would have been too late."

"Are you saying it was not his fault?"

"No, my lord. Unless he was spelled the entire time, he was responsible for his decisions. I meant that he may not have intended any evil when he joined the Company . . . may in fact have slipped into evil bit by bit. Perhaps the massacre that killed your wife was the first overt act of evil. The Marshal was killed, too: could it be that the Marshal was beginning to suspect something? That the attack was aimed as much at him as at her?"

"No!" The Duke stiffened, then sat back. "It couldn't be. Yet—"

"She might have noticed, too, my lord," said Dorrin. "Being as she was. And she would be more in the steward's way than the Marshal."

"But we still don't know why Achrya spends her strength here," Paks went on.

"The northern border—it was always important—" But Arcolin did not sound convinced.

"So long a time," the Duke mused. "If Venner was in truth part of a long-laid plan—by Tir, that's more than sixteen years she's been plotting. Against me? Against this holding? We know that she supported Siniava in Aarenis."

Cracolnya shifted in his seat. "If it's to clear this holding for another invasion from the north, why didn't she strike while you were in Aarenis with the whole Company?"

"That's when the orc trouble began—"

"Yes, but not enough to wipe us out. Just enough to discredit you. I'd like to know who Venner knew in Verella. And why you, my lord? I'm not saying you're no threat to evil in this realm, but I'd not have thought you that important, begging your pardon."

"Nor I," said the Duke with a smile. "By the gods, captains, I admit I've been trying to strengthen my position in this kingdom, but I wouldn't have thought I'd succeeded well enough to flurry a demon. Or, for that matter, that my deeds were so good."

"Why didn't Venner simply stab you one night?" Cracolnya went on. "Or is that my nomad heritage showing? It should have been easy enough, with all the hidden passages we've found."

"That's not Achrya's way," said Paks. "She prefers to spoil rather than destroy utterly. Her minions could have killed me in Kolobia, easily enough, but they wanted to make a spoiled paladin, or a useless coward, rather than kill me." She was surprised to find she could speak of this easily. "Whatever her plans here, they will be devious and intricate—the cleric's stab was desperation, not the original intent, I would say."

"Mmph. I wonder. The witch kept me from paying enough attention to the orcs. I should have been thinking why they would come, and why they acted as they do. I've fought orcs before, and they never behaved like this. If she sought to distract me long enough for them to burrow into the stronghold, what then? Death, I expect." He looked around the table. "We need not understand all her motives, I think, to know we are opposed. But how can we foresee what she will do? Will we be attacked by orcs, or by other monsters of her will?"

"My lord, she will not risk herself against a ready foe: Achrya sends others to do her fighting. Orcs we can expect. If she has men or kuaknom nearby, they may attack as well, or she may withdraw, and try to plan other coils. Most importantly, she may have other agents within the stronghold or nearby. Those we must find, and quickly."

"You found none among the servants—"

"No, captain," said Paks to Arcolin. "But I am not sure enough yet that I would. Great evil, yes, but—"

"That brings up another point," said the Duke. "How

did you happen to turn up here just when you were needed? And what are you? Can you tell me that you came merely to bring back my ring?"

"No, my lord." Paks looked at him soberly. "While with the rangers in Lyonya, I had a sudden feeling—a call, it seemed—that you had need of me. I did not know why, but I knew I must come."

"And did you know you had these powers? Making light, finding evil, healing?"

"Yes. But I am not sure how to use them all yet, my lord."

"*Are* you a paladin, then, Paks?" asked Dorrin, fingering her Falkian pin.

"Both the rangers I was with and the Kuakgan in Brewersbridge think so," said Paks slowly. "I have no other explanation for the powers. They must come from the gods—from the High Lord, I believe. But the limits of the gifts I do not know. I think, my lord," she said, turning to the Duke, "that you should call a Marshal or paladin from Verella or Fin Panir—someone who knows how to use these things—and be sure your Company is free of traitors."

"You do not trust your own gifts?"

Paks tried to think how to explain her reserve. "My lord, I trust the gifts, but not yet my mastery of them. You would be wise to make use of another's experience, as well."

"I see." The Duke looked around the table. Arcolin was frowning, rumpling a bit of cloth in his hand. Dorrin sat still, hands out of sight. Pont leaned back in his chair, looking half-asleep. Cracolnya glanced from the Duke to Paks and back. The Duke looked at Paks. "You may not know, but I refused to have a Gird's Marshal in the stronghold after my wife was killed. I have always blamed them for her death—for hiring me and most of the Company away, so that she was left without enough guard; for the Marshal's weakness that day, that he did not save her. It has seemed to me that they claim to protect the weak and helpless, but in fact do not."

"My lord, having lost your wife and children, such bitterness is understandable."

"Mayhap. You do not know all I said to the Marshal-General when I found out about you. For that, too, I blamed them. But you do not, I think?"

"No, my lord. As any Girdsman is the natural enemy of Achrya's plots, I went into that peril knowingly. Certainly Girdsmen—the Marshal-General included—can make mistakes, but those I have known were honorable, if sometimes narrow."

"But they did not heal you. They sent you out alone and helpless—"

Paks laughed. "My lord, you remember they would have sheltered me. I insisted on leaving when I did, despite the Marshal-General's plea. True, they did not heal everything. They did, however, heal the worst of the evil, though it left scars. And—look now. What have I lost? You've watched me fight. If there is wisdom outside the grange as well as within, the Marshals have never claimed differently."

"And you—having suffered under them—would ask me to call them in? Knowing what you do of my past?"

"I know little, my lord, but what you have said here. I cannot imagine them asking you to take the Company elsewhere if they had known of your lady's peril. I cannot imagine the Marshal here doing aught but fighting to the death to save her and your children. Your anger I can understand, and your bitterness—in all honesty, my lord, during those terrible months last winter, I was bitter myself. But it seems now that you—and the Girdsmen—and your family—were all victims of a long-laid plot. A plot so cleverly hidden that not until last night did anyone—even you—recognize the traitor within. I daresay Achrya was pleased when you barred Marshals and paladins from your gates."

The Duke had one hand before his face, and his voice was muffled. "By the gods, I never thought of that. I never thought—but—that she was dead, and I had not been here to ward. And the little ones—"

"And then," mused Dorrin, covering his confusion, "in all the years her influence could act to corrupt the Company. With no one here who could detect evil directly, we could slip, bit by bit, into her ways."

"But that didn't happen," put in Paks. "This Company is honorable—"

"Not as it was," said the Duke, looking up now. His eyes glittered with unshed tears. "Not as it was, Paksenarrion; you never knew it before. When Tammarrion was alive, and a Marshal lived here—" He stopped and drew a long breath. "Well," he said finally. "I have been wrong. I have made as big a mistake in this as any I ever made. It was not the fault of Gird or Gird's followers, and I was blinded by my rage." He looked around the table again. "Do you agree, captains?"

They responded to the new timbre of his voice, straightening in their chairs and nodding. Arcolin spoke first. "My lord Duke, we have followed you in all things—but I confess I was long uneasy with your quarrel with Gird, and I would be pleased to have a Marshal here again."

"I also," said Dorrin quickly, her face alight. "Even as a Falkian."

"I wonder if they'll come," said the Duke. "After what I said to the Marshal-General, she may let us stew awhile—"

"I doubt that," said Cracolnya, grinning. "She'll be too glad to be proved right."

The Duke shook his head. "It will be some while, after these years, before I can learn to think anew. But our enemy now is Achrya, not Gird, and at least we know it. Paksenarrion, you have saved more than one life here. And, with your powers, you must see that you won't do as a corporal. I want you with me—as squire, perhaps?—until this knot is untangled."

"That's right," grumbled Arcolin with a grin. "Just let me get her trained as a good corporal, and then take her away. What am I supposed to do now, conjure one out of thin air?"

"You have plenty of good soldiers. Until a Marshal or paladin comes, she's the only one who might be able to detect another of Achrya's agents." The Duke turned to her. "Paksenarrion, will you accept this?"

"My lord, I came to serve you in whatever need I found. I will do whatever you ask until the gods call me away."

"Good, then. Stay by me. Have you any idea where the nearest Marshal of Gird might be?"

"No, my lord. The nearest grange, as you know, is at Burningmeed, two days south of here. But when I came through, that Marshal had gone on a journey; I don't know when she'd be back. It might be quicker to send a messenger straight to Verella."

"I dislike such an open move—if Achrya's agents are watching, they'll surely know something has happened."

"I suspect Achrya knows," said Cracolnya. "That one would have spies everywhere, despite our care. 'Tis almost a full day's turn gone since her cleric was killed. She'll either strike, or vanish to plan again."

Chapter Eleven

An immediate consequence of her new assignment was separation from the rest of the cohort. Stammel was unsurprised when she came to pick up her things from the barracks that night.

"You aren't a common soldier any more," he said bluntly, his composure recovered. "You can't pretend to be. If you need a friend, I'm here, but I'll take your orders the same as I would Arcolin's or the Duke's."

Paks shook her head silently. She could think of nothing to say.

"One thing you've got to be clear on," he went on. "I saw you retreat from this in Aarenis. If you mean to be a paladin—or a commander at all—you must accept being alone, clear through."

Paks found her voice. "The Kuakgan said something like that. I know it's true—I can obey only my own gods, now. But—"

"It takes getting used to. Yes. And you're young. But not as young as all that. Our Duke commanded a cohort at your age—that was all the Company he had then. And Marrakai gave him command—have you heard this?"

"No," said Paks, interested suddenly. She knew very little about the Duke's past.

"You can't stay long, so I'll hurry the tale, but it's worth telling. His first independent contract with the crown of Tsaia was in support of an expedition to Pargun. The crown prince commanded in the field, and the Duke—a captain then—had wangled a direct contract so that he ranked with the other independent commanders, dukes and counts and such. They didn't like that, so I hear. Ask Siger, some time: he was there. They were at the Pargunese border, east of here, when the prince called a conference one night. All the commanders in one tent—and their bodyguards. A force of Pargunese made it through the lines from the rear, and killed nearly all of them. Our Duke was knocked cold; the prince was killed; Marrakai—the most powerful baron, then—was badly wounded.

"Marrakai was widely believed to have ordered the attack—no love lost between him and the crown, so most men thought. The camp fell apart—the prince's commanders quarreling over command, and the steward threatening to go back to Vérella with his body—and our Duke took command, just by shouting louder than the others, according to Arcolin. Then Marrakai called him in, and gave him command of the Marrakai troops—five fighting cohorts—to attack the Pargunese and avenge the prince. So he did, and routed them, and brought back the head of the Sagon, the Pargunese western commander. That was his first big command, and that's when he got this grant, and the title. The next year, it was, he began recruiting in the north, and I remember seeing him come through my home town. I was too young, then, but I didn't wait about long."

"I had wondered how he got this land," said Paks.

"You talk to Arcolin, now—he was our Duke's junior, hired away from the Tsaian Guards, when he first came to Tsaia. Siger knew him before that; he was one of Aliam Halveric's sergeants in the old days. That's where our Duke got his first training."

"Do you know where he came from? Before that?"

Stammel shook his head. "No. No one does, unless the Halveric. I tried asking Siger once, and near lost an arm. I wouldn't advise it." He looked at her, smiling now. "You go on now, and do what you came for."

Paks had hardly stowed her few belongings in a cupboard when she heard the Duke's voice in the passage, asking if she was back. She went out quickly, and followed him into his study. Cracolnya and Valichi were there; the other captains were not.

"The more I think about it," the Duke said without preamble, "the more I think Venner was involved in most of what happened here. Val mentioned that trouble you had with the corporal—what was his name? Stephi?" Paks nodded. "It seemed fairly clear he'd been drugged, and at the time that potion was the best source. But if Venner could become invisible, as I understand he did during the fight with you—" He paused, and Paks nodded. "Yes, then he could have drugged the ale as he brought it, and drugged the potion bottle as well."

"I still don't see why, my lord," said Cracolnya, after shooting a hard glance at Paks. "Why would he cause such commotion, and run such a risk, to get Stephi in trouble?"

"It wasn't Stephi, I daresay," said the Duke. "It was Paks—if she was going to become a paladin—"

"Why not just kill her, then?" Cracolnya sounded half-angry. "I'm sorry, my lord, but it seems entirely too roundabout—"

"He had no access to recruits," said Valichi quietly. "He never came out of the Duke's Court, but to visit the villages, and rarely then. He couldn't have marched into barracks without being challenged—"

"But if he could be invisible?"

Paks had said nothing, still uncertain of her status, but now she intervened. "My lord, there's more to it, I'm sure. As with all Achrya's plots, we must look for more than one gain, and for interlacing of design. To discredit any good soldier—Stephi and me both, perhaps—and cause dissension in the Company, between recruits and veterans, between men and women, between Dorrin's cohort and Arcolin's." She paused. Both the captains were nodding slowly; the Duke watched her closely. "Then the other recruits—Korryn and Jens, whom you never knew, my lord—"

"Bad 'uns," put in Valichi.

"Yes, sir. If they had stayed longer, they might have

done more harm by influence. Even as it was, the trial and the punishment drove some recruits away—you remember that, sir. And not the worst, either."

"True." Valichi nodded again. "And I daresay Stephi's friends in the Company didn't trust you, Paks, at first."

Paks remembered Donag's early unfairness. "No, sir, they didn't. Stephi did what he could—he was always fair—"

"He was a good man," said the Duke. "If we could have known—" he sighed and quoted a version of the old saying, "*If* never won a battle. We must go from where we stand. I've sent for a Marshal." He looked around at all of them. "Until the Marshal comes, Paksenarrion, we'll hope your gift is enough to warn us. Since you found nothing amiss in the servants, I'm willing to let them go back to their work. We don't need that many, actually, and I'd as soon send some of them away, but it's too near winter for them to find work elsewhere. I know how most places are about hiring in the late fall and winter." His voice sharpened on this last, and Paks wondered how he knew. She had certainly run into that reluctance the previous winter.

"You could board some of them out in the villages," suggested Cracolnya. "That would free your veterans for militia service if it's necessary."

"I could, but I'd want to be very sure they're harmless. We're better equipped to deal with traitors than the villages are. Another thing—are we likely to run into more of those spider-things, Paksenarrion?"

"I don't know." Paks frowned as she thought. "This is only the third one I've seen. The others were in Kolobia. I don't know how common they are. We ought to be ready for another—but I doubt there'd be many of them."

"Are they all shape-changed followers of Achrya?" asked Valichi.

Paks shook her head. "I don't think so. One—larger than the one here—almost seemed to be a pet, or mascot, to the blackwebs in Kolobia. They bowed to it, before the combats, and they said it was Achrya's servant. It—"

"Larger than *that*—?" Cracolnya seemed to have trouble speaking.

Paks nodded. "Yes, much larger. Each leg as long as I am tall, and the eyes fist-size, at least."

"Great gods! Did it—did it *do* anything?"

"It bound in silk and ate those I defeated."

He looked at her with new respect. "I had not realized—your pardon, my lord, for you told me, but I had doubts I never spoke—that Paksenarrion had faced such peril. In my own land we have many legends of the spider demons, and such a death is the worst we know."

"I don't know how it would fight outside its web," Paks went on. "Those that I know were shape-changed used fangs and spinnerets both, as that one did last night. They move very fast, and can leap higher than a man's head. If they have such, to lead the way through the tunnel, for example, archers might not be able to stop it."

"Did you ever fight against one directly?" asked Cracolnya.

"Not alone. Three of us—the paladin I trained with, a dwarf, and I—fought it together."

"What about the spinnerets?"

"It can't throw the silk ahead while moving; it trails a line, instead. But if balked, it can stand on its rear legs and throw the silk forward. Arrows in the fat back section ruin its aim. The legs are bad too—claws, but a single sword-stroke will sever them."

"Arrows in the eyes should work, shouldn't they?"

"Yes, but it moves fast, and that's a small target. The rest of the head end is hard armored; arrows glance off, as do swords."

"I keep thinking," the Duke said, "that unless Achrya is a very stupid demon, we'll see trouble very shortly. Tonight, I expect. If I were in her place, I'd be moving as soon as I knew of trouble, and she's bound to have had some way of keeping in contact. I wish Master Vetrifuge were here—some of his wizardy fire down there might fry a spider or two."

Paks said nothing, but was just as glad Vetrifuge was

elsewhere. Wizards and paladins worked ill together, but she doubted the Duke remembered that.

"We've oil enough in the stores," Cracolnya said. "I daresay one of those wouldn't like fire, wizardy or not. And that cellar is all stone and earth—it wouldn't menace the rest of the building."

The Duke nodded, and turned to Valichi. "Val, has anything moved outside today?"

Valichi shook his head. "Nothing, my lord. No reports of orc sightings from either village or any farmstead."

"That in itself tells me they know something." The Duke looked down at his desk, and shifted the sheets of paper. "Beyond doubling the watch, and keeping a close eye on that tunnel entrance—if that's what it is—I can't think of more for tonight. Can any of you?" Valichi and Cracolnya shook their heads, but Paks spoke up.

"One more thing," she said, and waited for his nod. "Suppose they don't attack here at all, but go past us to attack holdings south of here. Duke's East, or even beyond our lands. If Achrya's purpose is, in part, to discredit you—"

"I had not thought of that. Such a plan could include a small attack here, enough to convince us, with the bulk of them harrying south. Cracolnya—?"

"They couldn't have moved today, my lord, unless they swung wide of the ridge east of here. We had plenty of men out, and even some miles west on the road. But tonight or tomorrow—"

"To make it work, they'd have to show that they'd come past me," said the Duke. "If they entered from east or west . . . everyone knows I can't patrol the entire north line alone, and no one holds west of me this far north. Proof—they'd need some proof—"

"Neither of the villages could stand against a large force," said Valichi. "With plunder from there—even prisoners—"

"That's it." The Duke's voice hardened. "By the gods, I think that's it. Paks?"

"Yes, my lord. It feels right."

"Now what? Let me think. How many would they commit to an attack on us? In the dark, it wouldn't take much—some fire arrows, an attempt to break into the cellar—maybe fifty against the walls. Cracolnya, how few archers can you hold this place with?"

"Me? Tir's gut! Mmm—most of the cohort—all of it, if you mean hold it very long. There's that tunnel, don't forget."

"I haven't. Even so—I'll leave you a squad of Arcolin's, to back you on the walls, and take two of your archers. Paks, go find Arcolin and Dorrin; tell them to ready their cohorts to march out at once, and then meet me here. You ride to Duke's East—that's where they'll hit, because that's where the Verella road is. Rouse the militia, and tell them we'll be there as soon as possible. Heribert Fontaine, the mayor, has a great horn—blow it if you see any sign of orcs."

"Yes, my lord." Paks turned to go.

"And even if you are a paladin, don't try to take them on by yourself."

"No, my lord, I wouldn't." Paks grinned at him, and ran out of the room. She had not been able to sense clearly what was wrong before, but this plan felt right.

Dorrin and Arcolin, when she found them, understood at once, and by the time she had saddled a fast horse, the cohorts were arming for the march. Paks led the horse out the postern, and found herself alone in the dark on a cold, windy plain. She mounted, and turned the horse toward Duke's East. The north wind behind her carried the sounds of the Company roused. She legged the horse into a gallop, trusting its night vision over hers. The sounds fell away, as she rode, replaced by the thudding of hooves beneath, and the rush of wind.

She had never ridden in a night so dark. It was like being in a cave: heavy clouds shut out the sky, and she could see nothing, not even the horse's neck in front of her. When they came to the shallow rise a mile out, she knew it only because the horse lunged at the slope, the rhythm of its stride broken. Then down the other side, into the same blackness. She thought of trying to make light, but decided to wait until battle was joined. It would only make her obvious to any watchers to do it now.

At last the watchlights of Duke's East flickered ahead of her. The horse snorted and lunged ahead. The lights came closer: she could see them now as individual torches, streaming in the wind, on the low bank that had been thrown upon the north side of the village. She pulled the horse down to a long trot, and yelled for the watch.

"Stand and speak," yelled one of the sentries behind the bank.

She hauled at the horse, and it lugged to a halt. "I've word from the Duke for Mayor Fontaine," she yelled back. "I'm Paksenarrion—"

"Come on, then," said the guard. "What is it?"

She rode slowly into the circles of light, and slid off the horse in front of them. "You're to rouse the militia," she said. "The Duke's bringing the Company, as soon as he can—he thinks the orcs will attack here."

"Here? Why?" Paks recognized Piter, the innkeeper.

She shook her head. "It's too long to explain—but he's got reason. Be ready. Where's the mayor?"

"D'you know his house?" asked Piter. Paks nodded. "Go, and I'll call out the rest. Do you know how many?"

"No, but the Duke thinks it will be a large force." Paks started up the lane, leading her horse. Behind her she heard Piter directing the watch, then the clatter of boots as they went to rouse others.

In the mayor's house she found the Council of Duke's East eating a late dinner. Kolya smiled as Paks came in, then sobered quickly as she gave her news.

"When will the Duke come?" asked Fontaine, looking worried.

"The cohorts were forming as I left," said Paks.

"We can't hold a real force," he said. "That bank is just to slow them down and give our watch a chance to fire one flight of arrows. We have fewer than a hundred who can fight—"

"Most of the buildings are defensible," Kolya pointed out. "The Duke's insisted on stone roofs as well as walls, and we can't be burned out. My cottage won't hold, but it's on the south bank anyway."

"We'll move everyone but militia into a few of the strongest houses," the mayor said. "Is there time to bring in any of the farm folk? No, I suppose not. Forget the mill, and the south bank buildings: we'll try to hold around the square."

Paks had not met all the Council before, and did not know who the heavy-set black-haired man was who spoke next. "I'll see to gettin' the south bank folk in, Mayor—"

"Thanks, Tam," said the mayor, and the man went out quickly. The mayor turned to a man whose face was marked with a broad scar. "Vik, be sure the central houses are provisioned; use the winter stores, if you have time to move them. They'll do us no good anyway, if the orcs get them."

"Aye, Mayor—and what about slipping the millstones? If they burn the mill, it might crack the stones."

"Good idea. Tell the miller that. Kolya—"

"I know." She was already near the door, with a last grin for Paks. The mayor clambered up stiffly, and called upstairs to his wife.

"Get out the horn, Arñe, and bring it down here." He looked at Paks. "This house has too many doors; I'll send the family over to the square."

A glass had passed, and part of another. Paks waited at the northernmost angle of the bank around Duke's East, listening, with the others, for any hint of the orcs' attack. They knew it would take the Duke's Company another half-glass at least to march the distance in battle order . . . if the Company met no enemy on the road. Behind, the village was as secure as it could be. All who could not fight crowded in to the buildings that bordered the square, all of which had but one door each and narrow windows easily defended. Those who could draw a bow were on the upstairs windows. Paks raised her head suddenly and sniffed. She heard nothing, but with a sense of unease came a sour stench on the wind.

"They're coming," she said to the man next to her. He was, as most of them were, one of the Duke's veterans, and limped badly from a wound taken the last year in Aarenis. He'd been a farmer until the orcs burned out his farm. He grunted, passed the word to the man next in line, and drew his sword; she heard it rasp on the scabbard. They had torches ready to light, but until the enemy came, only widely-scattered ones were lit.

Paks felt something dire nearby; her skin crawled. Something more than orcs moved in the dark. She drew Tammarrion's sword. The blade gleamed blue. Paks squinted into the wind—was that a reflection? With a shout she called on the High Lord, and light swept up from her upraised arm, pure white radiance revealing two of the spider figures only a few lengths away, a mass of orcs behind them. Paks leaped for the top of the bank. She heard the cries of the watch, and saw the first gouts of flame as torches caught all along the line. The orcs broke into one of their marching chants, fierce and savage, and surged forward. Far back she heard the mayor's deep horn. The spiders had scuttered back at the first of the light, but now bounded forward.

As they came up the bank, effortlessly, Paks slashed at their heads. One sprang sideways, evading her. The one in front reared back, head out of danger, and raked at her with a foreleg. Paks dodged and drove in, striking for the vulnerable neck. Tammarrion's sword swung easily, and parted the black carapace as if it were butter. The head flew off, and the legs jerked. Paks jumped back to the top of the bank, looking for the other spider. It had disappeared: one of the militia waved an arm and Paks saw behind their lines a glossy humped back moving swiftly toward the center of the village.

"Look out!" yelled another man, and Paks whirled to face the first orcs. Swords rang on her blade; beside her the militia had climbed the bank too, and the clash and clatter of swords filled the night air. Paks killed the orc in front of her, and wounded another, but more filled the gaps. The pressure of them forced her back over the top of the bank. Here, for a moment, it was easier—as the orcs came over the top, the defenders could strike from below, where they were more vulnerable. But again, the orc numbers overwhelmed them, and they began to fall back toward the square. They could not even take their dead along, for the orcs poured over the bank in black waves, and they were almost driven out of line as it was.

Then from the left came a harsh blast of sound, and the roar of the Duke's Company's charge. Both cohorts struck the flank of the orcish advance. With the first flurry in the orcs' attack, Paks called the militia around her to fall into double lines. She and the others managed to thrust forward until one end of the line was anchored on the bank again. Beyond her, the line doubled back sharply along a lane, but the defenders had only a short stretch from the bank to the first building with no sort of parapet. While the Duke's charge pulled the orcish interest, they threw up a weak protection of furniture and barrels from that house, and stones from a garden wall. Beyond this, the orcs were pushed aside to stream past, on through the village.

The orcs had clearly not expected this kind of resistance. Once the line was in place, the militia felt at once the lessening pressure and orcs shifted to the right and beyond. Paks held the point until it was clear that the orcs no longer meant to dispute it. Then she called for reinforcements.

"But where are you—?"

"That other spider—I must find it." The innkeeper—for he had come at her call—grunted.

"You'd go for that? Go on, then. Gods go with you."

Paks made her way through the remains of the militia toward the square. Even with all the torches lit, it was hard to see clearly; black shadows leaped and twisted everywhere. She looked for the gleam of a hard carapace, or the telltale eyes.

Wagons had been overturned in the gaps between buildings in the square, but this protection had not been enough. Orcs had thrust them aside, and Paks found the square itself full of bodies, orc and human both. Two wagons burned in the middle of the square, lighting it well enough, but she saw no sign of the giant spider.

"Paks!" Kolya's voice came from a high window in one of the houses.

Paks squinted up. "What?"

"Are they gone?"

"Not all—I'm looking for that spider."

"It came over the wagon there—and left that way—" Kolya pointed. Paks waved and started to follow her directions. "Paks! No! Don't go by yourself!"

Paks looked back up at her, and something—a shadowy movement—caught her eye on the roof above the window. She tried to make it out, then realized what it must be. "Kolya! It's on the roof!" As she yelled, the thing dropped suddenly, its anchoring line gleaming. Two legs caught the sill of the window where Kolya had been, and it swung to crawl in. Paks yelled, "Someone drop me a bow!"

But Kolya or someone else inside rammed a torch toward the crouching form before it could get through the window, and it retreated, dropping swiftly to the ground. Paks ran to meet it, hoping to strike a blow before the legs found purchase on the cobbles, but the spider pushed off the wall to meet her.

Paks dodged the first leap, swinging at its head, but missed. It leaped again, sideways, and she followed. Quickly it scuttled sideways, turning so that the light of the burning wagon was in her eyes. Paks grinned, and ran wide herself, to snatch a burning length of wood from the fire. It retreated, still poised to leap. Paks moved in slowly, arms wide, ready to strike with torch or sword. She heard an arrow strike the stones, as someone in one of the houses tried to shoot the thing and missed. The spider leaped at her, forelegs spanning wider than her arms, and tried to clutch. Paks dove toward the belly, thrusting higher with torch and lower with sword. She saw the spinnerets facing her, and the pulsations that would drive out the poisoned silk. Then the spider flipped away from her, the head crisping already from the torch, and the abdomen gaping open. A single gout of grayish fluid struck her hand, burning through the glove; she gasped with the pain of it, but struck again, until the head and body were separated.

By then the Duke's men were coming into the square.

"These midnight conferences," said Arcolin, "are becoming tedious." Paks wondered if he was making a joke of some kind. Arcolin?

"Will the Duke be here?" Heribert Fontaine, back in his mayoral robes, paused as he set out mugs for ale.

"I doubt it." Arcolin rubbed the back of his neck. "Simmitt says he'll be fine, but insists he must rest for a night and a day. The gods know he needs it—"

"But he's sure—"

"He's sure the Duke will recover, yes. Flesh wounds and exhaustion—no more than that, he says, and Simmitt wouldn't lie."

Valichi came in, shutting the door carefully behind him. "Surprisingly little damage across the river, Mayor Fontaine. They broke into Kolya's place, but didn't burn it. Near as we can tell, only two trees were badly torn up. It looks like they panicked and ran on through. We've set up a perimeter for the night, including the south bank cottages, but not the outlying farms."

Paks found the rest as tedious as Arcolin had suggested, for they had to explain the events of the past days in sufficient detail to reassure the Council of Duke's East, no easy task when they kept breaking in with questions, comments, and reminiscences of past campaigns. The revelation that Venner had been closely involved in Tammarrion's death aroused a storm of indignation. But discovering that the Duke had sent for a Marshal silenced them at last. Paks could see relief and satisfaction in some of their faces, dismay in none.

Chapter Twelve

Late fall rain had chilled to sleet; from the parapets the sentries could see only a short distance from the walls. The last bonfires were hard to keep alight. Foul smoke whirled away from the orcs' bodies, but they would hardly burn. Finally the Duke had a barrel of mutton-fat melted and poured on, after all the remains had been dragged to one fire, and the ashes left from that smelled of nothing but ashes.

The next afternoon, a party on horseback came within bowshot of the gates before being seen; fog and sleet together hid them. Paks heard the alarm horn, and met the Duke heading for his stairs. She stayed beside him as he strode across the inner court. By the time they reached the Duke's Gate, the sentries knew who it was: the Marshal, they sent word.

"Name?" asked the Duke irritably. Paks glanced at him. She knew his wounds must be hurting him, though he wouldn't admit it. He had refused to let her "waste," as he put it, a healing attempt on him.

"Connaught, was one, and Amberion, and Arianya—"

"The Marshal-*General*?" The Duke glared at the sentry. "You're sure?"

"That's what they said, my lord, them names. I don't know—"

The Duke silenced him with a gesture and turned to Paks. "Is that likely? And why? Has she come to make mock of me, after all?"

"No, my lord," said Paks firmly. "It would not be that. If this is the Marshal-General, she has come because of the urgency of your message, and because she feels you may need her help. Mockery is not like her."

"No." He rubbed his shoulder, considering. The sentry waited, hunched in the cold. "Blast it! I can't get used to the idea— Go on, man, and let them in. Fanfare, but don't keep them out there waiting while the troops parade: it's too cold." As the sentry jogged back to the gate tower, the Duke strode across the main court, calling his captains. High overhead the fanfare rang out, the trumpeters' numb fingers missing some of the triples. The main gate hinges squealed in the cold, and the gates themselves scraped on blown sleet.

Through the gates, as the gap widened, Paks could see a dark clump of horsemen: sleet whitened the horses' manes, and the riders' cloaks and helms. They rode forward, ducking against the wind that scoured a flurry of sleet off the court and flung it in their faces. Paks could not recognize any of them, until they were less than a length away. The leading rider halted, and threw back the hood of a blue cloak.

"My lord Duke?" Arianya's weathered face was pinched with cold.

"Marshal-General, I am honored to receive you in my steading." Duke Phelan took the last few steps, and reached a hand to her. "By your leave, I suggest we continue our greetings somewhere warmer."

"Indeed yes." But she sat her mount a moment longer, looking around the court as if memorizing the location of every door and window. Then she looked back at him. "Gird's blessing on this place, and all within it, and on you, my lord Duke." The Duke stiffened slightly, but bowed. Then she dismounted, as did the other riders, and one came forward to take her horse. "I hope it will not inconvenience you—we brought some along to care for the gear and horses—"

"Not at all. Arcolin, find room for these, and the animals. If you'll come with me, Marshal-General—"

"To a fire, I hope. By the lost scrolls, this last day's ride seemed straight into the wind, no matter which way the road turned." Then she caught sight of Paks. "Paksenarrion! Is this where you—?" She broke off in confusion, and looked from the Duke to Paks and back again.

"Is this Paks?" Amberion, now, had come to stand beside her. "Gird's grace, Paksenarrion, I'm glad to see you looking so well." She saw that his glance did not miss the sword at her side. "Are you—?"

But Paks did not mean to discuss everything standing out in the cold. She knew the Duke was in pain, and needed to get back inside. "Sir Amberion," she said, nodding. "My lord's right, sir; we should get within."

The Duke led the way to the dining hall, and sent a guard to the kitchen for hot food. The visitors stood around the fireplace, their wet clothes already steaming. Within minutes, kettles of sib were on the table, and bowls of soup. Servants had taken away wet cloaks, and brought dry stockings for those whose feet were wet.

"I'm getting old for this," said the Marshal-General frankly. "It's been far too long since I left Fin Panir in wintertime. Ah! Hot soup. I may survive." She smiled at the Duke, then her gaze sharpened. "My lord, you are ill—or wounded. Why did you come out in that cold?"

"I'm not a child!" snapped the Duke. Paks looked at him, worried, but he had already taken a long breath. "I'm sorry, Marshal-General. I was wounded a few days ago—it's painful, but not dangerous. I would be shamed did I not welcome such visitors myself."

"And you want no advice on it. Very well. But, my lord, we came to help, and if you spend your strength on hospitality, we are a burden, not help at all." She took another spoonful of soup. "I would eat cobbles, were they hot like this, but this is good soup. You wonder, you say, why, in asking for a Marshal's aid, you got the Marshal-General. I was in Verella, having been called to a meeting with the prince and Regency Council." She drank some more soup and poured herself a mug of sib. "Then your message came, mentioning Achrya, and traitors, and a possible invasion of orcs. It seemed enough—the council was concerned already about your holdings here. I don't know why." She looked at the Duke, who sipped his own mug of sib and said nothing. "I did not, of course, read them your message, but I thought it would ease their minds to know I was coming."

Arcolin came into the room, followed by the other captains. The Duke looked up. "Marshal-General," Arcolin said, "we have stabled all your mounts, and assigned the rest of your party room in the barracks. Is that satisfactory?"

"Entirely," she said. "Two of them are new with us, and it will be well for them to see barracks life; they're nobles' sons, and convinced we stint them by assigning only single rooms, rather than suites."

Arcolin grinned. "Two of them did try to tell me something about their birth, but I didn't have time to listen."

"Good. Don't. While I'm glad to see the Fellowship of Gird expand, and as Marshal-General I can't pass up a single blade, I often wish the nobly-born would spend a few years of their youth where no one knew their birth. We do our best to knock some of it out of them, but as Paks knows, we don't entirely succeed."

Paks found herself laughing. She had wondered what it would be like to see the Marshal General again, and had not looked forward to it. Even though she knew she was cured, she anticipated an awkward meeting and difficult explanations. But this was easy. The Marshal-General looked at her, as did the others.

"Paksenarrion, I find it hard to believe what I see, yet by Gird's gift you are more than merely healed. Will you tell us, someday, how this happened?"

"Indeed, I would be glad to," said Paks. "But parts of it I don't clearly understand myself."

"I sense great gifts awakening in you, if not already come," said Amberion. "Are you still a follower of Gird?"

Paks nodded. "I am not forsworn, sir paladin. I gave my oath to Gird in the Hall of Fin Panir, and by that oath I stand. But much has happened that I did not anticipate, or you, I think, foresee."

The Marshal-General's eyes glittered with tears. "Paksenarrion, however you were healed, and by what power of good, matters not to me. We are all glad to see you so; we had all grieved over your loss. Gird witness that if you had turned to Falk or Camwyn and received healing there, I would be as glad, and would not condemn you for changing your allegiance. It was my error—not Gird's—that led you into great peril, and in the end near killed you. I am not mean enough to begrudge any healing."

"But," Paks began delicately, "the powers I have—and some have come—did not come with your dedication at the Hall—"

"We have not all forgotten how paladins began," said Amberion quickly. "The power comes from the High Lord—if he has lent it to the training orders, from time to time, that does not bind it there. If Gird spoke to you directly—" He looked a question at her.

Paks looked from one face to another. "I have not told anyone—not even the Duke—the whole story."

"Nor is this the best time, perhaps," suggested the Marshal-General "If this stronghold faces peril from Achrya—"

"I think it is past," said the Duke, slowly. "Paksenarrion unmasked the traitors within—when I sent for your aid, they were already dead. We had found a tunnel leading into a cellar from without, and expected an invasion of some sort. It came the next night. We burned the last of the bodies yesterday."

"You have wounded that need healing?"

"Yes—but they are not all Girdsmen."

"We'll try what we can. Are you sure your traitors are all found?"

"I hope so. Paksenarrion wanted me to ask more help; she is not sure she would find them all."

"We can help with that, certainly."

"I had not expected so quick a response—and you come from Vérella—"

"Your messenger, my lord, came to the grange at Burningmeed; the Marshal there, Kerrin—" she nodded at her, "had come to Vérella to meet me. Her yeoman-marshal forwarded the message as fast as he could—which, for us, is very fast."

The Duke nodded. "I remember." He coughed, and Paks watched him, worried again. He took a careful breath, and went on. "My message was short, Marshal-General, as word of peril should be. But you must know that I acknowledge—have already admitted to my captains—that I was wrong, years ago, to blame you for my wife's death—"

"My lord," interrupted Arianya, "in dealing with great evils, as you and I have done, all make mistakes. The High Lord grant I never make a worse—in fact I have made worse." She nodded toward Paks. "There is one, as you rightly said, and the elves said at the time. Certainly neither I nor my predecessor intended harm to your wife and children—or to Paksenarrion. But whether by error or overwhelming evil, harm came. If you can now believe that it was unintentional—that I sorrow for it—that is well enough."

"I make bold to contradict a Marshal-General," said the Duke, with a wry smile. "It is not—quite—enough." He took a long breath, staring into his mug, and none thought to interrupt him. "You may remember that in the years before my wife was killed, this entire Company fought under the protection of Gird."

"I do."

"After that, when I was no longer any way a Girdsman, I thought to keep, nonetheless, the standards of honor, in the Company and in my holdings, that were appropriate."

"So you do," said Marshal Kerrin. "You're known as a fair and just lord, and your Company—"

The Duke waved her to silence. "Compared to some, Marshal, that may be so. But compared to what this Company was—well, you can ask my captains, if you don't believe me." He nodded to Dorrin, Arcolin, and the others. No one responded. The Duke continued. "The last year I campaigned in Aarenis, even I had to admit the changes. We were short of men, through treachery—I expect you've heard the tale of Dwarfwatch—" The Marshal-

General nodded. "Yes. So I called back veterans, and when that wasn't enough, I hired free swords in Aarenis itself. That changed the Company. Worse than that, I used them as I'd never used them before, and when Siniava was caught, I—" he looked up as Paks stirred. The Marshal-General, too, looked at her. Paks wished the Duke would not speak of that time, but he smiled at her and went on. "I was so angry, Marshal-General, at his treachery, at his cruelty to my men and others, that I would have tortured him, had Paks not stopped me. And I was angry with her, at the time."

"But you didn't." The Marshal-General's voice was remote and cool.

"No. I wanted to, though."

"You could have—you, a commander, didn't have to listen to a— what was she then, anyway? Private? Corporal?"

"Private. I did have to—I'd given my word. If you want the whole story, ask her or the paladin who was there."

Amberion stirred. "That would have been Fenith. He died the next year, in the Westmounts."

"So." The Marshal-General took the conversation again. "You chose to honor your word, and by what you say gave up your anger at Paksenarrion—that sounds like little dishonor, my lord Duke."

"Enough," said the Duke soberly. "Enough to change the Company, to risk my people here—for that's what happened, what I left them open to, when I took the veterans that could fight. And then to fall under the spell of Venneristimon's sister—if that was his sister—"

The Marshal-General stood. "My lord, I would hear more of this, if you wish, but if you have wounded, we should see to them."

"As you will. If you'll excuse me, Dorrin can take you to them; if I go over there, the surgeons will scold."

"Perhaps we should begin with you?"

"No. I'm not in danger. Dorrin?"

"Certainly, my lord. Marshal-General, will you come?" Dorrin moved to the door, and the Marshal-General and

Amberion followed. Kerrin looked at her, but the Marshal-General waved her back.

"We'll send if we need you, Kerrin; keep warm in the meantime."

When they had gone, Kerrin looked at the Duke. "My lord Duke, I've seen you ride by, but not met you—"

"Nor I you. Yours is the nearest grange?"

"Southward, yes. West you might come to Stilldale a little sooner. It was but a barton until a few years ago." She drained her mug of sib, and poured another. "You won't remember, perhaps, but I had an uncle in your Company: Garin Arcosson, in Arcolin's cohort. He—"

"I remember. He was file-second of the third. Killed by a crossbow bolt in—let me think—the siege of Cortes Cilwan, I think, wasn't it? A lanky fellow, with a forelock that turned white early."

Kerrin nodded. "I'm impressed, my lord,, that you remember so well. That was years ago—"

The Duke shrugged. "It's important to know one's men. And I have a knack for names."

"Even so. I remember when his sword came home, and his medallion; the Marshal of our grange hung them there for all to see. And my aunt, my lord, lived well enough on his pension." She coughed delicately. "Do I understand, my lord, from what you've said, that you will be placing your Company under Gird once more?"

"That depends. In the years since the last Marshal here died, I have recruited many who were not Girdsmen—indeed, not Falkians, or following any of the martial patrons. Yet most are good men, hard but honorable fighters. I would not have them distressed—I owe it to them—"

"My lord, it would be far from my desire—and I believe I speak for the Marshal-General here—to coerce warriors faithful to another to change faith. I am aware that among your soldiers are those who follow Tir and Sertig as well as the High Lord, Gird, and Falk. And your responsibilities under the crown of Tsaia, I realize, will forbid any venturing of the Company for Gird. But should you desire such protection—even a Marshal resident here—that can be arranged."

"You seem confident." The Duke frowned at her.

"I am." Kerrin turned her mug in her hands. "My lord Duke, it may seem strange to you, who have been at odds with the granges for so long, but Gird himself mistakes no honest heart. We have never shared that quarrel, only watched from afar." The Duke started to speak, but Kerrin went on, heedless. "I swear to you, my lord, that if we had known anything definite—if we had been able to tell who or what was the source of that evil that tainted your lands and gossiped against you at court, we would have told you." The Duke settled back in his chair; Paks noticed that the remaining captains were rigid in theirs. "But," Kerrin went on, "without the right to come here, and investigate, we could do nothing. I don't know if you believe prayer to have any power—but I tell you that at the granges at Burningmeed and Stilldale prayers for you and your Company were offered at every service. We of Gird—and sensible nobles of the Council—well know that you and you alone stand between Tsaia and the northern wastes, and what comes out of them."

"You could have said something," muttered Cracolnya. The Duke shot him a look, but did not speak. Kerrin cocked her head.

"Could we? Think about it, Captain. How well would you have listened, had I come, or sent my yeoman-marshal, to tell you that something—undefined, but something—was wrong in your cohort or the stronghold? If I had seen the traitor—your steward, Venneristimon, wasn't it?" Cracolnya and the others nodded. "If I had seen him, I might have known. But how to convince you?"

"Prayer," muttered the Duke.

Kerrin gave a tight smile. "Just prayer, my lord. But Gird has more weapons than one in his belt, and he sent a fine sword." She nodded at Paks.

"True enough." The Duke sighed, leaning back in his chair. "With all respect, Kerrin, I would talk to the Marshal-General about this—"

"Indeed."

"Even though I was wrong to be so angry before, still the Girdsmen make mistakes."

Kerrin laughed. "My lord Duke, our legends say that even Gird himself made mistakes. We are but human. The Marshal-General admitted one to you herself. But we all fight, as best we know, against the powers of evil. We all try to strengthen our realm—whether steading or grange—in anything good."

"Yes. Well—" The Duke paused. Paks, watching, noticed a grayer tinge to his face. She glanced at Arcolin, who met her eyes and nodded. He stood and moved behind the Duke's chair.

"My lord, I must remind you of the surgeons' orders."

"Nonsense. We have guests—"

"Marshal Kerrin," Arcolin went on, "the surgeons made me promise to remind the Duke of their opinion. if you will excuse him—"

"Certainly." Kerrin looked concerned. "Should I call the Marshal-General?"

"No. Paks will fetch a surgeon."

"Viniet is upstairs, Captain."

"Good."

The Duke started to protest, then subsided, leaning heavily on the arm of his chair. "Tir's gut, Arcolin—excuse me, Marshal—it's just—"

"A mere cut. I know. I know as well that you were hardly in your bed enough to warm it before going back to work. And if we're truly, as the Marshal says, the one bar to the northern troubles, then we've no desire to lose you, my lord."

Paks did not witness the Duke's meeting with the Marshal-General in his study later that day. They were closeted for several hours; she spent the time talking with Amberion. He had been called to a border fort along the south border of Fintha, and had spent the summer convincing farmers in the area that they could indeed repel the mountain-dwelling robbers.

"Though most of those robbers were poor folk enough,"

said Amberion thoughtfully. "Some years back they'd left a barony in a mountain valley because of the great cruelty of the baron. There in the heights they could not grow enough food for themselves, and when they lost weapons in hunting, could replace them only by raiding. Some of them would be glad enough to settle in the farmlands, if there were farmland to spare. A few, though—" he shook his head. "It's easy for such demons as Liart to gain worshippers when men must live like wolves or die anyway."

"But why farmers?" asked Paks. "Couldn't the local lord—count or whatever—have held the keep and protected them?"

"No, not in Fintha. In Fintha nearly all farmland is freehold; our lords are those who hold enough that they can't work it all themselves. Even then there are very few with such estates as the Marrakai or Verrakai—or even your Duke—in Tsaia and Lyonya." When she looked puzzled, he went on. "Come now, Paksenarrion, you had more history than that in your months with us. Gird himself was a peasant. Fintha is the center of his cult. By Finthan law, each farmer owns the lands he can plow. Grazing land is usually owned in common, though in the north, where you came from, it may be held by the farmer. But the Hall never makes large grants of land, such as your Duke got, in return for raising a troop. Those who are given a grant must work it themselves, and each man owes service to Gird when it's needed. If someone has more land, it was inherited, perhaps from two families. The nearest lord to that border fort could offer only himself and his older sons to aid. Which he did." Amberion paused. "One of them died there."

By the time Paks had told him about her summer in Lyonya with the rangers, the Duke's conference was over. They were called in, along with the Duke's captains.

"We have settled more than one thing," said the Duke. He was somewhat pale, still, but seemed steadier. "First, it's clear to both of us that the Company cannot go back as it was. It's been fifteen years since my wife was killed, fifteen years during which no effort was made to screen out those who are not Girdsmen. The veterans of those fifteen years have served me well, and I will not change the rules on them now. Yet some of the changes in those years were for the worse, and we will work to reverse them.

"As far as my domain goes, the past fifteen years, again, have seen changes and growth in directions which Tammarrion and I had not planned. My relations with the Regency Council, my duties—these cannot be set aside.

"What we have agreed, then, is this: I will accept, in my domain, the influence of Gird. Granges will be built wherever enough Girdsmen gather; bartons will serve the rest. A Marshal will be stationed either here or on the plain between Duke's East and West, at the discretion of the Marshal-General, and I will grant sufficient land for the support of that grange. Girdsmen among the Company will be encouraged to be active in the grange. As for me—" He looked aside, then around at them all. "Most of you know little of my background. Until I came to live with the Halverics—" a slight stir at this; Paks had not known it until Stammel mentioned it; neither had most of the others "—until then, I followed no god or patron. I had heard of none I would follow." His face had settled into grim lines. "The Halverics were, as they are, Falkians, and from them and their example I first learned of the High Lord, and of Falk. I had served Aliam Halveric as squire for some years, and he sponsored me as a novice with the Knights of Falk, as a reward. Too great a reward, as I found later; he never told me of the cost of such sponsorship. He hoped, I believe, that I would swear fealty to Falk, and become one of them."

"But then—how did you end up a Girdsman?" Pont's long face was sober.

"Well—as to that—I didn't. Precisely." The Duke shuffled a scroll across his desk. "To go back: I was knighted after two years, in the Falkian order, but I had sworn no word to Falk. I'm not sure why, actually, but I never felt a call to do so. Then—again with Aliam Halveric's help—I began on my own as a mercenary captain in Tsaia. Arcolin remembers that. A couple of years here and there garrisoning forts no one else wanted to bother with. Caravan work. That sort of thing. Then my first big contract, as an independent with the crown. We didn't even have a full cohort; Arcolin had to scour the streets to make up our numbers. But out of that came this—" he waved his arm to indicate the domain, "and many more contracts. Then Tammarrion joined the Company, and we married, and she was a Girdsman in full." He stopped, and Arcolin moved quickly to pour him some wine. The Duke sipped, and went on.

"I had hired Girdsmen before because they were honest and hard-working. After her I hired them because she wished it. We married, as you know, in the Hall at Fin Panir—also her desire. But though I lived as a Girdsman, and gave freely to the Fellowship of Gird, I never took the vows myself." He took another swallow of wine. "Again, I don't know why. Tammarrion often asked me, and it's one of the few things I failed to do that she wished. I think I felt—" He stopped again, and looked past them all, as if across a field of battle. "I felt sometimes that another vow was waiting somewhere, and that I must be free to take it." He shook his head. "Foolishness, perhaps. Yet Tamar felt, or so she said, that until I made my vow freely and willingly, Gird would not begrudge my waiting. And after she died, I—" His head bowed for an instant. "I would not."

"And now?" asked Dorrin.

"Now is difficult. You, Captain, have argued that I disgraced my former allegiance." For the only time, Paks saw a flush on Dorrin's cheek. "You were right, except that I had none. I agree that I was wrong, and I am willing to amend—but I still feel a reluctance to commit myself to Gird."

"But surely—" Marshal Kerrin looked sideways at the Marshal-General.

"As things stand," she said firmly, "I do not ask Duke Phelan to join the Fellowship of Gird."

"But why?"

Her eyebrows arched. "Are you asking what we said to each other? For therein lies the reason. Since you have a nearby grange, I will assure you it is from no lack of trust in him. But I agree with him that the time for making such a pledge has not come to him."

"As for you, my captains," the Duke said, regaining control of the room, "you may choose freely to stay or go, with full honor. I will be trying to do what Tamar and I had once planned, within the limits I've mentioned. I have enough wealth, now, and enough land is in plow, that I need not take the Company to Aarenis again—certainly not for several years. Instead, I will try to make of this domain what our vision was: a fruitful land, governed justly, and serving as a strong ward between the rest of Tsaia and the northern waste. If you are not comfortable with that vision, if you are unhappy with the thought of a Marshal constantly among us, you may come to me at any time, privately, and leave with my thanks and a substantial reward."

"You know I will stay," said Arcolin quickly, and the others nodded.

"That offer stands, nonetheless," said the Duke. "If in the future you change your mind—any of you—you have served me well for many years, and you will not find me ungrateful."

"But when will you tell the Company?" asked Arcolin. "Do you want us—?"

The Duke shook his head. "No. They should hear it from me, I think. Rumors are flying already, I daresay. Tomorrow—no, for Keri may die tonight. The day after, I think. Plan a formal inspection; the Marshal-General may like to see them up close. And I'll tell them then. The same offer applies—I will be fair to my veterans no matter what their faith."

A sharp wind had scoured all clouds from the sky, and left it pale and clean. Paks, standing now as squire beside the Duke, watched the Company wheel into review formation, after an hour of intricate drill. She glanced sideways at the Marshal-General. Her eyes were alight in that impassive face. Paks looked back at the Company. It had never seemed so impressive. She felt almost like two people—one here beside the Duke, cold from the wind, and another in formation, file first of the second file in Arcolin's cohort, waiting for Stammel's brusque commands.

They halted, lines straight as stretched string. Paks scanned the faces she knew so well. Stammel, his brown eyes watchful. Devlin, somehow conveying grace even while standing still (hard to believe he had five children, one nearly old enough to be a recruit). Arñe, newly promoted to corporal, trying not to grin. Vik. Barra. Natzlin. Rauf, who would retire to his little farm as soon as they were sure the orcs had gone. The captains pivoted to face the Duke, and bowed. The Duke gestured to the Marshal-General, and they moved to the first cohort, Paks and the others following.

The Duke had a word for most of them. The Marshal-General, beside him, said nothing, but looked into each face. Paks felt very odd, walking along the lines, and knowing so well what it felt like to wait for the inspecting party to pass. When they reached the recruit lines, she was poised between laughter and tears. She knew the strain in the neck, the struggle to look only forward, the trembling hands that stiffened as they went by. One girl forgot to say "my lord," and blushed so that Paks remembered her own lapse as a recruit. A boy's voice cracked on the words, and he broke into a sweat. Another stammered.

At last they were done, and the Duke returned to his place before the Company. He waited a moment, as if for silence, though nothing had made a sound.

"Sword-brethren," he began, and Paks saw as well as felt the response to that old term. "You all remember what I told you after we defeated the orcs attacking Duke's East. You have seen the Marshal-General of Gird, High Marshal Connaught, Marshal Kerrin of Burningmeed, and the Gird's paladin Sir Amberion. Some of you have felt the healing grace of Gird through them. You have sensed, perhaps, that a change has come to me, and through me to the Company. Some of you, I hope very few, may be worried about it." He paused and looked slowly from one cohort to another. "You older veterans, who remember the days when Tammarrion Mistiannyi was my lady here, and our children were growing—" Paks saw the shock ripple across the faces of the older ones. "Yes, I can speak of that now. You will remember how the Company was then, when a Marshal of Gird lived here, in the stronghold, with us. Those days, my friends, are past these fifteen years. Yet good and evil have not changed, and I welcome, from this day on, Girdsmen, yeoman and Marshal, to this domain. I am not myself sworn to that fellowship, but I am sworn, as always, to the crown of Tsaia, and to the cause of good, as the High Lord and his servants Gird and Falk are.

"You have always served me well. You deserve, therefore, this choice: to stay, in spite of these changes, or to go, with my respect and a settlement reflecting your years of service. We will be in the north for a few years—no fat contracts in Aarenis, no chance of plunder. If you prefer such service, I will recommend any of you to any commander you name. Speak to your captains, or to me, and it will be done as you desire." He paused again, but no one moved or spoke. Paks found tears stinging her eyes. "I hope," he went on, "that none of you go. Girdsmen or no, you are all such warriors as anyone would be proud to lead. If you stay, we shall be making, by Gird's grace, a place of justice, a domain fruitful and safe, and a strong defense for the northern border. Whatever you decide, I am proud to have had you—each one of you—in my Company. You may be proud of your deeds." He stepped back, bowed to the captains, and they turned again to their cohorts. The Marshal-General nodded to him.

"You are as generous as just, my lord Duke."

His voice was slightly husky. "They are—they deserve it."

"If they do, I know where they learned it. By Gird's cudgel, my lord, I must say that even after your message I had not hoped for this reception. I thought that at best you would let us help you in the crisis. You are not a Girdsman, and yet you have done as much as if you were—while being more than fair to your soldiers. My predecessor, Enherian, spoke very well of you—told me, when I became Marshal-General, that one of his regrets was the breach between you and the Fellowship of Gird. Now I see why."

The Duke moved away, eyes distant. "I have no quarrel with Gird's view of things, as you know."

"No." She walked beside him, and Paks trailed, with the others. "I would like, my lord, to hear Paksenarrion's tale of her healing. Do you mind?"

The Duke looked back to catch Paks's eye. "It's her story, Marshal-General. If she's ready to tell it, I would like to hear it myself. But I will not command it."

"I would be likelier to command a stone to fly, than that. But I confess a professional interest in it—I was wrong, but I'd like to know how I erred so." The Marshal-General turned and grinned at Paks. "Will you tell us, or must we itch with curiosity the rest of our days?"

Paks found herself grinning, even though she had tensed at the question. "I will try, Marshal-General, but it's a tangled tale, and parts of it I do not understand myself."

Chapter Thirteen

The Duke led the way upstairs, past his study door to his private apartment at the end of the passage. Paks looked around as she came in. A fire burned in the small fireplace at one end of the chamber; several padded chairs were grouped around it and a small footed table. Tapestries hung on the walls. Behind a low divider at the far end of the room, a great bed loomed, but it had neither mattress nor hangings. A narrow bed, made up with a striped blanket, stood along one wall.

"Sit down," urged the Duke, as Paks hesitated. The Marshal-General had already chosen a chair, and propped her feet on a stool near the fire. Paks tired to guess which chair was his, and finally took one to the side of the fire. The armrests were carved, beyond the padding, into dragons' heads. The Duke took a seat opposite her and stretched his legs. "This is how it used to be," he said softly. "When we built this end of the stronghold, this is where we held council. The office I use now was the scribes' room. It's many a night I sat here with Tamar and Marshal Vrelan." He poured out three mugs of sib from the pot on the table, and offered them.

The Marshal-General glanced at him, her eyes bright in the firelight. "If you don't mind my asking, my lord, how old are you?"

"About fifty years. Why?"

"I had thought you younger, when you came to Fin Panir, but remembering that you and your wife had children who would have been, so you say, as old as Paksenarrion, I began to wonder."

The Duke grinned. "I was angry then. Anger makes me younger."

"Not only that. Most men your age are less vigorous, especially after such a life as yours. I have heard you were orphaned, but you must have come from strong stock."

"I don't know." His voice hardened, and the Marshal-General sighed.

"I did not mean to distress you—"

"It is not you who distresses me, Marshal-General, but the thought of it. I have no family—never knew who I was, really. I know nothing of my breeding, nothing of my heritage of strength or weakness, folly or wisdom. My name could come from anywhere in southern Tsaia or the Westlands: I thought when I met another Kieri, my first year in Aarenis, that I'd found a kinsman, but soon learned that Kir and Kieri are common as cobbles there."

"Your family name?"

"Phelan? I found one Phelan in Pliuni, in a wineshop; he said his kin were short and dark. Another in Fossnir, a tailor; and a woolsorter in Ambela. That's all: none like me, and none missing any children. By looks I should be northern; anywhere in the Eight Kingdoms you find tall men with red hair and gray eyes. So take your choice. Unwanted bastard's the easiest, fostered out somewhere and forgotten." Paks could hear the pain in his voice. "And then the family I bred was destroyed. Nothing before me—and like to be nothing after me. Who will I leave this to? I swear to you, it was that thought, and that alone, that let me fall to the spell of Venner's sister. Here I am, in the range of fifty years or so, and I have no heir. I have sworn to go back to building this domain—but for what?"

She nodded. "It is no easy puzzle, my lord. It is hard for any man to work years on such a project, and see nothing ahead—"

"But it falling apart when I die. In what—twenty years perhaps?—I will be too old to lead them, if not before.

Indeed, Marshal-General, I wonder that Achrya hurried so. Time alone will do her work here."

"My lord, no!" Paks found herself speaking before she thought. "That isn't so. You will find someone to take over here, I know it. And what you have done so far has been worth doing—"

The Duke smiled, a little sadly. "I'm glad you think so, Paks. I hope the High Lord thinks so, as well. But—forgive me—when I look at you, and think of Estil, my daughter—she would have been so like you—"

"My lord, by your leave, I will think on this, and perhaps be able to make some useful suggestion." The Marshal-General sat forward, hands clasped in her lap. "You have made a settled domain out of wasteland, and the holdings south of you no longer fear invasion every year or so. This in itself is useful, besides the rest. This will not disappear, if the Fellowship of Gird can save it."

"Thank you." The Duke sighed, and reached a hand for the poker to stir the fire. "Well, now, Paks, we've set you at ease, no doubt, with this other talk. Tell us, if you will, what befell you after you left Fin Panir."

Paks took a deep breath and set her mug on the table. "You remember," she began slowly, "how it was with me that last week—" They nodded. "I can see now," she went on, "that it was foolish to leave then, in winter, in that mood. It went as badly, Marshal-General, as you had feared."

"I had hoped sending word to the granges would help—"

"It might have, if I had been able to use them." Paks found herself breathing short, and tried to relax. "As it was, I feared the ridicule so that I could not, after the first time."

"Ridicule? I told them—"

"No, lady, not their fault." Paks tried again. "They did not mean to hurt me; the Marshal, where I stopped that time, tried to be kind. But my weakness is the very thing—they would have understood a missing leg," she said hurriedly. "Blindness, something they could see or understand. But Girdsmen are taught that cowardice is shameful, that it comes from within, and cannot be imposed from without."

The Marshal-General nodded slowly. "We ourselves caused you trouble."

Paks shook her head. "I don't blame you. It's the common thought anywhere, not only among Girdsmen. So I thought myself, even knowing how it had happened. I blamed myself for that weakness—"

"Paksenarrion, we told you it was not your weakness, no more than one choose to lose an arm to a sword."

"So you said, but I could not believe it." Even now, the memory of that misery made the breath catch in her throat. She stared at her right hand, gripping the armrest of the chair. "I—had a difficult winter." They said nothing, and waited. "What Venner's sister said, my lord, about my running away many times—that was true. I did." As quickly and baldly as she could, she told them about it: being run off by the shepherds, being abandoned by the trader when she could not fight against bandits. Her fear of everything, everyone, that reduced her to a shivering wreck.

"How long did this last?" The Duke's voice was gentle.

Paks closed her mouth on the rest of that story. "Until early spring, my lord." She decided to say nothing of the incident in the inn, or the nights she spent shivering in ditches. She glanced at the Duke, and it seemed as if he knew that without her telling; his eyes were bright with tears. "I came back to Brewersbridge," she said flatly, and stopped again. They waited. Finally she went on with the tale. Clearly the Marshal-General wished she had gone to the grange instead of the Kuakgan's Grove, but she listened without interruption as Paks told about the initial healing, and the days of quiet talk that had restored some of her spirit. Paks was surprised to see her nodding agreement when she heard the Kuakgan's comments on the nature of courage. Both the Duke and the Marshal-General were fascinated when she told about her service with the rangers in Lyonya. They seemed to know much that Paks had learned only that summer, asking questions about the relations of elves and humans and other matters Paks knew little about. When she told them of the daskdraudigs, and of the rangers' questions afterwards, the Marshal-General choked on her sib and sat bolt upright.

Paks nodded. "That's when I first realized that I had some of those powers given to paladins. They were surprised that I could sense the location of the daskdraudigs. And they asked me to try healing one of them—"

"Gird's grace! I wouldn't have thought—"

"And—it worked. I was as surprised, my lady, as if I'd sprouted wings."

"Mmm." The Marshal-General stared at her. "No wonder."

"Then, toward the end of summer, I began to feel a—a sense of something wrong here, that the Duke needed me. I came back through Brewersbridge." She went on to tell of that last night with the Kuakgan. Both the Duke and the Marshal-General were open-mouthed.

"Gird, certainly," murmured the Marshal-General. "A silver cup—the horse, the flowers—child, you could not have come closer to the gods and still been on this earth."

"And then what?" asked the Duke.

"And then, when I was aware of myself again, I found that all the old joy had returned, my lord."

"And you feel no bitterness, Paksenarrion, for that half-year or more of loss?"

Paks shook her head. "No, Marshal-General. The Kuakgan was right. Now I know what Gird himself knew—how those who cannot fight feel when in danger. And I know that the delight in battle, what we soldiers think of as courage, is not essential, even to a soldier. I need not call up anger any more—and the anger I called, in Kolobia, opened the way for Achrya's evil. I know that I can, if I but ask the gods, know what is right, and do it."

The Marshal-General held her gaze for some moments in silence. "Well," she said finally, "you told Amberion you were yet sworn to Gird—but I can tell, Paksenarrion, that you are no longer my blade to wield. You have gone beyond that. Gird and the High Lord know what they would have you do; I cannot direct you."

Paks smiled. "Yet I respect your wisdom and experience—"

"Don't fence with me, child. I believe you are truly a paladin, called in the old way by the gods directly. And not by one of them, but by several. If you can use any of my experience, you are welcome to it—but I expect you'll use it in ways I cannot foresee."

"If that is so," said the Duke, "then her mission here must have been at their bidding."

The Marshal-General shot him a quick glance. "Certainly. Can you doubt it?"

"But why? What—"

"To maintain the protection you built here. That's one thing. I don't know what else. I don't know if her mission here is finished. Do you, Paksenarrion?"

"I feel no call to go, at this time."

"Then you will stay—if you will."

Paks grinned. "I will stay."

"You have still a horse and armor in Fin Panir. They will be waiting for you when you come. Or ask, and we will send them where you will." The Marshal-General sat back with a sigh. "Duke Phelan, I cannot recall a more surprising day, and that includes my first half-year as a yeoman-marshal."

"Nor I. Not since—" he said, then stopped, staring into the fire. But when they looked questioningly at him, he shook his head. "One person's tale is enough for one time. Long ago I was saved, suddenly and unexpectedly, from great evil, but I will not speak of that now."

"Do you think many of your soldiers will leave, with the influence of Gird returning?" asked the Marshal-General, in what was obviously an attempt to be tactful.

"I hope not. You and your paladin found none who are truly evil, but some might still find our changes distasteful. Campaigning in the south meant excitement, a chance for riches, the company of other mercenaries—"

Paks herself had sometimes thought that Valdaire, full of mercenaries from a dozen companies or more, was the best place to be. She thought of the times she'd walked into the White Dragon with Vik and Arñe—and before then, with Saben and Canna, for a pleasant evening. They would miss that, with no city nearer than Vérella.

Even so, Paks was surprised when the first list appeared of those leaving. Barranyi, who had joined the same year that she did, headed the list. She realized now that Barra had not been around, those times old friends gathered to talk; she had wondered only briefly, and thought no more of it. Without saying anything to the Duke, Paks went to talk with her. She found her already packing her things, with Natzlin watching, stony-faced.

"You!" Barra said, as Paks came up. "I'm surprised to see you hanging around common soldiers, Paks. But I suppose you remember that I knew you before you became such a famous hero."

"Barra—!" Natzlin's voice shook.

Paks herself was shocked at the venom in Barra's words. "What are you angry about, Barra? I thought we were friends—"

"Friends! If ever we were, it was long ago. Before you started thinking you were the High Lord's special messenger. I saw through you a long time ago, Paksenarrion Dorthansdotter. I knew you'd cause trouble in the end, and so you have!"

"Barra, that's not fair!" Natzlin threw a quick look at Paks, then touched Barra's arm. "She's changed, yes, but so have you."

"We've all changed. She's just—" Barra folded her lips together as she rolled another tunic and stuffed it in her pack. Then she turned to Natzlin. "And you—what's she done to you, that you're staying, eh? Do you think there's room for more than one hero around here? As long as Paks is with the Duke, that's who's going to get the notice. You might as well come, Natzlin; you'll end up a scarred old veteran with nothing to show for it but a few measly apple trees, like Kolya."

"I like apple trees." Natzlin turned toward Paks. "I don't know why she blames you. I know it's not your fault—"

"Tir's gut, it's not!" Barra grabbed Natzlin's arms and

swung her around. "Who was it that let herself be banned when it was that man's fault? And who was the 'hero' of Dwarfwatch? And who talked the Duke out of handling Siniava as he should have? Who have we heard about, night and day, this past year? Who, but poor, brave, wonderful Paks! And I thought Effa was a sugar-tit, with her 'Gird this, and Gird that' all the time. And she got killed, and I knew what Gird thought of *her*. But Paks!" Barra flung her pack across the room, startling the junior privates who had been loafing there, and had not heard any of it. She turned to Paks, her face pale under its tan. "You!" she said again. "You were no better when we started. By Tir, I remember giving you plenty of lumps in practice, if you don't. You had no special powers—you said it yourself. But you had all the chances. Everything came to you, praise and plenty all the time—" Paks thought of Saben's death, and Canna's, and the bitter hours she'd spent in combat with dire and dreadful things—the elfane taig, the kuaknom of Kolobia, the daskdraudigs. Praise and plenty? After last winter's starvation and contempt? She said nothing, realizing that the facts meant nothing now to Barra, lost in her own bitterness and anger.

"I could have done better," said Barra harshly, not bothering to lower her voice. "I could have—and I'll tell you this, Paks—I wouldn't have gone craven, as you did, to become the laughingstock of half the north—" So those tales had come this far, Paks realized. At the moment, it seemed less important than Barra's rage. "I'd have died decently," Barra went on, "if I couldn't live decently."

Paks looked at her. Where had the young girl gone, she wondered, who had snatched the last plum tart from the table one night, and tossed it to Paks across the crowded mess hall? It had disintegrated, Paks remembered, after a dozen or so throws. What had happened, to turn someone who dreamed of being a hero, even a paladin, into this hard and bitter soldier? Had the kernel of evil always been there? An old conversation with Vik trickled out of her memory: ". . . you think she's good because you like her," he had said. "But people aren't like that . . ." Perhaps it had been there, even then, and her liking for Barra had blinded her. Certainly it was here now, and visible to her senses. She wondered how the Marshal-General and Amberion had missed it, when they walked among the Company searching for just such danger.

"I'm sorry, Barra, that you think this," said Paks quietly. "I expect you might have done better—many might have. But I was the one there."

Barra laughed harshly. "Yes—you were. You always got the chance. Do you remember the night you came into the camp in Rotengre? I wondered, after, why you were the only one to make it through. Did the gods help you, Paks, or was it something you did?"

Her meaning was unmistakeable. Natzlin gasped a protest, and Paks was suddenly breathless with rage. Without thought, she was alight, casting a white radiance that dimmed the winter daylight through the windows. Barra shrank, eyes squinted nearly shut. Paks fought the rage down, and damped her light. She merely looked at Barra, and Barra looked back. Natzlin, tears running down her face, turned her back on Barra and walked out of the room.

"You'll find, someday," Paks found herself saying, "that your own tongue cuts you worse than any blade. I cannot even offer you the satisfaction of a fight, for you could not stand against me—and you know it. Go make your peace with Natzlin before you leave her—she's been a true friend to you all these years."

"A lover isn't always a friend," said Barra, still clenched in her rage.

"Not always. But she is, and you know it. Leave here angry with me, if you will, or with the Duke. But do not leave Natzlin to bear the burden of it." And Paks held her gaze until Barra's rigidity eased, and she looked down.

"Tir's gut," she said crossly, but without the intensity she'd had. "You'd think she was *your* lover, the way you care about her feelings."

"Good luck, Barra, wherever you go."

"Just don't follow me, Paks!" The intensity was back,

the dark eyes snapping with anger. "Just get out of my way, give me a chance."

Outside the door Paks met Dorrin, who shook her head with a wry smile. They headed across the courtyard to the mess hall. "You won't stop that one," Dorrin said on the way.

"I had to try—"

"You were recruits together, I remember. But she wasn't your friend, was she?"

"I thought so."

Dorrin shook her head again. "Paks, Barra's had as few friends as anyone in the Company. Only Natzlin—"

"Well, she was always prickly—"

"She was always ready to take offense at anything, and she'd hold a grudge until it died of old age. She's a skilled fighter, and honest, and works hard—all good. But I've heard more harsh things about her, from my sergeants, than about the rest of your recruit year put together. She wasn't *bad*—not the way I could complain of—but she hadn't a generous bone in her, and she'd a way of talking that kept everyone miserable. She didn't just love women—that's no problem—but she hated men, as well. And she has the most dangerous of beliefs: that things are unfair for her. The High Lord knows things are unfair. But they're unfair for us all, That's the way the world is." She sighed, and leaned on the mess hall door. "It's Natzlin that will suffer, as usual. I don't know how many times Natz has apologized to others, and smoothed things over. I'm glad she's staying, but I don't know how she'll do."

"I didn't know others had had trouble—"

"No. You haven't been here, or in my cohort."

Paks did not seen Barranyi again before she left. Within a week, it seemed the Company had settled into its new routine. The Girdsmen volunteered to work on the grange on their time off. Others joined them, from time to time. Wideflung patrols, riding out on the frosty hills, had not found any concentrations of orcs, and the orc raids on farms had ceased. The last of the damage had been repaired in Duke's East, and the millstones were back in place. The Marshal-General held the first services for Girdsmen, and then declared she had to leave.

"If I don't go now," she said, looking at the sky, "I might end up wintering here. That won't do; I've work in Fin Panir. Thank you, my lord Duke, for your invitation and courtesy, and our prayers will be with you."

"I thank you," he said.

"Paksenarrion," she said, turning to Paks, "you know you are welcome in Fin Panir. You have friends who would be glad to see you. But I know you are under other orders than mine—so if I do not see you again this side of the High Lord's table, you have my prayers and my good will."

Paks bowed, and thanked her. It had taken but an hour for the Marshal-General's party to be ready for travel, and now they walked across the Duke's Court before a whipping north wind. Once in the main courtyard, the Marshal-General took a last look around the stronghold.

"Duke Phelan," she said, "a man who can bring this order out of the chaos that was the north borders need not fear his work will waste. I cannot say what will come, for I have no prophecy, but I feel that your power is only now coming into its strength. Gird's grace, and the High Lord's favor, on all you do." She mounted quickly, and turned her horse to the gate. Again the trumpets rang out. This time, the soldiers in the courtyard raised a cheer, and the Marshal-General and her party rode out onto the windy plain.

Chapter Fourteen

Over the next few weeks, Paks divided her time between attending the Duke and leading scouting parties of archers north and east from the stronghold. No orcs showed, but the Duke took no chances.

"I don't want to take the whole Company into the Lairs," he explained, pulling out the old charts of those tangled burrows and tunnels. "It would take the whole Company, at least—we never did follow these all the way to the end. We'll post a guard closer to the Lairs, and ride patrols, and let that be it in this weather." For hard winter had set in, with a bank of cloud to the north that promised storms of snow.

Although Paks was still uneasy about it, the rest of the Company accepted her unusual status calmly. On patrol, she wore the Duke's uniform and carried a short sword or bow; her friends had gotten over their shyness, and chatted with her easily. But she lived in the Duke's Court, with the captains, and ate at the Duke's table. His armorer was making a set of chain mail for her. She drilled on both sides of the gate: with the captains and the Duke himself at longsword both afoot and ahorse, and with Siger and the others for short sword and bow. She rode in with the Duke to meet with the Councils of Duke's East and West. Here she learned things about farming that she had never learned on her father's farm. She began to see how all the crafts and trades in the Duke's lands fit together, how he could know how much of what supplies to order from Vérella.

In the evenings, she listened as the captains and the Duke discussed not only his realm, but other realms around. She heard the story of his first visit to Kostandan—and why Soft Ganarrion was willing to help him in Aarenis. Gradually she learned more about the Duke himself—that he had been Aliam Halveric's senior squire once, that he had won his title and domain after taking command of the Tsaian army after the death of the crown prince, and defeating a Pargunese force along the border. Tammarrion's sword, she learned, was a wedding gift from Aliam Halveric; Tammarrion herself had been Finthan, from Blackbone Hill.

With maps and models, the Duke and his captains made clear the relationship of the Eight Kingdoms: the forests and hills, the non-human kingdoms of gnome and dwarf. They reinforced the things she'd learned in Fin Panir, and extended them . . . the correct forms of address for different officers in each kingdom, the insignia of all the knightly orders, the little niceties of etiquette at each court. And they asked for her tales, especially of Fin Panir and Kolobia. At first she was shy of speaking before them, but this soon passed.

Day by day, as the Duke recovered from his wounds, and the threat of orc invasion lessened, the mood of the Company changed. Paks thought it was for the better—more smiles, more laughter in the mess hall, but without any less intensity or eagerness in drill. The Duke himself seemed more relaxed, and at the same time more alert. He gave his whole attention to each problem that came up, from the restocking of orc-burnt farms to the blocking of the tunnel in the wine-cellar. Paks had always thought of Arcolin as stern, and Dorrin as remote and severe, but even these captains thawed, showing her the warmth and humor hidden behind their authority. Part of this was certainly due to the actions of the Gird's Marshal.

Before the Midwinter festival, Marshal Kerrin had transferred to the stronghold; her replacement had arrived in

Burningmeed. Frost was on the ground before the foundations of the new grange were finished, so she traveled from the stronghold to the villages for services. Paks sometimes rode with her. Although younger than other Marshals she'd known, Kerrin impressed her with her ability. She had served two other granges as yeoman-marshal before training in Fin Panir, and had seen action in western Fintha against the nomads. Her steady, cheerful ways attracted many to the new grange.

The day before Midwinter Feast, Paks rode out with Stammel and a patrol into the hills northwest of the stronghold. As often at midwinter, it was clear, and wind had scoured the snow from the ground. Only a light breeze sifted along the ground, sharp as a sword-edge. Paks kept her face tucked into the hood of her cloak.

A sudden flurry of hoofbeats caught her attention; at the same time the forward scout yelled. She turned to see a red horse gallop out of a gap in the hills.

"A demon horse!" yelled the scout. "It must be! Shoot it!" He yanked his bow from his shoulder.

"No!" Paks twisted to watch as the horse circled the group. "Wait. It's not evil—"

"Are you sure?" asked Stammel, at her side. She nodded, watching the horse, which had slowed to a springy trot.

"I don't feel anything evil in it. I would, if it were a demon."

The others turned their horses to watch. The red horse seemed too slick to have been out in the weather; their own mounts were shaggier. It had white stockings behind, and a white star on the forehead. It pranced around them, blowing long jets of white vapor. Paks noted the size—as tall as her black warhorse, but built more for speed, a little lighter.

"Let's see if we can catch it," suggested Stammel.

"Good idea." Paks waved the others out to form wings, and they tried to pen the horse among them. It flung up its head and bolted, kicking up gouts of snow and frozen earth and streaking past their horses with a mocking whinny.

"I think it's some kind of enchanted," said Stammel. "No ordinary horse—"

"Oh, it's cold clear weather, and he's playing," said Paks. "Just the same as these would, only he's faster—" She paused as the horse slowed again, out of reach, and looked back at them. "Gird's teeth, he's a beauty. I wonder who's finding that his tether didn't hold."

"If that horse has worn a saddle in the past month, I'd be surprised. Not a mark on him."

"True. And the wild horses north aren't built like that. Hey, there—" Paks spoke to the horse, which stood with pricked ears watching her and the others. "I wonder if he'd let me come on foot."

"Paks, you be careful—"

"He's not evil, I tell you."

"Evil or not, he's not acting like a normal horse. At his size, he could put dents in you if he stepped wrong."

"So could a pack mule." Paks slid from her mount, and handed the reins to Stammel, who heaved a big sigh. She gave him a quick grin before returning her gaze to the horse. "Don't follow me," she said. "Don't spook him."

"Did you ever hear about the demon horses that enchant men to ride on them, and then take them away?" asked Stammel as she walked forward.

"Yes, but he won't."

"Tir's gut, Paks, begging your paladin's pardon, but you're acting half-enchanted now."

"It's all right." Paks felt sure it was all right, and she moved slowly toward the red horse. It stood still now, balanced neatly on all four legs, watching her. Its long mane and tail blew sideways in the breeze, but it did not stir. She came closer, close enough to see the great eyes, purple-brown, with their oblong irises, and the long upper lashes. The white star was perfectly centered. She paused, looking at the straight legs, flat knees, deep chest—the horse whuffled at her. She felt a nudge of urgency. She took another step forward, and another. The soft dark nose reached out, bumped her hand. "Well," she said. The horse nudged her again, more firmly. She put a hand to the side of its neck, and it leaned into the caress.

She moved to its side, and it turned its head to watch. A long neck, well-arched; a sloping shoulder, deep heart-girth, long underline. Although lighter built than the black, those powerful hindquarters did not lack for strength. She laid her hand on its back; it stood poised, waiting. She ran her hands down the near foreleg, and asked for the hoof; it came to her hand without resistance. The unshod hoof showed no chipping or splitting, as if it had just been trimmed. When she stood back, the horse turned to her again, and snorted. It was clearly a challenge. Paks felt a surge of excitement. More than anything else she wanted to be on that horse, moving with that speed and power. Was it enchantment?

She walked around the horse, noting strong hocks, muscled gaskins, everything a well-built horse should have and nothing it shouldn't. She came again to the head, and started to reach for the lips, to check teeth. The horse threw up its head and gave a snort of clear disgust. Paks chuckled.

"All right. Your age is your business. Gird knows you can't be too old."

"Paks—" Stammel's call carried over the wind. "Don't get on that beast—"

"It's all right." Paks turned to yell back, and the horse blew warm on her neck. She jumped, and glared at it. "Listen, horse—" It whuffled again, and touched her softly. An invitation? A challenge? She raised her hand to its neck again, stroked along it. A real paladin, she told herself, wouldn't be fooled by a demon horse. So either it's not a demon horse, or I'm not a real paladin, and whichever it is or I am, I'm going to have one glorious ride.

With no real fear, she moved to the horse's side and put her hands on its withers. It stood still, merely watching her with one ear cocked back.

"If you buck me off," warned Paks, "and make me look like an idiot, I'll chase you from here to the Cold Waste." The delicate nostrils quivered; the horse did not move.

Paks took a deep breath and vaulted up, swinging her right leg wide. The horse stood still as she gained its back and settled herself. She glanced at Stammel, whose face was set in a disapproving scowl. Paks closed her legs gently, and the horse stepped forward. She had not ridden bareback since regaining her powers, and had nearly forgotten the complex shifting of muscles under her. But the horse made no move to bolt, and she adjusted easily. When she nudged with one heel, the horse turned smoothly, angling toward Stammel. Paks stiffened her back, and it halted, perfectly balanced.

"Well," said Stammel grudgingly, "it's not acting like a demon horse. They're supposed to charge off at a run and never stop."

"It's not a demon," said Paks, "but I don't know what it is." The horse threw up its head and whinnied loudly. She laid a hand on its neck. "Sorry—I really don't. Stammel, I'm going to try him out."

His eyebrows went up again. "With no bridle or saddle?"

"So far he responds to legs alone—we'll see. If I break my silly neck, you can tell the Duke I admitted it was my fault beforehand." With that she tapped with her left heel and the horse wheeled to the right. A firmer leg, and it broke to a long swinging trot. Paks took a cautionary handful of mane and asked for a canter. At this gait, smooth but longer-strided than her other horse's canter, she guided the red horse through circles and figures of eight with legs alone. It did everything she asked, with smooth flying changes of lead when necessary. And as for feeling—it was, she thought gleefully, the best horse she had ever ridden. Perfect balance, perfect rhythm, suppleness . . . she brought it back to halt near the others.

"All right," Stammel said. "I'm convinced. But what will you do with him?"

"I don't know. I—" The horse whinnied again, and Paks ran a hand down the glossy neck. "I suppose I'll ride him back to the stronghold. If he's someone's, they may come by—"

"I don't think it is. Whatever that horse is and wherever

he came from, I think he came for you. Not a demon horse, no—but where do paladins get their horses?"

Paks felt her jaw drop. She had forgotten about paladins' horses. In Fin Panir, when paladins were confirmed in the High Lord's Hall, they came out to find their mounts awaiting them in the courtyard. Everyone insisted that the horses appeared—uncalled, but by the gods—and that no one, from the Marshal-General on down, had anything to do with it.

"You're a paladin," Stammel was going on. "Stands to reason you'd have a horse of your own. You can't stay here forever, the way I understand it."

"No—that's true." Paks covered her confusion by smoothing the red horse's mane. "I—hadn't thought about it. Maybe—" She leaned over and met the horse's backturned eye. "Are you a paladin's horse? Are you my horse?" The head tossed, and a forefoot pawed the ground.

Stammel laughed, a release of tension as much as humor. "Gods above, Paks, we never know what will happen with you around. Can we finish this patrol, or does your fancy horse insist on going home?" The horse blew a rattling snort, and Stammel nodded to it. "Begging your pardon, beastie, but some of us have work to do."

"He'll go along," said Paks. "Let's get on with it." And she took the reins of her assigned mount from Stammel, and led the way along their patrol path.

Back at the stronghold that evening, the red horse caused plenty of comment. Paks was hardly through the gates when a crowd gathered to stare. The Marshal, on her way across the courtyard from one barracks to another, stopped short.

"Where did you get that?" she began.

"Came running up to us from far in the hills," said Stammel, before Paks could speak. "He pranced around as showy as a gamecock, then let Paks walk up to him. I feared it was a demon horse, but she said not, and proved it riding him."

The Marshal shook her head. "Not a demon horse—by the High Lord, Paks, you've surprised us again."

"Marshal?" Paks swung down, keeping her hand on the horse's neck.

"I had wondered how you would get your mount—or if you would. You're different enough that I had no idea— But I never thought one would appear here, in Midwinter."

"Then you think it is—"

"Your paladin's mount, of course. Of course it is." The Marshal held a hand out to the red horse, who touched it lightly with his nose, then turned to nuzzle Paks. "I only wonder why he didn't come at once."

The horse snorted and stamped. The Marshal looked surprised, then shook her head again. "Paks, paladins' mounts have powers of their own—I don't know if Amberion told you—"

"I've heard somewhat—"

"Good. Not all are the same. I wouldn't venture to say what this one can do—but don't be too surprised." The Marshal nodded briskly to both Paks and the horse, and strode off.

Paks looked around. No one else ventured to say anything, but she caught many intent looks. "I suppose," she said finally, "I'd better find you a place in the stable."

Somewhat to her surprise, the red horse went into a box stall willingly, and began munching hay like any ordinary horse. Paks hurried back to the Duke's court to tell him about it.

"I suspect," said the Duke, "that it means you haven't much longer to stay here. Your mail is almost finished . . ."

"Do you feel anything, any call?" asked Dorrin.

"No." Paks looked around the room. "Not yet. But you're probably right, my lord. There's nothing here I'd need a horse like that for."

"Well, you're spending Midwinter here, at least, unless your gods lack sense," said the Duke. "We've planned a feast to remember, this year, and I won't have you miss it."

Paks thought of her last Midwinter, cold and afraid, in

hiding from her past and future both, and smiled against that dark memory. "We will celebrate together," she said, and included the captains with a quick glance, "the victory of light over darkness, and courage over fear." The Duke started to speak, but nodded instead.

And when the recruits, freed for the festival days from their usual strict discipline, had the audacity to pelt officers, Marshal, and paladin with sticky fruit pastries, she laughed along with the others. They had been solemn enough when the fires were quenched, and the entire Company stood watch the whole night of Midwinter. On the second day, Paks rode out with the Duke to both villages for the ceremonial exchange of vows. She had not intended to ride the red horse for this, but found him waiting, saddled and bridled, in the forecourt when she came down. The Duke shook his head, then grinned.

"Your gods are pressing you, Paks—best be aware of them."

"I didn't plan to—"

"You keep telling me that paladins don't plan—the gods plan for them. If someone gifted me with a horse like that, I'd never walk."

"Yes, well—" Paks reached out to stroke the red horse's neck; it was as slick as if it had just been groomed. "I'd like to know who saddled him."

"We can ask, but my guess is no one."

"But horses can't saddle themselves—" The red horse snorted, stamped, and bumped Paks hard with the side of its head. "Sorry," said Paks. "I only meant—" The horse snorted again, and the Duke chuckled.

"Come on, Paks; mount the beast before you say something unforgiveable."

Paks swung into the saddle. It felt as if it had been made for her, and the stirrups were exactly the right length. Neither then nor later would anyone admit to have made the saddle (though she suspected the Duke, at first, of having supplied one), or having put it on the horse. Paks followed the Duke out the gate, puzzled but delighted. When they returned that evening, the horse permitted her to remove saddle and bridle, but despite a day's riding no mark marred that satiny coat. Paks hung saddle and bridle on a rack and went back to the Duke's Court, still slightly confused.

Chapter Fifteen

She felt that she had always run away before: from home, from the Company in Aarenis, from Fin Panir. Each time she had tried to escape something, and each time the thing she had refused to face confronted her again. This time, she was not running away—she was sent. She was less embarrassed than she'd expected by the troops in formation to see her off. It might be the last time she'd see them, the old friends who had made her what she was. That fanfare the Duke commanded, ringing through cold sunny air from the gate tower, honored the gods she served. And the Duke—his eyes alight as she had never seen them—they had said all they had to say. She wore Tammarrion's sword at her side, and he had nothing of hers but her prayers. And his life.

Riding through Duke's East, the red horse pranced, snatching his hooves off the cobbles as if they were coals. They all came out, men, women, and children—waving at her, shy to call. She knew the names, the faces, grinned at them and at herself. It was living the old dream, to ride through a town this way, and if it wasn't Three Firs, with her own brothers, sisters, and cousins waving and smiling, it was well enough. She felt the horse's amusement through her legs: he knew; it was why he pranced so, showing her off. He slowed without reining by Kolya's gate. Kolya nodded slowly, squinting up at Paks in the bright sunlight.

"So—it's as I heard. You're going. We'll miss you, Paks. The Duke, too—" she stopped, her eyes fixing on

Tammarrion's sword. She looked quickly back at Paks's face. "That, too?"

"Yes. He gave me that—I argued, but—"

"That alone?" Her meaning carried more by look than the words themselves. Paks thought of the talks she'd had, these past weeks, as she waited for the Duke's gift of mail to be finished to his satisfaction. He had insisted on helmet and shield as well, befitting a paladin of Gird. His offer had been as oblique, yet as clear, as Kolya's question.

Paks looked ahead, then back at Kolya. "I am not free, Kolya, to answer all calls. There's better for him." Paks hoped she was right to say that. "Even if I were free—and would marry—I'm not Tammarrion. It's not only age, Kolya."

Kolya sighed. "No. That's so. It's that likeness, though, that keeps the thought in mind. Maybe it's better that you're going, for that as well."

The red horse did not move, but Paks felt his eagerness to be gone, his certainty of which way to go. She glanced around a last time. "Kolya, I must go. I can't linger—"

"I understand. Can you accept the blessing of an old kuakgannir?"

"Of a friend, always."

"Then may the First Tree shade your path, and shed fruit for your hunger, and the wisdom of all wild things be yours."

"And may the High Lord's grace and Gird's protection be on you, Kolya, and the Lady of Peace bring plenty to your orchard." They clasped hands, then Paks straightened, and the red horse moved on. Paks did not look back.

Although Paks had imagined being a paladin, she had never seriously thought what it would be like to travel as one. She had had some vague idea that paladins knew from the beginning exactly where they would go, and what they were to do, that they stayed in granges for the most part. She did not know even yet how other paladins moved around, for her it was different. Besides a feeling that they should go south and east, she had no idea where they were going. The red horse chose his own trails, and these did not lead from grange to grange, or along the roads she knew.

South of Duke's East, they left the now-familiar road that led to Verella and struck southeast across wooded country. Paks had already found that the red horse had more speed and endurance than common horses, and she let him choose his own times to rest. That wasn't often. They came to the Honnorgat downstream of Verella in three days of hard riding. Paks was stiff and cold, and sat staring at the broad gray river while the red horse drew breath.

"Now what?" she asked it. "You aren't planning to swim that, I hope. And the bridges are all upstream, as far as I know." The horse flicked an ear back at her. Paks stretched and looked around. They were on low water meadows, now covered with frost-dry grass. Along the river itself, a fringe of trees thickened here and there into a grove. Downstream smoke rose from a clutter of huts. Paks thought of that den of thieves in Aarenis and wrinkled her nose. On a low mound still farther downstream a larger building bulked—a keep of some kind, perhaps. Upstream was yet another group of huts, with a stake fence. When the horse pricked his ears, pointing, she could see a herd of dun-colored cattle grazing.

Sound carried well near the river, and she heard the jingle of harness just as the horse threw up his head. A small band of riders jogged her way from the larger building—she had been seen. "I hope you know what you're doing," she said to the red horse. "I hope you haven't crossed the border to Pargun somewhere in those woods." But as the band neared her, she was reassured by their colors, the rose and silver of the Tsaian royal house.

"Ho, stranger!" They were just in hail. Paks sat still and let them come. The red horse was alert but unalarmed. She recognized the band's uniform now—Tsaian Royal Guard—but wondered what they were doing this far from Verella. The leader wore Gird's crescent on his chest, and the device of the Order of the Bells. A knight, then, and well-born. Six men-at-arms, trim and fit-looking, rode behind him. When he was within speaking range, he reined in. Paks nodded to him.

"Gird's grace to you, sir knight."

His eyebrows rose. "Gird's grace . . . uh . . ."

"Paksenarrion Dorthansdotter," said Paks pleasantly.

"You are from—"

"I have just come from Duke Phelan's stronghold," she said. "I am a veteran of his Company, but no longer, as you see, one of them." Her own garb, chainmail under the plain brown cloak she'd bought in Brewersbridge with her Lyonyan coins, gave him no clue.

"Hmm." He rubbed his chin, obviously confused. "On the Duke's business, are you?"

"No. On Gird's business." That got his attention, and that of the others; they all stared. Paks hoped she hadn't stated it too baldly, but she felt a push to do so.

"Are you a—a Marshal?" At his question, her horse snorted, shaking its head. That reaction made her grin, and the knight even more uneasy.

"No, sir knight," she said, trying not to laugh. "I'm no Marshal. Might I ask your name?"

"Oh!" He had clearly forgotten about introducing himself. "I'm Regnal Kostvan, third son of the Kostvan Holding. The Royal Guard has garrisons in an all the border keeps right now; that's why I'm here."

"Is there trouble along here with Pargun?"

He frowned. "Not to say trouble. Not more than usual. But the way things are going in Lyonya—" He looked hard to see if she knew what that meant. Paks nodded. He went on. "And so we're to make sure of travellers in this way. Were you planning to cross the river? Because you'd have to have clearance from me to hire a ferry."

"I have reason to cross, yes." Paks did not say more. How could she explain that she didn't know where she was going, or what she was to do when she got there?

"You'd best come back with me to the keep," he said. Paks felt rather than saw an increased alertness in the men-at-arms. They must have had some trouble, to make them so nervous. "My commander will want to speak with you."

"I'd be glad to," she said. "It's a cold day to talk out here." As she eased the red horse forward, she saw the men-at-arms tense and relax.

"I've heard of one Paksenarrion," began the knight tentatively. Paks could feel the ears of the others growing longer as he spoke. She laughed, surprised at how easy it was.

"Sir Regnal, it might have been you heard of me, though I claim no particular fame. But I served with Duke Phelan three seasons in Aarenis, and rode to Kolobia with the Girdsmen from Fin Panir—so if that's what you heard, you heard it of me."

He glanced at her sideways. His horse was enough shorter that she could tell little of his size. "Yes—I had heard of that. And of some other—" he paused, looking away, then back at her. She nodded.

"You may have heard truth and falsehood both, Sir Regnal. And the truth could be the more unpleasant. I do not speak of it much."

"I see." He rode a little way in silence. Then he turned to her again, as they neared a small stone keep whose gate faced the river. "But it is our duty to know what passes here—what manner of man or other being, and with what loyalties. I have heard such things of one Paksenarrion that I would not let that one pass. So these things must be spoken of, and your faiths proved."

The red horse stopped short at Paks's thought. She faced the knight squarely. "Sir knight, my faith has been proved already by such trials as I pray you never face." He reddened, but she went on. "I think you will be convinced, ere I leave, of what 'manner of man or other being' rides such a horse in such a way." She smiled, then, and nudged the horse on. "But it will be quicker to convince you and your commander all in one; let us ride in." And the long-striding red horse caught up and passed the knight's, and led the way into the keep courtyard.

* * *

Sir Regnal was stiffly correct in presenting Paks to his superior, a heavyset older man with the intricate corded knots of a cohort-commander on the shoulders of his velvet winter tunic. Ganarrion Verrakai: Paks recalled from the charts in the Duke's library that this was a second son of the minor branch of that powerful family, second only to Marrakai in influence at court. She bowed, and carefully chose an applicable honorific which recognized his family position as well as his Guards rank.

"Sir nigan-Verrakai."

His eyebrows didn't rise, but he did not miss the wording. "Paksenarrion Dorthansdotter. Duke Phelan's veteran?"

"Yes, my lord. Not presently in his service."

"Ah, yes. On Gird's service, you told Sir Regnal?"

"Yes." She wondered how far they would press.

"Have you any authorization from the granges? From Fin Panir, perhaps?"

"From Gird, my lord," she said.

This time his eyebrows did rise. Not all the Verrakai, she remembered, were Girdsmen. Some were Falkian, some kuakgannir, and some, it was rumored, followed less honored gods. "But you are not a Marshal, you said?"

"No." It was astonishingly hard to say, to actually open her mouth and claim what she was, among strangers. "I am a paladin." At least it sounded all right.

They stared. Finally the commander said, "A paladin." He sounded unconvinced. Paks was not surprised. She was uneasily aware that she was going to have to prove it to them. "Could you tell me," he went on, "why a paladin should come here, where we have no need of one?"

"Because you lie between where I was, and where I must go," she said crisply.

"Oh. And where is that, if you please?"

Paks met his gaze steadily, and his eyes fell first. "I don't think," she said finally, "that that is your concern. If you know anything of paladins, you know we must answer the call at once, and without question. Nor do we answer questions without need."

He nodded. "Yes. I knew that. I just—wondered. But—" he looked her up and down. "I had heard things, last year at court. I mean—no offense meant, but—I heard of a Phelani veteran who went to Fin Panir to become a paladin, and failed. Left Fin Panir. Was wandering around as a—" he paused delicately.

"Coward?" suggested Paks, amazed that she could. He glanced quickly at her, and nodded. "Well," she went on briskly, "you have heard a lot, it seems. Some of it was true. It is also true that wounds heal, and cowards can regain their courage. And it is true that now I am a paladin. When the Marshal-General came to Phelan's stronghold—"

"What?!" The commander looked even more flabbergasted. "The Marshal-General of Gird?"

"Yes. He summoned a Marshal, on my advice, and she came."

"Well. I would never have thought. Phelan hates the Girdsmen."

"He did at one time. No longer. A grange is being built there."

"I can scarcely credit it. And you—you say you are a paladin. Have you any proof?"

Paks smiled, and called light. It lit the room far more brightly than the meagre daylight until she damped it, and the commander nodded. The younger knight looked shocked, and blinked warily.

"I have seen such light before," said the commander. His voice had warmed. "Well then, Lady Paksenarrion—you may indeed go on Gird's business. But why do you conceal yourself?"

"I travel as I am bid, my lord; Gird himself was a plain man, and I am a sheepfarmer's daughter. When Gird chooses to have me recognized, I daresay I will be."

"A good answer. A good answer indeed. We are honored by your presence, and will do whatever we can for you. You will cross the river?" She nodded. "Then by your leave I'll send Regnal here to arrange a ferry. Can you wait until morning? I'd be glad to have you at our table this night."

Paks felt no restless urging, and was glad to stay the night. If she had to ride in another boat, she wanted to do it in daylight anyway. The commander set a good table, and Regnal had recovered enough from his surprise to be good company as well. They were full of gossip about the state of affairs in Lyonya.

"I'm not asking, you understand," said Ganarrion Verrakai. "But it will take a paladin, I'm thinking, or a company of them, to save Lyonya from years of chaos—even war. All I've heard for the last half year is how sick the king is. And how muddled the succession will be. And if Lyonya falls apart—our best ally— then it won't take long for Pargun to move, I'm thinking."

"Not long at all." Regnal drained his glass, and stared at the table. "My grandfather was killed by Pargunese—you won't know this, Lady Paksenarrion, but that was when the Tsaian crown prince was killed as well, and your Duke Phelan captured the Pargunese commander. That was before he got his lands. Pargun has always wanted this territory."

"Yes, but it's worse than that." Verrakai shoved his glass around on the tablecloth. "I remember my grandfather's tales of the old evil, before Tsaia and Fintha joined Lyonya and Prealith to fence it out. With Lyonya in trouble, it could erupt right in the middle of the Eight Kingdoms, instead of hanging about the fringes. It wasn't that long ago, when you think of it, that they fought at Long Stones. I daresay the Master of Torments would like another chance at the inner realms."

"Or *her*," said Regnal. He glanced at Paks. "By what I've heard, you know as much about the webspinner's ways as anyone can, and live."

Paks nodded. "Yes—and I see what you mean."

"By my thinking, *she* probably had something to do with the prince being lost like that," said Verrakai. "No one says so, true, but something evil came to the queen and the prince. If he hadn't been lost—"

"No, I think it was the king dying while the princess was still so young," argued Regnal. "She had the taig-sense, but with no guidance, she never learned to use it fully."

"But that was from grief. If the queen hadn't been killed—"

"When was this?" Paks had heard the story outlined, but was not clear on the earlier details. The rangers had concentrated on more recent problems, including the king's illness.

"Oh, let me think." Verrakai stared at the table. "I was only a boy when it happened. Forty years, it must be, or fifty. Somewhat around there. Do you know the tale at all?"

Paks nodded. "The queen and prince were going somewhere, and attacked. She was killed, and he was never found. Is that right?"

"Yes. He was a little child, and the princess only a baby; she had been left behind, being too young to travel."

"The thing is," put in Regnal, "that there's no one else in the line who has enough elven blood. And there's so many that don't want it, because they don't know what it does—" he glanced at Verrakai, who reddened.

"Don't look at me, young Kostvan. I'm no elf-hater; that's my uncle. I've met rangers enough, working for the court, and I know what they mean by taig-sense. I still think Gird's guidance is enough, for human folk at least, but I admit that Lyonya's different. It's a joint kingdom, and the elves have a right to be in the kingship. And where you have elves, you have taigin. But even in Lyonya there are humans who fear more elven influence. And so they don't care, and so they have had two kings, now, with not enough taig-sense to hear thunder before a storm, and no one coming who has any more."

Listening to this, Paks had a curious sensation, a tingling of the mind, which forced her attention more strongly on what was said. For some reason she did not yet understand, it was important to what she was to do. But now Verrakai was smiling at her.

"What they need, maybe, is a paladin ruler instead. That hasn't been tried yet. By Gird, if you can sense good and evil directly, I'd think that would work as well as taig-sense."

Paks knew from her own experiences in Lyonya that it was not the same, but didn't want to explain all that. She merely laughed a little. "Paladins are called to harder seats than thrones, good sir. Granted that rule is not easy; but we are not trained for rule and judgment, but for sharp conflict."

"It might be better the other way. But I am not one to quarrel with the gods' ideas, only I hope something changes for the better in Lyonya, and soon. We have had bands of orcs around here, and worse things seen at a distance. If there's serious trouble ahead, I'd as soon our allies were in shape to help."

In the morning, Paks and the red horse were ferried across the Honnorgat, its wide surface pewter colored between ice that still clutched each bank. On the far side she mounted, and rode on thoughtfully. She noticed that her mail shirt was brighter than the day before. No one had polished it, or the rings and buckles of her tack, which were also gleaming. She wondered if her gear were beginning to take on the gleaming cleanliness she had noticed on other paladins.

South of the Honnorgat the land was more settled and richer. She passed through many little villages, and by noon was riding into a larger town. The red horse came to a stop before a handsome grange just as a Marshal stepped out the barton gate.

"Gird's grace, traveller," said the Marshal, eyeing her keenly. "I'm Marshal Pelyan. And you—?"

"Paksenarrion," she answered. "A paladin of Gird, whose protection lies on all this land."

His eyes opened a little wider, but he merely nodded. "Welcome to our town. Will you take lunch with me?"

"With honor." Paks had already found that a paladin's hunger differed in no way from that of an ordinary soldier.

She swung off the red horse, and looped the reins over her arm. "Is there a stable?"

"Around here." He led the way to the back of the grange, and waited while she made the red horse comfortable in a box next to his own brown warhorse. "You have traveled hard," he said, as he preceded her out the stable door.

Paks shrugged. "Not too bad."

"Mmm. Some would consider any travel this time of year hard. But not you, I suppose." They had come to an inn, and he entered, waving his hand at several men who looked up. A landlord came forward, looking at Paks curiously. The Marshal forestalled any questions by asking him for a quiet table. When they were seated, he leaned forward in his chair. "I know I asked for assistance," he said softly, "but I didn't think it required a paladin. Is it really that bad?"

Paks was startled. She had had no feelings about this town at all, and no sense that she was called to do anything here. "Marshal, I'm not here in answer to your call—that I know of. It's true I'm on quest, but somewhere else."

"I see." He looked somewhat relieved. "Do you—would you know if my message was received in Fin Panir?"

"No." Paks shook her head slowly. "I haven't been in Fin Panir for over a year."

"Oh." Now he looked dismayed. "Blast. I wish I knew—" He stopped as the landlord came to take their order, and quickly told the man to bring stew and hot bread. When the landlord moved away, he began again. "Sorry—should have let you order. But I'm that worried, you see. And then you came in, just when I was thinking I'd have to ride at least to Vérella myself." The landlord came with their food, two huge bowls of steaming stew and two loaves of bread. Paks began to eat. The stew was good; she finished it all, and mopped the bowl clean with a hunk of bread.

The Marshal insisted on paying for their meal, and said nothing more about his problems until they were near the grange, and the street empty around them. "I don't mean to delay you," he said, "but if you have a little time, perhaps you could just tell me if I should ride out myself. It's very vexing, is what it is . . ."

Paks herself was curious what sort of problem could bother him so, and what kind of help he'd asked for. She agreed to take a cup of sib in his office and listen.

"This is solid old Girdish territory," he began. "Has been for generations; we had a grange here before Tsaia claimed it. So we've always had a strong yeomanry. But as we're close to Lyonya—Harway, maybe a half-day's walk east, is on the border—we've had plenty of Falkians, too. I've nothing against them; they're quiet, law-abiding folk, and brave enough in trouble. But this trouble in Lyonya—well, now, folk here are beginning to worry. When the first few Falkians came in wanting to join the grange, I admit I was pleased about it. After all, that's what any Marshal hopes to do, is increase the strength of the yeomanry. The Falkian captain even joked with me about it, wanted to know my secret. But along about last spring, it went beyond any jokes. They've closed their field—that's like our grange—and the captain's left. There's a sergeant now, for the few commons left. And our grange is stuffed with ex-Falkians."

"Why do you think they changed?" asked Paks. It still didn't seem much like a real problem to her.

"Lyonya. I think they wanted to show their loyalty to Tsaia, where the court's Girdish. They don't say so, of course. I wouldn't take 'em if they did. That's a bad reason to change patrons, just for policy like that. And that's part of my problem: all these so-called Girdsmen. I don't have the arms for that many, or the money and time to get arms. Of course the Falkian captain didn't send the arms along with them—very properly, too: I certainly never sent arms with a yeoman who left the grange. But they talk, talk, talk, all the time, worrying themselves—and me—and I have only one yeoman-marshal, and she's been sick. Then there's the visitors."

"Visitors?" Paks asked politely, since he had paused as if waiting for her question.

"Yes." He made a sour face. "Close as we are to the border, you see, families here and families there have intermarried and so on. With all this uncertainty in Lyonya, they've come over here until it settles down—if it ever does. As I said, we're a long-settled area. It's not easy to absorb several hundred more people all at once, and no knowing when they'll leave. Families going short call on the grange for help; we had a good harvest, but most of these people came just after harvest—not during the working season, when they could have made the crop bigger. I wrote Fin Panir back in the spring about getting another yeoman-marshal or Marshal, and maybe starting another grange. They said wait and see what happened. What's happened is that I've got a grange full of people, less than half of them my own, and not enough arms, or time to train, or anyone to work with. I suppose it's not a paladin's concern—" He looked at her sadly.

"Tell me about your yeoman-marshal," said Paks, trying to think what she could do in a short time. "Did you say she was sick?"

"Well, she's not so young any more, and she's had lung fever last winter and this winter both. This last time, she never really got well."

"Why don't I take a look?" said Paks. Then she thought again. "Of course, you've tried a healing—?"

The Marshal shook his head. "She didn't want one, she said. She's been low in her spirits this last year or so—and that's another thing, but I've had no one to talk to, and been too busy to go anywhere. Something's bothering her—"

"Would she talk to me?"

"I imagine so. A paladin, after all. On a quest. It might interest her."

"Can't you appoint another yeoman-marshal?"

"Well—yes, I could, but—everyone knows Rahel. She's been here since before I came. As long as she's—and it's not as if we were actively fighting—"

"Where is she?" asked Paks.

"Along here." The Marshal rose and led the way along a passage inside the grange. He stopped outside a door, and rapped on it. Paks heard a chair scrape inside, and a heavy cough, then a tired voice responding. "It's the Marshal," he said. "We have a visitor, Rahel—a paladin."

The door opened. Rahel, the yeoman-marshal, was a hand shorter than Paks, with heavy gray braids wrapped around her head; her face was thin, and she stood slightly askew, like someone with a stitch in her side. Paks was aware of a heavy feeling in the air. "Sir Marshal," said Rahel, in a voice without resonance. "Paladin—?"

"Paksenarrion," said the Marshal, with a gesture. "She is on quest, but stopped here for a meal, and a rest."

"Gird's grace, Lady," said Rahel, with obvious effort. "Will you come in?"

"Gird's strength to you," said Paks in return. "I'd be glad to sit awhile, if it won't tire you."

Rahel smiled without humor. "Nothing tires me, Lady, but living itself." She stepped back, and Paks followed her into a clean spare room with a small fireplace. Two comfortable chairs, a small table, and a narrow bed piled with pillows furnished it. A mail shirt hung from its stand, and several swords hung from pegs on the wall. That was all. Rahel sank into one of the chairs, clearly short of breath.

"How long have you been sick?" asked Paks.

Rahel shook her head. "I am not sure. I have an old wound—every year or so I used to have lung fever in winter or early spring. I can't remember when it was that it first started hanging on too long. But last year—it was near midsummer before I could walk to Harway and back in a day. And just after harvest, I got the lung fever again." She stopped, gasping. Her color was bad, an odd bluish-gray that Paks had seen on men with lung wounds. She coughed again, bending to it. Paks waited, wondering if there were any chance of a healing.

"The Marshal," Rahel went on when she caught her breath, "he thinks I should let him try a healing. But it's too late—too much is gone—I—" she coughed again. "I'm too tired," she said finally. "I fought—years—and I'm tired."

"Would you let me try to ease the pain for you" asked Paks.

"Ease—? Not heal?"

"If it can be healed, I will try to heal it. I think you are right, Rahel, that it's gone too far. But I can ease it for you, for awhile."

"I didn't want numbwine," muttered Rahel. "Can't think with that stuff—can't work at all."

"Not numbwine." Paks watched her, recognizing the heaviness for what it was, and wondered why the Marshal had not seen it—or if he had just not wanted to see it.

Rahel nodded. "If you will—I'm sorry, Lady—I can't say the right things—"

"No matter. Would you rather lie down?"

"Yes, if you don't mind. It's hard to—" She pulled herself out of the chair, and went to the bed, piling the pillows at one end. Paks wondered briefly if she should tell the Marshal first, and decided against it. Rahel lay against the pillows, her eyes sagging shut. Paks took a deep calming breath, and called on Gird and the High Lord.

As she touched Rahel's head, she knew at once that no cure would be given. She prayed quietly, hoping to ease the pain, and sensed that Rahel's breathing had quieted. After a few minutes, she felt a clear instruction to stop, and withdrew her hands. Rahel opened her eyes.

"That—is—much better. My thanks, Lady, for this and for Gird's grace." She looked better, even rested, and Paks fetched her a drink of water from the jug on the table.

"The power is the High Lord's," Paks reminded her. "It is lent me, under Gird's grace; it is not mine."

"True. Oh, it is easier. If it never got worse than this, I could—" she stopped suddenly, with a surprised look, and fell back. Paks knew at once that she was dead, as she had known that death was near. She straightened Rahel's body, and called the Marshal.

Chapter Sixteen

"So it has come." The Marshal did not seem surprised. "I knew it would be soon, but not how soon." Together he and Paks prepared the body for burial. Paks struggled with her own feelings; she was not used to death save by violence. The Marshal spoke softly as they worked. "When death comes in war, quickly, it is easily faced. So also with many illnesses—either life and health, or death. For most who grow old in peace, the weakness of age comes gently, and death is no longer an enemy. But for her—you saw that scar; I think she had pain from it all along. For two years every breath was drawn in pain. She was too strong to die soon, and knew it might last beyond her strength to face it. That fear—that she might not—began to master her. When you took the pain—"

"I knew it might end—" Paks ducked her head. He touched her shoulder.

"You are a young paladin, and so I will be bold to answer what you did not ask. And even to answer what you fear I might ask. Yes, what you did might have caused her death so quickly. Yet I know you intended neither evil nor her death, and I do not think you killed her. For the healing power comes, as you said, from the High Lord—from him comes the end of pain, not pain itself."

"You were listening—you knew—"

"I hoped. She wouldn't let me—and it had gone on long enough. She feared to be weak, and take my help; it had to be someone else."

"Why didn't—why didn't Gird heal that wound in the first place?" Paks was surprised at her own resentment. She knew the danger of that, fought it back. The Marshal finished folding the blanket around the body, laid Rahel's medallion on top of it, and looked at Paks levelly.

"She wasn't a Girdsman then. She—" he looked briefly at the body, and back at Paks. "She was a brigand; Gird knows what gods she followed, if any. The Marshal before me here found her near death, in a cave. The others had left her, after dragging her that far. The wound was too old to heal cleanly, even if she'd been a yeoman. Somehow she lived—he was a good herbalist as well—and, when she was stronger, he converted her. Had to, or the local Council would have hanged her."

"Oh."

"He made her yeoman-marshal not only for her ability, but to protect her from the yeomen and the town. And she served well, the rest of her life."

Riding east the next day, Paks thought about what the Marshal had told her. The land seemed settled enough; she saw none of the disruption that war had brought to Aarenis. Few travellers moved on the road, but it was winter, and cold. She came to Harway before noon. Here she was stopped by men-at-arms in Lyonyan green and gold, but they passed her quickly enough when she gave her name.

"Didn't you serve with the rangers last summer?" asked one of them.

"Yes, with Giron."

"That's what I thought. They send those names all around the border. Go on, then, anywhere you like—but if you go to Chaya, you should give your name at the court, and let the king know you're there."

"I've never seen Chaya," said Paks.

"Stay on this road and you will—it's south and east of here, more east than south. You've worked with elves; you'll like it."

"I'll ride that way if I can. How would I find the Halveric lands?"

"Which Halverics? That's a big family."

"Aliam Halveric—he has a mercenary company—"

"Oh. You were close enough to it last summer—didn't you know?" Paks shook her head. "Well, it's far in the south—I haven't been there myself."

As she rode into Lyonya, the amount of forested land increased. Bit by bit the fields grew smaller, and the blocks of wood between them larger. Near Chaya itself, a wide belt of forest had been left undisturbed; snow whitened the ground on either hand, though the road itself had been churned to frozen mud. Gradually the tress grew larger, and the spaces between them wider. At the inner edge of the forest belt, Paks reined in to look at the city.

Unlike Vérella and Fin Panir, Chaya had not been built for defense: no proud wall encircled it. Instead, it was as if a grove of noble trees had cleared the ground around themselves, and then been invaded by clusters of bright mushrooms. The mushrooms, Paks realized suddenly, were the buildings: of stone and wood both, brightly painted, with colorful tile roofs. The trees—she squinted upward—were immense, each larger of bole than most houses. The lower bark was cinnamon-red, breaking into plates partway up, where the branches began, and showing pale gray and even white above that. Off to one side of the grove a castle faced the widest part of the open ground, now a snowy field. It looked like a model next to the great trees.

"First time you've seen Chaya?" The voice held a little of the elves' song. Paks turned to see a part-elf in hunting leathers behind her.

"Yes—it's—not like anything else—"

"No, indeed. Those are the only such trees outside the elvenhome forests. They are a sign that this kingdom is of both kinships." The part-elf sighed. "As long as it is, they will thrive. But otherwise—"

"Are you one of the rangers?" asked Paks.

"Do you think that is all elven blood has to do in this kingdom?"

Paks did not understand the rancor in his voice. "I don't know," she said. "I was with the rangers in the south last summer, and merely wondered if you knew them."

His face relaxed. "Oh, well, then—I may indeed. I have many friends in the south." But as it happened he knew of them by name only. They moved on toward the city together, both silent for some distance. Then, as they neared the first buildings, he spoke again. "Have you come from them? Few travel so far in Midwinter."

"I'm a paladin of Gird," said Paks. "On quest." He stopped short, and Paks stopped in courtesy.

"A paladin? Have you come to heal the king?"

"I am not yet sure why I've been called here."

"It could not be for better cause. Go and see him, at least." He looked about, and hailed a youth in green and gold livery. The boy came near, eyes wide, and bowed. "Here—Belvarin will take you. This lady is a paladin," he explained to the youth. "She must see the king."

Paks followed the youth through the twisting lanes between trees and buildings to a gate in the castle wall. It surprised her with its size, and she realized again that the trees made it look smaller than it was. She dismounted inside the gate, and led the red horse across a wide court. A stableboy came, and she warned him not to tie the red horse. The boy nodded and walked off, the horse following.

Her escort led her into the main part of the castle, along wide passages. She noticed that the many servants bowed as they passed. She felt the slight tingle that indicated she was near to some act of power. She estimated that they had come to the far side of the castle, on an upper level, when they arrived outside double carved doors. Two nobles in rich gowns greeted her escort, and acknowledged the introduction.

"Paksenarrion—a paladin. Welcome, Lady, to the court of our king. I am Sier Belvarin; I hope my son has served you well." Paks saw a blush redden the youth's neck. His father was tall and fair, with a red tinge to his hair and beard.

"And I am Sier Halveric. Are you that Paksenarrion who served Phelan of Tsaia?" When Paks nodded, he smiled at her. "Then I daresay you know my nephew Aliam Halveric."

"Indeed yes, my lord." When she looked closely at him, something of the eyes seemed like Aliam, but he was much taller, with red-brown hair going silver.

"Have you come to heal our king, Lady?" asked Belvarin, with a sour glance at Halveric which Paks did not miss.

"I would offer my healing if it were welcome," said Paks cautiously. "But the High Lord's power comes at his will, not mine."

"I fear, my lady, that you come too late, if such was the High Lord's purpose in calling you here. Nonetheless, you shall see the king, if you will, and perhaps can ease him." Sier Halveric smiled at her, and turned to the door.

"Not so fast, Jeris. Have you forgotten what the surgeons said? He must rest, the little he can."

"Falk's oath in gold, Tamissin! He's dying anyway—what harm can a paladin do?"

"But the surgeons—"

"The surgeons! Hmph! And is he better for them, these last months?"

Their voices had risen; Paks was not surprised when the doors opened from within, and a man peered out, scowling. "Lords! Lords! Have you no better place to quarrel than before the king's chamber? He but barely sleeps at the best of it—" He caught sight of Paks, and stared. "And who's this? A stranger?"

"A paladin," said the Halveric quickly. "A paladin of Gird, a servant of the High Lord. The king must have this chance—"

"For healing?" The man sounded more than doubtful. Paks intervened.

"Sir, I am here, in Chaya, by the call of the High Lord, to serve his purpose. But as for the king, I can offer only such prayers as I am commanded to offer."

He looked her up and down, and relaxed. "Indeed,

Lady, it has been long since a paladin came to us. We are honored, and the king would wish to welcome you properly if he could. If you can forgive his inability, perhaps you might consider attending him."

Paks bowed. "By Gird's grace, and the High Lord's power, I will do what I can." She glanced at the other two, who avoided each other's eyes. "Gird's grace be on you," she said quietly, and passed through the opening.

Within, the large chamber was full of light from windows on either side. The king's bed stood on a low dais; besides a fireplace near it, several braziers filled the air with warmth and the scent of light incense. The king lay propped on pillows beneath a spread worked in gold thread; a matching canopy rose from the bedposts. Paks followed the other man closer. A woman sitting by the bed rose and came to meet them. She wore the insignia of a knight of Falk, but was dressed in robes rather than armor.

"My lady—you are a paladin? You can save him?"

"I don't know. I will do what the gods give me the power to do." Paks looked past her. The king's eyes were closed; he looked much older than she had been told he was, in his middle fifties. She watched closely as the woman went to the king's side and spoke softly. He opened his eyes slowly; they were clouded blue. His gaze shifted around the room and found her; he tried to sit up.

"Be welcome in Lyonya, Lady; we are honored to have you at our court. Pardon my inability to rise—"

"Certainly, sir king. May I approach?" He nodded, and waved a hand. Paks came up beside the bed. "May I ask the nature of your illness?"

"We do not know," said the man behind her. "I am Esceriel, the king's squire." Paks was surprised; he was of middle age. He read her surprise and smiled. "Lady, the king's squire is a knight of Falk; so also is Lieth here. But to answer your question, the king's surgeons know not what his illness is."

"What I feel," said the king softly, "is weakness, and pain here—" he touched his chest and shoulder. "My mother had the same thing, and also died of it. The surgeons speak of the heart, and then the lungs—for it seems the air fails me sometimes—and then as well nothing I eat stays with me these days."

Paks stood by the bed, and took his hand. The skin was thin and dry, a little loose on the bones, like that of a very old man. She almost feared to start her prayers, remembering Rahel's sudden death, but the pressure of her call forced her to action. When she released the hand, she had no idea how long she had stood there—but the afternoon had passed into evening. Her knees sagged; Esceriel was quick with a stool behind her. The king lay asleep, peaceful.

Lieth brought her a cup of hot spiced wine. "Lady," she said softly, "I never thought to see such—"

"Nor I," said Esceriel. "Your power was great."

Paks shook her head. It felt heavy as a stone. "Not my power, but the High Lord's. Ah, but I'm tired!"

"No wonder. You'll have a place here. And he's asleep, resting well, for the first time in days."

"But not healed," said Paks. They looked at her.

"But perhaps—" began Lieth.

"No. I'm sorry. I don't know why; I never know why. But he is not healed, only eased for a time."

"It's enough," said Esceriel firmly. "If you're strong enough now, I'll take you to your chamber."

"Are you sure—?"

He grinned unexpectedly. "You gave us hours to prepare, Lady. You stood there from just after noon until dusk. Can you come?"

Paks pushed herself up from the stool joint by joint. "I can come."

Her chamber was but two doors from the king's, a small room with a fireplace, its walls hung with tapestries. A single window looked out over the inner court and gardens, now white with snow. A high carved bed was piled with down-stuffed coverlets; a fur throw lay folded at its foot. Her pack had been set carefully on top of the carved desk.

"Lady, if you need anything, be sure to ask. Servants

are on the way with hot water and bathing things. Would you prefer to eat alone, or in Hall?"

"Alone, if that would not be discourteous here. I am somewhat tired."

"And no wonder," he said again. "With your leave I shall say you wish to rest undisturbed."

Paks nodded. "I thank you, sir. But if the king wakes, and wishes to speak to me, I am always at his service."

"We thank you, Lady, more than you can know. But, Lady—your pardon, but—I did not catch your name—"

"Oh." Paks realized that the quarreling nobles had not introduced her by name. "I am Paksenarrion Dorthansdotter. Once I was a soldier with Duke Phelan of Tsaia, but now I am a paladin of the High Lord and Gird."

He bowed. "Be welcome here, Paksenarrion. The Sier Halveric would no doubt have introduced you properly, or Belvarin would, but the two of them have little patience with each other."

"So I noticed." Paks shook her head.

"It is nothing for a paladin's concern, of course, but—" Esceriel broke off as two strong youths carried a deep tub of steaming water into the room. Behind them a wizened man bore a carved box on top of a pile of folded towels. "Ah," he said. "Here's Joriam with your bath things. I'll go now; ask Joriam for whatever you need; he can find me at any time." Esceriel bowed again and withdrew, as did the two youths. Paks met the old man's dark gaze, intent and curious.

"Well, Lady, we hope to please you," he began, setting the towels down on the bed, and opening the box to reveal several balls of scented soap. "Here are andrask, figan, and erris soaps; we judge these best for travellers in cold."

Paks had never heard of andrask and figan; she had once seen erris in a shop, a straggly yellow-flowered herb. The shopkeeper said it was used in soaps and wines both. She watched as Joriam laid the towels and soaps out in a neat row, his every motion precise and ceremonious. He pulled out a tiny drawer in the base of the box, and removed two combs, one of bone and one of horn, which he set above the row of soaps. He glanced at her.

"May I take your cloak, Lady?" When Paks nodded and reached for the clasp, he moved behind her to gather it up. Paks unhooked the scabbard of Tammarrion's sword—as she still thought of it—from her swordbelt, and laid it on the bed. She pulled the swordbelt over her head and tossed it on the bed as well, and began to unlace the fur-lined tunic over her mail. She turned to see Joriam staring wide-eyed at the swordhilt.

"What is it?" she asked, when he did not move.

"It's—by the High Lord, Lady, where did you come by that sword?" It was more accusation than question; his eyes blazed with anger.

"It was a gift," she said, watching him closely. "It was given me by Duke Phelan of Tsaia; it was his wife's sword."

"Phelan of Tsaia," he muttered. Then he looked closely at the sword hilt again. "Lady, my pardon—but does this sword have runes on the blade?"

"Yes," said Paks slowly. "What—"

"How old is this Phelan of Tsaia? Is he a very old man, as old as I?"

"By no means. He is of middle age, perhaps fifty."

"And you say this was his wife's sword? How did she come by it?"

Paks began to feel a little annoyance at all these questions, but Joriam's face was honest. "All I know of it, Joriam, is what I was told. It was his wife's sword, and was recovered after her death in battle against orcs. She was killed some fifteen years ago. Those who told me are as honest as anyone I know, and I am a paladin. Now—why do you ask these things? Do you know more of this blade than that?"

Joriam's face contracted to a mass of wrinkles. He shook his head slowly, but answered. "Lady, I can scarce believe my eyes, but—if the runes are the same, this sword comes from this Hall—from the queen's hand, I would have said, many years ago."

"What!"

"Yes, Lady. You would not be old enough to remember—you may never have heard. But when I was a young man, in service here, that king ruling was the older half-brother of our present king. He married elven, in the old way, to restore the taig-sense to the ruling line." Joriam looked at her doubtfully. "You are not afraid of elves, are you, Lady? Some Girdsmen are—"

"I am not," said Paks. "I have friends among the true elves, and I spent some time with your rangers in the south. I respect the taig of tree and forest, and the taig of the kingdom."

He nodded, satisfied. "Well, then, perhaps the rangers told you of it. Lyonya is both elf and human, kingdom and holder, root and branch—and in health it is ruled by someone who can sense the shift of taig directly. The old king—Falkieri's father and this king's father too, of course—his first wife was part-elven, and so Falkieri had enough taig-sense, but just enough. He was wise to marry elven, whatever they said afterwards. Their son showed such ability early, and their daughter too, poor lass."

"But what happened to them—the son and daughter—or does the throne go to brothers before children?" Paks wondered if the old man were mixed in his wits, for so far the tale didn't sound like that she'd heard from others.

"No, that's what I'm telling you. This king, and the one before, are from a different mother, half-brothers to Falkieri. The old king's second wife was all human; he didn't think it mattered, with Falkieri healthy and betrothed to a full elf. Anyway, when the first two children were born and weaned, the queen desired to take her son to see her own people. Some kind of elven ceremony; I don't know. I was too young to be told much. So the queen and the prince left Chaya for the Ladysforest, leaving the princess here with the king. And they were attacked, in the forest near the border, and killed."

"Killed?" So it was the same story, but told from a different view.

"Yes. When nothing was heard for too long—for the elves would send word of safe arrival, and besides the eastern taig was troubled—search was made, and the wagons and bodies were found. Most of them, anyway. They never did find the prince's body, but he was small—only four years—and perhaps it was carried off by animals." He paused to see if she had questions; Paks waved him to continue. "Well, then, you can imagine—I suppose—what it was like. The king was frantic. He and his wife had sworn life-marriage; he refused to remarry, even though it left only one heir, his daughter. And though he tried hard, he never mastered his grief; we think it killed him eventually. The princess was then about nine or ten; the king's brothers were still too young to rule without a regent, so the king's cousin was named regent for the princes." He paused again, and ran his hands over the towels on the bed. "Pardon, Lady, but your water will cool. This tale can wait until you bathe."

Paks looked at him. He seemed near tears; she would not have thought an old man would be so moved by a tale so old. "Perhaps what you tell me is more important than a hot bath," she suggested.

"Lady, I—I will continue if you wish; I but thought of you cold and tired—" Paks was indeed chilling again, and very tired. Her back felt like a bar of hot metal. She glanced at the tub, still steaming.

"Joriam, I want to hear this, but you're right—I'm tired and cold and I may not pay close enough attention. But until I hear it, I don't want you telling everyone about the sword. It may not be the same—and I'm still not sure whose sword you think it is."

"I will speak to no one, Lady. Only seeing the sword again—it brought back those terrible days—"

"I understand." She didn't, but it seemed the right thing to say. "I won't be long; why don't you bring something hot to eat—soup would be fine—and we'll talk again."

"I'll take your things to be cleaned," he said, nodding. Paks struggled out of her clothes while he pulled one tapestry aside to reveal a niche with clothes pegs and drawers set into one wall. From this he took a long soft robe, and hung it to warm by the fire. She wondered if he would try to snatch the sword and take it as he left, but he did not touch it, or the sword belt.

The hot bath eased her aching body, and she had stretched comfortably on a low seat by the fire when Joriam returned with a tray, followed by the same two servants who removed the water and damp towels. He had brought a deep bowl of soup, a plate of sliced meat in gravy, and two small loaves of hot bread, as well as a tall beaker and mug.

"Sit with me," said Paks, gesturing, "and tell me the rest of this tale."

"Sit?" he sounded almost scandalized. "Lady, I do well enough." He leaned against the wall, and went on. "The king died, as I said, when the princess was about nine or ten. His cousin was an honest man—" Paks could tell that Joriam was struggling to be fair to someone he had not liked. "I believe he did the best he could. But, Lady, you know some humans fear elves—have small liking for them—and he himself had no taig-sense at all. He blamed the queen for the young prince's death—taking that journey—and he disliked the elves at court who would have tutored the princess in taigin."

"But didn't he know that Lyonya must be ruled by someone who can sense the taigin?"

"I think he didn't believe it. Some men are like that—as if blind men could deny sight to others, lacking it themselves. Anyway, our young princess was a fine one, and he did honestly by her, but for that. Only he insisted, since she was the only true heir, that she must marry early. When the elves argued, he sent them away."

Paks thought back to things Ardhiel had told her. "But isn't it true that elves and half-elves—even to quarter elves—come late to such growth, and should not marry too early? Especially the women, I thought, for bearing children too young—"

"—can be fatal," Joriam finished, with some heat. "Yes. And that's what happened to her, poor lass. The regent and Council insisted she marry at the first legal age, and put it to her that such was her duty. She was as brave as could be, that one, and would dare anything for duty. So she married the year she was crowned queen—married the regent's son—"

"Scoundrel—" began Paks angrily, seeing a plot of the regent.

"No . . ." Joriam was more judicious. "I don't think so. He loved her well, and she had been fond of him from childhood. She need not marry elven, being half-elf herself—all her children would have taig-sense. And he renounced any claim on the crown, should she die. No, I think it was simply fear, fear of the elves—and then they made her marry early, and that killed her. And the child." Joriam looked down. Paks finished the soup she had started, and began on the meat, waiting for him to regain his calm.

"Then things really began to go wrong," he said quietly. "As long as she was coming to rule—even though she had no training, she had a strong gift, to sense the taigin. The regent would listen to her. He was honest, as I said, and did her bidding where he could. But after—the old king's second wife was all human, and from a line with no ability for taigin. With her dead, the Council decided to offer the crown to Falkieri's younger brothers, now of age, even so. They were both good men, please understand me—they were, as our king is now, honest, brave, and faithful to the kingdom. In another kingdom, that might be enough. In Lyonya, no."

"What about this king's heir?"

Joriam snorted. "He has none—not direct. One evil after another, Lady, has stalked this royal house for near fifty years. After him it goes to cousins and second cousins of the old king—half the nobles might have a claim, if it comes to that. War—by the gods, Lady, we have not had war in Lyonya, save along the borders only, since the Compact was made with the elves. Yet now all fear it. It seems nothing will prevent it—and to think of Lyonya at war, the forests fired, maybe . . . and we wonder what the elves will do. It is a joint kingdom, after all."

Paks nodded. "I see. Now—about the sword. Whose was it?"

"The queen's, Lady—not the young queen that died, but Falkieri's elven wife. She carried it; I saw it in her hand, on her wall, when I first came here to serve. That jewel in the hilt—the guards—"

"And runes, you said. What runes?"

"I don't read runes myself. I remember the shape of two of them, because once when I—" he stopped and blushed. Paks watched him, fully alert now. He blinked and went on. "I had broken something, Lady, and was scolded for it. She was nearby, with the sword partly drawn, and I found myself staring at it."

"What were the runes like, that you saw?"

"Like this." With his wetted finger, he drew on the polished wood tray a rude copy of the rune for treasure and something Paks could not read at all.

"Is there anyone else who would know the sword, and could remember all the runes on it?"

Joriam thought. "I'm the oldest servant here, now the elves have gone—"

"Elves gone? Why? How?"

"It was the regent, at first. Later . . . I don't mean there are no elves in Lyonya, of course, but few now come to Chaya, to the king. They are quick to resent a cool welcome."

"So would I be, were I an elf," murmured Paks. Then, louder, "But are there any others?"

"Yes, I think so. The Sier Halveric is older than I, though he doesn't look it—he's part elvish, you see. He was much at court in those days. A few others—old Lord Hammarrin, the Master of Horse—he's near ninety years. Sier Galvary. Tekko, he was Master Huntsman in those days, but he's been retired these fifteen years. All these would know the sword, but Tekko doesn't know runes any better than I do."

Paks had finished her meal; she stretched after pushing the tray farther away. "Well, Joriam, it seems to me that we'd best speak to these others. If I am carrying a treasure of your realm, it must come back to you—isn't that right?"

He stared at her. "But Lady—you're carrying the sword—"

"It's not the first I've carried; I doubt it will be the last. If it belongs here, I will give it willingly—"

"But that's not the point! Lady, please—" his face was troubled. "The sword alone will do us no good. It was her sword, the queen's, before our troubles began. What I meant was—" he shook his head. "I don't know. I'm old; I've never been anything but a servant here. But if we could find what happened to her—if her sword is still here, perhaps she was not killed. Maybe it wasn't her body they found. Perhaps she is prisoned somewhere, and could be freed, to return and rule—"

Paks in turn shook her head. "Joriam, I cannot think what could imprison an elf, a queen, for forty-five to fifty years, leaving no trace for searchers, and still leave her alive and fit to rule when found."

"The—the kuaknom? They say they can take elves—"

Paks felt her face harden, saw the shock on Joriam's at her expression. "I have been among the kuaknom, Joriam. It is a quick return, or none, from their realms."

"Lady, my pardon. I did not know."

"I was captive with the kuaknom for only a few days, and got more scars than in years of fighting in Aarenis. Scars of mind and body both."

"I am sorry, Lady—"

"No matter. But I must talk to these others. I was called here for some reason—your folk hoped it was to heal your king, but perhaps it was to return the sword instead. I ask your silence on this, Joriam, until those you mentioned are gathered together before witnesses. In such a matter all must be done properly."

"Yes, Lady. Will you speak with the steward first? Or Sier Halveric?"

Paks thought. She did not know the ways of power at this court; the quarrel between Sier Halveric and Sier Belvarin had not escaped her, nor the vigilant authority of the king's squires. And elves were involved, as well.

"I will speak to the king," she said. "It is his right, to

know first. After that, if he is able, he will call what witnesses are needed. But I insist that the elves, also, be here. Surely there is one—an ambassador, perhaps?"

Joriam looked worried. "Across Chaya, Lady, in their own Hall—they do not stay here any longer. But why—"

"Because you say the sword was hers. She was an elf. It is their right too, Joriam. She was one of theirs, and this was hers. Perhaps they have a claim to it." Paks moved the tray and table away, and pushed herself up. She was still weary, but the bath and food had refreshed her. And the call that had brought her throbbed in her head.

Chapter Seventeen

By the time Paks had dressed in dry, clean clothes, it was full dark outside. Starlight and torchlight glittered together on the snowy courtyard. Joriam waited outside her door, and escorted her to the king's chamber. Esceriel showed his surprise in raised eyebrows when he opened the door.

"Lady—I thought you were—pardon, you are welcome to enter—" But his voice still held questions.

Paks had put on her shining mail again, and belted on the mysterious sword. "The king?" she asked softly.

"He woke without pain, Lady, and ate with appetite. He has dozed off again—must you wake him?"

Paks met the eyes of both squires. "Let me explain, if you will." They led the way to a window alcove, and stood near. "My call brought me here," Paks began quietly. "I do not know the reason. When I found your king so ill, I hoped the call was for healing. As I found, and told you, it was not." The squires stirred, but said nothing. Paks went on. "While I was setting my things aside to bathe, Joriam noticed what he thought was a treasure of this realm."

"What! Old Joriam?"

Paks nodded. "Yes. If he is right, perhaps my call was to restore this treasure to Lyonya—perhaps it has some power to aid you that neither he nor I know of. Joriam named several others old enough to recognize it—if, in fact, that's what it is. But I thought the king himself should decide how this would be investigated."

Esceriel looked bewildered. "But—Lady—what would you be doing with a royal treasure of Lyonya? Surely Joriam didn't suggest—I mean, you cannot be a thief—"

"No. But I would like to know myself where this thing has been since it left here—if it did—and how it came where I found it. But you have not asked what it is."

"No." Both squires shook their heads. "If you wished to tell us, you would."

"Do you agree, though, that the king should know first?"

They looked at each other. "I suppose." Esceriel looked doubtful. "He has been able to do no work for some weeks. The Council—"

Paks shook her head. "No, if this is what Joriam thinks, it is a relic of the royal house. And it involves elves—high elves—and the king must decide what to do."

"Yes, I see. You're right. But could it not wait until morning? If the king can sleep through the night, even once—"

Again Paks shook her head, and saw that both of them took the meaning of that refusal. Nonetheless she stated it. "I'm sorry—truly sorry. But as I told you, I was not sent to heal him. He may not live that long, and this, I judge, is urgent enough to disturb even the last of his rest. I will do what I can to ease him again later."

They nodded shortly, and left her in the alcove, moving quietly to the bedside to wake the king. Finally Lieth beckoned, and again Paks approached the bed. The king's face showed less strain than before, but his color was no better. His lips quirked in an attempt to smile.

"Lady—I believe you must have some reason for waking me. I am in no pain, but—I feel no strength, either. What is it?"

"Sir king, your old servant Joriam recognized among my gear what he believes is a treasure of your house. If he is right, then the return of this treasure may be my reason here. And since it was elf-made, and belonged to the elven wife of your older brother, who was king many years ago, I believed you should know first, and decide how this is to be handled."

His eyes gleamed. A faint flush of color stained his cheeks. "A treasure? Elf made, and the elven queen's? That would have to be—" He paused, obviously thinking. "Is it a ring, Lady, or a sword?"

"A sword," said Paks. She did not take it out. He glanced at her side, and she drew her cloak back a little.

He nodded. "It might be—her sword had such a green jewel in the hilt. I remember that much, though I was only a boy when I saw it last. But how did you come by it?"

Paks repeated what she'd told Joriam. The king listened carefully. "I don't see how it could be the same," he said then. "How would such a treasure come to a Tsaian mercenary?"

"If I remember correctly," said Paks, "it was a wedding gift to his wife from Aliam Halveric."

"Halveric!" The king tried to push himself up. Lieth and Esceriel were quick to lift him and pack pillows behind him. "Could it be that the Halverics—no. I won't believe that of them!" But his voice held a measure of doubt. Paks was appalled.

"Sir king, I'm sure it doesn't mean that the Halverics stole it—or had anything to do with the attack. He isn't old enough—"

"Falk's blade! That's right—he's only a few years older than I am. He wasn't even at court. Forget I said any such thing—please. It is my weakness, Lady, and the hour. . . ." his voice trailed off. Then it strengthened again. "In fact, now I remember that we were pages together when it happened. Of course it couldn't have been Aliam."

"The Halverics, sir king, have always been loyal supporters of this house," said Esceriel quietly.

"Yes, yes—I know. That's why we were fostered as pages to the Halveric estates. I just—for a moment—"

"In such a surprise, sir king," said Paks, "anything may come to mind. But, my lord, I think it is important to identify this sword certainly. I have not taken it from the sheath since Joriam spoke; no one here has seen its blade. Can you describe it?"

"Oh yes." The king nodded. "The hilts—well, I could have seen that, since you've been wearing it. On the blade, as I recall, were runes. I don't remember exactly which. Averrestinil—the queen that was—rarely drew it. And I was just a boy, and seldom at court anyway. The elves would know—if you want to drag them in—and Sier Halveric. Perhaps the old huntsman, if he's still able to see. Averrestinil enjoyed hunting."

"Sir king, the elves *must* be told. They, more than anyone, can confirm whether this sword is the same or another. I know it is of elven make, and magical, but nothing else." Paks looked at the squires, to find both of them staring at her with glowing eyes. She looked back at the king. "I don't know, my lord, what good this sword will do—if it is the one that was lost when the queen and prince were killed—"

"Perhaps it will proclaim the heir—the true heir—" began Lieth. "I have heard of such swords—they take light when drawn by the one who is to rule."

Before she thought, Paks answered quickly, "It can't be that. It lights up when I draw it—" Then she realized how they might take her words. It was too late. Lieth nodded, smiling, and when she looked, the king was smiling too.

"If so, then perhaps your call was to save Lyonya by taking the throne."

"No, my lord!" Paks shrank from the idea. "I am a soldier—a warrior of Gird—not a ruler."

"At any rate, I agree that the sword must be identified and tested. And even by elves." He sighed. "Would that my cousin were still alive—he was regent for my niece before her death—and he was both cautious and wise with elves. I myself have had little to do with them."

"Sir king, do you wish us to gather these people here, in your chamber?" Paks felt the need to push for some definite action that night.

"It must be done openly," mused the king. "A thing of such importance must not be hidden. Yes—bring them here, but give audience to all the Siers, human and part-elven alike."

"But my lord," said Esceriel, with a worried frown. "You are not strong enough—"

The king managed a steadier smile. "Old friend, I will be as strong as I must—this grace the gods have given me so far. If this can leave my kingdom in better state—if it can prevent quarrels and bickering such as I hear through my doors daily—"

"We try, my lord—" said Esceriel.

"I know. I know, and I also know why they come. It will be well worth a day or so less life, Esceriel, to leave my kingdom with hope and peace." He drew a deep breath, that suddenly seemed to hurt, for he stiffened. Paks laid her hand on his, and he smiled again. "No, Lady—I need no more of your strength for the moment. I will save mine for what I must say when they come. Lieth, mix me a warming draught, and call Master Oscarlit. Esceriel, summon these: all the Siers in Chaya, and the kyllan-siers of those who are not here. Also the ranking elf—I don't know who that is, worse luck, but you can find out easily enough."

"I don't know if the elf will come—" said Esceriel.

"They will come if I summon them," said Paks. "May I, sir king?"

"Yes—do. Assemble them, if you will, in the Leaf Hall. If so many come that would be crowded here, you will carry me down."

"My lord—"

"Enough, Esceriel. I know I will die soon; I will die happier if this is behind me. Ward of Falk, Esceriel—be on your way."

"My lord and king." With a deep bow, and a flashing glance at Paks, Esceriel swept from the room. Lieth, having set some drink to warm on the hearth, bowed also and withdrew to find the surgeon. The king beckoned Paks to bend close.

"Esceriel, Lady, loves me too well. He is my son—a bastard, alas, of a human mother with more taig-sense than I—and the only son of mine to reach manhood. This he suspects, but does not know—and has never reached for power for himself. I love him well, Lady, and if you have comfort for him, I pray you give it."

Paks felt tears stinging her eyes. "Sir king, what comfort the High Lord permits, I will give. And now I'd best go, and seek the elves." His eyes sagged shut as she turned away.

Finding the elves in Chaya was not as easy as she had hoped, or as hard as she had feared. No one in the palace seemed to know just where they might be—"They're uncanny, Lady, and wander about—" She had feared they might all be withdrawn into elvenlands, where she had no entry. But after a cold, miserable trek through the streets of Chaya, she heard a few words of elven outside a tavern. She looked up. The sign, lit by a gleam of light from within, was a harp with a wreath of ivy, and beneath it was the elven rune for song. Paks shoved the door open and entered. Light seemed to fail as she came in, shifting in an instant from clear white to the dim reddish glow of a dying fire. Paks felt her bones tingle with magic. She looked around.

"You come late, traveller." The tavernkeeper loomed nearby, tall and stout.

"I am looking for someone," said Paks, in elven. Silence followed. She heard the faint rustle of clothing in one corner, the resumption of breath, where all had stopped for an instant.

"Art thou a true elf?" asked the tavernkeeper in elven. "Art thou of the house of the leaf, or the house of the fountain?"

"I am not," replied Paks, still in the same language. "Yet I have had friends of leaf and fountain, and have been graced by their wisdom and song. I am Paksenarrion Dorthansdotter, named elf-friend by Ardhiel. I have touched the elfane taig, and lain captive of the iynisin longer than I care to tell, and fought a daskdraudigs when my wounds were healed."

"I have heard of such a Paksenarrion," he said. "A servant of Gird Strongarm, so I've heard, and a friend of the Kuakgan of Brewersbridge, and of Kieri Phelan of Tsaia."

"That is true." Paks waited through another silence. Elves, she thought, could be just as slow as dwarves—but then they thought humans were hasty.

"And what do you search for here?" he asked finally. "You carry such magic with you as you would satisfy most humans."

Paks laughed easily. "I search for someone, not some thing. For someone who can identify what I carry, and tell me its tale. And not only me. I search, as you must realize, for the elves I thought to find in Chaya, the heart of Lyonya the Fair. For this, I was told, was a kingdom of men and elves together—"

"So it was, once, Paksenarrion," said another voice, from near the dying fire. "Long years ago. But evil betrayed that dream—"

"And good may redeem it," said Paks. She felt a nudge from within, and called light. In that sudden glare the room showed full of elves—many of them high elves, richly dressed. Her light glittered from jewels on fingers and belts and weapons, gleamed on the gold frame of a great-harp, the silver of buckles and mail. Around the walls ran a pattern of interlacement, set in gleaming tiles.

"You are a paladin, then." The tavernkeeper's voice was steady; she had not startled him, at least.

"Yes. And I have come to Chaya on quest, with a call from the gods I serve. This call sent me to find elves—elves who remember the better days, the days when King Falkieri had an elven wife, and two children—"

"Does anyone want those days remembered?" asked the elf in the corner. He sat in a carved chair that resembled a tangle of tree roots formed into a throne; his velvet tunic was embroidered heavily in gold and silver.

"The king does," she answered. "He sent me to ask."

"The king? The *human* king?"

"Yes. He knows he is dying; he wants to leave Lyonya in better hope than now seems likely."

They looked at one another; Paks felt the intensity of

those looks. "And on his deathbed he acquires wisdom that might have saved us had he found it earlier." That was a part-elf, squatting on the hearth itself.

"Peace, Challm," said the richly dressed elf. "Wisdom is always worth having, be it never so late. And for a human, whose soul lives after him, it is a priceless gift." He stood. "Paksenarrion, you will not remember, but you have seen me before."

Paks shuffled rapidly through her memories, but to no avail.

He smiled. "You were dying in the snow—you had taken such injuries from an evil power our best efforts were nearly too late and too little. And we did you a discourtesy, in casting a glamour on you that made you forget an errand—though I swear, lady, we took the scroll to Estil Halveric faster than you could have done."

Paks felt her jaw drop. "You! You are one of the elves who found me after—"

"You freed the elfane taig. Yes. Kinsmen, this is an elf-friend indeed. I am glad to see you with such powers, Paksenarrion. From time to time we heard that things went hard with you." She nodded, speechlessly. "You may withdraw your light if you wish; we have our own." He was smiling now, and as Paks damped her light, the elflight, similar but with a more pearly glow, radiated from the air around her. It had no source she could see, and cast no shadows. "You asked my name that night," he went on. "I judged you did not mean any discourtesy, though I was short with you. It went hard to admit that a mere human had done what many elves had tried and failed to do. But now—" he bowed. "Permit me to introduce myself. I am Amrothlin son of Flessinathlin, the lady who holds the heart of the Ladysforest, and brother of that queen you spoke of."

"The queen who—"

"Who disappeared with her son, the prince. Yes. And if my eyes have not faded—which they have not—you bear at your side the very sword—"

Paks had, in the past few moments, forgotten the sword.

Now she laid her hand on its hilt. "It is this, my lord, which—"

He nodded. "I know." His eyes swept the room. "It is time, kindred—time and more than time. We are not hasty, we elves, but the time for mysteries is past, and the time of truth is at hand. I will take six of you: Berris, Gyorlan, Challm, Adreath, Signys, Preliath." He came to Paks. "When does the king wish our presence?"

"As soon as may be, my lord."

"Then we shall come now." He made a gesture, and the elflight died. Paks blinded in the darkness, until her eyes adjusted to the red glow in the hearth. Then she turned, hearing the elves around her, and led the way back toward the palace.

They said nothing during that walk—nothing aloud, at least, though Paks surmised that their thoughts were full. At the palace gates, the guards' eyes went wide when they saw Paks and the others. But clearly they had had their orders, for they swung the gates open and stood at attention. They came to the far side, to the doors of the palace. Lieth stood there, now formal in armor and surcoat of royal green and gold.

"Lady Paksenarrion? It will be in the Leaf Hall; Esceriel called too many lords to fit into the king's own chamber."

Paks introduced the elves with her, and Lieth bowed. "Be welcome, my lords and ladies, in the king's Hall. He will be with you shortly." Lieth opened double doors into a long high room with panelled walls, now brightly lit by many candles. Paks estimated that some twenty men and women waited there. Fires blazed in both fireplaces, and at one end a long chair waited for the king. The elves moved into the room; Paks saw some faces light, and others freeze, to see them. She turned to Lieth.

"Will you need help to bring him down?"

"No, Lady. He insisted on donning his formal mail, and Esceriel and I, and two others of his squires, will bear his chair down. He asked that you stay here, until he comes."

"Then I will do so." Paks entered the room. Almost at once, Sier Halveric came to her.

"Well, lady paladin, you have tossed a torch into the oil barrel indeed. What is this, do you know?"

"My lord, I await the king's command to speak of it."

He eyed her shrewdly. "And think I should not ask, eh? Pardon, Lady. I've been on Council so long, and the king's been ill so long, that I am too hasty. The king's business has been our business these many months."

"I hold no anger, Sier Halveric."

He nodded. "I hope I am permitted to thank you for easing him. The word has gone that after your care he slept easily for the first time in months."

"I grieve, my lord, that I was not given healing for him." Paks wondered if she should say even this much; she knew that others were listening.

"I also." He bowed and stepped back. Sier Belvarin stood nearby, frowning, and came forward as Halveric left.

"I wonder, Lady, that you would bring elves to the palace. Perhaps you do not know how we feel—"

"I do not know how you feel, Sier Belvarin," said Paks, with an edge in her voice. "But I know this kingdom is both elven and human, and has been so since humans came here. Elves granted humans land-right here, but the precedence is theirs." Belvarin reddened, and Paks went on. "Besides, I obeyed the king's express command to bring them."

"The king *wanted* elves?"

"Indeed yes," said Paks, now with a smile. "I would bring no one here without his consent, human or other. He told me to find and bring them."

Shaking his head, Belvarin melted back into the crowd. Paks watched him, uncertain. She felt no warning of evil, as she had in Phelan's stronghold, but she knew something was wrong.

"Lords and ladies." At the door, four squires carried the king's chair; he was propped with pillows, gray-faced and gaunt. The speaker was a man in forest green whom Paks had not met. Everyone bowed, while the squires carried the chair forward. In courtesy, no one looked as the squires helped the king from the carrying chair to the one that awaited him. Then they took up their positions on either side of him.

"My lords—ladies—high elves of Lyonya and the elven-lands—" The king's voice was thin but steady. He took a long breath and went on. "This day a paladin of Gird arrived in Chaya—here, in this palace—and because she is here, I called this assembly." He took a sip from a silver goblet that Lieth held ready. "She bears with her what may be—*may* be, I say—a treasure of this house, lost since Falkieri's queen and heir were killed over forty years ago. If it is so, it may have returned to our aid in this time of need. I called you here to witness the examination of this object, and hear what she knows of it."

"In the middle of the *night*?" Paks did not know who that was—a tall dark woman on the far side of the room. But the king smiled.

"Yes, Jonnlith. You all know that I have not long to live. The paladin Paksenarrion asked healing for me; it was not granted." He lifted his hand to still the murmurs that ran around the room. "Enough, please. She eased my pain—more ease than I've had since last spring. If the gods have decided that my life is over, who am I—or who is she—to argue? I have no quarrel with her, only great thanks. But in what time is left me, I would learn what I can of this treasure. Paksenarrion, come forward."

Paks moved toward the king's chair, aware of the eyes watching her, and bowed. She felt, rather than saw, that Amrothlin followed her closely.

"Show them the sword in its scabbard," said the king quietly. Paks unbuckled the scabbard from her swordbelt, and held it flat on her arms before her. She saw nothing but interest on most faces, but a few suddenly seemed intent. Sier Halveric. An old man, somewhat stooped, in heavy woolens and a fur-collared cloak. And, of course, all the elves.

"How many think they can name this sword?" asked the king. The Halveric stepped forward.

"Sir king, by the jewel on the pommel, and the shape of the hilts, it is much like the sword that your elder brother

Falkieri's elven wife carried. That blade was rune-marked on the spine; is this?"

"Wait," said the king. "Anyone else?" A thin old man in blue shuffled forward, with a younger one supporting him.

"I saw that sword in her hand," he quavered. "The day she left, sir king, when I led her horse out, and set the lad up behind her, it was belted to her waist. If I can look at the hilts—there was a mark, inside the curve, where the boy had made a scratch with something. She laughed about it, said it was his first mark." He bent over the sword, and poked a bony finger into the place, searching with his fingernail. "Yes—there it is. Can you see it?"

Paks held the sword for the king to see, and he, too, found the scratch. "Thank you, Lord Hammarrin. Anyone else?"

Now the stooped old man came forward. His face was dark and weathered into a nest of deep cracks, but he moved more lightly than the other. He put out one gnarled hand, and touched the scabbard lightly. "I say it is the same, sir king. It—it feels the same, the way it always did. And the stone's the same—" he touched that, too, with a wary finger. "I've seen this sword many a time—at least, this grip and hilts. But it wasn't hers, as I remember, but the boy's—"

"What!" One of the younger lords cried out.

"That's right," said Hammarrin, turning toward them again. "I remember she said something about giving it to him someday. But what does it matter?"

"Master Tekko," said the king. "Do you know what runes would be on that blade?"

The old huntsman's face creased into a gap-toothed grin. "Me, my lord? Nay, the only runes I know are of track and trail. I can read red deer and wolf well enough. It had something on it, I know that, but not what."

"My pardon, sir king," said Amrothlin quietly. "May I speak?"

The king peered at him. "You are an elf, sir?"

"Yes." The elf's voice held none of the scorn that Paks knew it could convey. "That lady you speak of, the wife of your brother Falkieri, was my sister; this sword and its story are well known to me."

A scurry of sound like mice ran through the room. The king raised his hand again, and again took a sip of the cup Lieth held. "By your leave, sir elf, we will hear this tale."

Amrothlin turned so that the rest of the room could see his face. "Sir king, in the days when the queen bore her first child she asked her family, in the Ladysforest, to forge him a weapon. She foresaw that his life would be full of danger, and wished him to have the protection of such blades as elves are skilled to make. And so the smiths labored, and after that the singers, to bind into this blade what spells would serve him best."

"But *she* carried it," blurted someone. Paks heard the hushing hisses.

"You're right," said Amrothlin. "So she did. She judged her son would grow to be a tall man, as most half-elven are, and the sword was made full-size. But—" he looked for a moment at the sword Paks held. "It is possible for such a blade, forged to serve one person in particular, to change size and shape somewhat with need. Until he grew to carry it, she kept it in a form she herself could use. It was safer so, she thought, than lying unused. Another thing—although it was made for him, and sealed to him at its making by elven magics, a more formal sealing was planned for that very trip. After that, it could be used by no one else, but until then, anyone might use it. Should evil handle it, it might be corrupted. So she thought to keep it safe for him, and bind her own mother-spells into it as well."

"But how did it get to *her*?" asked Sier Halveric, looking hard at Paks.

"Please, Sier Halveric, Let me finish what I know. The runes on the blade are these: fire, treasure, ward, rejoice, mountain, royal." As he spoke, he traced them on the air in elflight. Paks saw many of the watchers flinch. He turned to Paks. "Are these the runes?"

Paks nodded, and spoke. "Yes, my lord. Those are the

runes on this blade." She glanced at the king. "Shall I draw it now, sir king?"

"Wait," he said, looking at the elf. "There is more to this?"

"Yes. The runes can be read several ways, but they were set in the pattern that high elves would read as 'Guard this royal treasure, and the mountains will rejoice.' The royal treasure, of course, being the prince himself. The exact shape and size you see is that chosen by the queen for her own convenience—that's why it looks slender for a grown man's weapon."

"I don't understand," said the king slowly, "how it can have been sealed to the prince, yet not sealed to the prince. And what difference does it make now?"

Amrothlin smiled, but gently. "Sir king, at its making it was spellbound with the prince's name. That meant that no other would ever awake its full powers. As well, the queen had sent, with her request, a bit of cloth with one drop of the prince's blood, and a few hairs of his head. But the final binding, which would make the prince the knowing master of the blade, had to wait until he was old enough to grasp it and speak clearly the words of the ritual. Had their journey been completed, the prince would have been master of the sword. As it was—the prince and queen disappeared, and the sword was lost."

"Yes, but it's here." Belvarin had pushed his way to the front. "It's here now. Where has it been?"

"As for that, Sier Belvarin, I don't know the whole story. For many years it was lost—perhaps stolen by the raiders who attacked the party, or perhaps thrown far into the wood by the queen herself. But I next heard about it when Aliam Halveric sent word to the Ladysforest that he had found an elf blade near three murdered elves, between Chaya and his own lands. His description was exact; it could be no other."

"But you didn't tell him what it was," blurted Paks. "He didn't know, did he?"

"No. Although—" Amrothlin looked away for a moment. "We did not tell him. At the time, sir king, your brother

Serrostin had recently come to the throne. We feared that such a relic, at such a time, might stir—might cause unrest. It seemed to us that elves were less and less welcome at court. We feared haste, and the consequences of haste."

"But—" Sier Halveric looked bewildered. "But Aliam never told me about any sword. If he'd told me, I might have remembered—"

The elf sighed. "Sier Halveric, we know that. Aliam had a distaste for talking to you about it."

"You kept him—"

The elf bowed slightly, his eyes glinting. "And if we did, Sier Halveric, it was many years ago, and for reasons we thought wise. We advised Aliam Halveric to give it to the one it was made for—"

"The dead prince?" the king broke in.

"You wanted it sent to his memorial?" asked someone else.

"As you wish," said the elf. Paks felt a curious twist in her mind. The elf's mouth was quirked a little, as if he were secretly amused. But he went on. "Then he told us he was planning to give it to Phelan of Tsaia, as a wedding present, because his betrothed's name was Tammarrion, or 'light of mountains,' two of the runes. We told him that was well enough."

"And when his wife was killed," said Paks in the silence that followed, "the sword was recovered, and hung on his wall until I took it in need."

"Why?" asked the king.

"My lord, Duke Phelan's steward of many years was actually an agent of—" she hesitated to speak that name, and paused for another one. "—the webmistress," she said finally. "He feared my power to detect evil, and tried to kill the Duke and me before I could expose him. No one wore sword to the Duke's Hall; the steward grabbed one from the wall, and I happened to take this one. It was happy to drink his blood."

"I see. And you, not knowing its past, bore it away, and

returned it here." The king leaned back, looking even more tired. He drained the goblet Lieth held.

"My lord king, I am sure, now, that I was sent here to return it to its rightful place." The elf stirred beside her, but Paks went on. "I don't know what it can do for you, but such a source of power must be—"

"No." The king shook his head.

"No?"

"No. You were sent here, Lady, that I do not doubt. And I do not doubt that you were sent here with the sword to some purpose. But just the return of it—no. What good will such a sword do, when the one for whom it was made has long died?" He rolled his head sideways to meet the elf's eyes. "Tell me, sir elf—what can such a weapon do, without its master?"

"It is as you see it, sir king. A fine weapon—I've no doubt the lady has found it so—and particularly apt against certain evils."

"Would it be useful to anyone?"

"I think not. It was made in good, for good; it has been used by good, to some purpose. It would not, I think, fight well in a wicked hand."

"How would it be different in its master's hand?"

"My lord king, I know not all its powers. I had no need to know, when it was forged; in fact, I was far away at the time. Like any elf-blade, it gives light when its master draws it: more, if dire evil is near, or if its master's name is in doubt." Paks shifted now, remembering the flare of light from that blade every time she'd drawn it.

"Then if someone drew it," said the king slowly. "If it lit, would that prove anything?"

"It might—I don't know what spells my sister—your queen—put into it."

"I don't remember it lighting up when *she* drew it," said Tekko suddenly. Everyone turned to stare at him. "Many's the time I've seen her with it, too, and I don't recall any light."

"I will tell you all my thought," said the king, raising his voice with an obvious effort. "Here is a paladin come to

Chaya, in our deepest need. You know I am dying; I have no heir. Lyonya faces many troubles—between human and elf, between our borders and our allies, with Pargun and Kostandan to the north. This paladin—" he reached out and caught Paks's sleeve, "—has been named elf-friend. She is Gird's warrior, and known to powerful lords in Tsaia and Fintha; this would make our allies happy. The rangers say she can sense the taigin, which I have never done, to my shame and sorrow. And she comes with a treasure of our house, with the sword my eldest brother's wife carried, and which was made, we now know, for her son, who should have been our king. Let her draw the sword—let us see whether it lights for her. If it does—and I believe it will—then I suggest we have found my heir. Can anything be better than a paladin, bearing an elf blade, a friend of elves with taig-sense, to rule in Lyonya?"

Paks turned to him, appalled. "My lord, no!" She heard the rising murmur behind her. "I am no ruler; I am not even noble-born."

"If the gods choose you as a paladin, should I quarrel with your birth?" His voice carried over hers and the hubbub. It stilled as he went on. "Lady Paksenarrion, you have been tested and tried in ways that prove your fitness to wear Gird's crescent—or a crown. I command you now: draw the elf blade made for the heir to this throne, and show us all what it says."

Paks looked around the room, seeing consternation change to anticipation on all the faces. She looked back at the king, soberly. "Sir king, as a paladin, I am bound to honor the gods' commands above all others. But your command does not conflict with theirs. In the name of the High Lord, and Gird his servant—" As she slipped the sword from its scabbard, it flared blue as it had since she first pulled it from the wall. A shout went up.

Chapter Eighteen

"You see?" said the king quietly, beneath it. Paks shook her head, felt the blood rush to her cheeks.

"My lord king," she said as the noise began to die down. "I fear you have chosen the wrong person even so. I feel no call from my gods to accept this task. Many paladins find their swords give light when drawn."

"Lady, your modesty becomes you." The king's eyes were alight. "Yet see what a solution you are to our problem. A paladin: therefore untainted by evil ambition. A paladin of Gird, which will reassure our neighbors to the west, and warn those to the north. You can sense the taig. You are acceptable, I daresay, to the elves—" he glanced up at Amrothlin. The elf bowed slightly.

"Paksenarrion is, indeed, an elf-friend," he said. "We do not advise on succession, as you know, sir king; but if she held the throne we would not object." Paks gave him a sharp look, seeking for something more behind the words, but his face was smooth and unreadable.

"But I'm not of your House," she insisted. "I'm not Lyonyan at all, or even part-elf—"

"No, but you're honest, brave, and have the power of paladins. These will serve well enough. What has my heritage brought?" The king sounded both tired and bitter. "My Council has not agreed these last two years on a successor. I have found one with more ability than any of their candidates." He looked out at the others in the room. "Would you dispute that, Council members?"

"Not I, my lord," said Sier Halveric quickly. Others murmured agreement, but Sier Belvarin frowned.

"What if she's an agent of Tsaia, my lord? She has been a member of that Phelan's company—he's a Tsaian Duke, after all."

"A paladin?" The king looked shocked. "Belvarin, she's an agent of the gods—that's all." Belvarin looked unconvinced, but nodded. The king turned back to Paksenarrion. "Lady, before the Council and assembled nobles of my realm, and the elves as well, I ask you—I beg you—to take the throne when I die. You can do no worse than I, and I think you must do better, with the gods gracing you as they have. This kingdom—this green land—is the strong heart of the four southern kingdoms. If it fails—then evil is free to ravage Tsaia and Prealith, not to mention the Ladysforest."

Paks knelt beside him. "Sir king, I grieve—for you, for this kingdom in distress. But—"

"Someone must, Paksenarrion," the king said more softly. Paks saw his eyes dull with approaching pain. "Please—save it—no one else—" His head sagged. She felt the mingled awe and terror of the others like a cloud.

"Sir king—" Her hand on his conveyed nothing; she had no power to give. She felt the live flesh stiffen, the skin hardening subtly under her fingers like cooling wax. A rustle filled the room. When she looked aside, they were all kneeling, even the elves.

Esceriel moved first. He took a corner of the king's cloak and covered the face. Paks looked up to see tears on his cheeks. He leaned his head against the dead king for an instant, then met her eyes. His gaze carried both challenge and admiration.

"My lords and ladies," said Esceriel slowly. "Our king is dead. He—"

"Our king," interrupted Amrothlin with the slightest emphasis on *our*, "was a brave and great man. We honor his memory."

The squires stood; Paks also rose to her feet. Esceriel finished arranging the king's hands beneath the cloak. He nodded to the group. "Our king has died; he made one last request. I am no longer King's Squire; I am on no Council. I have no right to know, but the king was dear to me, and I would ask whether you will honor it."

"I see nothing else," said Sier Halveric, clambering up from his knees. Others rose as well. "I thought it was a good idea then, and now—Falk rest him well—it's the only thing to do." A low murmur ran around the room, obvious agreement. Even Belvarin shrugged and nodded. Amrothlin gave Paks a keen glance, then a quick bow. "I have said already that the elves would have no quarrel with such a succession."

"Will you then accept this charge?" asked Sier Halveric, coming forward to confront Paks. "Our land is in need—desperate need—and you have been sent to help us. So much you have said yourself. We offer you the crown for your lifetime, knowing that no harm will come to us on your account."

Paks glanced at the dead king, then looked the Halveric full in the face. "Sier Halveric, I respected your king. I respect your need. But I am bound to obey the calls of my gods. I cannot discuss this here, with your king still—"

"I am sorry you think we have something to discuss," said Sier Halveric. "I had hoped—"

"My lord, if I took the throne, you might find me less biddable than you hoped."

A brief smile lightened his face and made him look more like Aliam. "Lady, if it would persuade you to save our kingdom, I would not mind if you crossed my every whim. Yet I understand; it is not seemly, if you cannot accept without reservations, to discuss it here and now." He turned to the others. "As senior Councillor present, I ask the steward to announce the king's death." The steward bowed low and withdrew. Sier Halveric turned back to the others. "And if the squires would stand guard, as we pay our respects, I will send for the others who should come." He was the first to kneel before the king, and lay his lips a moment on the cloaked face. The others came up, one by one, to do the same. Then they left, and the squires lifted him back to the carrying chair, to take him to his chambers for the formal laying out.

Paks stood until they were out of the room, then faced the group of elves who remained. Their faces were unreadable, even for her. Amrothlin spoke.

"You are very tired, Lady Paksenarrion. Will you council with them, or rest?"

Paks wanted to fall asleep where she stood. She reached in thought for the High Lord and the others. Strength flowed into her, leaching the tiredness away. She smiled at the elves.

"I can sleep when this is settled. The gods give strength when it's needed, as you elves know well, who rarely sleep at all."

"Few are the humans who drink from our springs," said Amrothlin gravely. "But then, few are the humans who have touched an elfane taig directly. Will you say what you have decided?"

"I will say what the gods would have me do, when I know what that is and the council is assembled," replied Paks.

Outside, Sier Halveric waited for her. "I am sure you are tired, Lady Paksenarrion. If you would rest and pray before meeting with us, we will wait. But the realm's great need requires that we not sit long in uncertainty—may I ask that you speak with us when you can?"

"My lord, if the Council is ready to meet, I will come now. But did you not say that you had messages to send? If some must come from a distance, I would sleep a little."

He nodded. "To assemble the full Council will take some hours more. Those here can make legal decisions, however; we have had to do so since the king's illness worsened. I have sent to all the Siers who are not present, and to the Knight-Commander of Falk. But in the matter of succession, I fear any delay. I myself resign my claim, to favor yours; at this moment most favor yours, but—"

"What action would be taken by a council of regents, had the king left a minor heir?"

"Oh—the announcement of regents, a proclamation of

the terms of regency and that the regents swore their honor to it. Continuance of the alliance, and its terms, and the authority of the courts as presently constituted—"

"Could not the Council act as a regency for awhile?"

"Regent for whom? For you?" He looked confused.

"Let us say, for whomever comes to rule."

"I hadn't thought of that." He gave her a shrewd look. "Falk's blade in gold, Lady, if you become our queen, as I hope, you promise to be not only good but wise. We could indeed. As well, it would be reasonable, since you are unfamiliar with our laws and customs, to continue as we have until you've time to learn them." He looked past her to the elves who had followed her out. "Would that satisfy you?"

"A temporary regency? That is a matter for the Council to decide, but it seems well enough." Again Paks had the impression of some hidden amusement.

"Then may I see you to your chambers, Lady?" asked Sier Halveric. "Whatever you need—"

Paks nodded, still thinking hard. He led her up stairs and along corridors; Paks realized that they were not returning to the room she'd been given. Before she could ask, he answered.

"The king's chamber is of course where he is being laid out. The room you were given is needed—and would not be quiet, either, in all the bustle. Your things have been moved to the old queen's chambers; servants await you there." He looked over his shoulder to Amrothlin who, with two of the elves, followed them. "Will you grace the palace by staying here for the present? Rooms are available nearby; I can—"

"I will stay near Lady Paksenarrion for the present," said Amrothlin. "Not to speak to her, or impede her rest or prayer, but merely to be present should she have need of any elven lore." Paks shot him a quick glance but nothing showed on his face. The Halveric nodded, as they came to the double doors of another chamber of state.

"The queen's suite has several chambers; I've no doubt you will be comfortable. Lady, if you will come—"

Paks entered. The fair-sized room, bright with firelight and candles, held several tables and comfortable chairs. Old Joriam was there, and two women in the forest-green livery of the palace, and Lieth, still in armor. Doors led into other rooms; Paks could see a tall canopied bed in one, book-lined walls in another. A steaming pot sat on the hearth. The Halveric bowed.

"I will leave you now, Lady Paksenarrion. Rest well, and I shall pray that the gods give you leave to grant our king's last request." Then he withdrew. Paks wondered what to do next.

Joriam had no such doubts. "You'll want out of that armor, I daresay," he began and came to her. "Sela, fetch that robe we've got warming. Sir elf, we've plenty of that good hot punch by the fire. Keris will serve you some, if you will—" The other woman went quickly to a cabinet and fetched out more silver goblets. Amrothlin smiled, and accepted one, as did his companions. By this time Joriam had helped Paks off with the sword, and out of her mail. She had never had such help; he made it easy. Before she knew it, she was wrapped in a warm robe and seated by the fire with a hot drink halfway down. She looked at Lieth.

"Lady," said Lieth carefully, "it was the Council's wish that you be squired as would befit our sovereign. I offered to come this night, having met you. Esceriel mourns."

"I am honored," said Paks. "You know I have given no commitment—"

"I know. But if you do, then it is fitting, and I am glad to serve you even if the time is brief."

"You do not always wear armor," Paks said.

Lieth smiled faintly. "No, Lady. But we are between reigns; you have not yet taken the protection of your crown. And so I thought better to be armed, lest any have secret thoughts."

Amrothlin smiled up at her. "You are a wise squire, Lieth; that was our thought as well."

"You feared for my safety here?" asked Paks, surprised.

"Lady, you are a paladin; you cannot be tainted by evil without your will. But a knife in the ribs will kill you."

"No one would kill her," objected Joriam. "She's—"

"Peace, Joriam. Do you argue that evil has not dogged this realm for many years? Do you think it will give up so easily? If she is, indeed, the hope of this realm, then that could draw the evil powers."

"For that," said Paks, "a paladin exists not to avoid conflict, but to bring it into the open."

Amrothlin nodded. "So I have heard. But here you will be warded by several loyalties: Joriam's lifelong honesty, Lieth's Falkian honor, and the elven sense of the taig. You will have peace for your prayers, and for your rest."

Paks nodded. "Thank you—all of you." A few minutes later, she let Lieth lead her to the bedchamber, and lay for the first time in her life on embroidered sheets beneath a costly canopy figured with flowers and vines. She slept better than she expected, waking in early dawn to a horn call from the palace gates. For a moment she lay still, staring at the pale shape of the window. Everything in the chamber was dark, shade on shade of gray without color. She could just see Lieth's form standing near the window, looking out. She stretched, rustling the covers, and Lieth turned.

"It is early yet, Lady, if you wish more sleep."

Paks felt more awake every instant. "No—I am rested."

"Shall I light a fire here?" Paks remembered that the bedchamber had its own fireplace, but she was not used to that luxury. She shook her head, then, remembering the darkness, spoke.

"No, Lieth. That's all right. Is there a quiet place, where I can be alone to pray?"

"Here—I can guard the door. No one will bother you."

"Very well." Paks pushed aside the covers and swung her legs over the side of the bed. Lieth had already gone out, closing the door softly. Paks padded over the carpets to the window and looked out. There was the courtyard, an eerie uncolored paleness in the dawn. She could see figures by the gate, dark against the dawnlit snow. To the east, the sky was luminous, a band of green beneath the blue. She pushed the window outward, and craned her head to look up. Winter stars still burned overhead, disappearing as she watched.

She looked at the courtyard again. A puff of smoke came from a chimney across from her window. Then another. She remembered watching for the smoke from the kitchens when she had the night watch at the Duke's. And this was what they would give her: this courtyard, to watch over, to have as her own. This land—the rich farmlands, the great forests full of game. For a few moments, leaning her head on the window frame, she let herself imagine being queen here. She could be good for them—she knew that. She could sense the forest taig, even here; she could let her mind reach out and sense the taig of the entire kingdom. It lay under her inner eye like a rich tapestry; she could see the places—here, and there, and over there—where something had soiled the fabric, or worn it thin. She thought of having those like Lieth and Esceriel for loyal friends and servants—of hunting in those forests, on a red horse that moved like the north wind. That stopped her. That red horse was no queen's mount, no horse to spend his days in a royal stable champing royal oats. He had not come out of the winter wind for that. She sighed, pushed herself back from the window, and went to sit before the fireplace with its neat pattern of wood waiting for a light.

Her mind emptied of thoughts of thrones and crowns, spilled its images and memories of councils and courts and ceremony. It stilled, gradually, as a forest pool stills when no wind blows. What did she really know? The feel of a sword in the hand. The sickness of fear, and that brother-sickness, rage. She knew the taste of bread to the hungry, the ease of warmth to the cold. One by one, the things she knew of her own experience flicked through her mind. And faces: Saben, Master Oakhallow, Sevri, Stammel, Aliam Halveric, Duke Phelan. These left her. A fire grew in her mind, a fire of both warmth and song, and a tree grew in that fire, burning and unconsumed. And a red horse crashed through the flames on a winter wind, taking her somewhere, taking her far away into laughter and flowers.

She came to herself hearing a knocking on the door, and the crackle of flames on the hearth. With a shake of the head, she stood, and opened the door. By then she had seen it was broad day, with sun spearing in the south-facing window.

"We were worried, Lady," said Lieth. Sier Halveric and Sier Belvarin were behind her.

Paks nodded. "My pardon. When the gods speak, it is difficult sometimes to come away." They stared at her, seeing something in her face she did not feel.

"When you're ready," said Sier Belvarin finally, "the Council will be pleased to meet with you."

"I won't be long," said Paks. She could feel her normal wits coming back; she felt strong and rested. The two Siers left the room, and Paks saw that Joriam had bathwater hot by the great hearth. The elves still stood near the outer door; Amrothlin nodded to her.

"I need not ask how you fared, Lady; it is obvious you fared well indeed in the gods' care."

"I have seen your Tree," said Paks. She did not know why she said so, only that it was true and important. Amrothlin stood straighter, if possible.

"Indeed? Then I hope you received the blessing of its leaves, Lady. You are more than welcome to it."

More quickly than Joriam intended, Paks was bathed and dressed; she soothed the old man, while refusing his embellishments.

"Joriam, you are used to serving royalty—and I am a paladin, a warrior of the gods, and not a king or queen. Would you get me used to your luxuries, so that I would miss them on campaign?"

"No—but—"

"You have given me great pleasure already, Joriam. It is all I can take, now."

He grinned at her suddenly. "Now, you say! Very well, then, another time. You'll see—the gods have no hatred for these things, and you are too experienced a warrior to misuse them. I'll wager you like good food well enough, yet can go hungry at need."

"You're right on that, Joriam. Mushrooms—" Paks laughed as Lieth helped her into her mail. "But see here—you save all this for your ruler, eh?"

He nodded. "May it be you, Lady—that's what I say."

"It's the gods' will, Joriam. Your kingdom has great need, and they know best how to fill it."

The Council met in the Leaf Hall. Most of those attending had been at the meeting the night before. Those new to Paks were introduced: the Knight-Commander of Falk, the widower of the half-elven queen, a few nobles. Paks had been ready to dislike the widower, but he was clearly as Joriam had described: a good man, though perhaps narrow-minded, and wholly without ambition. The Knight-Commander was another matter. Half-elven, slightly taller than Paks, he gave her a challenging look when they were introduced.

"Gird's paladin, eh?" he said. His grip was strong, but not painful. "You are not like the others."

"No." Paks said no more.

"I had heard of you," he went on. "Not the most likely candidate for a crown, I would have thought."

"As you will hear," said Paks, "I did not seek one."

"That's what they told me," he said. "If you say you did not, then you did not." He chewed his lip a moment. "I find that hard to believe, but perhaps Falkians emphasize command more than Girdsmen."

Paks thought of the Marshal-General and repressed a chuckle. "I assure you, sir, that ambition for command is found often enough among Girdsmen."

"And to that, as well, you are an exception?"

"It depends on circumstances," said Paks.

"Indeed. And in these circumstances?"

"Sir, when the Council is convened, I will speak to the whole Council of the outcome of my prayers."

"I am well rebuked, Lady," he said, lowering his eyes. Paks did not think he felt rebuked.

By this time everyone was standing behind one of the chairs that had been drawn into a great circle. Sier Halveric looked at Paks; when she nodded, he spoke.

"Sirs and ladies, we are met to discuss our late king's last council and request—and to settle the government of this realm for the time being. I believe you all know what our late king asked—that this lady, a paladin of Gird, who has come to us bearing the sword of Falkieri's heir, take the throne for her life. This she was unwilling to do without consulting the High Lord and Gird her patron. Yet most of us saw her draw that sword in council last night, and saw the sword take light." He turned to Paks. "I ask you now, Lady Paksenarrion, before the Council of Lyonya, acting in regency for the one who will be our ruler, to draw that sword again, and give us your answer."

Paks laid her hand on the sword, but did not draw it. She looked around the circle slowly, meeting each pair of eyes in turn. All were welcoming, as far as she could see, human and elf and those of part-blood alike. When she completed the circle, she nodded once and began.

"Lords and ladies of the realm, elves of the kingdom—I was honored beyond my due by your king's offer. But paladins are bound to the gods they follow. I came here on quest; I am on quest still. After long prayer I believe I now know what that quest is." She paused; the room was utterly silent. Even the fire on the hearth burned without sound.

"It is not to be your queen." At that, an outbreak of sound, rustlings and murmurs. Paks ignored this and went on. "I thought long on this—I would have been glad to take it—but it is not my quest, and I may not turn aside." Now they were quiet again. "But your kingdom's peril, Councillors, is my task, and I believe the gods wish me to find your ruler—the one who should be here, in the place you offered me. I think it was for this that this sword came into my hand. For this that it responds to me—" Now she drew the sword, and its blue glow lit the room. "Not that I rule myself," she said, slipping it back into the scabbard, "but that I find its lawful master."

"But he's dead," said Sier Belvarin. "It was made for Falkieri's son, and he's dead."

"Is he?" asked Paks. Heads turned; she saw the uncertain glances. She looked past them out the tall windows. "I am a stranger here perhaps I heard things new that you are too familiar with. You think he is dead—but what is the proof of that?"

"They searched—"

"Bodies—"

"—the queen—"

Paks stilled the gabble with a gesture. "They were attacked; the queen was killed. So much is clear. But the prince? His body was never found. What if he lived?"

"If he lived, then why did we never hear of him?" asked one of the others. "And how could a child like this live, alone in the forest?"

"I do not know how he lived, or where he is, or why no one ever heard," said Paks. "But I believe he was not killed. Last night much of this was new to me. So I listened to everyone—and heard what was said, not what I expected to hear." She turned to Amrothlin. "What did you say was the message sent to Aliam Halveric, when he offered to return this elven blade to elves?"

The elf's eyes flashed at her. "He was told to return it to the one for whom it was made."

"But—" Sier Halveric stopped in midsentence, and stared. "You—you knew the prince was alive? *You* knew?"

"The elves would know," said Paks, "if anyone would." She saw the mouths open, the start of an uprising, and spoke quickly. "You all assumed the prince had died in the attack; you all assumed the elves' message meant something or someone else. But if the prince were alive then—and that was how many years ago?—then the elves may have meant exactly what they said."

"*Was* he alive then?" asked Sier Halveric. Amrothlin nodded.

"He was," he said without any emphasis.

"Why didn't you tell us? Why—why, it could have saved—"

Amrothlin interrupted. "My lords and ladies, it could not be. At first we too thought he was dead; we could not sense his taig. When at last one of us saw him again, he was—" he stopped, and looked around the room before going on. "He was no longer a prince."

Silence filled the room. Then Sier Belvarin broke it. "What do you mean by that? Born a prince, he would always be—"

"No. He had changed. We judged he might never be fit to rule."

"You judged! How dared you—!"

"You forget, sir, that he was my sister's child!" This time Amrothlin's voice was edged with all the cold fury that elves could show. "My own mother's grandson, a flower of the Ladysforest as much as an heir to your throne—you know, or should remember, how rarely we elves bear children, and how we delight in them. We judged, yes—we, who loved his mother through such ages as you humans call infinite, we judged him. Had you seen him then, sir, you would have judged him too—and perhaps more harshly than we, for you would never have known him for his father's son. Or his mother's."

"What had happened?" asked Paks into the horrified silence.

Amrothlin, still angry, turned to her, speaking with delicate precision. "Lady, we do not know. He bore scars of body and mind, as if he had been enslaved to a cruel master. Far away, I would say, since we had not sensed his taig. Within was fear, but with a core of bitter anger."

Paks turned to the others. "So at one time in the past your prince still lived—years after you thought him dead. Perhaps he lived long enough to father heirs of his own." She looked back at the elf. "Is he still alive, Amrothlin?"

"Do you do well to ask, paladin of Gird?"

"Amrothlin, I ask what I ask by the bidding of the High Lord, if my prayers be true. Not for myself, but for this kingdom."

"As you will, Lady. Then I will say he is alive."

"Do you know where? Do you know his name?"

"I cannot help you," said Amrothlin. "You have not asked yet why he himself never claimed his inheritance. He has no memory of it; it was destroyed. If only—" Amrothlin looked down for an instant, then met Paks's eyes again. "We elves like not that phrase, but in this case, had the attack happened on the way home, the prince could not have been damaged as he was. The wakening of his elven powers would have warded him somewhat. But as it was, he knows not his own name or title. When he returned to the Eight Kingdoms, the man who took him in as a servant eventually guessed who he might be. But he saw no future for him at this court; he concealed what he guessed, and told the boy nothing."

"Who was that?" asked Sier Halveric quickly. "In Lyonya? In Prealith?"

"I cannot help you," said Amrothlin again.

"Cannot, or will not?" asked Paks.

"Lady, I have done what I can. We are not convinced he is fit to rule; he has had the chance to show such ability, and has turned away."

"Why didn't you heal him?" asked Belvarin suddenly. "Couldn't you have done that when you first met him again?"

Amrothlin put up his hand. "We could not heal—or attempt to heal—without risking great harm, both to him and to the kingdom. If we had restored, say, his memory of his name—and not been able to restore the taig of his spirit, would that have been well done? We judged not. Sometimes time itself heals what no magics can, elven or other. We waited. We watched from afar. We did not see the sign of growth we could foster; we did not wish to do more destruction to one who had been so harmed already." He waited until everyone was quiet again, then went on. "As for succession, we do not advise—but we will not help you find someone we think is too flawed to rule. If you find him yourself, against our recommendation, then we will see."

Paks, following all this, began to have a curious feeling that she had already what clues she needed—if only she had the peace and quiet to put them together. But for the next hour no one had peace and quiet. The Council roiled with excitement. They calculated how old the prince must be; they tried to guess who and where, and surprise the elf into an answer. Paks stood aside, listening, trying to think, trying to fix every word that had been said in her memory. Finally, when the same people began to repeat the same words, she raised her hand. They fell silent.

"Lords and ladies, high elves, Councillors: I say again that this is my quest. To find your prince, and restore the rightful king to your throne. I cannot make this quest without your support, for you must agree to accept the king I bring you—" She was surprised to find herself saying this, but went on; the gods surely knew what they did when they took over her tongue. "I will return with your true king, or his heirs. Is this agreeable?"

They argued a while longer; some thought they'd rather have a paladin already there than a mysterious lost prince who, according to the elves, wasn't worth finding anyway. But Paks insisted that she would not take the crown, and finally they agreed. Amrothlin looked long in her eyes before nodding at last.

"If you find him, and if you can show us that his anger will not break the kingdom to bits, we will accept him. And if we can, we will restore his elven powers."

"As the High Lord wills, and Gird gives grace, Amrothlin. I believe the prince will be found, and found able to rule, else this quest would not be laid on me."

"May it be so," said Amrothlin gravely. "May it be so indeed, that the powers of evil find their plots spoiled, and the House of the Fountain break forth in joy."

"I will ask questions," said Paks, "that you would be wise to answer." His eyebrows went up, and a mocking smile touched his mouth.

"You would teach wisdom to elves, paladin? Well, it may come to that, but we shall see. I will answer as I can, for our honor and his."

Chapter Nineteen

"Since you insist your quest is to find our prince," began the Knight-Commander of Falk, "we can only try to help you as we can."

Paks smiled at his expression. "Do you know Marshal-General Arianya, sir?"

His nose twitched. "Yes; I met her in Verella one time. A remarkable woman."

"She might enlighten you about my past," Paks suggested.

"Oh—" Under direct challenge, he seemed to deflate. "Ward of Falk," he said then. "I've no reason to doubt you're who or what you say—and I know a paladin cannot lie. To be honest, I suppose it galls a bit that the High Lord chose a paladin of Gird for this, when I would have thought a Falkian could do as much."

"Save that someone born and brought up here would have assumed the prince's death, sir. It is that ignorance, perhaps, which makes me suitable."

"I would have expected such reasoning from a kuakgannir, Lady, not a Girdsman. Emptiness calls fulfillment—is that what you mean?"

Paks shook her head. "Not precisely, though as you should know if you do not, the final healing of my wounds came from a Kuakgan. What I meant was that a commander new to a company can see what custom has hidden."

"Oh."

"Where will you begin looking, Paksenarrion? There are many men in the Eight Kingdoms of the right age—and many still when you leave out the black-haired, dark-eyed ones who cannot be the prince." Sier Halveric poured out mugs of sib as he spoke. They had gathered in the queen's chambers, the older lords who remembered the queen and prince, and the Knight-Commander. The elves had withdrawn, to pay their respects to the dead king in their own way, but promised to return if Paks called.

She thought a long moment, trying to feel her way into the gods' will. "I think," she said, "that I must begin with this sword's history. I must talk to your newphew Aliam—see the place where he found it, and hear from him the exact wording of every message the elves sent. They told him once to give it to the one for whom it was made—as if at that time he could have done so, and it would have been right. Surely if he had, the sword would have proclaimed the prince's identity. But he did not know who the prince was—how could he? Nor did he know the power of the sword—or so Amrothlin implied. I must ask him directly. In the meantime, tell me what you remember of the young prince—Joriam, you begin."

"Well, Lady, I was young myself then—I may have forgot—but I remember him as a lively little lad. Going on four or five he was then, a little scrap of a boy. Had reddish golden hair, much like his father's, but lighter, as a child's often is."

"Any marks you'd know him by?"

"No, Lady. I never tended him, ye see. Just saw him about. I remember once he climbed out on a window ledge and knocked off a pot of flowers—"

"I remember that," broke in Sier Hammarrin, chuckling. "By Falk, that little rascal had nerve—always loved to climb things. Down the flowers came, nearly hitting old Fersin, rest his soul, and shattered on the courtyard. He couldn't have been over three at the time."

"They sent you after him, didn't they, Joriam?" asked Sier Halveric. "I remember something—"

Joriam nodded, blushing. "Yes, my lord, they did. I was the closest, and lightweight too—I've always been small—they feared the ledge might go; it was before that section was repointed. And so I started out, and I was feared, Lady, of the height, and he saw it and said 'never mind, Joriam; I'll come in myself' and crawled right to me. Steady as a cat on a limb, he was."

"What else?" asked Paks.

"You mustn't think he was spoiled," said Sier Galvary, a bald old man with grey eyes. "Not more than any prince is. He was loved and wanted by both his parents—the pride of the palace—but his father insisted he be courteous. And he was, for such a little sprite."

"Not so little, really," said Sier Halveric. "For his age he was well grown. He seemed like to grow into a tall man. But I agree, he was mannerly. Do you remember when his father gave him the gray hound puppy, Galvary?"

Galvary shook his head, but Hammarrin began chuckling again. "I do. I certainly do. That dog was the worst nuisance . . . pick of the litter, indeed! Pick of mischief! He nipped everyone, and must have chewed half the harness in the stables."

"It made your stable boys keep the reins off the floor," said Sier Halveric. "But what I was thinking of was the boy—you know how boys are with dogs; he took a stick to it one day, and I came in on the end of that lecture. Two days later, I found him giving it word for word to some commoner's child outside the walls, who was tormenting a kitten. Word for word, his father's tone of voice, everything: 'It is not the act of a man or a prince to abuse helpless things, nor the justice of kings to give pain when it can be avoided.' It sounded funny enough, from that little mouth—and yet—"

"It sounds as if he would have been a good ruler," put in Paks. "If nothing had happened."

"I believe so." Sier Galvary nodded. "We had no doubts of it. Falkieri and his wife were mature; the boy showed every sign of ability. He did what normal boys do, mischief and all, but there was no meanness in him. And brought up to it, with good examples and good sense, there was no reason for him to go wrong."

"Look at his sister—the young queen—" said Hammarrin.

"She did well, even without her mother, with her father dying early, and all that. The same blood: brave, generous, intelligent—"

"I can't believe, whatever has happened, that if Falki lives he is completely unfit to rule." Sier Halveric took another sip of his drink. "The gods know people change, but he had such promise—how could it all be lost, without killing him?"

Paks thought she knew, but hoped it was not true. They had no need to know; she pushed her memories down below the surface. It hurt her to think of a child enduring anything like she had endured, a child living on with the hopelessness she had suffered for less than a year.

"What was his name?" she asked, distracting herself.

"The prince? The same as his father. We called him Falki. His parents had their own pet name for him, of course. His other names—let's see—Amrothlin, I just realized—that's for his mother's brother. Artfielan—for an uncle, wasn't it? Falkieri's mother's brother? And something else—we'll have to look it up. It's too far back for me." Sier Hammarrin shook his head.

"How many names do princes have?" asked Paks.

"Oh, it depends. Usually four or five. You want to please all the families, you know. But the names won't help; every Falkian family has a Falkieri or two, it's one of the commonest names in Lyonya. Artfielan—I've a son named that, a grandson and a nephew. Besides, the elves said he doesn't remember his name, and we don't know what name he's using."

"So," she began again to organize her thoughts. "You say he would be about fifty years old, with red or yellow hair—"

"I expect reddish," said Sier Halveric. "His was still reddish when he disappeared, and his father's had darkened."

"Tall, you think? And what color eyes?"

This began another argument. Paks found it hard to believe that no one had noticed the color of his eyes until she realized that she couldn't name the color of her own brothers' eyes either. Finally they agreed that they weren't green, gold, or dark. Blue or gray or something in between.

But this left almost nothing to go on. A tallish man of late middle age with reddish hair and blue or gray eyes—unless his hair had turned gray already, or he'd gone bald. Paks had trouble imagining a bald prince, but after all, he was old enough to be her father. According to the elves, he had been someone's servant once. She assumed that meant in the Eight Kingdoms, but it might not. He might be a woodchopper somewhere (Paks thought of Mal in Brewersbridge, but of course he was too young) or a farmer. He might be a merchant, a craftsman, almost anything. Paks thought of the number of red-haired men she'd seen in the north and felt depressed. Not only that, he might have gone to Aarenis. Or across the ocean. She found she was making circles on the table with one finger. Everyone had fallen silent; she could tell by the glum faces that they, too, had realized the size of her task.

"Unless the elves change their minds," said Sier Halveric, "I don't see how you can hope to find him in time to do us any good. There are too many—"

"It would help," said Paks, "if they would give me details—what he looked like when they saw him, and so on. But remember, sirs, that the gods have sent me this quest. If the High Lord wants your prince on the throne, can even an elf hide him from me?"

At this they cheered up, and Paks felt herself that somewhere in this she had learned something useful—if only she knew what.

The old king's funeral ceremonies took from sunrise to long after sunset. When it was over, Paks went to her chambers to pick up her gear, packed ready. There she found Esceriel, Lieth, and the other king's squires waiting.

"You are not the queen," said Esceriel, "but we have no ruler to squire. By your leave, Lady, we will ride with you on this quest. It may be that you will have need of us—or when you find our king, we can serve him well."

Paks looked at him searchingly. She had seen nothing of

Esceriel until now; the others had taken their turns in her chambers. But she felt nothing evil in him, and none of them seemed likely to put a knife in her back.

"I do not know how long I will be," she said finally. "Have you leave to be away from court for long?"

"We have no ruler to serve; it was the king who gave or refused leave to his squires, Lady. Other than that, we are all knights of Falk. Although we have stayed much at court, you will find us hardy travellers and able warriors, should such be needed." He turned aside for a moment, and one of the others handed him a bag, which he held out to Paks. "In addition, Lady, the court of Lyonya will bear any expense of our travels; here is the Council's gift to us, if you permit us to ride with you."

Paks looked each of them in the eye—all steady, all seeming good companions. She nodded. "You are welcome to come with me, as far as you will, as long as your will and the quest I follow travel together. Yet I will not bind you; since I cannot say where and how I go, it would not be right to take your oaths." They all nodded. "If for any reason any or all of you decide to leave me, I will give you no blame for it. But I was planning to ride tonight, squires—or should I call you companions?"

Lieth smiled. "By your leave we will be squires to you, Lady—it will keep us in practice for the king we hope to find. You know Esceriel and me; here are Garris, the oldest of us, but not too old for this, and Suriya, the youngest."

"And we also are ready to ride tonight," said Esceriel. "Our horses are saddled and ready; we have stores packed. We need only our cloaks."

"Very well," said Paks. "Then let us go."

They rode out through streets glittering with deathlights, twigs wrapped with salt-soaked wicks that burned green. The sharp smell of the burning twigs carried on the light wind for some time after they left the city. Garris, the eldest of the squires, who had squired for the previous king as well, led the way through the woods southward. They carried torches; light glittered off the crusted snow.

By daybreak, they were far from Chaya, among hills covered with forest. It was a gray morning, with icy mist between the trees, and Garris stopped them.

"We should wait for this to lift," he said. "I know where we are, but I cannot read the taig enough to keep direction in the fog."

"I can," said Paks, "but it will do us no harm to have a hot meal. If we travel today, Garris, can we come to shelter for the night, or must we camp in the snow?"

"If we keep to the way I know, we will come to a steading by midafternoon. But it would be easy to miss—the land is not so settled as that you may be used to in Tsaia."

"We'll see." Two of the squires built a fire; the others brought out pots and began to cook. Paks walked around, stretching her shoulders and watching their preparations. The night before she had not paid much attention to their gear; now she found that they were prepared for a long march in almost any conditions, with two pack animals along.

"When the king travelled," explained Lieth, "we cared for his things. Had you wanted it, we could have brought the royal tent as well." They had a small one; it would sleep all six of them if they crowded in.

"I shall feel like a rich woman yet," said Paks, as they served out hot porridge and sib. She noticed that they took guard duty in turns, two by two, even though they were in friendly country.

After the break, Paks led the way south, checking with Garris at intervals. She could feel a certain difference in the direction he thought the steading lay, a break in the forest taig. No one suggested stopping long at midday, though they rested the animals, and by midafternoon they had found a large farmstead. A log palisade surrounded a stone house; other houses clustered near it. Dogs ran out barking; a man in fur-lined leathers came out to look at them, and waved.

Esceriel and Lieth rode ahead. Paks had not realized

that they carried pennants until they lifted them: the royal crest on one, and—to her greater surprise—Gird's crescent on the other. By the time she rode up to the man, the squires had explained the quest, and the man bowed.

"Be welcome here, Lady Paksenarrion; luck to your quest. We sorrow for the king's death; the messenger stopped here on the way to Aliam Halveric's and told us of it."

"We thank you for your kindness, sir," said Paks.

"This is Lord Selvis," said Lieth quickly.

"Ride on in," said the man. "There's a barn inside the palisade. We've wild cats in the wood; we stall all the horses at night."

All day the red horse had travelled like any other, but when Esceriel reached for his rein, he drew back. Paks grinned. "I'll take him myself, Esceriel."

"He let the stablehands at Chaya—"

"I had asked—and after that perhaps he understood the emergency." They walked to the barn together, the red horse breathing warm on Paks's neck at every step. When she took off her saddle and bridle, she found him unmarked as if from a grooming. She picked up a brush anyway, but the horse nudged her hand aside. Esceriel stared.

"I never saw a horse like that."

"Nor I. He came out of the north, one day at the Duke's stronghold, in northern Tsaia. Slick-coated—as he is now—and full of himself."

"How long have you had him?"

"That was this winter—not long." Paks poured a measure of grain in the box, after sniffing it for mold. She pulled an armload of hay down and wedged it in the rack. "I had known that paladins had special horses, but—as you may have heard—I became a paladin in an unusual way. Not at Fin Panir. So I didn't know how—or even if—I would get mine."

"What do you call him?"

"If he has a name, he hasn't shared it with me."

* * *

The next day was clear again; they made good time along snowy trails that Garris remembered. That night they camped; the squires did not want to let Paks take a share of the watch.

"I'm not the queen," she reminded them. "And I'm used to night watches—and younger then most of you."

"But we depend on your abilities," said Garris. "You should take what rest you can."

In the end, Paks simply got up when she woke in the midnight hours, and went out to see stars tangled in the bare treelimbs. When she'd used the little trench they'd dug, she spoke to Suriya, the squire on watch.

"I'm wide awake, and I need to think. Go sleep; I'll wake the next in an hour of so." Suriya, the most junior and only a few years older than Paks, nodded and went into the tent.

Paks walked around the camp slowly. It was a windless night, so quiet that she heard every breath each horse took. Her own came to her, crunching the snow, and leaned a warm head along her body. She put her arm across his back and stood for a few moments. Then she pushed away, and went on. Her taig-sense told her that nothing threatened nearby. She caught a flicker of movement between the trees. Another. Some small night animals skittering over the snow. Remembering Siniava, she checked again, but it was nothing—just animals. When the stars had moved several hands across the sky, she shook Esceriel awake and rolled back into her own blankets.

The fifth day a snowstorm caught them between one steading and another. Paks had been uneasy since waking in the night, and had rushed the others through breakfast and farewells. She felt some menace ahead, which it would be well to pass early. But the storm began softly, so that they did not think of turning back until they were more than halfway to the next stopping place. A few flakes—a few more—a gentle curtain of snow that filled the tracks behind them. Then a wind that twirled the falling snow into eerie shapes. And finally the strong wind with miles of snow behind it, that turned their view into a white confusion.

If she had been alone, Paks might have trusted the red horse to fight through the deepening snow and sense dangerous terrain. But with four others, and two pack animals—

"Stop!" she yelled, as Esceriel's horse moved past her, drifting downward. He reined in; she could just see him. She got the others into a huddle. Slowly they moved into the lee of a large knot of cedars; snow had already drifted head-high on the upwind side. In the struggle of making camp, Paks found herself taking command easily. By the time they were huddled in the tent, which had been cross-braced with limbs against the snow-weight, she felt at ease with the squires for the first time.

"It's too bad we didn't bring lamps," said Esceriel. It was nearly dark inside the tent, and not far from it outside. Paks called light, and they did not flinch from it.

"Handy," commented Suriya. "You never have to eat in the dark, do you?" She dug into one of the packs and pulled out sausage and bread. "I don't suppose you can heat this as well, can you?"

"No," said Paks. "Unfortunately, this light won't even light a candle."

"Oh well. At least it's light." They ate by Paks's light, then rolled up to sleep.

The next morning they had to dig themselves out; it was still snowing, but not as hard. They stamped down a flat area around the horses, fed them, and Lieth climbed a drift to look around. She came down shaking her head.

"It's deep; I can't see the trail at all. And it's still coming down as if it meant to go on all day. We can try to get out, but—"

Paks shook her head. "No. We'll stay here. It'll be hard enough on the horses when we go; they don't need the bad weather as well. If you can't see the trail, you can't see the dropoffs either."

Lieth looked relieved. "I know you're in a hurry."

"Yes, but to find something. Not to fall into a hole in the snow." Garris laughed, and Paks grinned at him. "Gird's grace, companions, paladins are supposed to have sense as well as courage."

Suriya shook her head. "That's not what I've heard."

"You!" said Garris affectionately. "You're hardly old enough to have heard any tales at all. Why, you haven't even heard all of mine."

Suriya groaned, and the others laughed.

"I certainly haven't heard your tales, Garris," said Paks, still laughing. "We'll be here all day—when we've made a fire and have enough wood for awhile, I'll listen if no one else will." But it was some hours before they had time to talk. By then the snow had stopped, and the wind had died away, though the sky was still flat gray, like painted metal. They had trampled down a wide space before the tent, gathered wood, and started a large fire. The horses had been walked about, watered with snow melted over the fire, and fed again. A large pot of stew bubbled merrily; Garris had even set bread twists to bake in a covered kettle.

And then Esceriel, on watch, whistled a warning. Paks reached out in thought, and found nothing evil. The next moment, she heard the familiar trilling whistle of the rangers. Esceriel called out. A few minutes later, two half-elf rangers stepped down into their courtyard of trampled snow.

"We're glad to find you," said one, throwing back his hood. "We knew you were coming, and worried about the storm when you didn't show up at Aula's."

"We should have known that king's squires and a paladin would be safe," said the other. "But such storms can fool anyone."

"You'll share our meal?" asked Paks.

"Certainly." The first ranger turned to her. "You're Paksenarrion? Giron and Tamar send greetings; we met and passed two days ago. I'm Ansuli—no relation to the one you knew—and this is Derya."

"If you see them again," said Paks, "please tell them I am grateful."

"I will." He warmed his hands at the fire. "As late as it is, you might as well stay here tonight; we would be glad to guide you tomorrow, since the snow is so deep."

"Stew's ready," said Garris. They all ate heartily. After that, in the long dimming hours before they slept, they all told tales of other winter journeys. Paks had no tales she wanted to tell, so she listened. Esceriel told of a wolf-hunt, one year when the Honnorgat froze solid enough to ride over and they nearly found themselves in Pargun. Paks could not imagine anyone riding out on ice over cold black water. Ansuli countered with a tale of winter hunting in the mountains, against "things like orcs, only bigger" that came in tribes and used slings loaded with ice and rock. Lieth told of the time she had tried to go from her father's house to her uncle's in a snowstorm, when she'd been told to bide inside. She claimed her father warmed her so that she forgot all about the cold. Everyone laughed.

"Garris, I thought you had a story to tell," said Paks, turning to the older man.

"A story! Lady, I have stories enough to keep us up all night. But if you want a snow story—though why anyone would, in this cold—did your friend the Duke ever tell you about crossing Hakkenarsk Pass in the winter, with Aliam Halveric and me?"

"You?" Paks was startled. "I didn't know you knew Duke Phelan."

"Falk's blade, I do indeed. I mean, I did. We were squires together at the Halveric's. Until that year, anyway; my father decided it was too hazardous a way to make a man of me, that fighting in Aarenis with Aliam." He chuckled and poked the fire. "Or maybe it was Aliam finally losing patience with my clumsiness; I was a slow lad, in some ways."

"Well, what happened? I don't think you've told this one to me," said Esceriel.

"Or me," added Lieth.

"Maybe not." Garris nodded. "It's been a long time since I even thought of it—when I first came back I suppose I bored everyone in hearing for a couple of years and then forgot it, as boys do. But it was an adventure, all the same." He poked the fire again, and Paks saw determined patience on the other faces around the fire. Perhaps Garris was always this slow to get on with a tale.

"What happened was that Aliam was in a hurry to get home, one fall, and instead of going with his company through Valdaire, he decided to take the short way over the mountains." Garris paused; Lieth handed him a flask, and he took a drink. "Thanks. I was young, then—it was my first year to go into Aarenis with Aliam, though I'd been with him for nearly three. I suppose Kieri was a couple of years older—but then Kieri was always older. We could all tell he'd be Aliam's senior squire in a year or so, and we thought he might become a captain under him."

"Where was the Duke from?" asked Paks.

"Kieri? I don't know. I never asked. I'd never have asked him anything like that—not him. I was a little scared of him. Anyway, Aliam had taken us and four men and gone off north of Sorellin. There's a road partway, and then a sort of trail. And at the foot of the mountains, there's a village—or was. Someone told me it's gone now, and Sorellin has some kind of fort near there."

Paks realized with a shock that he must be talking about Dwarfwatch.

"It was coming on to dark," Garris went on, "and Aliam decided to stay in the village—they had an inn. Kieri and I were supposed to see to the horses while he ate. It was a mean-looking place; narrow stone buildings and a cold little stream between them. Ugly. Anyway, we had finished with the horses, and were bringing Aliam's things inside, when we saw through the window what they were doing. They had already killed two of the men, and knocked Aliam on the head. Kieri didn't hesitate. He sent me to saddle the horses again, and get them ready. Then he went after Aliam." Garris stopped again to drink.

"I don't know what happened inside. It seemed to take forever before Kieri came out with Aliam—I'd heard plenty of noise, too. Screams like I don't want to hear again. Aliam was dazed; Kieri helped me get him out, and sent me off leading an extra horse for him. He caught up to us some way up the trail, covered with blood. Horse blood, he said."

"Said?" asked Esceriel.

"You'll see. We took off uptrail as fast as the horses could go; that part of the trail is well traveled, and easy to follow. Aliam could hardly ride; we held him on his horse. When daylight came, I could see the bulge on his head with a crease in the middle—I would have sworn his skull was broken. Kieri coaxed him to eat and drink, and cleaned him up—I didn't know what to do but follow Kieri's instructions. Later that day, Aliam seemed to wake up—he talked sense to us, and told us which way to go when the trail forked. And I realized that Kieri was hurt, too. His saddle had fresh blood on it when he dismounted."

"How about you?" asked Lieth.

"A few bruises from someone who tried to stop us on the way out, nothing else. He had sent me off, you see. Anyway, I tried to help him tie it up; he'd taken a sword gash in the leg, and another in the ribs. That night a troop of dwarves come on us—we were near the top of the first pass, the higher one. Aliam was well enough to tell them what had befallen us; they were not pleased, and said they'd heard ill of that village. Aliam offered that treasure of his which had been left there if the dwarves would avenge his men and bury them; they agreed."

"So then what?" asked Lieth.

"Then it got colder. I swear to you, I have never been so cold in my life—and never hope to be, either. The next morning, Aliam didn't remember the dwarves. We got him on his horse again—he could sit a little better—and I had to help Kieri onto his. Then up, and up, and the snow began. The horses slipped and skidded. We got off and led them; we had to go one by one, and we were afraid Aliam would slip and fall. But he didn't. That night it was colder yet. We had nothing for a fire, and not much food left. The dwarves had said it would be a half day down, after the first pass, then a half day up, and then two or three days down to the nearest settlement. We stopped at the foot of the second pass. Aliam discovered that Kieri was wounded; he'd lost much blood, and had frostbite as well. By the time we got over the second pass, Aliam was better, but Kieri was fevered. Once we got below timberline, we had to stop. He couldn't travel. That's when he cried—it was the fever, of course. Aliam held him." Garris poked the fire again, sending up a fountain of sparks.

"Cried?" asked Ansuli. Garris looked up sharply.

"Oh. Something between him and Aliam, I daresay. I didn't understand, and Aliam didn't explain. But for awhile it worried me—I'd never thought of Aliam as a cruel man—"

"Aliam Halveric? Cruel?" The second ranger, Derya, sounded as shocked as Paks felt.

Garris shook his head. "I shouldn't have said that—he isn't, I know. But Kieri seemed so frightened. It's nothing. Fever—wounds—and anyway it happened long ago. We were only boys. Only I was the younger, you see—I'd always admired Kieri, from the first time I saw him at Aliam's. He was the best with sword or spear, the boldest of any of us. And to see him so frightened—well, it frightened me. And it means nothing. I daresay Lady Paksenarrion can tell us how brave he is."

Paks woke from a kind of reverie to find them all staring at her, waiting for an answer. "I never knew him to be anything but bold," she said finally. "I've seen him both in battles and in hand-to-hand fighting—he's the best in his own Company, and one of the best I've seen anywhere."

"You see?" said Garris. "The point is—I shouldn't have gotten off on that other, only it impressed me, being a boy back then—the point is that he got us all over the pass alive. And frankly, when I saw those villains bash Aliam in the head, and a foot of steel sticking out of Rollis's neck, I was sure we were all going to be killed. But he told me—just do what I say, and don't argue, and we'll see our lord alive out of this, gods willing, and so it came out."

By then it was dark, and they all retired to sleep. This time Paks did not argue about being left out of the watch rotation. She had plenty to think about without that.

Chapter Twenty

They arrived at Aliam Halveric's steading just after midday three days later. An escort had met them at the forest border, ten men-at-arms and a boy Paks thought had the family look. He introduced himself as Aliam, son of Caliam, son of Aliam; Paks thought back to Aarenis and realized that Caliam must have had children before that year. She was glad for him. The boy was in his teens, but already wearing mail and sword as if he knew how to use them. Paks was sure he did.

On the way in he said little, only pointing out the steading walls when they came in sight, the location of the mill, the drillfields and exercise lots for horses.

"There's a good ride south, up in the hills," he went on, eyeing the red horse with interest. His own mount Paks classified as good but aged. "If you stay that long—I mean—of course you're welcome to do as you please, but—"

Paks did not wait for his tongue to untangle. "If we are able to stay, perhaps you will show us that ride."

He nodded, not risking words again. Paks smiled to herself, but kept her face grave. As they neared the steading wall, she noticed the other houses scattered near it—only a few clustered together near the walls. She asked the boy about it. He explained that it served to prevent the spread of fire, and also made it easier for defending archers.

"On either side, I should think" said Paks. Near the steading, the forest was cleared back more than a bowshot.

"Yes. He said that's to give those inside a clear shot—the others have to expose themselves."

"Do you really expect trouble from the forest?"

"No." The boy shook his head. "Not for years. But my grandfather says to be ready for anything." He looked sideways at Paks. "Is it true my grandfather knew you before you became a paladin, Lady?"

Paks looked at him. "Yes. In fact, I had to yield my sword to him once." She saw by the boy's face that his grandfather had gained in his eyes.

"A paladin?" he breathed.

Paks laughed. I wasn't a paladin then. I was a common soldier, a private, in another mercenary company."

"Yes, but—" he looked confused. "I thought paladins were knights before they were paladins."

"Not all of them," said Paks. "I was a common soldier, and then a free sword, and then in the training company at Fin Panir—" she wished suddenly that she had not started this recitation. How could she tell a mere boy what had happened?

"But when my grandfather knew you—" He jumped into the pause. "You were just a common soldier then? Not a squire or knight?"

"No."

"Oh. What company?"

"Duke Phelan's, or Tsaia."

"Oh—I know him. Grandfather doesn't have that chance often, to capture one of Phelan's cohorts. And the last time he did, it all turned out bad—I don't suppose that was when you mean. It was only a few years ago." Now they were near the gates; Paks did not have to answer that. Ahead, in the opening, Aliam Halveric stood to welcome them, flanked by two taller men that Paks assumed were his sons. He was even balder than before, but he seemed as vigorous as when she'd seen him last.

"Well—Paksenarrion." He grinned up at her; Paks threw herself off the red horse and found herself wrapped in a bear hug. He let her go, and shook his head. "My pardon, Lady, if you mind it—but Kieri's told me so much of you,

I'd begun thinking of you as our family as well. It's good to see you looking so well."

She had never forgotten the warmth that seemed the essence of Aliam Halveric's character; here on a wintry day it blazed as bright. Now he grinned up at his grandson.

"Get off that horse, you young ruffian, and take our guests' horses. Will you sit there like the king come visiting?" The bantering tone took the sting out of his words. "Come on in, Paksenarrion—may I call you so? And you squires, of course—be welcome here. Paksenarrion, you've never met my Estil—she would have come out, but had something to settle in the Hall."

"My lord," said Paks, "I'd best take my horse to stable myself—he's not always easy to lead."

Aliam looked at the red horse with open admiration. "What a beauty. Paladin's mount, eh? I'm not surprised he won't lead to any hand. Well, come on, then. I'll show you. Cal, if you'll take the squires in and show them the rooms; Hali, see to the baggage." And he strode off, faster than he looked, leading Paks across a large outer court toward an arched opening to the right. She had just time to notice that everything was trim and workmanlike: the court swept bare of snow, the well-cover neatly in place, no loose gear or trash. The stable was equally well organized. Paks put the red horse into a box stall where water was waiting. As she had found usual, the horse showed no saddle marks. Aliam whistled softly through his teeth.

"Will he let grooms care for him? Or should I warn them off?"

Paks laid a hand on the warm red shoulder. "He hasn't caused any trouble yet—but if he doesn't want to be groomed, he'll push the brush away. Don't argue. And don't let anyone try to tie him."

"No. I'll tell them." Aliam went off to speak to the grooms, who were putting the squires' horses in nearby stalls. Paks looked down the wide aisle, well lit by windows set high in the inner walls. The red horse nudged her, and she poured the grain Aliam had given her into his box. Then she followed Aliam back across the courtyard into his Hall.

At the door, Estil met them. Paks saw a woman as tall as herself, dark hair streaked with silver, broad shouldered and lithe. She glanced at Aliam, as if for confirmation—he was grinning again, still a head shorter, his hands thrust into his belt.

"It surprises everyone," he said cheerfully. "Estil, this is Paksenarrion. She's a paladin now, you know."

"I know." Estil smiled, and gave Paks her hand. It was a strong hand, hard with work. "Come in to the fire; if you're not cold you should be. We have sib ready."

Paks saw Suriya and Garris already by the great fireplace on one side of the Hall. Garris was talking with one of Aliam's sons; a dozen other people scurried around, bringing food to the tables.

"It's a long way from our first meeting," said Aliam as they came to the fire. "By Falk, I remember you at Dwarfwatch, when you had to give up your sword. Thanks, Cal." He sipped at his mug of sib; Paks found another in her hand. Her eyes followed Cal Halveric as he moved away and joined Garris and the other Halveric son. He looked perfectly at ease, as if he had never been injured. Meanwhile, Aliam looked around at the others, gathering their attention. "She was in her first term of service then, and like all the young hotbloods. I was half afraid that when that sword came out, she'd use it—but Phelan's troops always had discipline. Then when the others dropped theirs, she stooped and laid hers down. Very carefully." He shook his head. "I've seen many things in my years of war, but that—that stuck with me. Damned cocky young idiot—and then I had to coax her into giving parole."

Paks felt herself blushing as she hadn't for some time. "My lord—"

"I'm not taking anything from you—just that you were already headed somewhere else than a sergeant's rank in that company. Or any other." He shook his head again and glanced sideways at her. "I'll wager it'd be a different matter if I tried to take your sword from you now."

In the little silence that followed, Paks pushed back her cloak, and shifted the hilt of Tammarrion's sword forward. Aliam's eyes followed that movement. Paks smiled. "My lord, I will hand you this sword if you can explain how you got it."

His face paled. "Gods above! That's—that's—Tammarrion's—"

"No," said Paks quietly. "This sword was given to her—but it was made for another, for the prince this realm lost many years ago, and the prince we go to seek."

Aliam sat abruptly, paler than before. "It can't be."

"It is. Old men at court recognized it; elves confirmed its forging."

"But it—but they—no one told me." His color had begun to come back; now he sounded annoyed. "I asked the elves, blast them, and they said nothing of a prince—"

"No. So they told us. They told you nothing, and told no one else, either. Until a few days ago, when the king lay dying."

"I don't—Paksenarrion, will you swear to me that this is truth?"

Paks stared at him, surprised. "My lord, I am a paladin; I cannot lie. I swear to you that what I saw is what I know, or have been told by those I speak of."

"I must believe you." For an instant, his head sank into his hands, then he looked around for Estil; their eyes met and conveyed something Paks could not read. He looked around at the others, whose interest was clear. "Enough for now. This is a grave word you have brought me; we will take close counsel, Lady Paksenarrion. But first you will eat, and we will speak of other things, less close than this, if you will."

Still a little confused, Paks nodded. "As you wish, my lord—but I may not delay long."

"No. I understand that. When we have eaten together, then—but come to the table now, and let us have this time together."

The meal was what she would have expected from the Halverics—generous, hearty, and far less formal than the

Hall implied. A score of soldiers ate at the lower tables—the current watch, Aliam explained. They looked like the Halveric troops Paks remembered: solid, disciplined, experienced fighters. From time to time a glance met hers, and shifted politely away. The king's squires has insisted, gently but firmly, on serving the high table—the younger lads, banished to the low, watched with relief and envy mixed. Paks, seated between Aliam and Estil, found the pair a fascinating combination. The tall woman kept up an effortless flow of conversation, while directing service and working her way through a plate piled with food.

"You were with the rangers, weren't you?" asked Estil. "Then you use a longbow. I keep telling Aliam what a marvelous weapon it is—"

"For women with long arms, yes," said Aliam a little sourly. "Just because I'm short, she—"

"Nonsense. You shoot well, love, and anyway—"

"I don't want a cohort of bowmen. No. I've said it before. Just because Kieri has one—"

"You see?" Estil smiled at Paks. "He almost started one, years ago, but when he found Kieri had one, he wouldn't."

"Had to let the lad do something I didn't do first." Aliam speared a slice of meat, and went on talking around it. "He'd have burst himself if I'd turned up with the kind of bowmen Estil would train."

"Aliam! I never said I'd train your bowmen." But her eyes were sparkling with delight. Paks eyed her broad shoulders and strong wrists: she *could* be a bowman. Certainly she was strong enough, and tall.

"And who else? Me? Gods forbid. I'm a swordsman who can shoot a bow when my sword breaks in half."

"I hadn't realized that the Duke—that Phelan—was with you so long," said Paks. "Garris was saying—"

Aliam broke into a laugh. "Oh, that brings back tales. Yes, indeed, Garris was a squire here—"

"And always glad to return, my lord," said Garris, passing by with a tankard of ale.

"Garris, you've been calling me Aliam to my face for

twenty years, ever since you were knighted—don't start lording me now."

"It's being here like this—"

"Then sit down. We've nearly more squires than eaters—and we're all nearly full anyway. Sit down, all of you—this is no royal banquet. You've all been riding in the cold. Eat." He waited until they had all found a seat, then turned back to Paks. "Garris, Lady, was the most hare-brained, witless, hopeless lad I've ever tried to turn into a warrior."

"My lord!"

"Until you call me Aliam I can't hear you, Garris. I nearly sent the boy home a dozen times, Paksenarrion. He was willing enough—generous—never a bit of meanness to him. But he couldn't keep his mind on anything—he'd fall over a stick in the courtyard, and then stumble on, not even picking it up." Aliam turned to Garris, who managed to look like a chidden boy despite his gray hair. "Not to say that you haven't turned out a fine man, either—I was young then myself, and had less skill at training boys than I thought. I was so damnably sure I knew what I was doing—of course I *had* to be sure. Any of them—boys or men—would have scented it if I hadn't, and the whole thing would have fallen apart." Aliam paused to pour himself ale, offered it to Paks, and then resumed.

"Anyway, there was Garris, amiable as a young pup and falling over his own feet, and there was Kieri, a few years older and made for war as a sword is." He ate silently for a few moments, then went on. "They made friends, of course. Actually it surprised me. Kieri made friends hardly, in those days; he kept to himself a good deal. Some of the lads I had were court-bred, and full of blood-pride until I sweated it out of them. But Garris followed him around, and followed him around, and in sheer self-defense Kieri began to teach him what I could not." He looked down the table. "I suppose you told her about Hakkenarsk Pass?"

"Yes, my—Aliam. What I could remember."

"Garris, I'd wager you remember every miserable step of that trail. I do, save where the knock on my head shook it loose. That's the trip that changed you, I believe, though you had grown so much that summer already—"

"I had?" Paks was sure Garris hadn't meant to say that aloud, or in such a tone.

"Indeed yes. Boys don't always know when they're changing, Garris, but I saw it. You surprised me all that summer—and so less in the crisis than you might have supposed." Paks noticed that Garris sat a bit straighter, with a curious expression. Aliam went on. "I had planned to ask your father if you could stay with me until you were ready for the knights of Falk; after Hakkenarsk, of course, your father insisted that you come away at once."

"Sir—I always thought you sent me away—I thought—"

"Good heavens, no! Where did you get that idea? Didn't he tell you?" Aliam shook his head. "I wish I'd known—no, he thought it was too risky, letting you fight in Aarenis any more. I'd have been glad to have you."

"He said that," Garris said. "But I didn't believe him . . . my brothers saw combat as squires, after all. I thought you had finally tired of me. . . ." He stopped short, embarrassed, and stuffed meat into his mouth.

"It startled me," said Paks into the silence that followed, "to hear Garris speak of Duke Phelan as your squire. I think I knew it—the Duke mentioned it this winter—but it didn't seem real to me. I never imagined him anywhere but in his own place or in Aarenis with the Company."

"It's always hard," said Aliam, "to realize that older people have had other lives before you met them. I remember an elf I knew once, who told me one rainy afternoon about seeing my grandmother picking flowers as a child. I was never able to relax with him after that." He sipped his ale. "Even though he said she was beautiful."

Paks opened her mouth, and shut it again. Twice she had tried to get Aliam talking about the young Phelan, as a safe topic they both knew, and twice he had evaded it neatly. She looked sideways at Estil, to find a worried look on the lady's face. Estil looked quickly along the table, and called to the kitchen for more sweet pies. Paks ate steadily.

* * *

As soon as the meal was over, Aliam and Estil led Paks to Aliam's study. She wondered if he would still hedge about, but as soon as the door was shut, and they were all seated around a table hastily cleared of map scrolls, he began.

"You are carrying the sword I gave Kieri to give Tammarrion at their wedding, the sword they found on her body after her death. And you tell me now that sword was forged for the prince that disappeared over forty years ago. And that the elves concealed this from me. Is there more?"

Paks told him the story she had pieced together, and ended with the elves' revelation that the prince had not only survived the attack, but was still alive.

"The true heir to Falkieri's throne, if he lives—and the elves say he's alive." Aliam looked down at his locked hands. "Did they say who he was, or where?"

"No, my lord."

"You, too, may call me Aliam. Kieri wrote me some of your story; I've heard more; you are not so young as your years."

"I would prefer—"

"Very well. Why didn't the elves tell me? Why didn't the elves tell anyone about the prince? Did they deign to say even that much?"

"Yes. They say that whatever damaged the prince made him unfit to rule."

"Umph. What do they mean by unfit?"

"They didn't say that."

"I suppose they wouldn't." Aliam got up and moved restlessly around the room. "And you are convinced this is the same sword?"

"My lord, your uncle and several other older men at court recognized it—could describe the runes on the blade without seeing them. Also the elf, Amrothlin, whose sister was the queen, the prince's mother—"

"I never told Jeris about finding the sword," mused Aliam. "I should have thought of that—but it never occurred to me that he might know anything. He's been at the court most of his life, and—"

"The elves said they—desired you not to speak to your uncle about it."

"Blast them," said Aliam, not sounding as angry as Paks would have thought. "They're always so clever. I've said often enough you can be too clever sometimes—clever enough to tie your own bootstrings together. And they are sure the prince lives?"

"So they say. But they will not say where or who. That is what I am to find out."

"You're sure that is your quest?" asked Estil. "How do you know?"

Paks shook her head. "My lady, the king, as he was dying, asked that I take the throne, because I had brought this sword, and was a paladin. Others agreed. But a paladin is not a ruler; I was not called to rule, but to save the realm by returning its rightful king. I am as sure of this as I am of the call I received in the first place, but I cannot tell you how."

Estil opened her mouth, but Aliam spoke first. "How do you hope to find him? And what do you think he will be like, after all these years?"

Paks recited the guesses they had come to in Chaya: age, hair color, eyes, and so on. That he had been a servant, and according to the elves had forgotten his past, even his name. "But so many men could fit that description," she said. "So I thought to trace this sword back, as I could. The elves reported that you had found it, and tried to return it to them."

"That's so," said Aliam, facing her again. "I found it near the bodies of three elves and many orcs. I sent word to the Ladysforest, by the rangers, and got back the message that I should give it to the one for whom it was made."

"And you had no idea who that was."

"No. All I knew of the sword was that it was elven."

"You hadn't seen it at court?"

"No." Aliam answered slowly. "I had not been at court yet, when the queen disappeared. "I was a page at my uncle's, along with the king's younger brothers—the old king's, that is: they were kings themselves later."

"Did you know of any such sword?" Aliam shook his head. "Then what did you think, when they told you that?"

Aliam frowned. "I thought it was typical elven arrogance, to be honest. They knew something I didn't, and were having a joke at my expense. I saw nothing on the scabbard, and then I saw the runes on the blade. It looked like a woman's blade, and from the runes I judged her name might have been elven. None of the runes fit Estil, or my daughters, and none of them wanted the sword, with that message hanging over it. I wouldn't sell it, of course, or send it out of my own Hall without telling the elves. I daresay they knew that. I thought I'd be left with it until some elven lady walked in to claim it. Then Kieri Phelan came to tell me of his wedding—and his wife's name was Tammarrion Mistiannyi. Two of the runes—light or fire, and mountains. I thought of that at once, and offered it to him as a wedding gift. Then I told the elves where I'd bestowed it, and they said it was well enough."

"Yes," said Paks, "but was it? Sir, this is what I've been thinking of. The elves think this sword, once held by its true master, will proclaim him and give him some powers he must have. They told you to give it to him—to the one it was made for. Doesn't that mean that you could have? That you knew the man who was actually the prince?"

She did not miss the sharp glance that sped between Aliam and Estil. "What would you have done, my lord, if you had known what sword it was? Would you have had any idea where to bestow it?"

"I—I am not sure." Aliam sat heavily across the table from her. "Paksenarrion, you have brought what you feel is great hope to our kingdom—the hope of finding our lost prince, our true king. But I believe you have brought great danger as well. What if the elves are right? What if this man—now near fifty years, as you said, and without practice at kingcraft—what if he is indeed unfit to rule?"

"My lord, only a year ago, no one would have thought

me fit to be a paladin. Not you—not Duke Phelan—not even myself. Least of all myself." For a moment she moved into those bitter memories, and returned with an effort. "Yet here I am, my lord, a true paladin, healed of all those injuries, and granted powers I had scarcely dreamed of." She called her light for an instant, and saw the last doubts vanish from Aliam's eyes. "The gods have given me this quest, to find your king. I do not think they would send me on a vain search. If he is unfit, the gods can cure him."

Aliam nodded slowly. "You may be right. I pray you are. Do you think the others—the Council and all—will agree to accept him? Assuming you do find him?"

"They have sworn to do so, my lord, and Amrothlin says the elves will at least consider it."

"Was the Knight-Commander of Falk there? What did he say?"

"He?" Paks considered a moment. She had not paid that much attention to him. "I think, my lord, that he was unhappy that the gods had not chosen a paladin of Falk for this quest."

Estil laughed. "That's probably true. But did he give any clues?"

"No—could he?" Neither of them answered, and Paks sighed. "I think, my lord and lady, that you know something you haven't told me yet."

"That's so." Aliam got up yet again. "Let me put it to you like this, Paksenarrion. If I once met someone who awoke in me a suspicion that he might be the missing prince—let's say I did—I had then no proof at all. Only that a boy was the right age, with the right color hair, and a face much the same shape as the old king's. Remember that I had never seen the prince myself; I don't even remember what his name was—"

"Falkieri Amrothlin Artfielan . . ." said Paks, watching him closely.

Aliam's hand dropped to his side. "Whatever," he said and waited a moment. "No evidence," he went on. "None from the boy—who remembered nothing to any purpose—

none otherwise. The princess was alive and well then, but an orphan. I could not see—I thought—" He stopped, breathing hard. Paks waited. "Gods above, Paksenarrion, I did what I thought wise at the time—what else can a man do? He might have been—might not—I couldn't tell. He didn't know. I didn't tell him—how could I? I was not ready to back his claim against his sister: she was well known, secure, growing into rule, loved by her people, capable. . . . She was my princess—would be my queen. When I was granted this steading, I had sworn allegiance to her father. What evidence did I have? He might have been a royal bastard—or a noble's bastard—or nothing at all. On the chance, I did what I could for him, kept him in my service, arranged his training, but—"

At that moment the truth blazed in Paks's mind. "Phelan," she breathed. "You're talking about Kieri Phelan!" Everything came together—his age, his coloring, his—

"Yes," said Aliam heavily. "I am. Kieri Artfiel Phelan, so he said his name when he came. Gods! If I'd only paid attention to Jeris—if I'd even known the lost prince's name—but I was a boy! Just a boy!"

"But he doesn't look half-elven," said Paks. "The others I've met—"

"I know. He looks so much like his father—in fact, that's what I saw first. I thought he was someone's by-blow, possibly royal, certainly well bred, one way or another. Even when I thought of it, it seemed impossible, and that was part of it: he didn't look elevn, or show any such abilities. And I was too young to be sure—"

"I don't know if the name would have convinced us, either," said Estil. "Falki's the common nickname, and we knew Kieri as a name from Tsaia or Aarenis."

Aliam shook his head. "What a mess!" Then he looked at her sharply. "But he can't be king. Tir's bones, I'd give my right arm to make him one, but he can't—"

"Why not?"

"If only I'd known about the sword back then," Aliam went on heedlessly. "Then, with Tammarrion alive—maybe he could have come back. But—and wait a moment! He can't be the one—I gave him the sword. Nothing happened."

"Did he draw it, my lord?"

Aliam thought long and looked at Estil. "I don't remember—no, I don't think so. I drew it, to show him the runes. I don't—now I think of it, I don't believe he touched it at all. I wrapped it for him—"

"I remember," said Estil suddenly. "Tammarrion told me, when her first child was born. When he gave it to her, he vowed never to draw it—"

"That's right; you told me." Aliam touched her hair. "I remember thinking Kieri was as sentimental as I am. He wanted her to feel that he was taking nothing from her as a warrior, Paksenarrion, and so he vowed never to draw her sword—it was hers, and only hers. But he was so close—surely it would do something—"

Paks sat for a long silent time with both of them watching her. Finally she shook her head slightly. "Perhaps not. Amrothlin said that although the sword was made for him, and would recognize him in some way, it was meant to be sealed to him by elven ceremony. That's one of the reasons the prince was being taken to the Ladysforest. Perhaps until that ceremony, it would proclaim him if he drew it himself from the scabbard."

"And he was so close—" Estil's voice was awed. "So close all those years—it's hard to believe he never did—"

"Not with him," said Aliam. "His word's been good, always."

"My lord," said Paks, leaning forward in her chair, "You see that I must know everything you can tell me about him. I must know why you thought he was the prince—and what was against it—and why you think he is unfit to rule—" Estil stirred, but Paks went on. "I must know what you know of his past—all of it—no matter how terrible. If he is the rightful king—"

"It would all fit," said Aliam. "The sword—they were telling me to give it to him—if I could figure out the riddle. They thought it was well enough, as they said, when I gave it to Tammarrion—perhaps they were sure he'd draw it in time."

"Well, my lord?" Paks persisted.

"All right. All right." Aliam sighed heavily. "Estil? What do you have? I know you know things about him he never told me." Estil ran her hands through her hair, and began.

"He came to us, Paksenarrion, near forty years ago. I can look it up in the rolls, but Cal was a baby just starting to walk strongly. That would be—let me think—thirty-eight years last fall."

"One of the woodsmen brought him in," said Aliam. "Found him wandering in the forest. I was butchering that day. Anyway, he said he wanted to work, and it was snowing and all." Aliam rubbed his nose. "He was a skinny, dirty, redhaired rat, to look at. All bones and rags. Said he'd come ashore earlier that year on the coast, at Bannerlith—he couldn't say what ship—and had worked his way inland. But no one wanted him through the winter. That's common enough." Paks did not say that she knew it. She waited for him to go on, but he nodded to Estil.

"It wasn't long," said Estil, "before we had him into the Hall. What I noticed was his neathanded way at the table. Most boys that age—that size—they knock things over, trip on their own feet. He didn't. I thought he'd make a fine page—we were out of the way and young to get fosterlings."

"And he was scared—if we have to have it all out, Estil, you can't deny that. The first night at my table, the lad takes amiss something I said and shrinks back like he thought I'd beat him." Aliam gave her a challenging look. Estil colored. Then she met Paks's eyes.

"He did, Paksenarrion. I don't recall what Aliam said, but Kieri flinched from him. I knew that would make Aliam angry; he's never mistreated servants, and to have the boy act like that before strangers—"

"—from Aarenis," Aliam broke in. "Guildsmen—that turned into my first contract."

"Anyway, I took him out, and spoke to him. That's when

I found he'd been in a Hall before, somewhere else. He thought—" she looked at Aliam as if afraid to say it, but he nodded. "He thought," she went on with difficulty, "that Aliam had meant him to sleep with one of the guests. As a—a—"

"I understand," said Paks. Estil nodded.

"I don't know any polite word," she said quietly. "Anyway, I told him no, and that nothing like that happened here, or would happen to him with us, and he—he seemed to come alive inside. Then I saw the scars on his head—and later the others he carried—"

"I knew about that," said Aliam. "He told me much later—that time in Aarenis. Some of it, anyway."

"Well, he came to the house, then, as a page, and we thought he was about fourteen. Old enough to start learning weaponry. At first we thought it wouldn't work—"

"I thought he was a hopeless coward," said Aliam frankly. "Couldn't have been more wrong; he didn't understand at first that he was allowed to hit back. Once he realized, nothing could keep him from it. He had no fear at all, as long as he could fight back."

"And he took in knowledge as a plant drinks water," said Estil. "And grew—keeping that boy in clothes was a loom's work in itself. And loyal—he would do anything for Aliam or me. Mind the children, even, which the other squires hated. Cal loved him—they all did."

"Anything but learn to think. D'you remember, Estil, the trouble we had with that boy? Daring—by all the gods, he had no fear and dared anything, but he wanted to impress everyone. He never broke out in mischief, but he was so certain of himself, so sure he could come out ahead—"

"And the fights," put in Estil. She smiled at Paks. "He wasn't a quarrelsome boy, exactly, but then he wouldn't give in. He didn't bully the weaker boys—but until he made senior squire, he was always pushing the senior ones. Nip, nip, nip. Then they'd get angry and jump him, and he'd fight until he was out cold or on top."

"And then I'd have to settle it." Aliam shifted in his

chair. "He took to tactics at once—strategy took longer. It was not in his nature to take the long view. And he wanted power—ached for it. He would never try to take it from me, but gods help the weaker squire—or even cohort captain. That Hakkenarsk Pass thing was typical—he thought out a good plan quickly, carried it out brilliantly, didn't forget anything vital, and then nearly killed himself trying to stay in control when his wounds went bad. Or the time in Aarenis, the next year, when I let him take that patrol out. The sergeant was supposed to be in command. Ha. Next thing I know, Kieri lost half the patrol into captivity, then enlisted some unaligned peasants, rescued the men, and fought a small battle—and as the sergeant said, it was like trying to lead a galloping warhorse on a thread. It did what needed to be done, but the risk!"

Paks smiled. "But why, my lord, do you think he is unfit to rule? Look at him now—he has a domain in Tsaia. It's gone from an orc-ridden, outlaw, uncultivated slab of northern hills to a settled, secure, prosperous land under his wardship. Isn't that some sign of his ability?"

"Yes, but that's not all. You are not Lyonyan; you may not know what we need in a king—"

"Taig-sense?" asked Paks bluntly.

"Yes, partly that. As far as I know, Kieri has no taig-sense. At all. And that impatience, that quick anger. You know that—you were there in Aarenis. If Tammarrion had lived—he was very different after their marriage. I wish you had known him then; she was well named, for she gave him light without changing what he was. But she died, and he turned darker than before. He banished the Marshals—I know he wrote something about talking to them again, after you unmasked his steward, but—"

"They're back," said Paks.

"What?"

"My lord, I think you do not know all that happened this fall when I returned to the Duke. He invited the Marshals back himself; he and the Marshal-General of Gird conferred in his Hall, and they have no differences between them."

"Well." Aliam sat back, pursing his lips. "Well. I would never have thought that. I don't know if it's enough, but—"

"My lord, I would agree with you that the man we both knew and fought with in Aarenis that last year would not make a good king for Lyonya—or any land. But that was over two years ago. Last year I was a homeless vagrant, afraid of everything and everyone—a true coward, my lord, as you thought Phelan was. Now I have been changed; now I know he has been changed, for I saw the change myself. At the time, I had no idea what the change might mean to him or to others—but it may have made him able to be your king."

"And the taig-sense?"

"I don't know. Perhaps the sword can restore it. Perhaps the elves can. If his rashness, his anger, are what they feared, and these have diminished, then maybe they will help."

"Do they know what you know of the changes in him?"

"I don't know."

"Then they should. The question is how best to tell them." Aliam turned to Estil. "What do you think?"

"I don't know. I can't think of anything but Kieri—as we knew him—and the sword, so near, and—"

"How far is it to the elven kingdom, my lord?" asked Paks.

Aliam looked startled. "Far? I don't know; I've never been. You can't go there, unless they want you to come."

"I know, but I thought maybe the rangers could guide me—Amrothlin claimed the queen was his sister; his mother is in the Ladysforest. If I convinced her—"

"Convince an elf?" Aliam looked at her. "Well, you might at that. But Paksenarrion, think: the elves love children as dearly as we do, perhaps more. And yet they knew he lived, and did nothing—they had some reason for that, but I doubt they liked it. For all we know they've been arguing that one out for all the years since. It's not like elves to leave one of their blood in trouble."

"Perhaps they did help," said Estil suddenly. "Aliam,

remember when Kieri was young here—we had a group of elves come by almost every winter. Sometimes they'd stay for Midwinter Feast. Kieri seemed to like elves as well as any of the squires, and he has said since that elves have done him favors from time to time."

"Maybe. I still think, though, that if he's the prince, and half-elven, they will be sore in mind at not having done him much more than occasional favors. Falk's oath, Estil, the elves of all races honor high birth—"

"When it's not been corrupted. Remember the bits of elven lore we know—about the kuaknom, and such."

"That's not the same thing at all." Aliam's face went red. "Kieri may have a hasty temper, but he's nothing like that. I can't believe that they let a prince of their blood—"

"Could they have done better than you, my lord?" asked Paks. "If they didn't want to interfere directly, they knew that you would take good care of him. By all accounts, you took a frightened helpless boy and made a strong man of him."

"I still—" began Aliam. He was interrupted by a knock on the door. "What is it?" he asked sharply.

Chapter Twenty-one

Cal Halveric looked in; Paks cold see that he was trying to control his excitement.

"Pardon, sir, but elves have come—"

"Elves?"

"Yes—I know you didn't want to be interrupted, but—"

Aliam nodded. "At once. Paksenarrion, will you come with me? And Estil, of course."

"Certainly, my lord." Paks and Estil followed Aliam down to the Hall, where a group of elves waited.

Paks recognized none of them. They were all wearing mail and furred cloaks, their faces partly obscured by the hoods.

"I am Aliam Halveric," said Aliam, going forward to meet them. "Be welcome in this Hall."

"My lord Halveric," said one of them, "you may not wish to welcome us; will you hear our errand first?"

Aliam froze where he was. Paks saw a band of color flush his neck. "Indeed, elves have always been welcome here, and all my guests are free to speak their minds."

"Your courtesy becomes you, my lord Halveric. But Amrothlin sent word to the Ladysforest that Paksenarrion of Three Firs, a Girdish paladin, had sworn to seek the lost prince. He feared, he said, that the two of you together might discover the prince's name and place. It is this we come to halt."

Paks stepped forward, sensing anger and unease in the

elf, but not evil. "Amrothlin did not interfere in the search," she said. "Why should you?"

The elf's eyes blazed at her. "You are that paladin, are you not?"

"I am."

"I have heard of you." That carried all the scorn an elf could put into Common, a cold serving of contempt. "I would not expect *you* to understand; you have no sinyin blood at all. But many of us have long regretted the alliance of men and sinyin in this realm. It was bad enough that our beloved sister wed that mortal king, and died by mortal hands. To lose her children to men's greed—one for money, and one for power—was far worse. And no human peasant girl, no sheepfarmer's child, is going to set a taig-crippled draudigs on the throne. Is that clear? I have come for that sword, paladin, which is none of yours."

Paks saw from the corner of her vision the king's squires group themselves near her, hands on swords. It seemed colder in the room, and every detail glittered. The elf went on.

"It is neither yours nor any human's. It was made for one of ours, and carried by one of ours, and to us it will return. Return it!" He held out his hand, commanding.

"No," said Paks quietly. "I will not."

"You would force me to fight in the Halveric's Hall?" The elf threw back his cloak, his own hand now on the hilt of his sword. Paks kept her hands in her belt.

"No, I do not force you to fight. If you fight, it will be on your own conscience." The elf started to speak, but Paks went on. "I will not return the sword to you; it is not yours. The sword belongs to the one for whom it was made—the lost prince, the true king, the one who shall rule in Lyonya, by the will of the High Lord."

"He is gone," said the elf. "He is no more."

"Amrothlin said he lived."

"Amrothlin lied! The body lives, that is all. The prince, the true spirit—that died in him." Now the voice was as pleading as angry. "We cannot accept that the throne be held by a hollow man—one empty of himself—"

"He is not," said Paks. She caught the slight movement as all the elves reacted to that.

"You *know* who it is?" More than the elves hung on her answer.

"Yes." Paks looked around the room, seeing humans as well as elves taut with suspense. "I know—and I know that he is not hollow, as you would say."

"But in Aarenis—" began the spokesman.

Paks held up her hand. "Sir elf, not all here know the name; I would not choose to publish it abroad at this moment—would you?"

"By the Singer, I hope it is never known!" The elf turned to his companions and spoke rapidly in elven; Paks could not follow his words. Then he swung around again. "You meddle in things you do not understand, paladin. It must not be."

"Sir elf, you also meddle in what you do not understand. Would you question the High Lord's judgment?"

"I question any human's ability to discern that judgment. As for you, I have heard of *you*, paladin. You were nothing but a common soldier, a mercenary, a hired killer, and then even lower—"

Esceriel stepped forward, his sword rasping as he drew it; Paks put out her arm and held him back. "No—put it by, Esceriel. I truly believe it is as I said—this elf meddles in what he does not understand. It is no insult to me, to speak truth, and I think his errors more ignorance than malice."

"By Falk!" Aliam burst out. "You cannot speak like that to a paladin in my Hall, elf, whoever you are. She was never a *common* soldier—"

"Peace, my lord. At one time I thought I was, and it satisfied me. Sir elf, my past is past; it may seem strange to you, for whom it is so brief, but to me a year ago is far away. Whatever I was then, I am now a paladin, chosen by my gods for this quest. If you dispute the truth of that, then I must make what proofs I can—but preferably outside. Even as a common soldier I disliked common brawls."

That got a laugh from the men-at-arms still in the Hall;

Paks saw Estil's mouth twitch, and one of the elves, in the rear of the party, grinned openly. The spokesman frowned, then shook his head. "If you will not yield the sword willingly—"

"I will not."

"Then I must try to convince you. I thought paladins were sworn to good—"

"I am sworn to the gods who chose me; as you have doubts that any human can discern the High Lord's will, I have doubts that anyone can know good without guidance."

He thought about that a moment, staring past her. "But you are a Gird's paladin?"

"I am a Girdsman, and a paladin, and Gird was part of my choosing. But the High Lord, the Windsteed, and Alyanya were present."

"Present!" The elf gaped. "You have seen—?"

Paks bowed. For a long moment no one moved or spoke; Paks could hear faint noises from the kitchens, and the hollow sound of hooves on the courtyard paving.

"Well." The elf looked at his companions for a moment and back at her. "If that is true—or you believe that to be true—then I must inform my Lady."

"The—?" Aliam began.

"The Lady of the Ladysforest." He eyed Paks doubtfully. "I find it hard to believe—"

"So did I, at the time," said Paks. She smiled at him. "So did the Kuakgan of Brewersbridge, who was also there."

"A Kuakgan! A Gird's paladin with a Kuakgan?"

"Yes." Paks nearly burst into laughter at the look on his face. "I never claimed to be a *common* paladin," she said slyly. Everyone but the elf laughed then, and he finally smiled.

"I fear," he said in a different tone, "that you will be hard to convince. So Amrothlin said, and so said Ardhiel, but—no matter. Will you come to the Ladysforest, then? I will swear no harm, and will guide you."

Paks remembered her first enchantment by elves, when she might have come to the Halveric steading but for their interference, however well meant. She had heard of men being lost for years in the elvenhomes, spending lifetimes there while seeming to enjoy only a few days of ease and delight. She shook her head. "I fear the turmoil of this realm without a ruler, sir elf. I must not delay."

"But our Lady must speak to you—"

One of the other elves spoke softly in elven; the spokesman stopped and turned to him. Heads were shaken. Paks took this chance to give her squires a reassuring look; Esceriel was still scowling.

"It's all right," she said quietly. "I won't give up the sword, and I think he's decided not to fight."

"He'd better," said Aliam grimly. "Sheepfarmer's child, indeed!"

"Well, I am, my lord."

"But that's not what matters! It's—" But the elf had turned back to them, his face now clean of all expression.

"My lord Halveric, I wished to make this easier on you by withholding my name—permit me to explain that I am Serrothlin, cousin of Amrothlin whom your paladin met, and the Lady's nephew. My companion has made a suggestion, which might serve all our needs."

"Oh?" Aliam did not sound enthusiastic.

"I deem it necessary for our Lady to speak with you and with this paladin. The lost prince, such as he is, is her grandson. It is on her that his acts will reflect the most strongly. It was with her consent that her daughter married your human king. She must know for herself what you think mitigates his behavior."

"I see." Aliam stared full at the elf, unmoving. "And so you propose what?'

"If the Paladin Paksenarrion refuses to come to the Ladysforest, it might be possible for the Lady to come here—"

"But I thought she never left the elvenhome!" Estil broke in.

"She does not. But the elvenhome—" he hummed a little tune, that Paks thought she remembered hearing from Ardhiel. "The elvenhome borders are other, as you know. Mortal lands in Lyonya are but clearings, as it were, in the fabric of the elven forests. If you granted your permission, Lord Halveric, she might be persuaded to come—to bring the Ladysforest with her."

"She could do *that*?" Aliam stared.

"Indeed, yes." The elf smiled. "We have not told humans all our powers." He looked around the Hall. "But before you agree, my lord—if you agree—I must warn you. If you grant this permission, and if she comes, then for that space of time your steading will be part of the elvenhome. No human can enter or leave unguided, and none should wander about in it. For the ways of the elvenhome forests are as perilous as any grove of Kuakgan."

"Hmm." Aliam looked down, then turned to Paks. "What do you think? I can see that the Lady has a claim to know what's going on."

"I agree," said Paks. "My concern is time: I will not imperil the quest to enjoy the delights of elven enchantments."

Serrothlin smiled. "Lady, I understand your fears. Indeed this might happen, but not without our will. Would you accept my word that we will not let it happen here?"

"It happened to Ardhiel without his knowledge—can you prevent it?"

"That was different. Have you never been in a trance of prayer? Even an elf can be enchanted by the gods. If you had not thought of the danger, I might indeed have been tempted to leave you ignorant of it, and solve this problem my own way. But although I dislike humans—as you may have surmised—I will not stoop to dishonesty. I will give my word that you will come from meeting our Lady no later than the time of conference demands."

"Are there many," asked Paks, suddenly curious, "who regret the alliance?"

"That number is growing," said Serrothlin, "as it has for some hundred years, as you measure time. It seems clear to some of us that humans have not abided by their word; others excuse them as too short of life to remember. But I remember when elves were most welcome in every Hall, when all the forest was open to our hearts, and the heroes you call saints sat at our feet to learn wisdom. Now to be free in our forest we must draw in and in, leaving more of the realm to humans. And lately we have been unwelcome even at court, at the heart of the realm."

"And what does your Lady say?"

He frowned. "I do not speak for our Lady; no one does. You will hear for yourself."

"If Lord Halveric permits." Paks looked at Aliam. "It is up to you, my lord, whether you will risk your steading this way. I believe his words; but it is your land."

"Not all humans distrust elves, Serrothlin," said Aliam. "Not all humans deserve your distrust. I will tell my people to stay close. Will you ask the Lady if she pleases to come?"

Serrothlin bowed and withdrew. Two of the elves in his party stayed, coming forward to greet Aliam and Paks.

"My lord—lady—I am Esvinal, a friend of Ardhiel's," said one. "It is easier if one of us stays, to form the bridge by which our Lady will shift the borders."

"Do you also dislike humans?" asked Aliam.

"I like them less than Ardhiel does, and more than I did when we arrived, my lord," said the elf smoothly. Aliam snorted.

"I'd best tell my people," he said. "If you'll excuse me—" and he left, taking his soldiers and Cal with him. Estil sent the others to warn those living in the Hall to keep their places. The squires stayed by Paks. The elf met Paks's eyes.

"I would not have known you from Ardhiel's last description, Lady Paksenarrion. You are not what he remembers."

"I daresay not." Paks was surprised to find herself so calm about it. "Yet what he remembers is not the worst of it. Will you believe that if I can change so, the prince is not beyond hope?"

"That is a hard saying. I saw him once myself." The elf looked quickly at the squires nearby, and Estil. "I—"

"By your leave, I think we should not discuss his past

until the Lady comes," said Paks. "Will it be long? How far is it?"

Both elves laughed lightly. "Far? Far is a human word for distances humans travel. And long is a word for human time. No, Lady Paksenarrion, it will not be long, for it is not far as we elves can travel within our own lands."

"Yet your friend Ardhiel rode and walked the same miles we did," said Paks.

"Oh—to be courteous, when traveling with humans—I've no doubt he did so. And that was outside the elvenhome forests, where other travel is difficult and perilous."

"As hard for you as travel in the elvenhome forest would be for humans?" countered Paks.

"Perhaps," said one of them. "I had not thought of it that way."

Estil came back to them. "Will the Lady stay for a meal, sirs? And what would be appropriate?"

One shook his head; the other looked thoughtful. "I doubt she will stay longer than to listen to Paksenarrion, my lady. If the household can offer something to drink—"

"What season is it, in the Ladysforest?"

"Ah—you are aware, then. It was late summer when we left, but the stretching may thin it."

"I have a good wine for that," said Estil. Paks looked at her in surprise. She had had no idea that the seasons were any different in the elven lands. Estil grinned at Paks. "Some good comes at last, of the time I listened at my great-aunt's door when she spoke with an elven friend. I thought for years all I'd got from that was a whipping."

Estil was hardly out of the room on her way to the kitchen when Paks felt the change. It was as if the room filled suddenly with water, and yet she could breathe. Her blood tingled. The air smelled of late summer, with the first tang of fall apples still unripe. It wavered, then thickened; common objects on table and hearth took on the aspects of enchanted things of song. It would not have surprised her if the table had begun to dance, or the fire to speak.

Paks looked at the squires; their eyes were bright. Suriya leaned forward slightly, her lips parted as if she saw an old friend. The door to the courtyard flew open. Instead of the gray winter sky they had ridden under, a soft golden light lay over the court. Paks heard birds singing, and the dripping chimes of snowmelt running off the roof. The elves in the room seemed unchanged in any detail. Yet Paks thought they moved with even more grace, and when they spoke the music of their voices pierced her heart.

So beautiful was that music that for a moment she could not follow the meaning of the words, and stood bemused. They waited, then spoke again, and this time she realized what they wanted. The Lady of the Ladysforest waited beyond the gate, and called her out. Paks glanced again at the squires. Esceriel's eyes were almost frightened; she knew he feared that she would give up the quest, release the sword, under elven power. She shook her head silently, and went out into the light.

Patterns of power. Paks remembered what Macenion had said about the elves and patterns—their love of them, the beauty, the strength of binding that they worked into them. Now the strange gold light of a late-summer evening seemed to accentuate the patterns of Aliam's steading. Stonework glowed, the joints making intricate branches up every wall. The arches of the stable cloister seemed ready to speak; Paks thought if they did they would sound like deep-voiced horns. The bare sticks of the kitchen garden, with its lumpy green heads of winter-kale poking from the snow, had sprouted a film of new green, lacy and vulnerable. Even as Paks looked, tendrils of redroot worked up the nearby wall.

Yet the light was not all golden. Through the open gate came the silvery opalescent glow of elflight itself. And in that glow, silver in gold, was the Lady of the Ladysforest, in form so fair that Paks could never after bring that face to mind. She was tall, as all elves are, and graceful; she wore robes that shifted about her like mists around mountains. And she conveyed without gray hair or lined face or age greater than Paks could well imagine, and immense authority.

Aliam Halveric bowed, welcoming, and the Lady inclined her head. She came through the gate, looked around, and crossed glances with Paks. Behind her Serrothlin and Amrothlin, not looking at one another, moved to stand beside Aliam.

"Lord Halveric, we have known you from afar; it is our pleasure to know you in your own steading."

Aliam bowed again. "Lady, you are most welcome here, as your kin have been and will be."

"As for us, we shall hope that your friendship endures, Lord Halveric." She looked around. "You have not walled out the trees entirely," she said, noticing the fruit tress trained against one wall. Under her influence their winter buds had opened into leaves and snowy blossoms. "I will mend them," she said, "when we must leave; it would be ill grace to leave you with frost-killed bloom. May we greet your family?"

"Of course, Lady." Aliam called them forward: Estil, then his children in order, and theirs. The Lady smiled at all, but Paks saw true joy in her face when one of the grandchildren reached out to her unbidden.

"What, child? Would you come to me?" She held out her hand, and the baby, still unsteady, toddled forward and wrapped chubby fingers around it. "Can you say your name, littling?" She looked up at the mother, Hali's wife.

"He doesn't say anything yet, Lady; his name's Kieri, for the Duke, Lord Aliam's friend."

"A good name, a brave name; gods grant he grows into it. He's bold enough now." She laughed softly, for the baby had grabbed her robe, and was trying to stuff it into his mouth. "No, child, that's not food. Best go to your mother; she'll find something better for you." She picked the baby up and handed him over in one graceful move; the child's eyes followed her as his mother turned away.

Then she turned to Paks. "And you must be Paksenarrion, who found the scrolls that Luap wrote long ago, and freed the elfane taig."

"Yes, Lady."

Her glance swept the courtyard, and cleared it without a word. The others moved quickly into the buildings; the two elves reappeared with seats, and she waited until they were placed. Paks felt the immense determination behind her courtesy, the weight of years and authority. With a fluid gesture, she sent her son and nephew away, and seated herself. With no less grace, the Lady set about to make her position clear.

"My son and nephew," she began, "brought troubling word of you, Paksenarrion, and of your quest. I had hoped never to face this hour. My daughter was dearer to me than you know, mortals with many children; when she died, and her son disappeared, my grief matched my love. Once that grieving eased, I laid their memories to rest, and hoped to find solace in her daughter. When first I heard of the boy again, it was that he had borne such injury as left him with no knowledge of himself, and none of his elven heritage. A lesser grief than his death, you might say, but not for me, nor for any who loved him. Patterns end; patterns mangled are constant pain. By the time we found him again, he was here, alive—" she glanced around the courtyard. "In this safe haven. If he could mend, it would be with such love as you gave. So I was told." Paks noticed that she neither gave Kieri Phelan's name, nor asked if they knew it.

"But why didn't you—?" began Estil. Aliam squeezed her hand. The Lady frowned slightly.

"The elf who brought word, Lady Estil, had it from a ranger first. Then he came himself: Haleron, a distant kinsman, much given to travel in mortal lands. The boy was badly damaged, he told me, in body and mind both. He found no trace of memory that he could use, only the physical signs that we elves read more easily than you. To be sure, he would have had to invade the boy's mind—a damaged mind—and risk more damage to it. As well as endure the pain of it himself." She turned away; Paks saw her throat move as if she swallowed.

"Then it was you, who sent the elves all those times," said Aliam. "And we thought they liked us."

The Lady met his gaze directly. "Lord Halveric, they—we—did. We do. You cared for a lost child, a hurt child, and one of our blood—healed him as well as you could. We are forever in your debt; do you think I would shift the borders of the Ladysforest to visit someone for whom I had no regard?"

Aliam shook his head, speechless.

"You ask, and rightly so, why we told you nothing and did nothing. First, for the boy himself. With such damage as Haleron believed he had suffered, we were as likely to harm as help, if we tried to stir his mind. I hear that Paksenarrion can attest to the truth of that—" She looked at Paks, who nodded. "And we judged it would not help him to know what he had lost if we could not restore it. We waited, watching him for some sign that he was healing in more than the body. If his memory returned, if any of his elven abilities came forth—"

"Could they, without your guidance?" asked Paks.

"Yes. Lord Halveric knew his sister, who without our aid came to her full powers. She was our second reason for saying nothing. You will remember: the year he came to you was the year his father died, of grief, we were told, for his dead wife and lost son. Already she had been brought up to bear the rule. Unless the prince showed that he was returned to himself, we would be unfair to her, and unfair as well to the realm, to champion a crippled prince over a princess of great ability. You thought that yourself, Lord Halveric, did you not? When you first suspected who he might be?"

"Yes." Aliam looked down at his clasped hands. "I had no proof—and she was just coming to coronation that next year— But how did you know what I thought? I never told—"

"You told the Knight-Commander of Falk. He is part-elven, one of my great-great grandsons."

"Oh." Aliam looked stunned.

"And of course he told me what he knew—which wasn't

much. I wish you would tell me now why you thought Kieri Phelan was the prince."

"He told me, finally, when he was my senior squire in Aarenis. I—don't want to go into all that happened, but he told me what little he remembered. Seeing him like that, looking older as men in pain often do, he had a look of the king . . . and his few memories made sense of it."

"What did he remember? Haleron said there was nothing in his memories but pain and despair."

"Well—" Aliam ran his hands over his bald head. "I'm not sure now I recall all he said. Little things, as a very small child might see them. A bowl he ate from, tall windows, a garden with roses and a puppy. A man who picked him up—I think that may have been the king, Lady; he remembered the green and gold colors, and a fair beard. He remembered riding with his mother, he said, and traveling in the woods—that's what caught me, you see—and being attacked."

"That's more than I thought he had," said the Lady quietly. She smoothed her robe with one graceful hand. "Haleron caught none of that."

"The older lords at court remember the puppy," said Paks.

"Yes, it knocked him down, or some such. He remembered that, and being lectured for hitting it." Aliam cocked his head at the Lady. "Forgive me, but one thing still confuses me. If he is the prince, and half-elven, why doesn't he look like it? All the half-elves I've seen show their blood—it's one thing that made me think he couldn't be the prince after all."

"A good question. Even then, there were humans who feared such strong elven influence, and so my daughter thought it would be easier for her children, if they looked more human. This is a choice we have, when we bear children to humans—how much the sinyin blood shows. As well, part of what you see in us is the practice of our abilities, as a swordsman's exercise with a sword shapes his arm and shoulder. Had the prince grown up with that training, he would show some of it—but he would still look more human than elven, as his mother chose." Aliam nodded, looking thoughtful.

The Lady frowned again, and leaned toward Aliam. "Lord Halveric, is it true that you did not know anything of the sword you found?"

"The sword? You mean, where it was from? No—nothing—that's what I wrote."

"Yes, but—" She rolled her robe in her fingers. "It's so hard with humans—you surprise us sometimes, with your gallantry and wit, and yet it seems you *know* nothing. That sword was famous at court; everyone knew it—"

"But I wasn't at court then!" Aliam's eyes snapped. "I was a boy—a page—at my uncle's. I never saw it!"

She shook her head. "I thought you were being courteous—offering to let us decide whether to try the sword or not."

"You were *what*?!"

"I truly did not know that you knew nothing. Amrothlin suggested you might not know, but it seemed impossible you could not. And when you said you were giving it as a wedding present—"

"To his *wife*," said Aliam.

"I thought that was your way of letting the gods decide."

Aliam stared at her a long moment. "Would you have told me," he said, "if you'd known I didn't know?"

"I—don't know. Possibly. At the time, as you said, he seemed as fit to rule as the new king, who had no taig sense and no way to beget any."

"But then when nothing happened, why didn't you—?"

She sighed, and moved her hands slightly. "Lord Halveric, I thought you had left it to the gods, by gifting his wife. Someday he would draw the sword; someday it would act—or, if the gods willed otherwise, it would not. What was I to do? We do not meddle much in mortal affairs, but we were never far from him. We never saw or felt aught to show that he had come to know who he was, or had found any of his elven abilities." She shook her head until her hair shimmered around her. "We were wrong in that, Lord Halveric—I say it; I, the Lady at the heart of my Forest and home. Wrong to think you knew, when you said you did not, and wrong to think we knew, when we knew only from afar. But believe me if you can, my lord, we intended no wrong."

"I believe you," said Aliam heavily.

"But the wrong was done," said Estil suddenly, out of her silence. "We all did it, and for us—for me, at least—it came from taking the quiet way, the easy way. Forget, I thought. Forget, put it behind, look to the future—as if the future were not built, grain by grain, out of the past."

The Lady looked at her with dawning respect. "Indeed, Estil Halveric, you speak wisely there. We singers of the world, who shrink from disharmony, may choose silence instead of noise, and not always rightly."

"And now will you help us, Lady?" asked Paks.

"I would do much to serve this land, Paksenarrion, and much to serve both you and the Halverics—but I am not yet convinced that my grandson can take the throne in any way that will serve."

"Because he has not remembered who he is?"

"Because of that, and because he turned to darkness after his wife's death. Even in the Ladysforest, we heard of that, and of his campaigns in Aarenis. We want no civil wars here, Paksenarrion, no hiring of idle blades to fill out a troop and impose his will where he has no right."

"It may not have been so bad as you thought," said Aliam.

The Lady turned on him. "It was indeed as bad—and worse than I have said. And the only bad I know of you, Aliam Halveric, is that you stayed with him through that and supported him."

"You mean Siniava?"

"I mean after Siniava. Do you think we get no word at all?"

"Lady—I don't know if you can understand—" Aliam's hands knotted together.

"I understand evil well enough," she said crisply, "even in my own family. It stinks the same everywhere."

"I would plead, Lady, that things happened which rubbed

the same scars. When Siniava tortured his men and mine at Dwarfwatch—"

"Lord Halveric, there is always an excuse. I know that. Such a man does not do wrong for no reason. But there are always reasons. Are we to set him on a throne—in *this* kingdom, set between Tsaia and Prealith and the Ladysforest—to have him find excuses to turn mercenaries free in the forest, as he turned Alured free? You will pardon my saying this: I know of your son Caliam's loss; I know how that angered you. Had it been only the torturing of Siniava—"

"But they didn't!" Paks burst out. "They didn't—"

"Because you withheld them, isn't that so?"

"Well—yes—but—"

"If you want to talk policy with elves, Paksenarrion, you must be ready to see all the truth and speak it." She turned back to Aliam. "Had it been only that, I would worry little. But you know—all of you here know—that it went farther than that. Much farther. We do not want—*I* do not want—the man who helped Alured reduce the coastal cities to show the same character in Lyonya. We would agree to no one's rule, who had done such things, elf or human. Elf least of all, for in this realm where so many fear us, even hate us, an elf's misrule could finally breach that old agreement between human and sinyin. Should we prove ourselves what so many already say we are? Arrogant, cold, uncaring, quick to anger? Should we risk confusion with the iynisin, to give space to his taste for cruelty?"

"Lady, no!" Again Paks broke in. "Please—let me tell you what I know of my own experience—"

The Lady looked at her without smiling. "Paksenarrion, I will listen. But I realize he is capable of love, and caring, for a few. You remind him of his wife, I daresay, or even his daughter; you have seen the private side of tenderness which all but the worst men have. As a king, it is the other side, the outer, that concerns us here."

Paks, immersed in the power that flowed from the Lady as steadily as water from a spring, inexhaustible, nonetheless found herself able to perceive more clearly what indeed the elven nature was, and what its limitations. Firstborn, eldest of the Elder Races, immortal, wise as the years bring wisdom, elves were due reverence for all this . . . and yet not gods or demigods, however powerful. Created a choir of lesser singers by the First Singer, they were so imbued with harmony that they endured conflict only in brief encounters, resolving such discords quickly, in victory or retreat. It was not weakness or cowardice that made them withdraw, again and again, when evil stalked their lands, but that they were made for another purpose. This was their gift, with living things or elements or pattern itself to repattern into beauty, endlessly and with delight. From this came their mastery of healing, of the growing of plants, the shaping of the taigin, for they alone, of all peoples of the world, could grasp the entire interwoven pattern of life the High Lord designed, and play with it, creating new designs without damage to the fabric. So also they enchanted mortal minds, embroidering on reality the delicate patterns of their imaginings.

Yet powerful as they were, as powerful as music that brings heart-piercing pain, tears, laughter, with its enchantments, they were as music, subordinate to their own creator. Humans need not, Paks saw, worship their immortality, their cool wisdom, their knowledge of the taig, their ability to repattern mortal perceptions. In brief mortal lives humans met challenges no elf could meet, learned strategies no elf could master, chose evil or good more direct and dangerous than elf could perceive. Humans were shaped for conflict, as elves for harmony; each needed the other's balance of wisdom, but must cleave to its own nature. It was easy for an immortal to counsel patience, withdrawal until a danger passed . . .

She took courage, therefore, and felt less the Lady's weight of age and experience. That experience was elven, and not all to her purpose. Kieri Phelan himself was but half-elven; his right to kingship came with his mortal blood. And as she found herself regarding the Lady with less awe, but no less respect, the Lady met her eyes with dawning amazement.

"I will grant your ideas," Paks began slowly. "Others have said I look much like Tammarrion. It may well be that he has turned a kinder face to me than to strangers. But I am not speaking—now—of his treatment of me." The Lady nodded, and Paks described the Duke's generosity to his own, from recruits to veterans, and to others who had served him, however briefly.

"That last year—" Paks took a breath before she said it. "He was wrong, Lady. I will say that, and Lord Halveric knows I bear the Duke no grudge. He was wrong to support Alured as long as he did; I think from what I saw that he was unhappy about it, but had given his word, not knowing what Alured would do. Any man is wrong to be unjust, whenever he is. But did you not say, a little bit ago, that you had been wrong? And the Halverics said they had been wrong?"

The Lady stiffened; Paks heard the Halverics gasp. Before the heavens fell, she rushed on.

"He was wrong then; I have been wrong, too. But he has asked the Marshals of Gird back, Lady, and apologized for sending them away. He said before the whole Company that he had erred, that he had been hasty in anger. Does that sound like an arrogant man, a man eager to judge harshly, delighting in cruelty?"

The Lady sat long without answering; twice Paks opened her mouth to speak, and shut it again, fearing she had already said too much. Finally she gave a little shake, like someone waking from a reverie, and turned to Paks with a smile.

"It speaks well of any man to gain the love and respect of a paladin. You are not lying about this, though you may have put the best face on it that you could. I did not know he had called in the Marshals. If he admitted his errors—then—I have less fear, though I am not confident. At least he might not be an evil king."

"Kieri's a knight of Falk, too," said Aliam. "At least, he was knighted, though he never took the vows and wears no ruby. Good things, too, or it'd have given him a fit of conscience when he became a Girdsman."

"He's not a Girdsman," said Paks.

"What? Of course he is—or was—and I suppose is again, if he's made his peace with them."

Paks shook her head. "No, my lord. He talked to the Marshal-General in my presence. He supported Tammarrion in the Fellowship, and encouraged it, but he never took the vows. He told the Marshal-General that he had always felt withheld from such vows."

The Lady sat forward, eyes bright. "He said what? Say exactly what you remember, Paksenarrion."

"He said that he had been drawn to both—to Falk and to Gird—but that he felt something about other vows awaiting him, and he could not swear with a free heart. And the Marshal-General told her Marshals that she was content—that she did not seek his vows."

"Ahh."

"But why does that matter?" Paks looked at her curiously.

"I am not sure. If it means what it could mean—" the Lady smiled again, and shook her head. "I speak in riddles, you think, as elves are wont to do. Indeed I do, for I have nothing but surmises. But if—and remember that I said *if*—what has withheld him from these vows is a memory of his true nature, even a slight memory, that can be, perhaps, restored."

"But I thought Lyonyan kings could be Falkians—can't they?"

"It has been so—and true of the last two kings, indeed. They were but human. A king of elven heritage, aware of the taig by that blood, would follow the High Lord, as you call him, directly." She sighed, then moved her shoulders. "You have told me much I did not know. It may be that he can become king. I accept, Paksenarrion, your description of your quest: to find the true king of Lyonya and restore him. I accept your decision to prove my grandson, whom you know as Duke Phelan, by the sword's test. But before I agree to his crowning, I wish to see him myself. If he can become what he was meant to become, my powers will aid him. If not—we shall hope for better things than I fear."

The Lady rose; Paks and the Halverics, trying to stand, found themselves unable to move. The Lady's voice was kindly, now, its silvery music warmer than before.

"It will make your task no easier, that all know the Ladysforest has moved to enclose your steading; as I shift the border in return, you will find that none of your people remember a summer's afternoon in winter. For you, I leave you such memories as you need—and from Paksenarrion I withhold no truth. You will not be troubled by any elves of my Household—"

Paks suddenly thought of the evil plots Achrya had woven for the Duke before now—had all this, for near fifty years, been one—? She wanted to ask the Lady, wanted to explain—but gentle laughter filled her mind.

"Be at ease, paladin; others, too, can see a web against the light."

A knock came on the door; Paks and the Halverics looked blankly at each other. Between them a bowl of apples and a tiny glass flask with a spray of apple blossoms filled Aliam's study with the mingled odors of spring and fall.

"What is it?" Aliam finally croaked.

Cal Halveric put his head in. "It's getting late, sir—did you wish to dine here? Shall I sit for you in Hall?" Paks looked at the small window; outside it was full dark.

Chapter Twenty-two

The three of them looked at each other, still dazed; Paks saw Caliam look at the apple blossoms with disbelief, and then at her. She inhaled that delicate odor, then shook her head. Aliam took a long breath, then thumped the arms of his chair with both hands.

"No—we'll be down. In a few minutes. Cal—do you—?" But he stopped himself, and turned to Estil. She smiled, and touched his hand, holding her other out to Paks.

"I thank you, my dear, for a very—interesting—discussion," she said. Paks could see in her eyes the memory of the Lady's visit. "I am sorry you must leave as soon as you say, but in the meantime, enjoy our hospitality."

"With all my heart," said Paks. Estil laughed, in her eyes, and they rose, less stiffly than Paks had expected.

The squires looked curiously at them as they entered the hall, where everyone waited at the tables. Now, at evening, more of the seats were filled. Cal and his brothers and their wives sat at the head table with their parents and Paks; the older children fitted in where they could, and the little ones tumbled around them. The hall rang with laughter and talk. Paks did not miss the many glances sent her way; she knew when one of the younger children sneaked behind her and boldly touched the hilt of the sword. Estil saw that, and snatched the girl back.

"You! Suli, you rascal—you do that with the wrong person someday, and you'll lose a hand, if not your life. You know better than to touch a warrior's weapon."

"It's pretty, grandmother—I just—"

"You just indeed! If you want to speak to a paladin, go ahead—there she is—speak—" And Suli, both frightened and thrilled, was thrust forward to face Paks, who had turned to watch this.

"I-I'm sorry," she quavered. Paks heard one of the boys giggle from a safe distance. Suli threw a sulky glance that way, and then stared at Paks.

"Your grandmother's right," Paks said, bending down to face the child. "I will not hurt you, but another might. And did you know that some weapons are magical? A sword might hurt you, if you were not its true master. You have a bold heart, and that is good—only learn from your grandmother to let a wise head guide it." The child blushed, and Paks turned to see the other children beyond her. "And for you others—it is easy to laugh when another is in trouble—but another's folly does not make you wise. In this family I would expect you to defend one another." To her surprise, a boy about Suli's size came forward at once.

"I only laughed because she is never afraid," he said stoutly. "If that was wrong, I'm sorry. But if you had tried to hurt her, I would have come."

Paks smiled at him. "I'm glad you would help. I said what I did because when I was helpless and in trouble, some laughed at me."

"You? I thought—can a paladin be helpless?"

"I was not born a paladin, lad. Even now, I expect there are things I cannot fight except by faith."

"I will not laugh again," said the boy seriously. "Suli—"

"It's all right." Suli put her arm around him. Paks realized suddenly that they were twins. Both of them grinned at her, and then Suli poked her brother in the ribs. They tumbled back, laughing and sparring.

"Ruffians," said Estil calmly. "Those two are wild as colts."

" 'Tis because you spoil them, Mother," said a woman down the table. "Every time I come, you—"

"Well, they're good-hearted ruffians," said Estil. "And

the only twins in the family. Gods grant we don't have more, the way they are, but still—"

"At home," their mother went on, looking down the table to Paks, "I keep them in more order—when they aren't running off in the woods. But since we spend half the year here, why—"

"Now that's unfair," the tall man beside her grinned. "Shall I tell them all what you said when we packed this time to come?" The woman started laughing, and he went on. "She was so glad we were coming, because then when the twins did something, she could blame you."

"Yes, but—"

"And, she said, they were better behaved when we left than when we came." He tapped his wife's nose. "So you see what you get?"

She shrugged, grinning, and made a face at Paks and Estil. Paks was amazed. She had never been in such a family—had not, she thought suddenly, been in any family since leaving home. There were at least a dozen children in the hall, and more had been carried off after falling asleep. Three or four generations lived here—happily, as it seemed. She looked at Estil—grandmother certainly, and maybe a great-grandmother—and still tall and broad-shouldered. A formidable bowman, her husband said. How had she done it? Paks could not imagine having all those children (for there sat Caliam, Haliam, and Suli—married to a Tsaian but home for a visit—and she had heard of others), managing such an estate, and still finding time to stay fit in weaponscraft. She shook her head; Estil noticed and turned to her.

"Is it too noisy for you, Paksenarrion? We're a noisy family; always have been. Aliam and I love talk and music as much as life itself."

"No, I just—I never—this is very different," said Paks lamely.

"It's just a family. Bigger than most, I suppose—and when you count in the others—" she looked around. The side tables were still full: Paks saw men and women in working garb.

"Does everyone eat here, my lady? Every meal?" She had thought that in rich houses, the master and mistress and family ate alone.

"Oh no. Some live in their own cottages; some prefer to eat somewhere else. But in winter, we keep a good fire here, and anyone is welcome. Evening meals in winter are usually a crowd. My sister from northern Lyonya says it's like a barracks, but we like it." Estil smiled. Paks heard the chime of harpstrings from somewhere, and looked around. Caliam's oldest son had brought a harp to the hall, and now tuned it. The tables began to fall silent. When he was ready, he brought the harp to Aliam, and bowed.

"You first, young man," said Aliam. "I'll let my fingers warm to your music first."

The boy began to play, a jigging dance tune that soon had hands slapping the tables. Someone knew the words, but had a flat voice; others took up the tune with better grace. After that, the boy played a slow song like summer afternoons before haying time; Paks felt her eyelids sag. Then a love song, which half the men sang along with. Then Cal took the harp.

"Get the lo-pipe," he told the boy. "Garris, do you still play?"

"I haven't blown a pipe for over a year," said Garris.

"Well, you need the practice."

Young Aliam carried in the long, polished tube of a lo-pipe, and set it before Garris. Cal plucked a note. Garris took a breath and blew; the sonorous mellow note Paks expected came out sour and cracked as a strangled goose. Everyone burst into a roar of laughter.

"Gods' teeth, Garris, I said play it, not break it."

"I told you—" He tried again, producing a deep, hollow sound that rattled dishes. "Now, if I can find another note—" It began well, a rich sound above the other, but it faded and split as he held it. He stopped and looked up, rubbing his lip. "I'll have a blister," he said. "But if you're willing to laugh over it, I'll try 'Cedars of the Valley.' "

"Hmmph. Child's play," said Cal, fingering the harp-strings. The silver dancing harp-notes began to work a pattern on the slower, lower lo-pipe. Garris had trouble; the notes broke again and again, or slid off-key, but Paks could hear what the music was meant to be. Then Hali took the lo-pipe, and Aliam the harp.

"For the paladin who has come on quest," said Aliam to the rest, and the silence was absolute. "You all know that much; I will tell you this much more—she is on quest to find Lyonya's true king, and when she leaves us will go with all our goodwill and hope. And so for her, and for the quest, Hali and I will give you this, which we do not sing here often. 'Falk and the Oath of Gold.' "

Paks had never heard it sung, though she knew the story of Falk, bound by oath and chains together, held captive many years then riding into the city of despair to free his kindred.

"Oath of blood is Liart's bane
Oath of death is for the slain
Oath of stone the rockfolk swear
Oath of iron is Tir's domain
Oath of silver liars dare
Oath of gold will yet remain . . ." The refrain first, set to a different tune, and sounding like part of something else. All of them sang it, but at the first verse, Aliam Halveric and his sons sang alone.

"Far the shadows fall,
far on the distant wall.
Under the weight of stone
the lost prince toils alone.
Far they have gone away;
bound by an oath to stay
the true prince toils alone . . ." As Aliam and his sons sang it, the music drummed in her veins, and it became the song of Kieri the lost prince. She smiled at him; his eyes acknowledged that meaning. Harp, pipe, and voices together wove the long spell, ending with

"His oath at last fulfilled
his captors' blood is spilled
but nothing can restore
the youth he had before.

Yet gold outlasts white bone,
blood, iron, silver, stone:
his honor is his own . . ." as they sang the final verses, and let the music die away.

"Now," he said. "I do not know how long Paksenarrion can stay—for us, as long as she will—but all of you remember that she is welcome to go or stay as she pleases, and take whatever she needs. If any of you can aid her, do it in my name. Is that clear?"

"Yes, my lord," came the response. Aliam nodded to them, then turned to Paks. "And now you will want to rest, you and your squires. Come and go as you will; I will always be glad to speak with you, but if you must go without my leave, know you have it."

"I thank you," said Paks, bowing. She followed him from the table and Hall. Estil and the squires came with them.

She woke from comfortable sleep—warm, clean, grateful for a good bed—to the awareness of danger. Starlight outlined the window; the room was dark but for the faint glow of a dying fire. She could hear the squires' breathing; all seemed asleep. Slowly, silently, Paks eased out of bed, taking up the sword which lay beneath her hand. She did not draw it; she did not need its warning. Out of the narrow window she could see nothing; its lower half was patterned in frost ferns. Still barefoot, she went to the door and opened it. A black passageway faced her; she could see nothing at all. But the sense of danger increased, pushing at her mind.

Sighing, she turned back to the room and woke her squires. As they rose, she dressed quickly, arming herself. Her sense of menace deepened. She opened the door again, and on an impulse, called her light.

The entire passage was filled with webbing, strand after strand looped in an intricate pattern that centered on the door of Paks's room. And a black presence hung in the web, scarcely an arm's length away.

"Well, are you less eager to meet me?" The voice was

strangely sweet. Paks could see no detail of the presence, could not tell shape or even size. She drew the sword. Its hilt comforted her hand.

"I am always eager to meet evil," said Paks, "with a blade."

"You will not be eager when you know what you have done," said the voice. "You vermin—I have warned you often enough, and yet you kill and kill. You have torn my webs, you have robbed me of my prey—"

Paks laughed; the shade seemed to contract and grow more solid. But it was large, larger than she had imagined it could be. "I have done no more than any good soldier," she said. "In keeping the barracks clean, the webs are swept away."

"Fool!" The word howled in Paks's ears, echoed in her head. She leaned against the force of it. "You think you can stand against me? Mistress of all webs, the spinner of wise plans—"

"Not I, but Gird and the High Lord."

"Who left you open to me: silly girl, I had you in Aarenis, and in Kolobia. You are tainted with my venom already; when I call, you will answer."

"No." Paks heard the squires behind her, and waved them back with her free hand. "By the power of the High Lord, and the grace of Gird, I am not your creature. And by that power I command you to leave this hall."

"If I leave, where do you think I will go, sheepfarmer's daughter? You are mortal still; you cannot be with all you love. You can save yourself: can you save them?" Paks saw her home in that instant: father, mother, brothers, sisters, and thrust the thought aside. If they were doomed, her failure here would not help them. But the sweet voice went on. "And there are others, wiser than you, who will hearken to counsels of caution . . . who will not welcome a warrior's bloody hands on the crown. Even your squires: dare you trust strangers at your back against the powers you know oppose you? I know their secrets; I can use—"

"You can use nothing here; you cannot even hide your intent." Paks drew that belief around her, palpable as armor, against the doubts and concerns the creature sent. "When you must appear openly, you are weakest," she went on, as much for the squires' benefit as anything. "As light shows traps, the truth will reveal your rumors and plots for what they are." She sensed a movement in the darkness, and braced herself.

The darkness thickened, leaped forward; Paks raised the elf-forged blade to meet it. She felt something tangle her arm, shake it, but with a screech the darkness passed. Only the webs remained, swinging to and fro. Paks looked at her arm; it bore no mark, and the sword still shone clean.

"Thanks and praise," she said quietly.

"What was that?" asked Lieth, who was nearest.

"I think it was a servant of Achrya," said Paks. She feared it had been Achrya herself. Its power echoed in her mind, a wailing certainty of doom, but she fought off that sending.

"Where did all that—those—is that web? Or what?" asked Esceriel.

"It's the web-stuff that Achrya's servants spin. Don't touch it; it burns." Paks touched the sword tip to one of the strands; it shriveled and parted. "I'll have to clean all this out."

She had cleared half the passage when Aliam opened his door suddenly. "What's going—" He stopped, staring at the webs.

"My lord, don't touch them; I'm clearing them. I'll tell you what happened when this is done."

"Will a torch help?" Aliam reached back into his room and brought one to the door.

Paks had forgotten about torches. "It will indeed," she said. "Just be sure not to let it touch you." With his help and Estil's, the passage was quickly cleared of web. But they found it was not the only one. All the passages were trapped with it, though not as heavily.

"How quickly can they spin this?" asked Aliam, as they finished. "That thing must have worked since we went to sleep!"

Paks shook her head. "I don't think so; I wakened knowing evil was near. I believe it was done very quickly indeed."

"And why didn't I waken? Or one of the guards—Falk guard us—the guards!" Aliam darted off to the main doors.

"Wait!" Paks yelled. "Don't call an alarm—if others are trapped, they'll blunder into the webs."

"But I must—"

"Garris, go with him; you know the steading. Go quietly, my lord, along the guard posts—be ready to destroy any web. My lady, take Esceriel, and go through the kitchens and storerooms— be particularly careful of places where a person might hide. I will pray, my lord, and see if any evil stays near us."

They moved off as Paks directed; she could feel no evil as strong as that which had left. But she and the others checked each separate room in the main part of the building, in case web had been left to trap sleepers. Aliam and Garris returned soon; the guards had been asleep but unharmed.

"They were spelled," said Paks, when Aliam would have scolded them. "As we were in Aarenis, when Siniava came out—remember? Thank the gods it was no worse than this. My lord, we bring peril on you—we must go."

"But into that?" Aliam stared. "What will you do, beyond the walls?"

"Go swiftly. It was to keep us here, to threaten you and tempt me to delay, for the care of you and yours, that such evil invaded. My lord, I will not tell you exactly where we go—although you surely know, in the main—and I suggest that you tell no one that you know so. Ward this place well; don't let the children wander—"

His face whitened at that. "Falk, no! Not another—"

"Watch them well. Keep together, keep faith. Ask the rangers—perhaps the elves will help you, since they value your aid in the past. I wish I could stay to guard you, but I think the danger will be less when I am gone."

He nodded; Estil, who had come down the stairs, longbow in hand, came up beside him.

"Paksenarrion, surely you can stay until dawn—"

"By nightfall, my lady, I would be far from here—very far."

"As you wish. Is there anything—? I have plenty of stores—"

"Thank you. Suriya, Garris—if you'll pack, I have a few words to say to the Halverics." Her squires moved away, toward the kitchens, where Paks heard the stirring of servants and cooks. The Halverics came near, and they stood together at one side of the Hall. "If you recall anything else—anything at all—about the Duke's past, please tell me now."

Aliam rubbed his head. "After this? Let me think—"

"Anything that would tell us where he was, those lost years?"

"No—not really. Why? You know where he is now."

Paks sighed. "I know. It's just—I'm not sure how to go from here. If I take the king's squires into Tsaia—"

Aliam relaxed. "Oh, that. I can help you there." He grinned at her expression. "Diplomacy . . . I've been marching foreign troops through Tsaia for years, haven't I? You're right, you can't take Lyonyan king's squires through Tsaia on a quest without causing lasting trouble. You'll have to go to Vérella first—"

"But the Duke—if someone realizes, and goes for him—"

"If the gods want Kieri on this throne, they'll watch out for him that much. He's in the midst of his own people, safer there than anywhere. After the trouble you've told us about, do you think they'll fail to watch out for him? And not because he's a prince, either." He shook his head. "You go to Vérella. Tell the Regency Council about your quest. You needn't name Kieri, not then. Tell them you must consult him about the sword: that's true, and logical since you found it in his Hall, and his wife used it."

Paks nodded slowly. This felt right, far better than trying to reach the Duke secretly.

"Paksenarrion," said Aliam, touching her arm. "If you

are killed, what then? Shall I try to tell Kieri, and hope that good comes?"

"My lord, if I am killed on this quest, then my advice is not worth much. I can tell you nothing you could not think of yourself—and you have the advantage of me in experience. Your land will go ill until an able ruler holds the throne; I believe the Duke is able. In the meantime—" Paks found herself reaching out to both of them; for a few moments they embraced. "Guard yourselves; try to hold the kingdom together until I return with him."

"You fear trouble here, as well?"

"My lord Halveric, you saw what tangled in your halls this night. If that one is spinning webs of distrust in the kingdom, how long will that patched-up Regency Council satisfy everyone? Too many people know something bad about the Duke; it will be easy to convince the fearful that he is grim and terrible. Were I you, I would be ready to aid Sier Halveric and the council at need."

"I will be ready," said Aliam.

Paks looked around and saw that her squires were ready to ride; Lieth and Esceriel had saddled the horses and had them by the door, while Garris and Suriya packed all their gear and food. She bowed; the Halverics bowed in response.

"My lord—my lady. Gird's grace be on this house, and the High Lord's power protect it." At those words, her light came, and blazed through the Hall as she and the squires walked out into a cold night. She did not damp it there, deeming it wise to maintain that protection.

So they rode off, in the turning hours of night. Paks, looking back for an instant at the gate, saw two small heads at one window, and wondered if they would remember, in older years, the night they saw a paladin ride away, light glittering on the snow.

Chapter Twenty-three

Dawn found them far north and west of Aliam Halveric's steading. Paks had chosen the direction, which took them across a low rolling ridge of forest toward the Tsaian border. As they rode, she tried to think which path north would bring them to Vérella with the least interference. She thought of going through Brewersbridge again—the Kuakgan might know more of the Duke than he'd said, might know if he could be healed. But Achrya knew she had been there before, knew where her friends were. She could not bring that danger to Brewersbridge. There would be blood in plenty before this was done; she would not start there. In first light, with the low sun throwing long blue shadows across the snow, she turned north.

"Lady?" Garris turned to her. "Are you sure? Where are we bound?"

She rode on some little time before answering. No one hurried her. Finally she halted; they formed a close group around her.

"You all saw what we faced last night," she began. They nodded. "It will have occurred to you that evil powers prefer that the true prince not be found. I had hoped we would be further with the quest before they noticed us; but paladins are not the spies of the gods, but their champions. I do not bring peace with me."

"I understand," said Suriya quickly, then blushed as the others looked at her. Paks smiled.

"Suriya, I believe you. I, too, before this—I would have

said the same. Now let me go on. I have not told you all I know—nor will I. Believe that it is not my lack of trust in you, but the command of the gods I serve, that prevents me."

"But—if you're hurt—" Garris looked worried.

"Garris, if need comes, I will tell you. But for now, if you will come with me, you will ride into uncertainty."

"We will come," said Esceriel, looking around at the others. All nodded. "We trust you."

"Trust the gods, rather," said Paks. "You follow Falk; I honor him." She looked at the lightening day. "Now," she said. "The Webspinner is a creature of darkness; she toils in secret to plot the downfall of good. I think we will not have much trouble with her as long as we keep close watch by night, and travel swiftly. She does not much like forests, especially not these, where the elves and rangers have sung the taig so often. It is another I worry about more. How many of you know of Liart, the Master of Torments?"

"I do," said Garris, shuddering. "In Aarenis—" Paks looked at each in turn.

"We were told, in the knight's training," said Lieth, "that he was evil, but not much more. No one follows him in Lyonya; I didn't pay much mind."

"I thought he came only where there was slavery," said Suriya.

"No," said Paks. "His followers may be anywhere. Liart sometimes allies with Achrya, in large plots. He's hastier. More active. I fear that we have attracted notice in that direction. Liart's followers practice torture as a ceremony; he delights in the fear of those victims. I say this not to frighten you, but to warn. If through some mischance we are separated and any of you is taken, your only shield is prayer. Do not despair; the High Lord will protect your soul, if only you can keep your mind on him."

Their faces were set; none of them asked how she knew. Paks looked at them for a moment. Then she stretched, feeling the return of strength with the morning sun.

"In the meantime," she said more cheerfully, "we have a

clear day and far to ride. Gods grant they miss us after all—it's likely enough. And together—well, they'd have a hard fight. Ride for an hour, companions—then it will be warm enough to stop for a meal." And she legged the red horse into a spurt of speed, the snow flying up in cakes and lumps from his feet. Behind her she heard the other horses whinny and run. In a few minutes they slowed again, but everyone was in a lighter mood. The horses jogged on, snorting. Paks started humming "Cedars of the Valley," and Suriya broke in, singing the words.

"Cedars of the valley, oh—
firtrees on the hill
where's the lad I used to love
and does he love me still—"

The others came in on the chorus: "Cedars of the valley, oh, cedars in the wind."

Paks sang the second verse. "Cedars of the valley, say, if I wander far, will I see my home again, or die in lands afar?" Again the chorus. Garris went next.

"Cedars of the valley, sing—tell us all a tale—"

"That's almost as bad as the lo-pipe, Garris," commented Esceriel, grinning.

"You made me lose my place," said Garris. He started again, where he'd left off, and finished the verse: "—and dressed in shining mail."

Paks listened with one ear to the singing, as the song wound on through its many verses (for it had been a marching song a long time), and with the other to whatever set the red horse's left ear twitching sideways. Finally she held up her hand, and Lieth stopped in the middle of a word. Nothing now but the crunching of snow, the jingle of harness and breathing of the animals. They halted. Paks could still hear nothing, but the red horse stared at the woods to their left as if he could do better. He blew, rattling his breath; Paks felt the tension beneath her. Esceriel raised his brows.

"I don't know," Paks answered the look. "But with such a horse, I don't ignore the warning, either." She drew the elf-blade; its blue flash was a warning in daylight. She heard the scrape of scabbards as the squires drew their own weapons. The red horse snorted. Paks looked around. They were in a wide glade with a frozen stream to their left, forest beyond it and on their right. They moved on again, more slowly, the pack horses on short reins.

If the red horse had not kept watching to the left, Paks might have decided that nothing menaced them, for they rode a good distance without any sign of trouble. Then the forest closed in on their right, and the streambed plunged into a rocky hollow. Paks slowed, looking for a safe way down through the drifted snow. Ahead and below seemed rougher country, with the tops of boulders showing above piles of snow. She peered into the forest on their right. It was thick here, heavy with undergrowth even in winter, and she could see little but a tangle of leafless stalks and stems. Still, it looked like the way down was gentler off to the right. She reined the red horse toward the forest edge.

"Paks!" Garris's shout brought her head around. Three huge white wolflike creatures hurtled across the frozen stream, roaring. They were pony-high at the shoulder, with pale green eyes. The pack horses plunged wildly, and Suriya fought to control them. Lieth charged between the creatures and Suriya, striking at one. Garris and Esceriel too were trying to attack, but the creatures were as fast as they were big.

The red horse wheeled; Paks leaned low from the saddle and plunged the elf-blade into one of them. Its howl turned to a scream; she had severed its spine. Another had hamstrung a pack horse and was fastened to its throat. The third raced in and out, slashing at the horses with its long teeth. Esceriel forced his horse close to the dying pack animal, and stabbed that one. The creature turned, with a terrifying howl, and flung itself upward against the sword. Lieth buried her sword in its back just as the third beast attacked her mount. Her horse bucked wildly, and Lieth flew off, landing in a shower of snow.

Paks legged the red horse into a standing leap; they came down beside Lieth, who was just scrambling up. She caught Paks's hand and swung up behind the saddle. Garris had finished the one that attacked Esceriel, but the third was racing after Lieth's horse. Lieth whistled, but her mount kept going.

"Get down, Lieth—get up with Suriya. I'll try to catch—" As she spoke, Paks sheathed the sword, and pulled her longbow from its case to string it.

"Not alone, Lady," said Garris. "That may be what they want."

"But we need the horse—" said Paks. She closed her legs; the red horse surged forward, back down their trail. Garris and Esceriel followed her. She could see the loose horse running flat-out beside the stream; the beast was hardly a length behind. Paks slid an arrow from its case, sparing a thought of thanks to the gods that she'd brought her bow along. Despite her weight, the red horse gained on the other, racing over the snow as if it were a smooth track. Paks drew and released. Her arrow sank into the beast's hindquarters; she saw it flinch and slow. As she set another arrow to the string, the red horse gained still more. Her next shot was easier; they were nearly abreast of it, and she placed her arrow in its ribs. The beast howled, slowed more, running partly sideways now. Blood spattered the snow. She heard Garris and Esceriel yelling, and looked back.

Cutting her off from them were four riders, all in gray armor, with the spiked helms she remembered from Aarenis. One of the riders faced her, a leashed beast at his side; the others attacked her squires. Paks sent a last arrow at the beast she'd been chasing, and tossed her bow aside into a tree. The elf-blade flashed as she drew it again; she leaned from her saddle to behead the wounded beast, then sent the red horse charging at the gray riders.

The one facing her sent a piercing cry across the distance. It meant nothing to Paks, but she saw her squires wince and stagger. That rider unleashed his beast, and the white wolflike thing flew toward her. But Paks had expected that; she had already gathered her horse, and when the wolf was a length away, they leaped high over it. By the time the beast reversed to follow them, Paks had attacked the first rider.

This close she could see that the gray armor was black, daubed with white paint or stain. He carried a jagged sword in one hand; Paks met that with the elf-blade, which rang to the blow but held. Her mount shifted suddenly; she glanced down just long enough to see that the other horse had hooked barbs on its harness. The rider struck again, laughing. Paks laughed too, a different sound, as she met it, then slipped her blade under his and thrust it into his side, where the armor jointed. Just then the red horse leaped, a sideways jump of some feet, and Paks nearly lost her grip on her sword. The white beast, which had leaped across its master's mount, fell to the snow, off-balance for an instant. In that moment the red horse jumped again, coming down with all four hooves on top of it, then jumped away. Broken, it screamed at them, helpless.

But Paks had no time to kill it. Her squires were driven back, into a knot around the dead pack horse. Lieth fought on foot; Suriya's horse was lame, hobbling on three legs. Esceriel and Garris tried to protect them, but one of the other riders carried a hooked lance, long enough to reach past their guard. She saw blood on all of them, and had no time to worry whether it was theirs or the horses'.

The rider she had wounded could still fight, but Paks went on to the others. She had to get that lance away. Before she could attack, two of them turned, leaving the lance-bearer to immobilize her squires. Both of them howled at her, screams of threat meant to terrify.

"Gird the Protector!" Paks yelled back. "The High Lord's power is with us!" She charged one of the two directly, knowing that opened her quarter to the other but trusting the red horse to jump when necessary. The one she charged fell back, luring her away from the squires. She knew better than that. She spun the red horse on his hocks, and caught the second a solid blow across the chest as he tried to attack from behind. His armor rang, and he rocked in the saddle. His horse rushed by.

Paks spun again, to meet the first rider blade to blade. Her horse reared, driving into the other horse's neck with both front hooves. Paks deflected a blow that would have severed tendons, and stabbed for the rider's neck. He flinched and parried wildly. Under the pointed chin of his face-guard was a gap above the body armor. As the horses squealed and fought, the weight of the red bearing the other down, Paks stabbed again for this gap. The rider tried to lean away, just as his horse staggered, backing away from the red but falling to one side. The rider lost his seat and fell half under his mount.

But as the red horse reared away, Paks felt a heavy blow on her back that nearly unseated her. Her left arm fell from the reins, useless, and she felt the pain tingle in her fingers. Just in time she got her sword in place, and met the first rider. He was a skillful swordsman, and strong; Paks felt every exchange all the way to her shoulder. From the corner of her eye, she saw the rider she had wounded ride up slowly; he sagged to one side, but still held his weapon.

"Ward of Falk!" she heard from one of the squires.

"Gird!" she called in reply. "Gird and Falk, the High Lord's champions!" Her blade rang on the other's, again and again. The red horse shifted; Paks thrust at the wounded rider, opening a gash on his leg. Now the other; she aimed a slash at his neck. He jerked aside, swinging for her face. Suddenly Esceriel was there, swinging hard at the rider's back. When he turned on Esceriel with that voice of fear, Paks thrust deep in his side. He slid from the saddle; his own horse trampled him. Paks slammed into the wounded rider again, blow after blow, until he, too, lay in the blood-stained snow.

Now the lance-bearer was alone. But he did not flee. He backed his horse a few steps, and swung down his lance, facing Esceriel.

"Get back," said Paks urgently. "Pray, and get back." He stared at her.

A bolt of light shot from the lance catching Esceriel full in the chest; he fell without a cry. Quick as a snake's tongue, the rider turned the lance on the others, standing in shocked stillness. Paks had already sent the red horse forward in great bounds, but she could not intercept the bolt that struck Garris from the saddle. The lance swung toward her; the rider mouthed the same dread words. Paks called out, and a light sprang from her sword to meet the other; the noise of that meeting shook her ears. Then she was close enough to strike directly.

At the first touch of his weapon on hers, Paks knew she faced one whose powers would test her limits. Back and forth they fought, their horses trampling the snow to a stained rag. Again and again Paks narrowly escaped a killing blow; the pole of the lance was spiked, and she could see that the spikes were poisoned. As the fight went on, she could feel through her legs that the red horse began to tire. Sweat broke out on his neck, and then foam rose in white curds. Yet he turned and twisted beneath her, saving her time after time. The sun rose out of their eyes, and glared from the snow. Then the red horse slipped, skidding down onto one hock. Before he could scramble up, the lance caught Paks between arm and body and flicked her out of the saddle like a bit of nutmeat from the shell. She landed rolling; somehow the barbed hooks had not caught in the mail, and she was free. The rider laughed, and charged. But she was up, with sword in hand, and the days were long past when a horse running at her could make her freeze. She dodged the point of the lance and jumped, grabbing the rider's arm with one of hers, while her sword arm swung.

Both of them fell from the running horse, Paks on top as she'd hoped, and the rider lost his grip of the lance in that fall. And before he could resist, she had cut his throat from ear to ear.

It was suddenly very quiet. Paks pushed herself up, feeling the blood chill and dry on her. His blood. Her blood. She shook her head, feeling cold and tired. A few lengths away, Lieth and Suriya held Garris in the snow. They were staring at her, white-faced. Esceriel lay where he'd fallen, to one side.

Paks took a long breath. "Thanks be to Gird and Falk, and the High Lord himself." She wiped the elf-blade on her cloak. Then she walked over to the squires. "Is Garris—?"

"He's alive," said Suriya. "He breathes—" She bowed her head, fighting back tears.

"You did well," said Paks gravely. "All of you. Are you wounded, Suriya?"

"No, Lady." Her voice was muffled. "And I—I didn't fight—as I should—"

Paks stripped off her bloody gloves and laid a hand on Suriya's shoulder. "Suriya, you did well. Believe me. These were such as most fighters never face. Lieth—how about you?"

The older woman nodded. "Not badly, Lady, but a few cuts from that lance, and from one of the swords."

"I must check Esceriel. Suriya, you come with me, while Lieth stays with Garris. Then I will do what I can for your wounds."

Esceriel lay on his back, arms wide, as he had fallen; he was cold to the touch, but Paks thought she could feel a breath when she bent near.

"Come—we'll carry him over there." She lifted his shoulders, and Suriya picked up his feet.

"Do you know what that was—that light?" asked Suriya.

"In a way. It's an attack these evil ones have, that strikes as lightning out of the sky. Sometimes it kills; it always stuns." Paks laid her hand on Esceriel's face, then Garris's. "They are both alive, but I cannot yet say whether they will live. We must get them into shelter, out of the cold; even if I can restore them, they will need rest and warmth." She looked up, startled to hear hoofbeats on the snow, and saw her red horse jogging slowly away. For a moment she was terrified—why would he leave?—but a reassuring nudge to her mind calmed her. She saw far along the frozen stream Lieth's horse standing uncertain and nervous; her own had gone to bring it in. She looked back at Suriya, whose face was less pinched, and told her to unpack the dead horse and ready the tent.

Paks turned to Lieth. "Lieth, your wounds are serious; those weapons are poisoned. I must try to heal you, before the others, so that you can help Suriya with the tent; we'll need shelter and food." Paks took Lieth's hands in hers and prayed. She could sense the poison in the wounds, slow-acting to sap her strength and cause pain, eventually killing days later. But the High Lord's power entered her, and spread from her to Lieth. When she let Lieth's hands fall, Lieth had regained her color. "How is it?" she asked.

"Well—very well, Lady. It—I've not felt like this since before the king's illness." Lieth got up slowly, and stretched. "Thank you—and the gods—"

Paks turned to Esceriel, who was in worse state than Garris. He had taken the full force of a deliberate attack. She laid her hands on either side of his face, trying to feel what damage had been done. His skin was stiff with cold; he made no response. Paks let herself sink deeper into awareness of him, calling again on the High Lord's power.

When she looked up again, Lieth and Suriya had set up the tent some little distance away. All the horses but her red one were tied to a picket line. A fire crackled in the afternoon light, and something savory bubbled in a pot over it. Beneath her hands, Esceriel's face held slightly more color; he lived, but did not waken. Garris was gone.

"We took him inside, and wrapped him up," said Lieth quickly, as Paks looked around. "Suriya's with him now."

Paks nodded. "Come help me with Esceriel." Together they carried him into the tent. Suriya looked up from her place beside Garris.

"Is he better?"

"A little. Not enough." Paks shivered, suddenly feeling the aftermath of the fight and her attempts to heal. Suriya unfastened her blood-drenched cloak, and wrapped a dry one around her shoulders.

"Sit, Lady. I'll bring you something hot." Paks sank down on a pile of bedding, glad enough to rest for a moment. Lieth smiled at her.

"Lady, even if Esceriel dies—even if I die—I am glad to have been here—to have been part of this."

"Why them?" asked Suriya, coming in with a mug of hot soup. Paks wrapped her hands around it and savored the heat. "Why did he strike at Esceriel and Garris? Why not me?"

"If you're asking why not you, Suriya," said Paks, "all I can say is that I asked the same question of my sergeant, my first year in Phelan's Company, and never did like the answer I got. But I think that Liart's priests value physical strength so much that they assume big men are a worse threat than women. He struck at Esceriel and Garris for that."

"And you," reminded Lieth.

"And me—but I have certain protections, as you saw. Unfortunately, I don't yet know all my abilities. Perhaps if I had, none of you would have been touched." Paks shook her head. "But we've no time to spare for such guilt. Tell me, how are the horses?"

One pack horse was dead, and the other injured. Two of the squires' horses were injured as well. They had caught two of the attackers' mounts, who seemed ordinary enough, and might do to replace their own. Paks took another long swallow of the soup, and felt its virtue warming her to the toes. Her injured shoulder was stiff, but she had recovered the use of her arm sometime in the fighting. Lieth was checking Garris and Esceriel; both were breathing, but unconscious. Paks and Suriya went to care for the horses.

When they were done, Paks looked back toward the site of the battle. "What did you do with the bodies and their gear?"

"Nothing—should we? We took the horses' tack off where we caught them, and left it."

"Good: you shouldn't handle anything of theirs."

"Do you think we'll have *more* trouble?" Suriya's face paled again. Paks smiled at her.

"More? Certainly we'll have more—but not, I hope, tonight. Suriya, think: already you've met and survived as dire a threat as most Marshals of Gird. And we live, and they are freezing out there—" She waved her arm. "By the grace of Gird, and Falk, and the High Lord, you and I have met trouble—and trouble found us too tough to swallow. Don't fear trouble—be ready for it."

"Yes, Lady." Suriya's eyes came alight again.

"And since we're traveling like this, can you relax enough to call me by my name? My fighting companions have called me Paks since I left home."

"Call you—Paks?" Suriya looked shocked, but pleased. Paks thumped her shoulder.

"Yes, call me Paks. It's the best way to get my attention—as you saw, when Esceriel yelled. When you say 'Lady,' I look around to see where she is." Paks looked over the trampled snow, shaking her head. "What a mess. I'll just make sure of them—"

"They're all dead—Lieth looked—"

"I'm sure she did. But they can fool you, beasts and men alike. That priest, for example—" Paks walked over to the lance-bearer, sprawled where she had left him. "The armor may be enchanted. If it is, we can't leave it here for someone to stumble over." She extended the sword; its glow intensified. "See that? Some peril remains. Ask Falk's aid, Suriya, and I will ask Gird's." Paks touched the dead man's armor with her sword. Through the smear of white and gray that had disguised it, black lines emerged, angular designs that conveyed terror and menace. Paks called her light; the designs seemed to burn, then die away to white ash. Then the armor and body fell in, collapsing to a shapeless heap.

"What happened?" Suriya's knuckles were white on her sword hilt.

"The gods helped us prevent trouble," said Paks soberly. "Let's see what else." All the helmets reacted to her sword's touch, as did two of the other corselets, but the men's bodies did not disappear. The wolflike beasts, dead, were simply dead beasts. They dragged them into a pile. Wood from the frozen stream bed, caught against the rocks of the falls, provided fuel for a pyre.

"Now what?" asked Suriya, when it was alight.

"Now I go find my bow, in case we need it, and then we

get cleaned up and see what we can do for Garris and Esceriel."

Paks turned and found that the red horse was already mincing toward her. "Give me a leg up, will you?" She waved as she rode off, enjoying Suriya's open mouth.

She found her bow easily, hanging from a branch, and retrieved her arrows from the body of the beast she'd killed. By the time she was back at their little camp, the sun was already low against the hills.

Despite her prayers, Esceriel died that night without opening his eyes or speaking. Garris, however, recovered enough to wake and look blankly at them before sleeping again. Paks turned away from them, too tired to weep.

"I'm sorry," she said, aware of Lieth and Suriya watching. "I was given no healing for him—but he died bravely."

Suriya nodded. Lieth unfolded a blanket across Esceriel's body, looking long at his face before covering it.

"He was always that way," she said. "He would always do things for others—" She turned her head aside, choking back tears.

Paks reached out and touched her shoulder. "Go on and cry for him, Lieth. The King spoke of him to me, his beloved son that he could not acknowledge, who never sought anything for himself, even a name. He has earned more tears than ours, and more reward than this."

Lieth turned back to her, eyes streaming. "You're tired—you need sleep. Yes—I'll watch. I'll take care. Sleep, Paks." And Paks fell asleep almost instantly, to the sound of the others mourning.

It was broad day when she woke, another clear morning, with frost furring the inside of the tent. There was Esceriel's body, covered with a blanket, and his sword laid across his chest. She could hear voices outside. When she turned her head, she saw Garris's eyes, still a little blank, watching her.

"Lady?" He spoke with difficulty, running his tongue over his lips. Paks remembered that feeling.

"Garris. You're doing well." Paks pushed herself up; she

was not as stiff as she'd expected, but she could feel the blows she'd taken. "I'll bring you something."

His head rolled from side to side. "I don't remember. Did I fall off my horse?"

"Among other things, yes."

"Hunh. At my age, to be thrown—"

"What do you remember, Garris?"

His brow furrowed. "We—were at Aliam Halveric's, weren't we? Then—we had to leave. In the night. Something—" He shook his head, and moved an arm. "I don't know. I can't remember beyond riding out in the torchlight."

Lieth looked into the tent. "Paks, are you—oh. Garris. Can I bring you something?"

"Anything hot and liquid for Garris. And me, too." Paks stumbled upright. "Gird's arm, I slept as heavy as a hill." She yawned, and pushed off the helmet she had not removed the night before. Her braid thumped her back as it fell.

Lieth came in with two mugs; Suriya followed with bowls. The food and sib smelled delicious. Garris reached for his mug, then looked around and saw the blanket-shrouded form across from him. The hot sib sloshed over his wrist.

"Falk's oath! Is that Esceriel?"

"Yes," said Paks. "It is. Garris, we had a fight yesterday—we were attacked on the trail. You and Lieth were wounded and Esceriel was killed—"

"But I don't—but what—" His hand shook; Paks took the mug from him and set it down

"Garris, you had a serious wound—that's why you don't remember."

"But I'm all right now—I don't feel any pain—"

"The gods sent healing for you, Garris. Not for Esceriel. I'm sorry." Paks watched the pain on his face. When it turned to anger, she spoke again. "I warned you this was dangerous. I told you that you didn't have to come. You chose that; Esceriel chose that. He chose more—he chose to come to me, when I needed him, and he killed one of them. Then he faced the same weapon that struck you down, and it killed him."

Garris nodded, his eyes filling with tears. "And you could do nothing?"

"No." Paks sighed. She felt slightly affronted; he expected too much of her—she had, after all, fought all of the enemy. She mastered that feeling, and went on. "I prayed for him, Garris, as for you. I was taught in Fin Panir that some brave deeds so delight the High Lord that he calls the warrior at once to his service—as a reward. So I think it was for Esceriel."

"I see." Garris pushed himself up on his elbows, rolled to one side, and took his mug of sib. After several swallows, he looked back at her.

"Will you tell us yet where we're going?"

Paks thought about it. She had not told them at Aliam's, where someone less wise than Aliam might overhear, and mention that name carelessly. And in the woods, that day, she had felt unsure, aware that the woods might hide enemies. But now, with those attackers dead, now surely she could tell them. She nodded. "I will tell you all, before we go on." She turned to see Lieth and Suriya both watching from the entrance. "Come in, both of you—you might as well hear it all at once." Suriya stayed where she could watch outside; Lieth squatted near Paks.

"We have a space of safety, I believe: those attackers are dead, and our enemies have nothing else close to us. So now I will tell you the prince's name, and where we must go. But that name must not be mentioned aloud—not even in the deep woods. Such evil as assailed us has the great forest taig under attack as well; it is broken into many taigin, and in places the fabric is threadbare; we cannot count on the forest to ward us. Enemies can get through—have gotten through—and the little creatures, if no other, may spy on us and pass along our words to each other. More than that, we shall not ride in forest forever; we must pass among the towns of men. There the many agents of evil will have their chance. I have some protection—nothing evil can change my mind or master my tongue—and you share that protection when you are with me—but you must not say the name aloud, or leave my protection once you know it. Do you understand?"

"I will stay with you," Lieth said quickly.

"And I," said Suriya. They both looked at Garris.

"Oh, I'll stay." He shook his head, then grinned at Paks. "Falk's arm, I might as well—how could I ride home alone and miss the rest of this tale. But I feel as I did the night Kieri started us over the Hakkenarsk Pass—it's a cold road ahead, and no sure fires, it seems to me."

"It is indeed," said Paks. "I am honored that you choose to come; alone I would not have much chance on this quest, and I think it worthy enough to cost all our lives if that becomes the choice." She took a deep breath, and glanced from one grave face to another. "Now . . ."

They started off again at an easy pace after noon, having built a mound of rocks over Esceriel's body. Paks had found a good way down to the lower ground, and none of the horses had trouble with the snow-covered rocks. Garris, though pale, insisted he could ride, and was able to saddle his own mount. Lieth and Suriya rode the grays, who were unharmed, and the injured animals carried their light packs.

Day after day they travelled the snowy woods, a journey that seemed to Paks later a strange interlude of peace, despite the dangers and discomforts of such travel in winter. Hour after hour they rode unspeaking, only the crunch of the horses' hooves in snow and the creak of leather breaking the forest silence. Behind and around them cold stillness lay untouched. The patterns of branches and twigs, the colors of snow and ice seemed to sink deep into her mind. The only warmth was the blazing fire that the squires kindled every night; the only warm colors were the things they carried. That small company, closer with each evening's campfire talk—it was a return to the close-knit companionship she had valued so much as a soldier. Yet not quite a return. For where once that campfire would have been all she knew of light and warmth, now she felt that magical flame within, a light still flickering across the landscapes of her mind, no matter how cold or dark the outer night, how uncertain her vision of what lay ahead. As the squires comforted each other, and looked to her for comfort and guidance, she found herself reaching within, more and more aware of that flame, and what it meant to her.

Chapter Twenty-four

Once they reached Harway, they travelled to Vérella with far less difficulty than Paks had feared—though with far more publicity than she'd hoped. Marshal Pelyan, whom she'd met on the way to Lyonya, had heard of the quest before their arrival. Travellers, he said, had brought word as soon as it came to Harway. And he himself had passed the word on through the granges. So their arrival in any town caused excitement but not curiosity. Paks enjoyed the crowds of children that followed them, the flurry when they entered an inn, but hoped the admiration was not premature. As well, she remembered the winter before, when she had stumbled into such towns as a hungry vagrant, whom the children tricked and harassed instead of cheering.

In each town, they spent the night in grange or field, for Paks wished the king's squires to have such protection at night. The Marshals each had a measure of news or advice; she listened to all. She did not tell them the prince's name, but she told what she could of the quest so far. The nearer she came to Vérella, the more recent the news became. In Westbells, just east of Vérella, Marshal Torin told her that the Duke had been summoned to the Council. She had not asked, but it seemed Phelan's call to court was of interest even to a neighboring town.

"What I heard," he said between bits of roast chicken, "was that after the Marshal-General went up there, and whatever passed between them, his friends on the Council thought he should come speak for himself. You know, I suppose, that there was a motion to censure him."

Paks nodded. She had heard about this from the Marshal-General.

"I never thought so bad of him myself," Marshal Torin went on, "for it seemed to me that if over half my yeomen were killed by treachery, I'd take risks enough to stop that. But they say by his charter he's bound to have a hundred fighting men on his lands, and the word was that this was not the first time he'd left the north unguarded." He ate steadily for a minute, then put down the bones and wiped his hands. "I can't believe that, or there'd have been more trouble. Kostvan, who holds south and east of him, has never complained. But then there was word about how he fought in Aarenis—even rumors from a Marshal down there, so I hear. And last year, instead of staying quiet at home, he went haring off to Fintha because of—" he stopped short and turned dark red. Paks smiled.

"Marshal, he went haring off to Fintha on account of me—and that may have been foolish, but showed a warm heart."

"Warm heart or not, it made some on the Council angry. They'd bid him stay on his lands, and—"

"But his men stayed," put in the yeoman-marshal, a young man who reminded Paks of Ambros in Brewersbridge. "His captains, and all the men—they could have handled any trouble—"

"I didn't say they were right, Keri. I said they were angry."

"Some of them would be angry no matter what he did." The young man's face had flushed. Paks wondered why he was defending Phelan.

"Court gossip, Keri. Nothing to do with us. You can clear now." The Marshal waited until Keri had left the room before saying more. Paks used the interval to ask her squires about their readiness to ride the next day—an unnecessary question, but they answered without surprise.

"You're going to the Council," said the Marshal, when

she had dismissed them to rest, and did not wait for her answer. "You'll find them in a flutter, I don't doubt," he said, shaking his head. "That's why I mentioned Phelan—you know him, and he's likely there, and that's why. He's got friends and enemies both on the Council, and until they've settled themselves about him, they're likely to be skittish with you. The thought that Lyonya had sent a paladin to search in Tsaia for an unknown prince—well, you can see how that will suit. Will they have to acknowledge someone as sovereign of a neighboring realm who has been thought base-born here? How if he's a slave, or a servant?"

"He's not," said Paks quietly.

"You know who it is?"

"Yes, but I am not at liberty to say, until I have spoken to him."

"I see. That makes sense." He chewed his lip a moment. "Someone highborn? How could that be, unless—no, I should not ask. You have your own guidance from Gird and the High Lord, and I pray their grace and strength for you. I doubt your task will be easy, even knowing for whom you go."

"Could you tell me," asked Paks, "which of the Council is the right person to approach?"

"Hmmph. Right for what, is the question. As you have dealt with me, so must I deal with you. I have no right to tell you all that the Marshals of Gird suspect about some families on the Council; we have not the proof, and we are bound not to illspeak without it. Yet I would not talk freely with anyone, and certainly not with the Verrakai family. Kostvan is utterly loyal, but has less power. Marrakai—Marrakai has the power, and I believe is loyal, but the Marrakaien have long had a name for secret treachery. Yet you know that the name is not the reality: the real traitor may not have the reputation. Clannaeth is flighty—they say it's his health, but I have a cousin down there who says it's his second wife. Destvaorn is bride-bound to the Marrakaien, but none the worse for that, if the Marrakaien be sound. Konhalt—there's another I'd go clear of; I know nothing against them, but that three times the neighboring grange has had to chase evil things from their hills. The rest are small, of little power compared to these, or closely related. I might speak to Kostvan first, or Destvaorn, and then to Marrakai. Phelan wields power, but not at the moment; your past connection would be suspect there."

Paks got from him the descriptions of these various lords, and committed them to memory. Then she chanced to mention the Verrakai captain she'd met north of the Honnorgat—a Girdsman, he'd said.

"Oh, that branch is sound," said the Marshal cheerfully. "I don't wonder you thought him well enough. That's the trouble with some families—and the Verrakaien aren't the only one—you can't tell by the name. Take the Marrakaien, now: true or treacherous, they're all of one brew, and that a heady one. There's naught to choose one from another, barring looks. But others—well, you have dreamers, drunks, daring men and dour men all in one heap, like mixed fruit."

"I'll keep that in mind," said Paks.

Their entry into Vérella was far different from the first time she'd seen the city. The guards at the first gate had heard of her quest; they saw her coming and held traffic (light enough at this season) to pass her through. She had long forgotten the way from the south gates to the court, but the guard sent an escort to guide her, an eager young soldier whose bright face reminded her of all the recruits she'd ever seen.

On horseback, she could see over the parapets of the bridge; the Honnorgat here had a skim of ice even in midstream. At the inner gate, on the north bank of the Honnorgat, a guard captain waited, mounted on a horse decked in the rose and silver of Tsaia; he dismissed the escort, and led them to the court himself. For a little they rode alongside the tall bare wall that Paks remembered, then turned left, and left again, and came to open gates that gave on a wide courtyard. Here they dismounted, at the captain's directions, and liveried grooms led the horses away. Paks warned the groom assigned to her horse, and the horse trailed him without a hand on his reins.

"Lady Paksenarrion," said the captain, with a low bow, "I have orders to convey you at once to the Regency Council, if you are not too fatigued with your journey." His voice conveyed the secure belief that they would indeed be too fatigued.

Paks returned the bow. "Not at all. It is in answer to Gird's call that I seek the Regency Council; it cannot be too soon."

To her surprise, the captain reddened slightly. "Well—ah—Lady—the Council assumed you would wish to take refreshment, whenever you came, and—in fact—they are in session now. But when they come forth, I am sure—"

Paks followed the pressure she felt. "By your leave, Captain, I would not intrude, but by the gods' commands. If you will, guide us to the Council, and make known to them that I would see them."

"They know you're coming—" he blurted, completely flustered.

"Yes, but not when—nor exactly what I have come for. Sir, the matter is urgent—" she felt this intensely, as if every moment now mattered. "I believe they will agree on the necessity for this, when I give my message."

"Well, Lady—" Clearly he did not know how to argue with a paladin on quest. Paks smiled at him.

"Come, Captain; take me to the Council, and let them decide if they have time. We do no good standing here in the cold."

At that he bowed, and led the way across the courtyard. The three squires followed Paks closely. She noticed, even in that rapid walk, how different this court was from that in Chaya. Fluted columns of pinkish stone supported a portico on three sides, and rose to frame a pointed arch opposite the gate. Above were walls ornamented with half-pillars separating pointed windows, several rows of them, up to the fretwork of stone that hid the roofs from those below. A lacework of frost or snow glittered from every roughness of the stone, making the palace shimmer with the rose and silver of Tsaia. Suddenly, from far over their heads, a sweet powerful clamour broke out. For a moment Paks could not think what it might be: then she remembered the Bells. The captain turned to her, speaking through the sound.

"You have heard our Bells before, Lady?"

"No." Paks could not say they were beautiful; she wanted only to listen. In the song they were gold, "the golden bells of Vérella"; she wondered if they truly were. The captain talked on, heedless.

"The elves gave them, when Vérella was founded. To look at they are pure gold, but of course they cannot be all gold, for it would not stand the beating. But the elves had them cast, and their voices are sweet to hear." His last words rang loud; the Bells had ceased.

"How often do they ring?"

"It depends on the Council. Always at true dawn, as the elves have it, and sunfall, and at midday when the Council is sitting. And for any festival, of course: Midwinter, Summereve, Torre's Eve, High Harvest, Gird's Victory—for those."

They had come to steps leading up to tall doors under the arch. Guards in rose and silver nodded to the captain and he led them in. Here the floor was set with polished blocks of silver-gray stone. Paks looked around the wide hall; wide stairs rose ahead of her, where the hall narrowed to a passage still wider than the main room in a cottage. To right and left were tall doors folded back to reveal great empty rooms opening into other rooms. Tapestries hung on the walls; the lamp sconces were polished silver. The captain had paused for a moment, looking around. Paks saw a youth in a green tunic with red piping over red hose—Marrakai colors, if her memory served—come into the room on the left. The captain hailed him.

"Pardon, Kirgan—is the Council still sitting?"

The young man—a squire, Paks was sure, though the title was that of eldest son—nodded. "Yes, Captain. Why?"

Paks saw his eyes rake over her and return to the captain's face.

"It's this—Lady Paksenarrion, a paladin. She is on quest, and must speak with the Council, she says."

"At once?" The boy's eyebrows rose, and he met Paks's gaze with surprising composure.

"I must ask them to hear me," said Paks quietly. "It is in their power to refuse."

He laughed shortly. "They will hardly refuse to hear a paladin, I daresay. It's better than what they have been hearing—"

"Sir!" The captain's tone chilled.

The boy's face reddened. "I beg your pardon," he said formally. "I spoke as ill befits a squire."

"If you will follow me," said the captain, turning to Paks. She nodded, but watched the boy's face stiffen as the captain snubbed him.

"I took no offense, Kirgan," she said to him.

She and the Lyonyan squires followed the captain through two large rooms and down a wide passage to a deep alcove. Here four guards in rose and silver stood before doors inlaid with silver and enamel. The captain spoke to them softly, in a dialect Paks did not recognize. One of them stood aside, and the captain knocked softly at the doors.

At once they were opened slightly from inside. The captain conferred with someone. Paks was aware of tension in the room beyond: it seeped out the open door like a cold draught. Then a louder voice spoke from within, an order, and the captain turned to Paks, clearly surprised.

"They will hear you now," he said.

"Thank you, Captain, for your guidance and help." Paks walked forward; the guards stood aside from the doors, now opened wide. She felt rather than saw the Lyonyan squires following.

Within was a room smaller than those they had passed, well lit by high windows on both sides. At the far end an empty throne loomed on a dais; on either side were tiered seats behind a sort of fence, rising up to the base of the windows. These were nearly empty, though a few squires lounged there, and—Paks squinted a moment against the light of the top tier—two elves. Taking up most of the floor space was a massive table of dark wood, heavily carved and inlaid with silver. Around this sat the lords she had come to see: the Regency Council of Tsaia. In the seat below the throne, the crown prince, who would be king by Summereve. Paks thought he looked man-grown already. His brother, younger by almost three years, sat to one side; he had no place on Council, and looked as bored as any youth locked into adult discussions of policy when he had rather be hunting. At the prince's left, a burly man in green and red, who reminded Paks of the boy outside: that was Duke Marrakai. Duke Mahieran, in red and silver. Baron Destvaorn, in blue and red. Kostvan in green and blue. Verrakai—she let her eyes linger a moment on Verrakai—in blue and silver. Sorrestin in blue and rose. Clannaeth in yellow and rose. And alone at the near end of the table, facing her now, Phelan in his formal dress: maroon and white. He smiled at her, then moved to one side so that she could approach the table.

The man who had opened the door, a silver-haired old man in the royal livery, announced her.

"Lady Paksenarrion, Paladin of Gird."

Paks bowed toward the prince.

"Your highness, lords of the Council: I thank you for your courtesy in thus allowing me an audience."

The crown prince spoke quickly. "It is our honor, Lady, to receive any paladin in this Court. Pray tell us how we may aid your quest."

"I will be brief." Despite herself, her eyes slid a little towards Duke Phelan. She almost thought she could feel the sword's desire to come to him. "You already know, I believe, that the king of Lyonya died without an heir of the body." They nodded. "I was called to that court, to Chaya, as paladins are called, but not, alas, to heal the king. Instead I bore unknowing a treasure of that realm: this sword." She pulled back her cloak; they peered at the sword hilt. Duke Phelan, as the others, merely looked puzzled.

"What sword is that?" asked the High Marshal into the brief silence that followed. Paks was sure he had already heard the tale, but she merely answered him.

"According to the testimony of lords in Chaya who remember, and the elves themselves, it was made for the son of King Falkieri—the older brother of this king, whose wife and son were lost while traveling to the Ladysforest. Because I bore the sword, the king—the one who lay dying—thought perhaps the gods meant me to take the throne after him, and so he spoke. But this, too, was not the quest for which I was called."

"He would have given his kingdom to *you*?" That was Verrakai. Paks could feel the scorn from where she stood. "To a—a—commoner? A peasant's child?"

From the corner of her eye, Paks saw Duke Phelan's face whiten with rage; before she could speak, the prince did.

"Peace, Verrakai. Gird chose her paladin; whatever her past, she has been given abilities that would grace any throne. And we will not have any guest insulted at this table." He smiled at Paks. "You will forgive Duke Verrakai's surprise, Lady? Those of us who live in the midst of families graced with every talent may find it difficult to credit such talents elsewhere." Paks thought she caught a bite of sarcasm in that; so did Verrakai, who first paled then reddened.

She bowed. "Your highness, I can take no offense for truth spoken. I am a commoner, a sheepfarmer's daughter, and I found the thought of myself on a throne as outlandish as Duke Verrakai might wish. Indeed, that is not my destiny, nor do I seek it. But the dying king, loving his land much, thought a paladin might bring peace—that I can understand. And his lords, your highness, loving their land and peace more than pride, would have agreed." She waited a moment for that to sink in; some of the Council found it hard to believe, by their expressions.

"Instead of that, I was called to search for the rightful

king. By bringing this sword where its true nature could be known—by tracing its history carefully—by searching for the man who was once the prince of Lyonya—by all these means I am to find the rightful heir to that throne and return him to his place. In warrant of this, I am accompanied by these king's squires of Lyonya, who will witness the identity of the man, when we find him, and escort him to Chaya."

"Only three?" That was the younger prince, now listening alertly.

"Four began the quest with me," said Paks. "One died. We have been beset by evil powers, lords, who do not want the rightful king found."

"How will you know?" asked the High Marshal again.

"By this sword." Paks laid her hand on the pommel; it felt warm to her touch. "It was made for the prince, partially sealed to him in its forging. Had the journey they were on been completed, it would have been completely dedicated to him, and no one else could have drawn it. But that did not happen; the journey was never finished. So I have used it, and so have others—but according to the elves, who made it, it will still acknowledge its true master when he draws it."

"And where did you get it?" asked Verrakai, still sour.

"From Duke Phelan," said Paks.

"That thief—" muttered Verrakai. Paks heard it clearly. She laughed.

"Thief?" she repeated. "Not unless he took it as a babe in arms. It was lost from Lyonya over forty-five years ago. He was given it, Duke Verrakai, by Aliam Halveric of Lyonya, who had found it near a dead elf in the forest."

"So he says." Verrakai's insistent distaste was not mellowing.

"So also the elves themselves say," said Paks. "Aliam Halveric told the elves when he'd found it; they did not ask its return, but told him to give it to the one for whom it was made. They thought he knew what sword it was; alas, the elves have trouble remembering the brevity of human lives, and that he had been too young to see the sword at court."

"But then—" The crown prince's voice topped a sudden burst of talk; it stilled, and he went on. "But then the elves knew—they knew who the prince was? Why didn't they simply say?"

"And how did they know?" asked the High Marshal, with a sharp look at the two elves who sat high in the tiers.

"You will remember that Falkieri's queen was elven; the prince was half-elven. It seems that when the tragedy occurred, everyone assumed the boy had been killed. Instead, he was stolen away—beyond the seas, the elves think, since they could have sensed his presence anywhere in these realms."

"Even in Pargun or Kostandan?" asked Duke Marrakai.

"I am not sure, my lord."

"Yes," came a silvery elven voice from the seats above. "Anywhere in these realms or Aarenis, Duke Marrakai, elves could have found him."

"So you see," Paks went on, "the elves also thought him dead, when they could not sense him. Then some years later, he returned to Lyonya: how, I do not know. But elves found him there, fairly quickly, and—"

"And did nothing? Do you ask me to believe that?" Verrakai led the rush of noise that followed. Paks waited until the room quieted; this time the prince had let them talk themselves out.

"The elves said," Paks went on, "that the prince had been treated so badly that he had no remembrance of his past. He knew nothing of his name, his family, or his elven blood. They found him so damaged that they feared he had none of the taig-sense left; they feared to try any intervention lest they damage him further."

"And so they did nothing." The crown prince's voice was calm.

"Not quite nothing, your highness. They watched. Remember that at that time, the prince's younger sister was alive and well—"

"But now," said the crown prince, "Lyonya has no king,

and no clear heir, and the elves want a part-elven ruler. Is that the meat of it?"

"Not quite. They do not want this man to rule unless he's fit for it—and they doubt his fitness." Paks waited for the silence. Then she spoke. "I do not doubt it."

"What!" The crown prince leaned forward; all of them stared. "You know—you *know* who it is?"

"I do."

"Then why haven't you said? Why this nonsense about a quest?" Verrakai again, sneering.

"Because, my lord, I have not been granted leave to speak by the gods—or by the king himself. What, would you have me place an innocent man in danger, by blurting his name out for the world to play with? Already one king's squire is dead, killed by a priest of Liart, to prevent my finding him. Already the powers of evil in Lyonya are massing to keep him from the throne. Suppose I had said his name openly, from the time I first suspected who it would be—would he be alive this day, to take the sword and test his heritage?"

"Well said," said the High Marshal. "Well said, indeed."

"I came here," said Paks, more quietly, "to tell the Council of Tsaia that my quest leads me into your realm. I must go where the quest leads, but in all courtesy, I ask your leave to travel as I must."

"Is he here?" asked the crown prince. "In Tsaia?"

"He is," said Paks, weighing the danger of that admission.

"Can you tell us now who it is?"

"No. Not at the moment, your highness. I must ask Duke Phelan some questions about the sword's history in his house: who handled it, and how."

"We all have questions for Duke Phelan," said Verrakai. "I hope, Lady Paksenarrion, that his answers to your questions are more to the point than his answers to mine."

The crown prince shot a glance at Verrakai that silenced him. Then he smiled at Paks. "We shall defer our questions until you are through, Lady Paksenarrion. A paladin's quest—and such a quest—is a matter of more moment than the Duke's response to matters of law." He rose, and the others rose with him. With a bow, he led them from the room, through a door Paks had not noticed behind the throne. The squires in the tiers followed, and the two elves climbed down to stand near Paks and Duke Phelan.

"Are you certain, Lady, of the rightness of your judgment?"

"I am certain, sir elf, of the rightness of the gods' commands; my own judgment is not at issue."

"Be joyous in your certainty, paladin of Gird," said one of the elves, eyes flashing.

"I hope you are right, indeed," said the other, "for I would see no fires rage in the forests of Lyonya, as have raged in other lands." He turned to the other elf. "Come, cousin—we shall know all soon enough; we might as well leave the paladin to her work." And with a bow, the elves also withdrew.

Meanwhile, Duke Phelan had recognized Garris, and come to grip his arm.

"Garris—by the gods, so this is where you ended up. King's squire—a good place for a good man."

"Well, my lord, I—" Garris struggled with his knowledge and the Duke's ignorance.

"You can't my lord me, Garris. Not when we were boys together. Have you told Paks here about all our scrapes?" Phelan turned to Paks, grinning. "Garris was a year or so younger than I, Paks, at Aliam Halveric's, and I got him in more trouble—"

"That's not what I heard," said Paks.

"It's true enough," said the Duke. "But come—let's sit down. Have you been here long? When did you arrive? I had heard nothing until I came to Vérella, where I found word that the King of Lyonya was dead, and you were coming here on quest."

"We have just come, my lord," said Paks, settling gingerly in the chair Duke Verrakai had vacated. "We rode this morning from Westbells."

"Have you had any refreshment? I can certainly have someone bring—"

"No, my lord. Please. We shall have time enough after."

He gave her a long look. "So. It is that urgent, eh? Well,

then, Paks, ask what you will, and as I know, I will answer."

Paks began with what she knew of the sword's history, and the Duke nodded. He affirmed what Aliam Halveric had said of the sword when he took it. Without prompting, he spoke of his vow to Tammarrion.

"You see, she had been—was—a soldier, as I was, and she was not giving that up." The Duke glanced quickly at Lieth and Suriya. "You will understand that. So I felt—in giving her a sword—that it would be but courtesy to promise it would always be hers alone."

"What happened when she first drew it?" asked Paks.

"It showed a blue light, much as any magic sword may. Not as bright as when you draw it, Paks, but Tamar was not a paladin. Though as one who loved and served Gird to her death, she might well have been."

"Did anyone else in your household draw it?"

"No. Not that I know of. Tamar was proud of it, and no wonder. Little Estil—our daughter, that was killed—she wanted to, but I remember Tamar saying she'd have to grow into it."

"And even after her death—"

"No. Someone took it and cleaned it, when they found—found them." His voice shook an instant, then steadied. "By the time I came north again, she was in the ground, and it was back in its scabbard, lying across her armor, for me to see. I hung it on the wall, where you found it, Paks, and there it stayed until you took it. I don't think that it would have suffered Venneristimon to mishandle it."

"No, my lord, I don't think so." Paks sighed. She hardly knew what to do; she could feel the stiffness of the squires, waiting for her to do—what? Tell him? Hand him the sword? What? She looked at his face; it was more peaceful than she'd seen it before. Was that peace a kind of defeat? But no—his eyes still held fire enough, and his hands and voice were firm. Now that she knew, she thought she could see the shape of elven blood—not as much as expected, but there. And for a man of fifty, he was remarkably lithe and young. Beside her, Suriya stirred, her cloak rustling a little.

"My lord," she began again, "what do you remember of your childhood?"

The Duke's eyes widened. "What!" An instant later he had shoved his chair back, and was standing, pale of face. "You don't—Paks—no." He put a hand to the chair; color seeped back into his face. "I understand. You want to help me, do something for me, but—"

"My lord, please." Paks forced his attention. "Please answer."

"Nothing good," he said grimly. "And you cannot be right in what you surmise."

"I can't?" Paks surprised herself with the tone of her voice. "My lord, I ask you to listen and think of this: the elves, when they heard from Aliam Halveric that he had the sword, told him to give it to the prince. And when he replied that he was giving it to you, they said it was well enough. They erred in thinking that Aliam knew the sword and its properties. But they knew that he suspected who you were."

"Aliam?" Now the Duke's face was white; he clung to the chair with both fists. "He *knew*? Aliam?"

"He suspected, my lord, and had no proof, nor any way to find some. And your sister was betrothed, soon to be crowned."

He shook his head, breathing hard. "I trusted him—Aliam—he said—"

"He said that he did not think your parentage could be proven, or your place restored; indeed, that's what he thought at the time. He was not sure; he had been too young when it happened, and he dared not ask anyone." Paks had feared his wrath with Aliam more than anything, but he was already nodding his head slowly as she spoke.

"I can understand. A boy with no background—what could he say? And my memories—so few, so far back. But—" he looked at Paks again. "Are you sure, Paks? Are you certain it's not your regard for an old commander?"

"My lord, it is not my thought only. I have talked to Aliam Halveric, and to elves of high degree—"

"And why didn't they—?" The Duke stopped in mid-sentence, his voice chopped off from a rising cry. His hand dropped again to the chair. "Because I was unfit—am unfit—"

"No, my lord. You are not."

"I am. Paks, you know—you have seen—and Lyonya requires abilities I don't have—if ever I did."

"My lord, you are half-elven, with abilities scarce less than the elves, but constrained by a mortal life. I believe you have them still, buried by what you have endured. Why else would the High Lord and Gird have sent me to find you? Would they choose an unfit king?"

"No—"

"And if they can make a paladin out of me, my lord, after all that happened, they can make a good king out of you."

"Perhaps." The Duke sat again, pulling his chair to the table so suddenly that its legs scrapped loudly on the floor. "So—you are sure, and the elves are sure, that I am a prince born, and the rightful heir to Lyonya's throne. Is anyone else convinced?"

"Aliam Halveric."

"And any others?"

"We have not used your name, my lord, for fear that evil would come on you before I could reach you. But the lords of Lyonya, gathered together after the king's death, agreed to accept the sword's evidence. The elves had admitted that the prince lived, and might be found. I think most of the lords, if not all, will accept you." She watched him; his eyes had fallen to the table, where he traced some of the silver inlay with his forefinger.

"It would be a matter for laughter, if I could laugh," said the Duke quietly, "that I am born a prince, and of better birth than those lords who have scorned me as a bastard mercenary. They were so sure of my lack—as was I, most times—and now—" His finger paused; he looked up at Paks. "You assume, Paks, that I *want* to be king."

"No, my lord. I only know that you are the rightful king, and must be."

"Hmmph." His gaze went past her to meet each of the squires. "Garris—Lieth—Suriya—if Paks is right, then I am your king. But I must say this, however it seems to you. Many years have gone by since I was a lost and lonely boy, tramping the fields of Lyonya looking for work. Aliam Halveric took me in, taught me my trade of war, taught me respect for the gods, and what I know of right and wrong. Garris, you knew me then—you know what sort of boy I was. Did you ever think I might be a prince?"

Garris blushed. "My lord—sir—I thought you were special, then—you know I did."

"As a younger boy to an elder, yes. But birth?"

"Well, my lord—you *acted* like a prince—"

The Duke's mouth curled in a smile. "Did I? I was trying to act like Aliam, as I recall. But what I mean is this. I had nothing when I came to Aliam. He gave me my start—as you all know, I'm sure. But from there, I made it myself. That land in the north—my stronghold—that is mine. My money, yes, but more than that. I built some of that wall myself; barked my own knuckles on that stone; left some of my blood on the hills when we fought off the orcs. Years of my life—dreams—Tamar and I, planning things. My children were born there, in that chamber you saw, Paks, the night we talked with the Marshal-General. I fought in Aarenis, yes—for that's where the money was, the contracts that let me improve my own lands. The money for that mill came from Aarenis, the food I bought all those years before the fields were large enough. Stock for farmers, fruit-trees for Kolya. But what I cared for—what I gave my heart to—was that land, and those people. My people—my soldiers." His fist was clenched now, on the table before him. "Now I find I'm a prince, with another land, and other people. But can I leave this, that I have made? Can I leave the Hall where Tamar ate, and the courtyard where our children played? Can I leave those who helped me, when they knew nothing of princes or kingdoms, only a young mercenary captain who dreamed of his own lands? Already this year they have endured one upheaval. Those that stayed are *mine*." He looked from face to face. "Can you understand this?"

Paks felt the tears stinging her own eyes. When Garris spoke, she heard the emotion there. "My lord, I understand. You were always that way—even at Aliam's, you would take responsibility. Of course you care for them—"

Suriya had pushed back her chair, and gone around Paks to stand beside the Duke. When he glanced up at her, she spoke. "Sir king, if you were unfit to be our king you could not have spoken so. I am most junior of your squires, but by your leave, I will not leave you until you sit in your own throne."

The Duke's face furrowed. "By the gods, Suriya, were you listening at all? I am not sure I want this!"

"Sir king, on Falk's oath I swear, you will be king, and until that day I will ward you." Paks had never seen Suriya like this, completely calm and certain. She smiled at Paks. "Lady, you told us we would have a king worthy of our service; so I find him. If he cannot find his heart in this yet, it will come, and I will await it."

"Gird's grace rest on your service, Suriya," said Paks. And to the Duke, "My lord—or should I say, sir king—I believe it is the gods' will that you take this crown. Surely if you follow their will, good will come even to your lands in the north."

"Think you so? Think you so indeed? It would not be the first time a man has followed what he thinks is the gods' will, and had things go ill indeed."

"You mean your wife's death," said Paks bluntly. "My lord, that was not the gods' will, but Achrya's; I believe her plan was laid longer than you have yet realized. Do you think you were stolen away by chance? Do you recall the words of her agent that night, when she said you were not born a duke?"

"Yes." The Duke sighed heavily. "Damn. All those years I worried because I did not know who my father was, and now—" He looked at his closed fist and opened it deliberately. He sighed again, and looked up at Suriya. "You are right, of course, as is Paksenarrion. If I am Lyonya's king—though to my mind that's not yet proven—then I must *be* the king; I cannot sulk on my own estates, and leave Lyonya to suffer evil." Paks felt the tension ease; Garris and Lieth moved from her side to the Duke's without a word. He smiled at them. "So—you would leave Paks unwarded? I assure you, squires, I am in no peril here."

"Paksenarrion is a paladin, and well fit to guard herself," said Lieth. "Though when she goes out alone, one of us will go with her, by your leave."

"Indeed so," said the Duke, as Paks still thought of him. "Until this is settled, I wish that. But now what?" he asked Paks. "Your test is that sword, is it not? Should I draw it here, or before the Council, or in Chaya? What is your word?"

"I do not know," said Paks. "You know more of statecraft than I: here are three witnesses to speak of what happens. Do we need more? I think you should not travel without testing it; the sword will be a mighty weapon for your defense, once you have held it."

"And will leave you swordless," he said, with a small smile. Paks shrugged. "No," he said, "we must find you another weapon; I will not have a paladin of Gird unweaponed for my sake. Let me think. The prince should know as soon as anyone. His father granted my steading, and was my friend; I would have sworn allegiance to this boy with all my heart. Indeed," he went on, with a broader grin, "it's as well you came when you did, Paks. They were urging me to swear now—before his coronation this summer—as proof of my loyalty. And so I might have done, and been bound by that oath, if you had not come in. For I tell you I had no reason to do otherwise."

"Sir king—" began Garris tentatively.

"Garris, you must not call me that—any of you—until the sword proves me so. Please. Your service I accept, but we must observe the courtesies of this court as well. Paks, it must be before them all, I think: the whole Council. To do otherwise would arouse suspicion. Then if it fails—"

"It won't," said the squires at once.

"If," the Duke repeated firmly, "then all will know, and will also know that I made no secret trials. Paks, if you will speak to the lords yourself, it will be better. The prince has no vote, but the Council defers to his wishes where it can; he will determine the hour."

"As soon as may be," said Paks.

"As he wills," said the Duke. "You will find him certain of mind. As were all of us, at nearly twenty."

"How shall we explain the service of the king's squires?" asked Paks, thinking how it would look to have the Duke trailed by those green-and-gold tunics.

"You asked them to look over some scrolls—old accounts—I had brought with me. I have brought the Company Rolls, at the Council's request. Will that do?"

"Certainly." Paks rose, with the Duke, and preceded him to the door. Outside, the elderly man who had announced her waited. "Sir, might I ask an audience with the prince?"

"With the crown prince, Lady?" he asked.

"Yes."

"Come with me, then. Is Duke Phelan free to meet with the Council?"

"Sir, I have asked him to look up something from his records; the squires go with him to take notes. By the time I have spoken to those other lords I must see, perhaps he will be free."

The man bowed. "I will inform the Council, Lady." He called to a page, and gave that message to be taken to all the lords in turn.

Chapter Twenty-five

The crown prince received her in his private chambers; Paks found herself face to face with a tall, self-assured young man of nearly twenty. He waved her to a seat with grave courtesy, and handed her a delicate rose-colored cup of some hot, aromatic liquid.

"I know you are used to sib," he said as she tasted it. "This is brewed from two of the herbs in sib, and another from the far southwest mountains. I like it better, but there is sib in this pot if you don't. They tell me you did not stop even to take refreshment."

"No, your highness. I could not delay."

"And then you asked Duke Phelan some questions, and now you wish to speak with me. I assure you, Lady, that I am too young to have knowledge you need."

Paks cocked her head. "I think you do know what I need, your highness. May I tell you?" He nodded, and Paks finished the drink before going on. "I think that Lyonya's king is in your court at this time. For his safety and reputation, the sword's test should be conducted openly, before your Council."

"He is *here*? Not merely in Tsaia, but in my court—and you know who it is? Whatever you asked Duke Phelan, then, confirmed your knowledge. Perhaps you asked who had come with him?" Paks had not thought to ask that, but the prince seemed not to notice. "It must be someone he knows—a captain of his, or—" he stopped short. "You are not saying it is—"

"I am not saying anyone, your highness, at this time."

His eyes were bright, watching her. "No—you aren't saying, but I have wits enough to guess, I think. Gird's cudgel, this will stir the Council." He laughed, a boy's clear open laugh, and poured her another cup. His face sobered. "And give us a problem, as well. The north—"

"Your highness, I pray you, do not speak of it until the time."

"Oh, very well. But you want a Council session, and it must be before we resume our previous business. You may not be aware that certain lords have been asked to swear their allegiance directly to me even before the coronation. In this case—" his lips twitched, but he controlled the smile, "it might prove inconvenient to your purpose." He poured another cup for himself. "So. A Council session called on special business. The High Marshal will support me there. You will want it as quickly as possible? Yes. Tomorrow morning, then: it will take several hours to arrange, and tonight, as you no doubt recall, is the Feast of Luap. We will all be in the Grange-Hall until late, for the High Marshal is knighting a score of youths."

Paks had forgotten about the Feast of Luap. "It could not be put off?"

His eyes widened. "Luap's feast? The knighting? Gods, no. Relatives of these boys have travelled days to be here. Not if a dragon sat smoking in the inner court. If you have concern about the—ah—person, I can assign guards, though—"

"No, your highness. Only if anyone asks, could you explain that the king's squires are looking into the Company Rolls for a name?"

He nodded. "That I can do, and will, right gladly. Now, if you'll excuse me, I will summon the High Marshal on this matter we spoke of."

Paks rose quickly and bowed. "Is there aught I can do, your highness, to help with this?"

"I think not. You will confirm your request, of course, to any lord who asks you—but I think they will not ask."

He nodded, and Paks withdrew, to find a page ready to escort her back to the rooms she'd been assigned.

Once there, she found Lieth in attendance; her things had been unpacked, and a hot bath was ready for her.

"I thought—" Paks began, but Lieth smiled and put a finger to her lips.

"With Garris to look, and Suriya to keep notes, they didn't need me. Here, Lady, let me take that mail." Lieth set it aside, and helped Paks strip off the last of her clothes and climb into the tub. "And I thought," she said very softly, "that you would want no one else near the sword. I chased two chambermaids out of here when I came."

"Thank you, Lieth," said Paks. The hot scented water was delightful; she felt she could acquire a taste for bathing this way. When she was done, Lieth handed her a robe of heavy rose-colored wool that had been warming by the fire. Paks put it on, wrinkling her nose at the silver clasps. "A rich house, the Mahierian," she commented.

"Yes," said Lieth shortly. She went to the door of the next room, and gestured. Two maids came through. "They've set a meal out in there," said Lieth. "Will you come?" She had already gathered the armor; Paks took the sword, and followed Lieth, leaving the maids to clear away the bath things.

The meal of sliced breads, cold meats, and fruit was spread on a round table beneath a narrow window. In this room as well a fire crackled on a clean stone hearth. Yet another room opened from it, this with a narrow canopied bed. Paks sat down with an appetite.

"Come eat, Lieth, unless you've had something in the meantime," she said.

"Thank you." Lieth sat across from Paks. For awhile they ate silently, each thinking her own thoughts. When Paks finished, and sat back, she found Lieth watching her.

"What's wrong, Lieth?" Paks hoped Lieth had not taken a dislike to the Duke. Her first words fed that fear.

"I came to serve the king," she began slowly. "I knew nothing of him, but that you knew who he was."

"Yes?" prompted Paks, when she said nothing more for a moment.

"I am glad to have seen him. I don't know what I was expecting, but not that—and it's better than I expected." She stopped again; this time Paks merely looked her question. Lieth shook her head, answering something Paks did not ask—perhaps a question in her own mind. "I am a king's squire," she said finally. "A Lyonyan. A knight of Falk. Here, in Tsaia, among Girdsmen, with my king unknown and disregarded, I am out of place. Lady, if I heard in Lyonya what I have heard this day, I would know how to answer—" her hand had crept to her sword. "But I am a stranger. I have no rights at this court."

"Lieth, what is it? What are you angry about?"

"Paks, do you know how many enemies the ki—the Duke has?"

Paks, frowned. "No. Some, but not so many, I'd thought."

"Then they must all be here. Verrakai—I had words with one of his squires, and a servant or so—"

"Words?" Paks was startled. Lieth had seemed the most placid of the king's squires.

"Just words—so far. They had plenty to say about the Duke, and all of it bad. That your coming here today was his doing, to avoid swearing an oath of loyalty to the prince. That you were no true paladin—and that I argued, telling them I'd seen you fight myself—but they would not believe. They think their lord has a witness who will make it obvious that you and the Duke are both liars and traitors."

Paks felt a chill down her spine. "I wonder how, since we're not. Did Garris and Suriya hear any of this?"

"I don't think so. They're with him; I was looking for your rooms."

"Anything from the royal servants?"

"No, not really. Some think the Duke's wild and uncanny, but none seem to harbor any malice. But the Verrakai weren't all. I ran into the whole group together: Konhalt, Clannaeth, a Sorrestin page, and the Verrakai. They were eager to tell me the worst they knew of the Duke—and of you."

"That could be bad indeed," said Paks placidly. She did not fear Lieth's opinion.

"It was bad to hear," said Lieth grimly. "Girdsmen. I'd have thought even Girdsmen would have more respect for a paladin."

"Even Girdsmen?"

Lieth flushed. "Lady, your pardon. It was unseemly."

Paks shook her head. "Lieth, these may not have been Girdsmen. While you are here, try not to remember all you were told of Girdsmen by the Falkians, eh? I'm a Girdsman."

"Yes—I know. I'm sorry, truly." She looked suddenly worried. "Is he?"

"The Duke? No. But his wife was."

"And she is dead. He must marry again. Will he, do you think?"

Paks thought a moment. "Lieth, if he has given his word, he will do more; he is that kind of man. He has said he will take the kingdom; I daresay he knows what that means, and will do more than his duty. But I am not one to speak of kings' weddings."

"You spoke to the crown prince?"

"Yes."

"And what is he like, may I ask? Will he be an ally of Lyonya?"

"He seemed nice enough." Paks did not know how to explain that she could sense only strong evil and good—not the average mixture most men carried. As well, she had no experience of princes. If he had been a recruit or a squire, she would have been well pleased with him, but as a prince she had to hope the same qualities would serve.

They were interrupted by a polite knock on the outer door. Lieth rose at once to answer it; Paks waited at the table. Lieth came back with a curious expression on her face.

"It's a boy—he wants to see you. He says he knows you."

"Knows me?" Paks looked down at herself quickly; she

couldn't receive anyone in a bathrobe, even with silver clasps. But Lieth was already handing her a clean undershirt.

"Here—says he's a young Marrakai. Aris Marrakai—did you ever meet such a one?"

Paks remembered the boy she'd met her first night in Fin Panir—and often thereafter. "Aris—yes. Fourth son, I think. Thanks." She looked at the mail and decided against it, pulling on her swordbelt over her clothes instead. Then she went through to the front room.

Aris had grown even taller, and looked much older in his squire's livery, the dark green and blue of Kostvan House, piped in the red and green of his father's colors. His black hair was longer, cropped just below his ears, but he had no facial hair. He stood stiffly by the door until Paks was halfway across the room, then grinned as widely as ever.

"Paks! I mean, Lady Paksenarrion—I'm sorry. But they said—and I kept telling them you would come back. You look—" he paused, examining her with his head cocked. "Fine," he finished. "But don't you have mail? Silver mail?"

Paks found herself laughing; even Lieth was smiling. "I have mail, Aris, but even paladins take it off now and then."

"Oh." He looked crestfallen. "I was hoping—when Juris, that's my brother who's Kirgan, said he'd seen you today, I wanted to come—and then I could say I saw it, you see?"

"I see. You wanted to make an impression on the other squires, eh?"

Aris blushed as red as the clothes he had worn that first night. "Well, Paks—Lady Paksenarrion—it's like this—"

"You're the youngest squire," said Paks inexorably, "and they tease you, and when you told them about your three estates someone pounded you, didn't they?"

"Yes, but—"

"And you think this will get you out of some scrape?"

"You didn't used to be like this," said Aris.

"No, and you used to be a little boy. Now you're a

young man, not my pet brother. You are the fourth son of a powerful Duke, and you should have better things to think about than impressing other squires by claiming acquaintance with a paladin."

Aris nodded. "I'm sorry."

"I'm not. I'm glad you came to see me, and if the others think it's because you're a vain young boy trying to shine by reflection, perhaps they won't pay too much attention to you."

"What?"

"Aris, listen. I know you've wits enough in that head." With that he stood still again, eyes gleaming. Paks went on. "Yes, indeed. As someone told me recently, Marrakaien are all one brew, and that a heady one. I'll tell you what, young Marrakai—you keep your wits about you and you'll have something to hold up your head about—and I'll see that it's known."

"Can I do something for you? Really? What can I do?"

"I want to know the extent of the division in the Council—who opposes your father on what issues, and why, if you know."

"Oh. Right now?"

"If you have anything to tell. But come into the next room; you can take a look at my mail, and have something to drink."

Once seated at the table, Aris recovered his usual ebullience, and told Paks what he knew of Council business with expressions that had Lieth on the edge of laughter. Paks did not correct him, for she wanted his first impressions, scurrilous though they were.

"Part of it's the Red Duke," he said, coming to what interested Paks without any prompting at all. "They call him the fox, and I can see why. Oh—that's right—you know him. Well, then, you know what I mean. My father says it's not slyness, just intelligence, but some of the others don't trust him at all. They say he got too rich too fast. No one could be so lucky as that. Someone had to be helping him, and of course they think it's Simyits or something. Even worse." He took a swallow of ale from the mug Paks had poured him, and went on. "But Lord Verrakai, the Duke's brother, he told his page that he had proof of Duke Phelan's wrong. Someone who had been with him in Aarenis, and seen it."

Paks managed not to move, merely raising an eyebrow. Aris scurried on through his tale.

"A veteran of his, who left because she didn't want to stay with such a man, or he mistreated her, or something. And she's supposed to prove you aren't really a paladin, too."

"That may prove difficult," murmured Paks.

"Well, of course. You are one." Aris snorted. "I haven't seen her, but Dorthan—that's the page—swears he has. Big and black, he says, and shoulders like an ox. But then Dorthan's so skinny he thinks I have big shoulders."

Paks could not think of anyone matching that description. "Do you have a name for this witness?" she asked.

"No. He didn't know that. Why? Would you know her by name?"

"I might, if she fought in the Company the same years I did. Go on."

But that was all Aris knew of the mysterious witness. He told a long involved story going the rounds of the squires concerning a second son of Clannaeth's younger brother, and Konhalt's heir, and a girl of the Destvaorn household, which supposedly explained why Konhalt was supporting Marrakai's position on the size of the Royal Guard, but Paks found she couldn't follow either the positions or the reasons. She was about to send him away when another knock on the outer door drew Lieth. Aris looked scared.

"If that's Juris, do you have to tell him I'm here?"

"Would he be angry?"

"That I came? Yes. When I told him today that I knew you, he said to let you alone."

And then Lieth announced the Kirgan Marrakai. Paks got up and jerked her thumb at Aris. "Come on, Aris, and see what the protection of paladins is worth."

In the other room, the Kirgan looked both embarrassed and annoyed.

"My pardon, lady, for disturbing you, but I feared my brother might—aha!" as he caught sight of Aris behind Paks.

"Kirgan Marrakai, your brother has given me information I greatly needed, and being unacquainted with the household, I knew not anyone else to ask."

"You *asked* him here?" The Kirgan's eyebrows lowered. Paks smiled.

"Not precisely, no. But I may say I valued his loyalty in Fin Panir, as I do here. I should not have kept him so long, perhaps, without asking leave of Lord Kostvan—"

"I had leave for the afternoon," Aris piped up. Paks and the Kirgan both stared him down. She looked back at the Kirgan and smiled again.

"And now that he has quite finished," said Paks, emphasizing the words, "I hope you have a few minutes to give me."

"I?" The Kirgan was clearly astonished.

"You. There are things the pages and junior squires know, and other things which heirs to titles know. Would you?" She waved a hand to the other door, and the Kirgan came forward, throwing a last glare at Aris as he hurried out the door.

"Did you really need him," said the Kirgan, "or were you in league with the scamp?" Despite the words, Paks could feel a warmth in his voice.

"A paladin in league with a scamp?" She spoke lightly. "No, he was a pestiferous little mischief in Fin Panir, and no doubt still is—but he was always loyal and honest, even in his worst moments. I asked, Kirgan, for gossip—because I needed to know it—and he told me what he knew, which I needed to know, and could not ask."

"And from me?"

Paks looked searchingly at him. Earlier in the day, he had seemed to have the same arrogant enamel as some of the boys at Fin Panir, but perhaps he had the same warm heart as Aris. "I will ask a few questions," she said then. "Please remember that I am not of this court, and speak only of what I have heard—not in condemnation or even suspicion. Is your father loyal to the crown? Are you?"

His lips thinned. "I should have expected this—you came from the east, didn't you? Through Verrakai lands. My father's inmost heart is his own, Lady, but to my knowledge he is and has always been loyal to the crown. As for me, I love the prince as a brother. Indeed but I cannot speak of that. I will serve him, Lady, as his loyal servant, when I become Duke."

"Very well. Then another question. Would you know who the witness against Duke Phelan is, that Aris spoke of?"

"No—not by name. I've heard there is one, that's all. A veteran, which surprised us all; his veterans all love him."

"So I would have thought," said Paks. "Then a final question. What do you think of Phelan?"

"I?" He smiled. "I've always liked him. My father does; he says Phelan has more breeding than any noble in the land, say what they will of him. He has always been courteous to me. You were in his Company; you know more."

"I know what I think," said Paks. "But I needed to know what you thought—what others think. When I came in this afternoon, it seemed almost that he was on trial. While I am on quest, I may not delay—but you can understand that after what he's done for me—"

"You would defend him? Good—I mean, it's none of my business, but I can hardly bear it when Verrakai gets started. Gird's blood! I was about to boil over when father sent me out on an errand."

"Tell your father to take care, Kirgan," said Paks seriously. "I will not always be in a position to help the Duke; he will need all his friends before long."

"I will, Lady," said the Kirgan steadily. "May I go?"

"Yes—you may say I have saved your little brother a scolding."

"More than a scolding, if I get my hands on that scamp," said the Kirgan, laughing. "You don't know what he did to my sister's room."

"Nor want to know," said Paks, waving him off. "That's between you—but remember, Kirgan," she said as he opened the door. She saw two servants not a spear-length away down the passage. "If young Aris wants to visit me, I have granted him leave. He was my friend in Fin Panir, and I don't forget my friends, even the young ones. He must have his lord's leave—but not yours." The Kirgan's face, as he bowed, was remote, as if he'd been scolded, but his eyes danced. Paks shut the door behind him, convinced that the Marrakaien were all a heady brew indeed.

Lieth was watching her, brows raised. "That will explain his visit, to all those listening ears."

"So I thought," Paks sighed, stretching. She would like to have rested, but felt she could not take the time. She wondered if the Duke would be at the Grange-Hall that evening. Yet another tap on the door interrupted her thoughts. Lieth answered, opening to a page in royal livery.

"Please, I am to give this to the Lady Paksenarrion's hand, and await an answer."

"Here." Paks took the single folded sheet, and opened it. The High Marshal Seklis wished a short conference before the evening's ceremonies. He would be at the Grange-Hall until dinner, if she could find the time. Paks handed the message to Lieth, who read it quickly and nodded. Paks turned to the page. "I'll come, of course," she said. "Can you guide us?"

"Yes, Lady."

"You'll want your armor," said Lieth quietly; Paks smiled at her.

"In the Hall?"

"Yes." Lieth could convey firmness very quietly, and she did it. Paks did not argue, and retired to the other room where Lieth helped her into it. "I'm coming with you, too," she said before they rejoined the page.

"As you will," said Paks.

The same High Marshal she had seen in the conference earlier met her at the side door of the Grange-Hall.

"If the circumstances of your quest permit, Lady Paksenarrion, I would be glad of your participation in tonight's ceremony."

Paks frowned. "What participation, Marshal—?"

"I'm sorry—I forgot that we hadn't met; I'm High Marshal Seklis. I've been attached to the court for about a year. Well, you probably know that the Order of the Bells advances its novices to knighthood at the Feast of Luap. We have a score of them this time. And since it's a Girdish order—with a few exceptions—a trial of arms is part of the ceremony. It would be an honor for the candidates to meet your blade in this trial. Of course, we have other Marshals, and senior knights of the Order also help out, but—"

"I thought only knights could act in the trials," said Paks.

"Well, of course—but paladins are knights first, and so—"

Paks shook her head. "No, Marshal; I'm not a knight."

"You—! But you must be—I mean I heard that you were different, but—"

"Marshal, let me explain. I was not at Fin Panir long enough to qualify; the Marshal-General admitted me to the order of paladin-candidate before I was knighted—as is sometimes done."

"Yes, but—"

"And after the expedition to Kolobia, I was unable to continue the training. I believe all Marshals were informed—?"

He nodded, reluctantly, it seemed to Paks.

"So I left Fin Panir, without being knighted—indeed, completely unfit for any such honor."

"But—you *are* a paladin?"

"Yes. By Gird's grace, and the gifts of the High Lord, I am a paladin—but not through the candidacy at Fin Panir. Marshal, I do not understand the gods' ways or intent; I know only their commands and gifts."

"I—see." He chewed his lip. "I don't know of another case such as this."

"In the event, I might be an embarrassment to you—"

"No. No, indeed." His voice steadied, and he gave her a

sharp glance. "If the gods see fit to make a paladin of you, am I to quarrel with your qualifications? You are their champion—their knight, if you will—and that is enough for me, and for the rest."

"Another problem," said Paks slowly. "I have no blade of my own—this one I carry on quest, as you heard, to test the identity of Lyonya's king. I dare not use it for any other purpose."

"Easily solved," grinned Marshal Seklis. "A Grange of Gird holds ample weaponry, I would think. Choose a sword from the armory that suits you. But if your quest forbids, I cannot insist."

"Then I would be honored. Only you will have to tell me how the ceremony goes."

"Like most such—but I forgot. Here, then—" And he led her into the Grange-Hall proper and showed how it would be set up. Although somewhat smaller than the High Lord's Hall in Fin Panir, the Grange-Hall was built to the same basic design. Tiers of seats rose on either side of a broad central aisle in which the trials would take place. Candidates would enter through a door at one end, and prove themselves against at least two of the examiners.

"Ordinarily," said Seklis, "we know that each bout will be short, and we don't expect the examiners to have much trouble. It's like the ritual exchange—merely public proof that the candidates are able to face an armed opponent. Even so, some of them surprise us. Last year we had a lad that outfought two Marshals and cost me a hard struggle before I got the winning touch. He's in Marshal's training now, and he'll be a strong arm for Gird in the future. But this time we may have real trouble. Many of them wanted to be in this ceremony because of the prince's coronation this year—to say they were knighted in the same year. So we have twenty zealous and very capable candidates. Beside the honor alone, that's one reason I asked you—I've scraped up every Marshal around, and the best of the senior knights, just in case, but we still have only fifteen examiners. That's more than two bouts apiece, any way you look at it."

Seklis explained the details of scoring, and introduced Paks to some of the pointers, who would keep track of each bout. Then he took her to the armory, and left her to choose a sword from the racks. They were all of similar design, with Gird's seal deeply graven in the pommel, and well-shaped hilts. They varied only in length and weight. When Paks had chosen two, Seklis told a yeoman-marshal to put them aside for her that evening, then turned back to her.

"Oh—by the way—unless your quest requires it, I would ask that you not wear that mail: for the trials, all wear the training armor, and all examiners are in the colors of their orders. You, of course, are entitled to Gird's colors, and there are surcoats enough, as well as the bandas—"

"I see." Paks thought a moment. She could think of no reason why she should be the only participant in full mail, but was yet reluctant to leave it aside. "I hesitate to question the custom—"

"And I the conditions of your quest." The High Marshal cocked his head slightly. "Lady, you know best what evils you face; I would not have them come on you unawares, yet I think they will not brave the Grange-Hall full of Marshals and knights. The candidates—"

"What about the challengers?" asked Lieth. "Or is not that the custom here?"

The High Marshal frowned. "Challengers? Oh, you mean outsiders? Well—I doubt there will be any—"

"What is that?" asked Paks.

"It is the custom," he said, "that anyone having a grievance against the court or any examiner can present a champion for a trial of arms at this knighting. But when any such is planned, it's usual for me to know ahead of time."

"Would that bout be fought on the same terms?"

"No—as a full trial of arms. Do you suspect anything of that sort?"

"To be honest, Marshal Seklis, I don't know what I suspect—besides trouble. We have been attacked already by Achrya's minions and several priests of Liart with their beasts. Until I see the rightful king of Lyonya safe on his throne, I cannot be easy about anything. I am willing enough to test your candidates without armor, but if it comes to protecting the king—"

"Ah. I see."

"If someone came in, claiming to be an outside challenger, could they challenge anyone there, or just the examiners, or what?"

"Anyone."

"Umm." Paks chewed her lip a moment. "I could keep my armor here—nearby—if Lieth will squire me here—"

Lieth nodded, and Seklis smiled. "That's permissable; we'll all have squires to freshen us between rounds; she can keep your mail in case of need. And on my word as High Marshal, I shall be watching for any trouble, and will ward whomever you say."

Chapter Twenty-six

Paks came to the Grange-Hall in the padded training armor and surcoat Seklis had provided. Lieth carried her paladin's mail and the elven blade. Light blazed from the Grange-Hall windows: candles on frames hung high above the floor, more candles set in brackets along the walls and the railing separating the seats from the open space. Paks peeked into the Hall on her way to the High Marshal's study: already the seats were filling.

Seklis grinned when he saw her. "Ah—Lady Paksenarrion. Come, meet your fellow examiners. Here's Marshal Sulinarrion, of Seameadow Grange—and Marshal Aris, of Copswith Grange—and Marshal Doryan—" Someone pulled at his sleeve, and he turned away, leaving Paks with three Marshals: a tall brown-haired woman and two men, both gray-haired and dark-eyed. By the time she had them sorted out (Aris was taller, with a wide scar on his forehead), the High Marshal was back, to complete the introductions. Paks was not sure she had them all straight in her mind, but there was no time to worry about it. The great Bells began to peal, and everyone moved into line, with Seklis rearranging as he saw fit.

"You, Suli—and then Seli here—and Paks, you get behind him. There. Gird's grace on all of us."

"Gird's grace," came the response, and they walked quickly into the Hall, ranging themselves across the width of it just below the platform.

The seats were filled. Candlelight glittered on jewels,

slid along the folds of satin and silk, caught the flash of an eye that glanced, and shone steadily back from the few motionless hands. From the far end of the Hall, a fanfare of trumpets followed the Bells into silence. Then the pointers, who would judge the trials, entered in their spotless white uniforms. They came forward, bowing once to the examiners in line, then withdrew in two files to either side. Another blast of trumpets, and the candidates entered in two files, still wearing gray training clothes and training armor. They faced the examiners, bowed, and waited. High Marshal Seklis stepped forward.

"Who presents these candidates for trial?"

"I do." A heavy-set man in the green, rose, and white of the Order stepped into the Hall. "Sir Arinalt Konhalt, Training Master of the Order of the Bells."

"Their names?"

As the Training Master spoke each name, the youth bowed. When he had finished, the High Marshal spoke again.

"Here in the very Hall where Luap spoke, and witnessed to the deeds of Gird, Protector of the Innocent and Helpless, we meet to test the fitness of these youths for knighthood. Each shall demonstrate in at least two bouts that he or she is skilled in swordfighting and brave enough to face a naked blade before others. Do you all agree to submit to the judgment of the pointers?" A murmur of agreement came from them all. "Then here is the order of the examiners." Seklis introduced each examiner.

"Because we have so many candidates," Seklis went on, "we cannot accommodate all bouts at once. The first five candidates will now choose their examiners."

As the candidates moved forward, Paks watched their faces. They seemed very young; she reminded herself that they had had at least two years of knight's training, besides serving as squires. None of the first five chose her; she watched as the examiners and pointers led the candidates back down the Hall to the fighting areas. The candidates waiting for their turns began to fidgit. They could not turn around and watch; they had to face the remaining examiners and try to feign calmness.

At the sound of trumpets, the first bouts began. Swords rang together, and stone echoed the stamp of booted feet. The nearest bout seemed evenly matched at first. Seklis had said that the examiners began by trying standard stroke combinations. No bout could end (except in emergencies) before fifty strokes, no matter what points were scored; most, he said, took between that and a hundred. Paks tried to keep count, but lost it when someone down the Hall cried out. Heads craned, but the bouts went on. Paks looked back at the pair she'd been watching; now the examiner, a Marshal whose name she'd forgotten, was moving the candidate around the area, gaining points with every stroke. The candidate rallied a moment, lunging again and again. But a final flurry by the Marshal broke that attack, and the pointers called the bout just after another one down the Hall.

As soon as a candidate finished one bout, he had to choose his next opponent. This time Paks was chosen, by the only candidate to win his bout. She followed her challenger halfway down the Hall to their assigned area. For the second bouts, the pointers gave the starting word. Paks grinned at the young man; his look of confidence faded. When he lunged, she caught his blade and shed it quickly from hers, then forced him back with a quick attack. He looked startled, as if he had not expected such a strong attack. Before he could recover his timing and balance, Paks pushed him back again, working him around the edge of their space. But he steadied himself, biting his lip, and managed to hold his ground. Paks tested all quarters of his range, probing but not using her full skill against him yet. She let him move into attack again. He quickened; she matched him, saw his surprise, and finished with a decisive rattle of strokes that got past his guard again and again. He would have bruised under his padding. But he bowed politely, and thanked her.

"Lady, it is my honor to suffer defeat at your hands."

"May it be your only defeat, Sir Joris—" for she had

been told his name, the ritual greeting: the first use of their title was by the examiner who passed them.

He grinned. "Lady, if I can learn to fight as you do, it will be. But I thought I had not so much to learn. Are you still learning new things?"

"Joris!" That was his proud father, come from the seats to grip his son's shoulder.

Paks smiled at the older man. "Indeed I am, Sir Joris—and that's a good question. You will learn as long as you know you need to."

"Thank you, Lady Paksenarrion," said the father. "He—"

"Please—" the pointers touched the older man's arm. "Sir—please—not here—we have long to go." Paks returned to the front of the Hall, and the new knight joined his successful comrades in the rear.

Paks lined up behind someone who had not yet been chosen—Seklis's suggestion, so that each examiner would have a short rest between bouts. The second five were already on their first bouts, although one bout from the first five was still going on. She looked around the Hall, trying to spot the Duke, but in that mass of color and movement, she could not find him at first. She tried again. "He's fine," said Lieth in her ear. "I saw them come in."

A few minutes later, another candidate chose her, and she fought her second bout, this one much shorter. At the fiftieth stroke, the spotter named her the victor. This candidate had taken a hard blow to the left shoulder on her first bout, and Paks suspected she had a broken collarbone. Her face was pale and sweaty, but she also managed her bow, and thanked Paks for the honor.

By this time, two of the examiners were out, one with a collarbone, and one with a cracked wrist. Paks made her way past three bouts going on, and lined up again. She did not feel particularly tired, and so put herself in line for immediate choice. She had another easy bout, which she drew out to near a hundred strokes for the candidate's benefit, and then watched the last two finish. Now the family sponsor for each new knight carried out the new armor which the knights had earned. While the knights changed into their armor (Paks hoped the woman with the broken collarbone would not have to struggle into a mail shirt), the examiners also changed. Then the crown prince formally greeted each new knight by name and presented the tiny gold symbol of the Order. When he was through, the High Marshal stepped forward once more.

"We welcome these new knights to the Order of the Bells, and ask Gird's grace and the wisdom of Luap to guide them in their service. At this time, any outside challenge may be offered: is it so?"

"Challenge!" A voice called from the far end of the Hall, near the outside door. A startled silence broke into confusion; the High Marshal stilled it with a gesture.

"Name your challenge," he said.

A figure in plate armor with a visored helm stepped into view; at the same time, someone in Verrakai colors stood in the seats.

"High Marshal, I call challenge on Duke Kieri Phelan. My champion is below: a veteran soldier from his Company."

Again the hubbub, stilled only when the High Marshal shouted them down. By then Phelan was on the floor, surrounded by the king's squires and his own companions. Paks recognized Captain Dorrin and Selfer, the Duke's squire.

"Phelan?" said the High Marshal. "How say you?"

"For what cause do you call challenge, Verrakai?" The Duke's voice was calm.

"For your treachery to the crown of Tsaia," he yelled back.

"I protest," said the crown prince, from his place. "This is not the occasion; the matter has not been settled by the Council."

"It is my right."

"You are not the Duke," said the crown prince. "Where is he?"

"He was indisposed, your highness, and could not attend."

"Do you claim to speak for him?"

"He would agree with my judgment of Phelan," said the

other. "As for challenge, and this challenger, that is my own act."

"Then may it rest on you," said the prince. "I will not permit Phelan to take up this challenge."

"Your highness—"

"No, Duke Phelan. As long as you are a vassal of this court—" Paks saw the Duke's reaction to that; he had not missed the prince's emphasis. "—you will obey. You may not take it up. You may, however, name a champion."

Paks was moving before any of the others. "If my lord Duke permits, I will—"

"A paladin?" asked the Verrakai. "You would champion this Duke—but I forget—you also are his veteran, aren't you?"

"And nothing more," said the other fighter. Paks wondered who it was; she did not quite recognize the voice.

The Duke bowed stiffly to the prince, and the challenger. "I would be honored, Lady, by your service in this matter. Yet all know you came on quest; I would not interfere."

The Verrakai and his attendant had also climbed down to the floor, and now stood opposite the Duke. Paks and the mysterious fighter advanced to the space between them. She noted that the other matched her height, but seemed to move a little awkwardly in armor, as if unused to it. The High Marshal raised his arm to signal them. When it fell, Paks and the stranger fell to blows at once.

The stranger was strong: Paks felt the first clash all the way to her shoulder. Paks circled, trying the stranger's balance. It was good. She tested the stranger's defense on one side, then the other. It seemed weaker to the left, where a formation fighter would depend on shield and shield partner. Perhaps the stranger was not as experienced in longsword—Paks tried a favorite trick, and took a hard blow in return. So the stranger had fenced against longsword—and that trick—before. She tried another, as quickly countered. The stranger attacked vigorously, using things Paks knew could have been learned in the Company. Paks countered them easily. She had no advantage of reach, against this opponent, and less weight, for she had chosen a light blade (as the High Marshal requested) to test the candidates.

They circled first one way, then the other, blades crashing together. Paks still fought cautiously, feeling her way with both opponent and the unfamiliar sword in her hand. She could feel its strain, and tried to counter each blow as lightly as possible, reserving its strength for attack. Suddenly the stranger speeded up the attack, raining blow after blow on Paks's blade. Paks got one stroke in past the other's guard, then took a hard strike on the flat of her blade. This time the sound changed, ringing a half-pitch higher. Warned by this, Paks danced backwards, catching the next near the tip, which flew wide in a whirling arc. She parried another blow with the broken blade, and then dropped it as it shattered, and backed again from a sweep that nearly caught her in the waist.

"Wait!" shouted the High Marshal, but the stranger did not stop. Paks knew Lieth had her second blade ready, but she was backed against the far side of the space. Dagger in hand, she deflected a downward sweep that still drove the chainmail into her shoulder.

The stranger laughed. "You are no paladin. You had the chances, that's all—"

This time Paks recognized the voice. "Barra!" At that, another laugh, and the stranger raised her visor to show that familiar angry face.

"Aye. I always said I could take you—" Again the sword came up for a downward blow.

But Paks moved first. As fast as Barra was, she had the edge of initiative, and slipped under the stroke. Her fingers dug into Barra's wrist, and she hooked her shoulder under Barra's arm, flipping her over. Barra landed flat on her back, sprawling and half-stunned. Paks had her own sword's tip at her throat before she could move. For an instant, rage and excitement nearly blinded her; she could have killed Barra then. But her control returned before she did more than prick her throat. When she could hear over the thunder of her own pulse, the High Marshal was speaking.

"Your challenge of arms, Lord Verrakai, is defeated."

With ill grace, the Verrakai bowed. "So I see. My pardon, lord Duke."

Duke Phelan bowed, silent, and waited while the Verrakai turned to go. Then the Verrakai turned back. "I should have known better," he said, "than to believe one of your veterans. Are they all such liars, lord Duke—and if so, can we believe this paladin of yours?"

Phelan paled, but did not move, and the Verrakai shrugged and walked out. Then Phelan looked at the High Marshal. "Sir Marshal, my defense is proved by arms, but at the cost, it seems, of something I hold more dear—the good opinion of my veterans."

"Or one of them, lord Duke. It is a rare commander who has not one bitter veteran. And you were defended by one."

"Yes." The Duke came to where Paks still held Barra at sword's point. "Lady, if you will, permit her to rise."

Paks bowed, and stood back a pace, still holding Barra's sword. The Duke offered a hand, which Barra refused, scrambling up on her own, instead. She scowled at him.

"Will you say, Barra, why you chose to serve my enemy?"

"I think you're crazy," said Barra loudly. Someone laughed, in the tiers overhead, and she glared upward, then back at the Duke. "You could have been rich—you could have done more, but you let others take the credit. And I was as good as Paks, but you gave her all the praise. She got all the chances—"

"That's not true." Dorrin strode across the floor to her side. She gave a quick glance at the tiers and went on. "You and Paks were recruits together—true. And back then, that first year, you were probably her equal in sword-fighting. But in nothing else, Barranyi, and after the first year not in that."

"I was—you just—"

"You were not. Falk's oath, Barra, I'm your captain; I know you inside out. You made trouble every way you could without breaking rules. You quarreled with everyone. Paks didn't—"

"That mealy-mouth—"

"Mealy-mouth!" That was Suriya, across the floor.

Barra turned dark red. "Damned, sniveling, sweet-tongued prig! Everyone on her side! Everyone—"

"Barra." Something in Paks's voice stopped her. "Barra, you do yourself an injustice here."

"I? Do myself an injustice? No, Paks: you did that. Make a fool out of me in front of your fancy friends. Think you're such an example—" Barra jerked off the helmet and threw it at Paks, who dodged easily. "I'll show you yet, Paksenarrion—you sheepfarmer's daughter. I know about you. You're a coward underneath, that's what—or you'd have had the guts to kill me. Why don't you, eh? You've got the sword now. Go on—kill me." She threw her arms out, and laughed. "Gird and Falk together, none of you have any guts. Well, chance changes with the time, yellow-hair, and I'll have my day yet." She turned away; Paks said nothing, and waved the guards away when they would have stopped her.

"Well," said the crown prince into the horrified silence that followed her exit, "if that's the best witness Verrakai can find against you, Duke Phelan, I think your defense in Council is well assured. That's her own heart's poison brewed there, and none of your doing." An approving murmur followed this. Duke Phelan smiled at the prince.

"I thank you, your highness, for your sentiments. Indeed, I hope nothing I have done has provided food for that—but I will think on it." Then he turned to Paks. "And you, again, have served me well. Paksenarrion—"

"Lord Duke, in this I am serving my gods, and not you; I am no longer your soldier, though I will always be your veteran. I pray you, remember that: although you have done me the honor to treat me almost as a daughter, I am not. I am Gird's soldier now."

Although the trouble had come, and apparently gone, without actual danger to the Duke, Paks was still uneasy that night. When the Duke finally retired to his chamber, she held a quick conference with the king's squires. On no account must the Duke go anywhere—anywhere—without their protection. If she was not available, they must all attend him.

"But Paks, what is it you fear?"

"The malice Barra feels, directed with more skill," said Paks, frowning. "Companions, we have not crowned our king yet; until then trust nothing and no one." When she returned to her own chamber, with Lieth, she found it hard to sleep, despite her fatigue.

Yet in the morning she found nothing amiss. After breakfast in the Duke's chambers, they went to the Council meeting together. Paks noticed, as they came in, that Duke Verrakai was present, and his brother absent. The two elves were there, sitting lower down, this time. She wondered what they had thought of last night's events; they would have to agree that the Duke had kept his temper under trying circumstances.

"I asked for this special session," began the crown prince, "at the request of Lady Paksenarrion, whom you met yesterday. You are aware that she is on quest, searching for the true king of Lyonya. She believes she has found him, and asked that you witness the elf-blade's test of his identity."

"And who is it, your highness?" asked Duke Verrakai.

"I will let the paladin speak for herself." The crown prince waved for Paks to begin.

"Lords, I will give you my reasons briefly, and then the prince's name," She repeated her reasoning, now so familiar, from the elves' claim that the prince had forgotten his past, to the meaning of the message they sent Aliam Halveric about the sword. "As well, when Aliam Halveric gave the sword to Kieri Phelan, to give his wife, the elves replied that the gift was satisfactory. That seemed, to me, to mean that the prince was someone with whom Kieri Phelan, as well as Aliam Halveric, came into contact. Then Garris, one of the king's squires who accompanied me on quest, told me of his own boyhood times with Aliam

Halveric, when Kieri Phelan was Halveric's senior squire." She saw comprehension dawn on several faces around the table, and turned to Duke Phelan before anyone else could speak.

"Yesterday, lord Duke, I spoke openly to you of this reasoning, and of your past; now, before the king's squires of Lyonya, and the Regency Council of Tsaia and heir to the throne, I declare that I believe you are the rightful heir to Lyonya's throne, the only son of King Falkieri, and half-elven by your mother's blood." She turned to Lieth, who had carried in the elven blade, and took the sheathed sword from her. "If it is true, then this blade was forged for you by the elves, and sealed to you with tokens sent by your mother. When you draw it, it will declare your heritage. Is it true that you have never laid hands on this sword to draw it?"

"It is true," said Duke Phelan steadily. "I swore to my wife that I would never draw her blade, when I gave it to her, and until you took it from the wall to kill Achrya's agent, she alone drew it."

"I ask you to draw it now," said Paks, "in the High Lord's name, and for the test of your birth."

Duke Phelan's gray eyes met hers for a long look, then he reached out and took the sword's grip in his hand. His expression changed at once, and at the same time a subtle hum, complex as music, shook the air. In one smooth move, he drew the sword free of the scabbard. Light flared from it, far brighter than Paks had even seen, more silver than blue. The blade chimed. Outside, the Bells of Verella burst into a loud clamor, echoing that chime until the very walls rang with it. Phelan gripped it with both hands, raising it high overhead. Light danced around the chamber, liquid as reflection from water. As Paks watched, the blade seemed to lengthen and widen slightly, fitting itself to the Duke's reach. Then the light still blazing from the blade condensed, seeming to sink into the blade without fading, and the runes glowed brilliant silver, like liquid fire. The green jewel in the pommel glowed, full of light. Phelan lowered the sword, resting the blade gently in his left palm. When he met Paks's eyes again, his own were alight with something she had never seen there. When he spoke, his voice held new resonance.

"Lady, you were right. This is my sword, and I daresay no one will dispute it." A ripple of amusement softened his voice there. "Indeed, I had never thought of such a thing. What an irony this is—so many years it hung on my wall, and I did not know of it."

"Sir king." The crown prince had risen; with him, the rest of the Council stood. "This is—" Abruptly his mannered courtesy deserted him, and he looked the boy his years made him. "It's like one of the old songs, sir, like a harper's tale—" The prince's eyes sparkled with delight.

"As yet, your highness, I am not king. But your congratulations are welcome—if it means that you do not object."

"Object! I am hardly likely to quarrel with the gods about this. It is like a story in a song, that you should be a king without knowing it, and have on your wall for years the sword that would prove you."

"But—but—he's just a mercenary—" Clannaeth burst into speech. The High Marshal and the crown prince glared at him.

"Gird's right arm," said the prince crisply, "if you'd been stolen away as an infant, how would you have earned your bread? As a pig farmer?"

"I didn't mean that," began Clannaeth, but no one listened.

Paks, watching the Duke's face, was heartened at the transformation. She had feared his lingering doubt, but he obviously had none. Whatever the sword had done for him, it had given him the certainty of his birth. So he listened calmly to the short clutter of sound that followed Clannaeth's comment, until the High Marshal hushed them. Then he addressed the Council.

"Lords, when our prince's father first gave me the grant I now hold, I told him I had no plans for independent rulership. That was true. But now I find I have another land, a land which needs me—yet for many years, as you know, I have given my life and work to my steading in

Tsaia. I cannot expect that you would allow the king of a neighboring land to hold land from this crown, but I do ask that you let me keep it for a short while, and that you let me have some influence over its bestowing. Your northern border—for so long, *my* northern border—is still a perilous one. It will need a strong hand, and good management, for many years yet if the rest of Tsaia is to be safe. Now I must travel to Chaya, and relieve the fears of my kingdom, but my senior captains can manage well enough in the north, with your permission."

The crown prince and the High Marshal approved this, and the others agreed—Paks thought by surprise as much as anything.

She looked at the elves. Their faces were as always hard to read, but she did not see the scorn or refusal she had feared. One of them caught her eye, and made a small hand signal she had learned from the rangers: approval, the game is in sight.

"Do you remember any more now?" asked the High Marshal. Phelan nodded.

"A little—and better than that, it makes sense. I had memories of my father—a tall, red-haired man with a golden beard, wearing a green velvet shirt embroidered with gold. Now I know that the embroidery was the crest of our house. And the court I remember, planted with roses—that will be at Chaya, and I daresay I can lead the way to it."

"Your name?" asked Verrakai.

"I am not sure. Your highness, your father once asked me of my heritage, and then swore never to speak of it. But now, with my birthright in my hand, I will speak willingly. My earliest memories are those I have just mentioned. Then, as you know, the prince—I—was stolen away while traveling with the queen. After that, for many years, I was held captive far away by a man who called himself Baron Sekkady. He was, your highness, a cruel master; I remember more than I would wish of those years."

"What did he—" began one of the lords. Phelan turned toward him.

"What did he do? What did he not do, that an evil and cruel man could think of! Imagine your small sons, my lords, in the hands of such a man—hungry, tired, beaten daily, and worse than beaten. He would have trained me to the practice of his own cruelties if he could."

"Did he know who you were?"

"I believe so. He used to display me to visitors. After one such banquet, the visitor seemed to recognize me, and the Baron put silence on him."

"Put silence—?" asked the Marshal.

"He was some sort of wizard, sir Marshal. I know little of that, but he could silence men, and hold them motionless, by his powers . . . though what he enjoyed most was hearing them scream. That visitor, whose name I never knew, had some strange powers himself, for he woke me, while he himself was being tormented in the dungeons. He sent me away."

"How?" asked the High Marshal, after a long pause.

"I'm not sure. By then I had tried escape—and been so punished for it that I had ceased to hope for anything but death. But this man took my fear, and sent me: 'There is a High Lord above all barons,' he said. 'Go to his courts and be free.' And so I climbed out the baron's window, and down the wall, and ran through the woods until I came out of that land. When I came to the coast, I stowed away on a ship . . . and eventually came to Bannerlith, where they set me ashore with their good wishes. I worked my way inland, to Lyonya, at any work I could find, until I fetched up at Aliam Halveric's on a cold winter day, half-starved and frozen. He took me in—first as a laborer, then as a page in the household, and then—when I showed aptitude for fighting—made me a squire. The rest you know. Anyway, it is from that man—Baron Sekkady—that I got my name as I know it. He told me it was Kieri Artfiel Phelan; he called me Artfiel. I use Kieri. What it really is—"

"Is Falkieri Amrothlin Artfielan," said Paks.

"Falkieri—" he breathed. "So close—like the sword—"

"He must have known," said the High Marshal. "He must have known who you were, and delighted in that knowledge. Some scum of Liart's, no doubt. Would you could remember where that was."

"If I could remember that, sir Marshal, I would long ago have freed his domain of him."

"Vengeance?" asked one of the elves.

"No—not vengeance alone. He was cruel to many others, not me alone. It would lighten my heart to know the world free of him."

"My lord," said the crown prince. "You do not wish me to use your title yet, but I must call you something—what will you do now? Will you travel at once to Chaya?"

Phelan looked at Paks, who nodded. "I think I must, your highness. Lyonya has been too long without me."

"Will they accept you?" asked Duke Marrakai. "Lady Paksenarrion said something about the elves—"

"Their council swore, the night I left, to accept as their king the man the sword declared," said Paks quickly. "At that time I did not know it was Duke Phelan. As for the elves, the Lady of the Ladysforest wished to see him before the coronation: the elves had their fears, as I said."

"And do you still, cousins?" asked Phelan of the listening elves, slightly stressing the last word.

"Lord Falkieri, what the elves feared in you was not to your blame. We feared the damage done by your wicked master. Will you deny your temper, and what has sometimes come of it?"

"No. But I asked if you still feared it."

One of the elves laughed. "Lord, you are not the furious man I had heard of. Here I have seen you accept insult with dignity, and remain courteous and capable of thought to all. For myself—but I am not the one who will decide—I would trust you to govern humans."

"But your realm is not all human," the other elf added. "For too many years Lyonya's ruler has lacked any feel for the taigin. This lack hurts us all. You have shown no such ability."

"You believe this, too, was destroyed by Baron Sekkady's cruelty?"

Both of them nodded. "If the small child is not taught—if instead all such sense becomes painful—then it can be lost, for a time, or forever."

"I see. But being half-elven, will not my children carry this ability by heritance, even if I lack it?"

"I suppose—I had not thought—" The elf looked genuinely surprised. "I had heard you swore never to remarry."

"I said so; I never took formal vows, not being in the habit of breaking my stated word. Clearly I cannot refuse to sire heirs for Lyonya, and old as I am, I daresay—"

"Old!" The elf laughed, then sobered quickly. "My pardon, Lord—and lords of Tsaia. I meant no disdain. But Lord Falkieri, you are not old for half-elven. You are merely well grown. You have many years yet to found a family, though your people will be glad the sooner you wed."

"But I'm—"

"Fifty years—and what of that? No elf-born comes to full powers much before that. Your sister would yet live had she waited to wed and bear children until fifty. Fear not death from age yet awhile, Falkieri; blade and point can kill you, but not age alone until your sons' sons are come to knighthood."

When the elves said nothing more, the crown prince spoke again. "We would honor you with an escort into Lyonya, my lord. Lady Paksenarrion speaks of peril; our lands are old allies. Will you accept it?"

Phelan nodded; Paks saw that he was near tears from all this. He struggled for a moment and regained control. "I brought with me only a small escort, as your highness knows. I would be honored by a formal one. But when could they be ready to leave?"

The meeting dissolved in a mass of details—which unit of the Tsaian Royal Guard would travel by which route, who would take word to Phelan's steading in the north, how best to plan the march, and on and on. Paks listened, starting as the High Marshal touched her shoulder.

"If you have a few minutes, Lady Paksenarrion, I'd like to see you in the Grange-Hall."

"Certainly. I see we won't be leaving for some hours, if today—"

"Not today," said Phelan, catching her last words. "Tomorrow at best—I'm sorry, Paks, but there's too much to do."

She bowed, and beckoned to Garris, who followed her a few feet away.

"Don't leave him, Garris—any of you—for any reason—for even a few minutes. I cannot name the peril, but we know that evil powers do not want him crowned."

"I swear to you, Paks: we will not leave him."

"I will return shortly." And Paks followed the High Marshal away from the chamber.

High Marshal Seklis ushered Paks into his study, and seated her near a small fire. A yeoman-marshal brought a tray of sweet cakes and a pot of sib, then withdrew.

"I understand your concern, Lady," he began, "but it will take the rest of the day to get a troop of the Royal Guard ready to ride on such a mission. Your things, no doubt, are simpler. And the king's squires will guard him. Now that you've handed over that sword, you'll need another, and I want a favor in return—the story of your quest so far, to write into the archives for the Marshal-General."

Paks told her tale, from leaving Duke Phelan's stronghold to her arrival in Vérella, as quickly and completely as possible, but the pot of sib was empty when she finished. The High Marshal sat back and sighed, then smiled.

"Now I understand your haste. Come—I have no elf-blades here, but we can find something more your weight than the blade that failed you last night." He led her into the armory, where Paks tried one blade after another until she found one to suit. Then they walked back into the palace, to find the Duke's suite a chaotic jumble of servants, gear, and visitors. Paks saw Kolya and Dorrin across the outer room, and worked her way towards them.

"He's not here at the moment," said Dorrin, "but he'll

be back. Before you ask, all the king's squires went with him, as well as Selfer—don't worry. Falk's oath, Paks, if we'd known what you would do someday, I don't know if we'd ever have risked your hide on the battlefield."

"Oh yes, you would," said Paks. "How else could you test a weapon? Not by hanging it on the wall."

"We'll miss him," said Kolya soberly. "The best master a land ever had, and I'm not the only one who thinks so. I'm not ill-wishing—I just wish I could pick up my trees and move to Lyonya."

"He'd find you a grove."

"It's not the same. Those Westnuts I struggled with, learning to dig one-handed—I can't move that somewhere else."

"And he feels it too," said Paks quietly.

"I know. And I'm glad for him. All those years of hearing the others pick and pick—hedge-lord, they'd say, or base-born moneybags—they'll sing a new song now. He was never less than kingly with us; Lyonya's lucky, and he deserves the best of it."

"Who's going with him? For that matter, who's here?"

Dorrin numbered them on her fingers. "Arcolin's commanding back north; Selfer and I came along, and we'll go on to Lyonya. Kolya, you know, and Donag Kirisson, the miller from Duke's West, and Siger. And Vossik and a half-dozen solid veterans. Plus the usual: carters and muleteers, and that. I expect he'll take his own veterans, and I doubt we could peel Siger away from him with a knife."

"And how many of the Tsaian Guard?"

"A score at least. The crown prince would like to send a cohort, but you know what that means in supplies. The Duke—the king—always said the Tsaian Royal Guard travelled on silk."

The High Marshal nodded. "It's court life—I've argued again and again about it, but to no avail. They're good fighters—well trained and disciplined—but any decent mercenary company can march them into the ground."

"It's too bad the Company can't be here," said Dorrin. "They'd be proud of him."

"What is it—a week's march? I agree with Lady Paksenarrion; he must not wait that long to travel. Although his own Company would be a fitting escort."

"If it didn't frighten the Lyonyans," said Dorrin. "They aren't used to troop movements there."

Paks looked a question at her, and Dorrin blushed.

"I trained there, you know," she said. "But I was born a Verrakai."

"You?"

"Yes. They don't admit it any more." Dorrin grinned, shaking her head. "My cousin is furious. I remember getting in fights with him before I left home."

More messengers and visitors arrived. Someone came to Dorrin with a handful of scrolls and a question; she shrugged helplessly at Paks and moved aside to look at them. Servants carried in trays of food. Paks thought of her own rooms, and wondered if Lieth had packed her things before leaving with Phelan. She wormed her way through a cluster of people to ask Kolya when he'd be back.

"I'm not sure—he said not long, but not to worry if it was a glass or so. Some Company matter. He'd already had to talk to his bankers, and draft messages to Arcolin. Why?"

"I'll go down to my rooms, then, and pack up. It won't take long." Paks worked her way out of the suite, past a row of squires bearing messages, and hurried to her own quarters. Lieth had not packed, but she found two of the palace servants straightening the rooms. In a short time, she had rolled everything neatly into her saddlebags or Lieth's. She went back along the corridors with the bags slung over her shoulder. It was midafternoon, and most of the outer court was in shadow. The bustle in Phelan's suite seemed less. A row of corded packs waited in the outer room. Kolya, Dorrin, High Marshal Seklis, and Donag Kirisson sat around a low table near the fire in the sitting room, eating rapidly. Paks joined them, dumping her saddlebags nearby. She reached for the end of a loaf.

"Where is he? Isn't he back?"

"Not yet," said Kolya. "Are you worried, Paks? He has four good squires with him."

"Did he take the sword?" asked Paks without answering Kolya.

"No," said Dorrin. She pushed back her cloak to show the pommel. "He asked me to keep it here—said he didn't want it on the street."

Paks frowned, her worry sharpening. "I wish he'd taken it. I should have said something."

"Why?"

"If nothing else, it's a remarkably good weapon. But more than that, in his hands it has great power, and none of us can use it."

"You can, surely."

"Not now," said Paks. "Not after he drew it—it's sealed to him completely now. I would not dare to draw it."

Dorrin looked at it. "If I'd known that—"

"Excuse me, Lady—I was given a message for your hand." Paks looked up to see a page in the rose and silver house livery holding something out. She put out her hand, and took it. The page bowed, and quickly moved away. It was a small object wrapped in parchment. Paks folded the stiff material back carefully. When she saw what it contained, she felt as cold as if she'd been dipped in the ice-crusted river.

Chapter Twenty-seven

There on her hand lay the Duke's black signet ring, the same ring she had carried from Fin Panir to the Kuakgan's Grove in Brewersbridge, the same ring she had taken back to the Duke that fall. The others had leaned to see what it was; Paks held out her hand, and watched the faces whiten. No one spoke. Paks flattened the parchment, and saw thin, angular writing she knew at once to be in blood. She shivered; she knew it must be *his* blood.

Alone, or Lyonya will have no King.

This too she showed the others, handing it around.

"By the Tree—" Kolya was the first to find speech. "What can you do, Paks?"

"Find him," said Paks grimly.

"But how?"

"They will guide me; they intend it." She was shaken by a storm of rage and grief, and struggled to master it. For what must come she had to be calm. She took the ring from Dorrin, who was staring blankly at it, and slipped it on her own middle left finger. "Kolya—" The one-armed woman met her eyes, blinking back tears. "Find the nearest Kuakgan—is there one near enough Verella?"

"For what?"

"To aid him when he travels. I want the taigin awakened for him."

"Great lords above!" muttered the High Marshal. Paks shot him a quick glance and went on.

"Tell the Kuakgan to ask the taigin of Master Oakhallow:

and tell him the three woods are fireoak, blackwood, and yellowwood."

"You want him to raise the highfire for the Duke?"

"For me," said Paks quietly. She turned quickly to Dorrin. "Make sure they are ready to ride at once. Whatever it takes, Captain Dorrin: the High Marshal will help you."

"Indeed I will." The High Marshal's expression was as grim as she felt. "Every Marshal in Verella—"

"And on the way. Sir Marshal, I must speak to you alone." Dorrin and the others left quickly. Paks took a deep breath but before she could speak, the High Marshal asked:

"Do you foresee your own death, paladin of Gird?"

"I see nothing, sir Marshal, but the direction of my quest. It seems likely that this summons means death. But Girdsmen are hard to kill, as you know—" He nodded, with a tight smile. Paks went on. "Sir Marshal, I ask you these favors. Would you ask the Marshal-General to send a sword to my family at Three Firs when she thinks it safe for them, and such word of me as she thinks it wise for them to have?"

"I will," he said. "You are sure you will never return there?"

"I knew that before now, sir Marshal. However this ends, I cannot return; I would like the Marshal-General to know my wishes in this."

"I will tell her," said Seklis. "Be sure of that. What else?"

"This time I will not have Gird's symbols defaced," said Paks. "I will arrange to return my arms and medallion. If you will leave these in the grange at Westbells, on your way east—"

"You expect to follow?" The High Marshal's voice was completely neutral.

Paks shook her head. "I expect to follow Gird's directions, sir Marshal. I hope to follow, but—to be honest—I expect not."

He lowered his voice. "It is not the way of the Fellowship to sacrifice any Girdsman—let alone a paladin—without a fight."

Paks managed a smile. "On my honor, sir Marshal, they will find they have a fight—though not the one they expected, perhaps. And as well—" she found herself grinning at him, "as well, imagine if one paladin can spoil such a long-laid plot. How many years has that black web-spinner been preening herself on the completeness of her webs? And the Master of Torments must have enjoyed what happened to a helpless child. Yet now the rightful king returns, and their attempt to sever Lyonya and Tsaia will fail."

"If you can find him." The High Marshal held her gaze. "If you can pay the price."

"I can find him," said Paks. "As for the price, what I have is the High Lord's, and I will return it as he asks."

"Gird's grace be with you, paladin," said the High Marshal formally.

"And Gird's power rest in your grange," replied Paks. She bowed and strode quickly from the chamber.

She hardly noticed those who moved out of her way in the passages outside. She was wondering how Phelan had been trapped. Were all the squires dead? Was he himself dead, and this message no more than a trap for her? But she did not believe that—else her quest would lead somewhere else. She would find him easily enough; those who had sent the ring would see to that. She came into the outer court and glanced up to see what light remained. In another glass or so it would be dark. No one questioned her at the outer gate, though the guards greeted her respectfully. She nodded to them and passed into the wide street beyond.

Here she slowed to a stroll, and looked around carefully. The street seemed full enough of hurrying people, hunched against the cold and ducking into one doorway or another. Directly across from the palace gate was a large inn, the Royal Guardsman. On one side was a saddler's, with a carved wooden horse, gaily decked, over the entrance. Beyond that was a cobbler's, then a tailor's shop.

On the other side was a scribe-hall, then a narrow alley. Paks walked that way, past the ground floor windows of the inn's common room. She was aware when someone came out the inn door behind her. She felt the back of her neck prickle with another's attention. But she walked on, steadily. The footsteps behind quickened. Paks slowed, edging toward the front of the scribe-hall.

"I think," said a low voice at her shoulder, "that you must be Paksenarrion?"

Paks turned; the follower was a tall redheaded woman, in the garb of a free mercenary. Paks saw the hilt of a dagger in each boot as well as one at her waist.

"Yes," she said quietly. "I am Paksenarrion."

The redhead gave her a scornful look up and down. "You are just as Barra said. Well, and did you get our present?"

Paks raised an eyebrow. "If you mean a certain ring—"

"Don't play games with me, paladin," the woman sneered. "If you want to see him alive, follow me and keep your hands off your sword." She turned away.

"Stop," said Paks, not loudly but with power. The woman froze, then turned back to her, surprise in her eyes. "Before I go one step, I will have your word on this: is he alive? What of his squires?"

"They are all alive, Phelan and the squires, but they will die if you are not quick."

"And I should follow so we can all be killed at once, is that it?" Paks forced humor into her tone, and again the woman's eyes flashed surprise.

"No," she said sulkily. "The Master would be glad to kill all of you—and will—but you can buy your lord some time, if you dare it."

"And where do you go?"

"You would not know if I told you. There are places in Verella that none but the Guild know, and places known only to few of the Guild." She looked hard at Paks for a moment, and shook her head quickly. "I wonder—perhaps Barra has erred—"

"Is this Barra's plot?" asked Paks. "Or Verrakai's?"

"You ask too much. Come." The woman turned away and walked off quickly. Paks followed, her heart pounding.

To her surprise, they did not enter the alley Paks had seen, but kept to the main streets until they were in the eastern end of Verella. Then the woman turned into a narrower street, and another. Here was the sort of poverty Paks had seen in every city but Fin Panir and Chaya: crowded narrow houses overhanging filthy cobbles and frozen mud, ragged children huddled together for warmth, stinking effluvium from every doorway. She was aware of the curious glances that estimated her sword's worth and the strength of her arm rather than a paladin's honor. The redhead ducked into a narrow passage between two buildings, scarce wide enough for their shoulders. It angled around a broad chimney and opened into a tiny court. Across that was a double door, painted black with red hinges. On this the redhead rapped sharply with her dagger hilt; a shutter in the door scraped open.

Paks looked quickly around the open space. It was already draped in shadow, overlooked only by the blank rear walls of the buildings that ended here. Paks wondered at the windowless walls, then saw that there had been windows once—they were blocked up, some by brick and others by heavy shutters. She could hear the red-headed woman muttering at the door, and something small scuttling among the debris across the way. Aside from that, and the distant rumble of street noises, it was ominously quiet.

One leaf of the double doors opened, squealing on its hinges. "Come on," said the woman sharply. Paks did not move.

"I want to see him."

"Inside."

"No. Here. Alive." Paks called light, and it cast a cool white radiance over the grimy stones, the stinking litter along the walls. Several dark shapes fled squeaking into holes.

The woman turned back to the doorkeeper, and muttered again. Paks waited. The door slammed shut, and the woman turned back to her.

"I told you he was alive. You're only making it worse."

"On the contrary," said Paks. "I do what is necessary."

"Necessary!" The woman spat. "You'll learn necessary soon enough."

"That may be, but I will see him alive and well before then."

"As the Master answers, you will see." They waited in heavy silence for some minutes. When the doors opened, both sides gaping wide, two files of armed men emerged. The first was dressed in dark clothes, and carried short swords. Behind them came two priests of Liart, their hideous snouted helms casting weird shadows in Paks's light. But for one being slightly taller, she could see no difference in them. The redhead bowed deeply. The two faced Paks; one of them raised a spiked club.

"Paladin of Gird, have you come to redeem your master?"

"He is not my master, but the rightful king of Lyonya, as you know."

"But dear to you."

"To bring him to his throne was laid on me for my quest," said Paks. "He is no longer my lord, for I am Gird's paladin."

"But you are here because of him."

"Because of Lyonya's king."

"The Master of Torments desires otherwise.

"The Master of Torments has already found that the High Lord prevails."

A howl of rage answered that, and a bolt of blue light cast from the second priest. Paks laughed, tossing it aside with her hand. "See," she said. "You have said that he lives, and that you have some bargain in mind—but I am not without power. State your terms, slaves of a bad master."

"You will *all* die in torment—" began one, but the other hushed him and stepped forward.

"You killed our Master's servants in Lyonya," he said. "You killed them in Aarenis before that. The Master will have your blood for that blood, or take the blood of Lyonya's king."

"Death for life?" asked Paks.

"No." The priest shook his head slowly. "Torment for it, paladin of Gird. Death is easy—one stroke severs all necks, and our Master knows you paladins expect a long feasting thereafter. You must buy the King of Lyonya's freedom with the space of your own suffering. This night and day one will suffer as our Master demands—either Lyonya's king, or you."

"And then you will continue, and kill in the end." Paks kept her voice steady with an effort.

"It may be so, though there is another who wants your death. Uncertainty is, indeed, an element of torment. But the terms are these: you must consent, and come unresisting to our altar, or Lyonya's king will be maimed before another dawn, and will never take the throne."

"Prove that he and his squires live."

"His squires! What are they to you?"

"You would not know. Prove it."

One of the priests withdrew. In a short time, the priest and more armed men appeared, bringing Phelan and the squires, all bound and disarmed. One man carried their weapons.

They gaped across the tiny yard at Paks's light. Phelan's face hardened as he saw her. Garris sagged between his guards, as if badly hurt. Suriya's right arm was bandaged, and Lieth's helmet sat askew above a scalp wound. Selfer limped.

"Paks. I had hoped you wouldn't come to this trap." Phelan's voice barely carried across the court.

"Your ring worked as we hoped." That was one of the priests.

"A paladin on quest, my lord, has little choice," said Paks, ignoring the priest and meeting Phelan's gaze.

"Now you see that we have what we claimed," said the first priest. "Will you redeem him?"

"All of them," said Paks. "The squires too."

"Why the squires?"

"Why should any be left in your hands?" Paks took a long breath. "I will barter for the king, and these squires, on these grounds: one day and night for each—you to restore their arms, and let them go free for those days."

"Paks, no!" Suriya leaned forward; her guards yanked her back.

"You have no power to bargain," said the priest. "We can kill them now."

"And you are beyond your protection," said Paks, "and I am within mine. If you kill them, Liart's scum, I will kill many of you—and your power here will fail. Perhaps I cannot save them—though you would be foolish to count on that—but I can kill you."

"So." The priests conferred a moment. "We will agree on these terms: one day and night for each—that is five you would redeem?"

"Have you more in your power?"

"No. Not at present. Five, then: five days and nights. We will restore their arms and free them when you are within."

"No." Paks shook her head. "You know the worth of a paladin's word. I know the worth of yours. You will free them now, and on my oath they will not strike a blow against you—"

"Paks—"

"Be silent, Suriya. As it is my choice to redeem you, so you are bound by my oath in this. Take your weapons and return to the palace; guard your lord on his journey and say no more." She looked from face to face. "All of you—do you understand?"

Phelan's eyes glittered. "Paks, you must not. You don't understand—"

"Pardon, my lord, but I do understand—perhaps more than you do. I am not your soldier now. I follow the High Lord, and Gird, the protector of the helpless, into whatever ways they call. Do not, I pray you, make this quest harder than it is."

He bowed as much as he could. "Lady, it shall be as you say. But when I am king—"

"Then speak as the king's honor demands," said Paks, meeting his eyes steadily. She looked back at the priest. "You will not harry them for the days of the bargain."

"We will not."

"Then I take oath, by Gird and the High Lord, that when I see them safely freed and armed I will submit without battle to your mastery for five days and nights."

"Unbind them," said one of the priests.

"Wait," said Paks. They paused. "I have one further demand. They shall carry away my own arms, that Gird's armor be not fouled in your den."

"I have no objection," said the priest curtly. He nodded, and the guards untied the bonds. Garris slumped to the ground; Suriya and Selfer struggled to lift him.

"Is he dead?" asked Paks.

"Not quite," said Selfer grimly. Paks prayed, certain the Liartian priests would not let her touch Garris to heal him. She felt a drain on her strength, as the healing often seemed, and Garris managed to stand between the other two. Suriya looked at her, and nodded slowly. When they had all been given their weapons, Paks spoke again.

"Come here—near the entrance—and I will disarm." Lieth and Phelan warded her as best they could while she took off her weapons and mail. She folded everything into a neat stack, covered with her cloak against curious eyes, and tucked her Gird's medallion into it. Then she took off Phelan's signet ring and handed it to him. "My lord, your ring. Take your royal sword, and keep it to your hand after this. Lieth, High Marshal Seklis will take my gear. My lord, you must go at once."

"Paks—"

"Gird's grace on you, sir king." Paks bowed; Phelan nodded, and started up the passage with Lieth guarding the rear. She watched just long enough to see them around the chimney, then turned back to the others. They had not moved.

"It is astonishing," said one priest, "that Girdsmen are so gullible." Paks said nothing. "For all you know, that man may be a convert to our Master's service."

At that, Paks laughed. "You know better than that of paladins: if he were evil, I would know. I can read *your* heart well enough."

"Good," said the priest, his voice chilling. "Read it

closely, paladin, and learn fear." He nodded, and the swordsmen came forward on either side. "Remember your oath, fool: you swore to come without a battle."

Paks felt her belly clench; for a moment fear shook her mind and body both. Then she steadied herself and faced them. "As I swore, so I will do; the High Lord and Gird his servant command me."

The priests both laughed. "What a spectacle we can offer! It's rare sport to have a paladin to play with—and one sworn to offer no resistance is rarer yet."

Paks made no answer, and when the swordsmen surrounded her, stood quietly. None of them touched her for a moment, daunted by her light, but when the priests gave a sharp command they prodded her forward, across the yard and into the doorway. Once inside, the priests grabbed her and slammed her roughly against the wall of the passage. Her light had vanished. She felt their assault on her heart at the same time, but trusted that no evil could touch her so. Guards bound her arms behind her and her ankles with heavy thongs, drawing them cruelly tight. Then they dragged her down one passage and another, down steep stairs where every stair left its own bruise, along wide corridors and narrow ones, until she was nearly senseless.

That journey ended in a large chamber, torchlit, half-full of kneeling worshippers. The guards pulled Paks upright, supporting her between them so that she could see the size of the room and the equipment gathered on a platform at the near end. It was grim enough; Paks had seen such things before. She would never come out of here; she would die of it, and worse than that, she would be watched, taunted, ridiculed, as it happened. She tried to think of something else—anything else—and felt a nudge in her back, warm and soft, as if the red horse had pushed against her. When the priests confronted her, she knew her face showed nothing of her fear.

When they introduced her to the waiting crowd, she heard the reaction, the indrawn breath—half fear, half anticipation. A paladin—would the high gods intrude? But the priests reassured them: the fool had consented. Her gods would not interfere. Paks saw the gloating eyes, the moist-lipped mouths half-open. At the back, a dark woman who might have been Barra gave her a mocking grin. As the priests talked on, she saw more and more slip into the hall, drawn by rumor and held by delight. A sour taste came into her mouth; she swallowed against it, praying.

Unlike her ordeal in Kolobia, most of what happened in the next five days and nights remained clear in her mind.

They began predictably, by ripping her clothes off and scattering the pieces as the worshippers laughed and cheered at the priests' urging. Paks stared over their heads at the back wall of the chamber. Then one priest handled her roughly all over, squeezing and pinching as if she were a draft horse up for sale. The second one began, slapping her face with his studded gloves, pinching her breasts sharply.

Now they called the worshippers forward, encouraging them all to feel and pry, slap and pinch. It was petty, but not less disturbing for that. The sheer enmity of it—the number of sneering faces, strangers to whom she had never done harm, who snickered and giggled as they ran their dirty fingers over her face, poked her ribs, felt between her thighs. She could not imagine being such a person, taking such pleasure. What could have made them what they were?

One youth reached up and yanked at her hair; that began a round of such antics. One would take a single hair and pull it out; others took a handful and pulled again and again. They pulled other hair, jeering when she flinched, and looking to the priests for approval. She felt the first blood trickle down her face; someone with a jeweled ring had scraped it deliberately across her forehead. But the priests stopped him.

"Not yet," one of them said. "The Master has plenty of time for this one, slave, and more skill than you know. Draw no blood, slaves, at this time—be obedient, or suffer his punishment." The man in front of Paks paled, trying to hide his bloodstained ring. The priest laughed. "Do you think to hide from the Master, fool? Yet you share our vision: you are only hasty. You will taste her blood later—be obedient." He confronted Paks, pushing the spiked visor of his helm into her face. "And you, little paladin? Do you fear yet? Do you begin to regret your bargain?"

"No." To her surprise, her voice was steadier than her limbs. "I do not regret following the commands of my lord."

"Then we will instruct you," he said, and made a sign to the guards. "You have seen the punishments in Phelan's army. See how you like ours." As he spoke, the guards forced her back over a small waist-high block, looping her wrist bonds through a hook on the floor of the platform. One of them leaned a fist on her chest, and two others pulled her knees down and apart. Paks felt her back muscles straining. The priest who had been speaking slapped her taut belly and laughed again. "It bothered you when our servants pulled your hair? Then we will ease you this far, paladin: you will have no hair to be pulled. You know the term *tinisi turin*?" The crowd laughed obediently and the second priest came toward her with a razor.

"It may not be as sharp as you would like," he began, "But it has certain—advantages—for our way—of doing things." As he spoke, he yanked on her braid and sliced roughly at her thick hair. In a moment or two, it fell free; Paks could feel the ragged ends stirring, the cool air on her scalp. He walked away. When he came back, two assistants were bringing with him the little brazier she had seen, and the razor he held was glowing hot. "It cuts well this way," he said, laying it lightly along her ribs. Paks tried not to flinch. But by the time he had shaved her head and the rest of her body hair, leaving raw burned patches that the chill air rasped, she was shaking. The watching crowd talked and laughed, like people watching a juggler at a village fair. The priest watching her nodded.

"You will learn despair, little paladin; even now you are finding what you did not expect. And now we will brand you with Liart's mark, that you feel in your own flesh his Mastery." One of them seized her ears, bracing her head, and the hot iron came down, its horned circle held before her eyes a moment before it pressed her forehead. For an instant it felt cold, as it hissed, then searing pain bored through her head. Tears burst from her eyes; she choked back a scream. The priest laughed. "Now you are Liart's. You may stay there, while we attend to other matters that need the Master's touch."

Paks could see nothing of what happened next; she fought to keep control of her own reactions. She heard a name called, and someone cried out in the crowd. A flurry—a frightened voice, a boy's voice, and another one pleading, a man's voice, older. The priest made some accusation; Paks did not attend to the words, but the tone came through. Then the boy's voice again, frightened and rising to a scream of pain. She heard blows—a whip, she thought—and more screams, then the man's voice sobbing. Then the priest—cold, arrogant, demanding, and the man's voice again, in submission. The priest returned to her, and grabbed her by both ears, holding up her head so that she could see the child who hung from his wrists, bloodstreaked.

"See? If we treat children so, think how much worse it will be for you."

"Gird's grace on that boy," said Paks quietly. "The protector of the helpless grant him peace."

The priest dropped her head abruptly. After that came several torments, repeated careful blows of a slender rod, cuffs and blows with padded sticks and weighted thongs. Then she was untied and thrown to the floor, kicked and prodded and beaten again, not enough to break bones, but until she was dizzy and sick. All the time the crowd watched, jeering at her whenever she cried out. Paks fixed her mind on Gird and the High Lord, on the magical fire the Kuakgan had raised, on the feel of the red horse's nose in her back.

Next she was shoved over to the platform where the boy hung, now stirring again and moaning. Blood spattered the floor, streaked his body. The guards untied him and tossed him aside. Paks winced at the hollow thud his body made, hitting the floor, and muttered another prayer for him. The priest slapped her. "Pray for yourself, fool! Better yet, beg mercy of our Master, who is the only one who can help you now."

"The High Lord has dominion over all the gods," said Paks, again to her own surprise. The priest signalled the guards, and Paks was jerked off her feet by a rope from her bound wrists over the crossbar. It nearly took her shoulders out of their sockets. The guards untied her ankles, and spread her legs, tying them to either side of the frame, then hauled on the rope until all her weight came on her wrists.

"You," the shorter priest said, "are not a god, and therefore our Master has dominion over you—or would you dispute that?"

Sweat ran into her eyes, stinging. Paks gasped, "I am Gird's paladin—your slavemaster has no dominion over me."

"Gird is not helping you now, paladin," sneered the priest. "Nor will you hold a sword again, if we disjoint both shoulders and leave them so."

"Nor is that the limit of our skill," said the other. "Trussed as you are, we can do anything—and you cannot prevent it."

Paks answered nothing; she could not breathe evenly. Pain wracked her shoulders and back; she hardly felt the burns and welts that had hurt so earlier. How long had it been? How much more?

"I will show you," he said. His gloved hands began to move over her body, gentle at first, in mimicry of lovemaking. The crowd laughed loudly as he exaggerated his movements for their benefit. Then his fingers probed her body, finding points that radiated spikes of pain. She could not stand it—had to writhe—could not, for the pressure on her shoulders. Soon she was panting, gasping for breath, tumbled in a roil of pain that brought back the night she'd been attacked at the inn. He stood back, then, and waited until her breathing quieted. Then he did it again. And again. The third time, she passed out.

When she came to, her arms were tied overhead to corners of the same frame, and the shorter priest was lecturing the crowd.

"—you see, you need not maim or kill—not at first. It is the skill, the knowing where to touch, and how hard. Knowing, for example, which child is a father's favorite." A pause; alert silence from the crowd. "Knowing how much punishment to give." Another long silence. "But some of you would already have killed this paladin of Gird—and spoiled our Master's pleasure by so many hours. Watch and learn—enjoy with us, the power of our Master over *all* mankind. Not even the hero-saints of old can save this paladin in her pain. We can do anything—anything at all—and we come to no harm, as you see. Our Master has the power—the only power. Our Master shares his mastery with his slaves, if they are obedient. You, too, can have power over even a paladin. Watch—learn—do as we say, and you can make a paladin bleed and cry out. And if a paladin falls to us, how much more easily an ordinary man, eh?"

He prowled the front of the hall, menacing, predatory, and Paks saw those in front shrink back slightly. Their eyes followed him, wary.

"What power is it you want? Is it money? We have her gold. Is it blood? We have it all—you will see it fall for our pleasure. Is it lust? You will have your chance. Is it mastery itself? You will see her cringe before us, and before those of you chosen to assist. Our Master has power—real power—and you can share that power. Everyone else is helpless in the end—helpless like this paladin. Would you have feared her once, with her big sword, her fancy armor?" His voice dripped contempt. The crowd shifted, not quite answering. "Yes, admit it! You would have feared her, up there on the street—yes you would, unworthy slaves! You might have cringed from her—but look now. There she hangs, bound and helpless. What she has, she has because we left it to her." He waved an arm back at Paks, and some eyes shifted to meet hers and as quickly shifted away.

"You—*you* there in the third row—you could blind her, couldn't you? And *you*—you could cut off her ears. Who would stop you but our Master? Who could punish you but our Master? Who is worthy of your service but—" he paused; the answer came quickly from the crowd:

"Master—Master—*Master*." The faces Paks could see were tight with fear, not so avid for the spectacle as before. She felt a surge of pity for them.

"Yes. Our Master: Liart the strong. You must never say his name, unworthy slaves, until you come to his altar to swear your souls to him forever. But you know who he is." He raised his hand, fist clenched.

"The Master," came the response.

The priests noticed her open eyes and came to her again. She met their gaze evenly.

"And you are still with us, little paladin?" asked the taller.

"The High Lord is still with us all," she said. Someone in the crowd hooted, and others laughed. The shorter priests reached out and stroked her sides.

"He hasn't done well by you, with these scars," he said. "I'd almost think you'd been given to our Master already."

"No," said Paks recklessly, "that was Achrya's work."

He slammed his fist into her belly. "Don't say that name aloud, scum."

Paks gasped for breath. "You—*fear*—her?"

Again a blow that took her breath away, and another to her face. One of the priests took up the barbed whip they had used on the boy, and showed it to her. "This will teach you something of our Master; he is bolder than that webspinner." He slashed it across her body, then her legs, and walked behind her. Five rapid blows split the skin of her back, hot blood sheeted down, dripping from her legs. Paks clenched her jaw against the fiery pain. Before it dulled, they had brought the next torment, a heated chain held carefully in tongs. First around her waist—then each thigh in turn. Paks could smell the charred skin, *her* charred skin.

Again the crowd was invited up, in groups, to participate. Now the men were urged to arouse themselves. "Not yet," the priest said, to those fumbling at their trousers. "Wait for that—but go on and enjoy what you can." They traced her scars and the whip welts with their fingers, poked and prodded every orifice. She saw one man lick his finger after wiping it in her blood. The thought of it made her sick. The priests laughed. "Good, eh? It's blood like any other—taste it." Several others did the same thing. Paks thought briefly of the many soldiers she had killed—the blood she had shed—but she had never tasted their blood, never seen soldiers as wantonly cruel. Yet some, she could tell, were more frightened than eager: they took no pleasure in it, their eyes downcast, their faces tense. It seemed a long time before the priest ordered the crowd back to their places.

The taller priest held up an iron that had been heating in the brazier, and flourished it.

"Now that you carry Liart's brand, we must do worse than threaten your beauty. But if we decorate you with deep burns here—" he touched the inside of her thigh. Pain flared along her leg. "—you might never ride or walk again." She could not tell how bad the burn was; her whole leg felt afire.

"There are other ways," said the shorter one, conversationally. "If we show you all of them, I fear you will not be able to appreciate the artistry involved. Perhaps we should demonstrate—" and he signalled to the guards. Paks did not notice where they went. Soon they were back, dragging with them a girl Paks had never seen. She looked to be in her mid-teens, someone's servant by her clothes. She was gagged and bound, her eyes wild; as soon as the tall priest ripped the gag roughly away, she screamed.

"Shut up!" He slapped her face. "If you scream again, I'll—" he did not finish the threat; she choked off her cries, and watched him, eyes streaming with tears. He turned to Paks. "From time to time we find our sacrifices in the streets—this girl loitered in an alley, and as we had need, we—borrowed her." As he spoke, the girl turned her head and saw Paks; her eyes seemed to bulge from her face in panic, and she struggled wildly. One of the guards twisted her arm, and she subsided. "Now, paladin, let me offer another bargain."

Paks said nothing.

"You are bound to endure five days and nights—let us say, five days and four nights, now—of our Master's pleasure, whatever comes. But if you will agree that our Master has dominion over all, then we need not waste this girl's limbs showing you the range of our skill. If, however, you still insist that your gods—whatever you name them—are more powerful, then we must teach you your weakness through her. Did you not name Gird protector of the helpless—and you claim to be his paladin? Yes—but you, a paladin of that so-called protector of the helpless, you cannot save this girl from anything, except by our Master's name."

"Please—" the girl's voice was faint, but she looked straight into Paks's eyes. "Don't let them—"

Paks looked away, scanning the crowd, then the priests, then the guards, and finally looking back at the girl. "No," she said steadily. "I can't."

"So," said the tall priest. "You begin to enjoy our entertainment then? You would like to see more, is that it?" Someone in the crowd tittered.

"No," said Paks again. "I take no pleasure in giving pain, or seeing pain given." The girl's mouth opened again, but Paks spoke first. "I cannot forswear my gods, child. I will pray for you—that Gird and the High Lord protect you, comfort you, and strengthen you, that the Lady of Peace bring you peace in the end—but the Master of these slaves is evil, and I will not praise him."

"Then she will suffer, and it is your doing," said the tall priest.

"No. If you harm her, she will suffer because of you. I am not a torturer: *you* are."

"But you could stop it, and you refuse to help her."

"Could I?" Paks managed a smile that seemed to crack her face. "*Could* I stop it? Have I any reason to trust your word? As long as I am trussed here, you can do as you like—and you like to do evil. Besides, your Master is a paltry fellow; I cannot call him great. Liart the strong, indeed! Liart the coward is more like it!"

"Girdish slut!" The tall priest snatched up the barbed whip again, and laid two strokes on her before the other grabbed his arm.

"She is stronger than you thought, brother—she taunts you into just such haste. See—if she faints, she rests."

"She will not faint." The tall priest swiped his hand down the bleeding welts and rubbed it over Paks's face, then licked his hand. "And if she does we will add every hour to the length of her bargain. Your blood tastes sweet, paladin. Before long we will try your flesh as well." He turned back to the girl, and his voice calmed.

"There are several ways to cripple without killing, paladin. Some are more . . . artistic . . . than others. Consider this—" He used tongs to pull from the brazier a fist-sized cobble. "A hot stone. Applied to the inside of a joint—say the knee—and bound there, it will burn deeply, and the scars contract, pulling the limb awry. It works best at knee, crotch, elbow, and armpit, choosing the size of stone to conform, of course—" The guards had forced the girl onto her face, and pulled up her skirts. Now the priest set the hot stone against the back of her knee, and the guards quickly forced her leg back against it, and bound it tight with heavy thongs. Her screams echoed off the stone walls. The guards let her go, cutting the thongs that bound her arms, and she thrashed on the floor, shrieking and clawing at her leg.

Paks fought down nausea. She could do nothing; she closed her eyes, trying to concentrate on Gird, trying to pray. But she heard the crowd shouting, jeering now at the struggling girl. Something tugged at her, sending a wave of pain through her. She opened her eyes to see the girl clutching at her ankle, trying to drag herself upward on Paks's body. "Please!" she begged. "Please—stop them!"

"I can't—" muttered Paks, "But Gird—"

"No! You—!" the girl screamed, clawing now. "You won't help—*curse* you—!" She threw herself upward, shaking Paks back and forth in her bonds. Then she collapsed, still screaming. Paks shook her head; tears burned her eyes. Her heart seemed to falter in her chest. The priests waited until the girl's screams died to sobbing, then the guards pinned her again, cut the thongs, and pulled her legs straight. She gave a final shriek as they knocked the stone loose; it left two charred wounds in her leg as it rolled to the floor; smoking bits of her flesh clung to it.

"Well, paladin—did Gird protect *her*?" The taller priest nudged the sobbing girl with his foot. Paks did not answer. She fought the black despair Liart sent, forcing herself to think of the king riding eastward, his squires around him. She would not have spent someone else's pain for that, but even so she did not repent the bargain. After a long pause, he asked, "Do you think he will protect you? Will you fight well, Paladin of Gird, with your leg twisted like this? Or imagine your arm—your sword arm—drawn up with scars." He touched the hollow of her elbow, and her armpit; Paks shivered. "I see you do understand. We need not be in haste to show you, then." He turned to the guards. "Tie that one, and leave her; we will want her later."

"No," said Paks.

"No? You dare give orders here? Or are you agreeing that our Master has dominion?"

"I am not. I am telling you not to hurt her more—she has done you no harm."

"What of that? It amuses us—and teaches you to know your helplessness. You can save her only by accepting our Master as yours."

Paks prayed, trying to convey what healing she could across that space, as she had with Garris. But she had known Garris, touched him with healing before. This girl was a stranger. She felt a comforting touch on her own head, as if a firm but gentle hand cradled it for a moment, but nothing that let her suspect she had healed the girl. She could not see the girl's face, where she lay, but the sobs quieted, and the heaving back was still.

For some time after that, she was left hanging before

the crowd; she noticed that it ebbed and flowed, and individuals came and left, to return after an interval. From time to time the priests came to her again, repetitions of the torments already begun. Once they tried to rouse the servant girl, and found her dead; they dragged her body aside. Paks could not be sure of the pass of time. Pain and thirst confused her. Whenever she fell into a doze, they roused her, until she longed for rest more than anything. Then the crowd thickened again.

The guards lit new lamps, and set pungent incense burning in a row of censors. The smoke swirled back and forth. Paks watched it, half-tranced by its intricate patterns that seemed to make pictures in the haze. She had managed not to listen to the priests' words, even reciting to herself the ten fingers of the Code of Gird. But now as they approached her again, her concentration wavered. Her belly knotted; her tongue seemed too large for her mouth. Two guards cut the thongs that held her wrists, and shoved. She fell forward, slamming into the floor with stunning force. She was just aware when they cut the ankle thongs and her feet thudded down.

The relief in her shoulders lasted only a few moments. Guards yanked her up by the arms and dragged her to the rough stone altar that centered the platform. They bound her again by wrist and ankles, with the rough-hewn stone rasping her lacerated back. The taller priest laid a single flat stone on her belly. He stood back, and the second priest laid another similar stone on her chest. Paks waited; the stones were uncomfortable, but not painful, except where they lay on the burns. She was too relieved to have her head supported at last, and the weight off her arms. Then returning blood seemed to dip her hands in fire for a few minutes. The priests called the crowd forward.

"We will show you a torment that lasts long only with strong sacrifices, such as this one," said the first. "We will add weight to those stones, a heavy link of chain at a time, until she can scarcely draw breath. Then time alone becomes the tormenter; in the end her breath will fail. And you will help. As you have given to the Master, so in your name will the links be added."

And each person who came by dropped a coin or so into a pot, naming the number; the guards fed a heavy chain from its coil onto the stones, link by link, one or two or three at a time, as the worshipper gave. One heavy man in a silk robe gave a large silver, and twelve links at once dropped onto Paks's chest.

The weight forced her back into the stone; before half the crowd had passed, she was finding it hard to breathe. When she tried to keep her chest expanded, they added links to the lower stone, forcing her to use chest wall as well for breath. Her sight dimmed; she let her eyes shut, concentrating on breath alone. She heard the priests' voices, but could not follow their words. No more links dropped. She struggled, fighting for every breath. Air rasped in and out of her throat. Cold water drenched her face; she choked on it, tried to cough, and could not manage it. Before she quite passed out, they took off a few links. Then they watched as she struggled with that weight. When that, too, exhausted her, they removed a few more links.

She longed for rest, for sleep, but could not sleep with that weight; whenever she dozed, she could not breathe. Again, she had no idea how long this lasted; each painful breath seemed to be an hour away from another. She could hear the voices, hear the clank of metal as they played with her, taking off a link or so, and dropping it back on. She felt other pains, as the priests and worshippers prodded her, spit on her, and tried to provoke some reaction, but all that really mattered was air: the struggle to suck it in, the weight that forced it back out too soon.

As the torment continued, a part of her mind was aware of the differences between this and the earlier captivities she'd endured. That night in the Duke's cells, when she'd been so sunk in her own misery that she had not even imagined worse than Stammel's anger. The pain had been real, the fear overwhelming . . . but as the pain and fear of a child stung by a wasp is real. Lost in the moment, the child cannot imagine that the pain will end, or that any pain could be worse. The adult knows better; she pitied the child she had been, so miserable in the dark, alone and afraid, convinced that her chance to be a hero was lost forever. And how Korryn's punishment had shocked her with its cruelty! She had trembled for days at the thought that she might have been whipped and branded instead. Being stripped publicly had been bad enough.

And from that she had gone to a soldier's endurance, learning to stave off pain and fear with anger and defiance, linking hope to vengeance. That righteous anger served well against Siniava, or seemed to, when she avenged her friends' deaths. Yet in Kolobia, that same anger betrayed her to deep evil. She remembered too well that mood, black rage edged with madness, so much less innocent than the panic of the beaten recruit. Under it had been the same fears the child had, disguised but not controlled, a willingness to deal the pain she suffered.

Again, as so often before, her mind filled with the vision of her childhood dream, the bright figure in shining mail, mounted on a prancing horse and waving a sword. It flickered in and out of her sight, shifting in tides of pain and weakness, as it had flickered in her mind's eye these several years. Now she could see its shadow, the dark nest of fears which had brought it to life. Helplessness, humiliation, pain, a lonely death, and nothing after—she had feared these, and made of that fear a dream of power, of freedom, of untouchable strength and courage. *She* would never suffer that, because she would be the hero, the one with the sword, the one who was above such suffering.

And here she was, bound helpless before enemies who enjoyed her pain, an example, as they said, of Liart's power. An example to teach more fear, more hatred, proof that the dream of glory had been false: no power, no bright sword or prancing horse, no protection, even for herself.

But the image of her dream steadied, and did not fade. No one whole wanted to be hurt, wanted to be the victim of such cruelty as held her now. Her fears were as common as a taste for salt or honey, as healthy as the desire for comfort, for love. So much she had learned from the Kuakgan. Now, at last, she accepted her right to share those fears: she did not have to deny them, only master herself.

And this, she saw, her dream had done. She had built against that fear a vision of power not wholly selfish—power to protect not only herself, but others. And that vision—however partial it had been in those days—was worth following. For it led not away from the fear, as a dream of rule might do, but back into it. The pattern of her life—as she saw it then, clear and far away and painted in bright colors—the pattern of her life was like an intricate song, or the way the Kuakgan talked of the Grove's interlacing trees. There below were the dream's roots, tangled in fear and despair, nourished in the death of friends, the bones of the strong, the blood of the living, and there high above were the dream's images, bright in the sun like banners or the flowering trees of spring. And to be that banner, or that flowering branch, meant being nourished by the same fears: meant encompassing them, not rejecting them.

She did not know herself when these thoughts linked at last, forming the final pattern, bringing up into her mind the self she had become. It was then as if several selves were present, mysteriously separate and conjoined. Trapped inside her body was the same child she had been, feeling each new torment as a wave of intolerable pain, each ragged scream as a fresh humiliation. The seasoned soldier watched with pity as her body gave way to exhaustion and pain as any body would, feeling no shame at the sight or sound or smell of it, for this was something that could happen to anyone, and she had never inflicted it on others. And someone else, someone newer, refused the soldier's tactics of defiance, anger, vengeance, and looked into her own fear to find the link to those around her, to find the way to reach those frightened tormentors, the ones not already lost to evil.

In the rare respites, when the priests stopped to harangue the crowd and revive her for more torture, she felt curiously untroubled. Not free of pain, nor free of fear, but free of the need to react to that fear in all the old ways. She had no anger left, no hatred, no desire for vengeance, nothing but pity for those who must find such vile amusements, who had no better hope, or no courage to withdraw. It would all happen to her—all the things she'd feared, every violation of body, everything she'd taken up the sword to prevent—and she consented. Not because it was right: it was never right. Not because she deserved it: no one deserved such violation. But because she *could* consent, being what she was, and by consenting destroy its power over her and others, proving in her own body that fear's power came from fear, that greater power could from the same dark roots find another way to the light.

This quietness, this consent, formed a still pool in the center of that violent place. At first, only the priests noticed, and flung themselves into a frenzy of violence against it. But it was not brittle steel to break, or crystal to shatter, but a strength fluid and yet immovable, unmarred by the broken rhythm of her breath, or even by her screams. The quietness spread, from gray eyes that held no hatred for those who spat at her face or tasted her blood, from a voice that could scream in pain yet mouth no curses after, that spoke, between screams, in a steady confirmation of all good.

Those watching could not deny the wounds: they had seen them being dealt: they had helped deal them. They could not deny the sight of blood, the smell of it, the sticky feel of it, the salt taste on too many tongues. They could not deny the stink of burnt flesh, the sight of scabbed and crusted wounds, the dead servant girl, the boy's back striped and bleeding. This was not the quietness of inviolable protection, for she suffered all that was done to her. They had seen a virgin raped, a soldier's scars mocked and redrawn in fresh blood. They had heard a paladin scream, as the priests promised.

And yet she did not hate, and yet she did not fear, and yet she said, when she had breath to speak, that the High

Lord's justice would rule in the end. The priests shouted threats, promised more torments, blustered and postured: the silence spread, as a pool rises silently above a new-broken spring when the dry season ends.

One by one the crowd fell still, or joined the mockery with less eagerness. She was so small, after all, broken like that . . . they could think of sisters, cousins, friends they had known, who might be where she was, if she were not there. They had thought it would be satisfying to see a paladin, one of the proud and powerful, brought low. But they knew her story, from the year that cruel rumor spread the tale of her cowardice. She was only a peasant girl, born into poverty. What did it prove to shame a sheepfarmer's daughter who had known shame already? Some among them had been soldiers, and recognized the scars of a common soldier who has seen hard service. They felt no braver for breaking a soldier's scarred hands. And those who had first laughed to see a virgin raped—and even those who had joined in eagerly—now looked from the dead servant girl to the other, and found something pitiful in both, something shameful in themselves, that they could take pleasure in such pain. She was no threat to them—why had they ever thought she was a threat? Paladins never threatened the helpless. The threat was elsewhere, in those who wore Liart's horned circle, who flourished the barbed whips and the heated chains.

By such small degrees the crowd's mood changed, shifting back in sudden fear when the priests turned their weapons on individuals chosen not quite at random, but slowly, inexorably, turning away from the praise of cruelty to some vague sympathy with suffering. Glass by glass, as the torches burned down and were replaced again and again, as the day passed into night and another day, and another night and day, one and another of those watching came slowly and without intent to a new vision of the world.

Of all this, Paks was hardly aware. At best, she knew what she must do, and why, but those moments seemed few. Pain followed pain in sickening procession; at times even her new insight failed, leaving her adrift in self-disgust or despair. For the most part she concentrated on refusing anger and hatred, accepting the pain as a necessary part of something chosen long before. When they broke her hands, each bone a separate torment, she struggled against her old fear of crippling. She had clung to the hope that if she lived, she would still be whole, able to fight. But she knew better, knew from having lived through it that she was more than a hand to hold a sword. She could live, being Gird's paladin, with no more than breath, or die whole, of old age, and be nothing at all. The difference lay in her, *was* her, was what she had become: no one but she could change it. The rapes, that she had feared before as both violation and torment wholly unknown, were then nothing but physical pain, no worse than others. She lost nothing, for she had had nothing, had never invested herself in that, or hoped for that kind of pleasure. It seemed to her that Alyanya came in a dream, and comforted her, but dream, vision, and reality were by then too nearly mixed for clear memory.

Then they held her up once more for the crowd to see. The chamber was crowded with worshippers who had come to see the end of the spectacle. At the priests' command the guards threw her to the floor.

"Will you admit that our Master commands your obedience?" asked one of the priests, nudging her face with the toe of his boot.

"I am Gird's," said Paks, forcing the words out. Her voice was clearer than she would have thought possible.

"You are meat. You are the sacrifice our Master demanded." The priest's voice was cold. "If you will not acknowledge our Master, the stones are heating for you." Paks said nothing. "Do you want to be a helpless cripple?" he demanded.

"No," she said. "But I do want to be Gird's paladin." Again she felt the lightest touch on her head, and a soothing haze came between her and her pain.

The priest snorted. "Gird's paladin! A bloody rag too

stupid to know the truth! Then you will suffer it all, Paladin of Gird, just as you wish."

Pain exploded in her legs as the burning stones were dropped in the hollow of both knees, and her legs bound tightly around them. She clenched her fists, forgetting the broken bones until too late. The pain was sickening, impossible; she retched, trying not to scream.

"And now, paladin? Where is your lord's protection now?" The priests hauled her up by both arms, forcing weight on her knees.

"The High Lord has dominion," gasped Paks. "Gird has upheld me here; I have not failed." She felt herself falling, and willed to fall into that darkness.

The guards held a bloody wreck between them. The crowd smelled burnt flesh, and shivered, not hearing the priests' final lecture. What had she meant, "I have not failed?" The paladin's head hung down, slack against her chest, the brand of Liart dark on her forehead. Then the priests gestured, and the guards turned her around. The taller priest cut the cords around her legs, and her feet thumped down. With tongs, the priest yanked the stones from their place, ragged bits of skin clinging to them. The hall stank of it. The paladin did not move, or cry out; she might have been dead. For an instant, no one moved or spoke.

Then those in front saw, and did not believe, but recoiled even in disbelief against those behind. For the burnt bloody holes where the rocks had been disappeared, as a wave swept across lines on sand erases them, gone without mark or scar. At the movement, the priests turned, saw, and gaped in equal disbelief. One by one, other wounds healed, changing in the sight of those watching to unmarked skin. Finger by finger, her misshapen hands regained their natural shape. With a cry, the two guards dropped her, flinging themselves back. One of the priests cursed, and raised his whip, but when he swung, it recoiled from her and snagged his own armor. The other drew a notched dagger, and stabbed, but his blade twisted aside. She lay untouched, unmoving.

Now turmoil filled the hall: those behind wanting to see what had happened, those in front frantic to escape the wrath of Gird they were sure would come. The priests called other guards, who yanked her upright, head still lolling—now all could see that Liart's black brand no longer centered her forehead. Instead, a silver circle gleamed there, as if inset in the bone itself. At that, the priests of Liart shrank away, their masked faces averted from the High Lord's holy symbol. The terrified guards would have dropped her, but the priests screamed obscenities louder even than the crowd's noise, and sent them away with her, out the same entrance through which they'd brought her earlier. And then they drove the crowd away, in a rage that could not disguise their own fear.

Chaos scurried through the warrens of the Thieves' Guild, panic and disruption, as those who had seen tried to convince those who had not, and those who would not listen tried to find someone to believe. Some fled to the streets: black night, icy cold with a sweeping wind, and patrols of cold-eyed Royal Guards sent them back into the familiar warrens, even more afraid. Factions clashed; old quarrels erupted in steel and strangling cord. Those who had arranged to take the paladin's body outside the city walls wrapped her in a heavy cloak and carried her gingerly, carefully not looking to see if that healing miracle continued, eager to get this terror out of their domain.

And at every grange of Gird, the vigil continued until dawn.

Chapter Twenty-eight

Kieri Phelan rode away from Vérella that dark night in an internal storm of impotent rage and frustration. He had been captured by a ruse he should have seen through—taken in by the plea of one of his veterans. That was stupidity, and he didn't excuse himself that he was distracted by the day's events. So he was Lyonya's king—that didn't mean he could let his mind wander. And then he'd been rescued—beyond his hopes—by another veteran—by Paksenarrion, now a Paladin of Gird. She had freed him, and his squires, but she herself was now a prisoner—for five days, she had agreed to suffer whatever torments the priests of Liart inflicted. And he had agreed to that, because he could do nothing else. She made the bargain with the Liartians, and her oath bound him. He shifted in the saddle, glad of the darkness that covered his expression. What must they all think, of a king that would sacrifice a paladin to save his own life?

And yet—he had to admit she was right. He knew who he was, now: the rightful heir to Lyonya's throne, a half-elf, torn from his birthright by slavers. No one else could do what he must do—restore the frayed taig of Lyonya, and the alliance of elf and human, clean the forests of evil influence. Lyonya needed its king—needed *him*—and he could not deny a paladin's right to follow a quest to its end. But Paksenarrion—dear to him as his own daughter—his heart burned to think of her in their hands. All he had seen in thirty-odd years of war came to him that night, and showed him what she must endure.

He forced his mind to his own plans. If she had bought his life, he must make use of it. Selfer would be far north of Vérella by now, riding hard to meet Dorrin's cohort and bring them down. Dorrin herself, in Vérella, would have fresh mounts ready for them, and a royal pass to follow him. Kostvan had agreed to let Arcolin pass through, if it came to that, and would be alert in case the Pargunese tried to take advantage of his absence. He thought ahead. Surely the enemy would strike before he reached Chaya—but where? Not in the Mahieran lands close to Vérella, nor in the little baronies of Abriss or Dai. East of that, in Verrakai domain? At the border itself? In Lyonya? He thought over what Paks had said about Achrya's influence there—some thought of him as a bloodthirsty mercenary. He had no clear idea of the river road in his mind; he'd always gone south to visit the Halverics, cutting eastward from below Fiveway to go through Brewersbridge and avoid Verrakai altogether.

At Westbells, the High Marshal and Phelan both stopped to wake Marshal Torin and hand over Paks's gear. Seklis did not explain much, and Marshal Torin, sleepy-eyed and bewildered, did not ask. Kieri touched that bright armor for the last time, as he thought, and prayed to all the gods that Paks might be spared the worst. The first glimmer of light seeped into the eastern sky as they rode away. Around him the ponderous hooves of the heavy warhorses—twenty of them—shook the earth. Behind were the lighter mounts of the infantry and bowmen, and then the pack train. Kieri's mouth twitched, remembering Dorrin's sulfurous comments on the pack train. He would have minded more, except that their slowness gave Dorrin a better chance to catch up. He thought where Selfer would be, on the road he knew best—changing horses, gulping a hot mug of sib, and starting off again, faced with Crow Ridge to climb.

As the day brightened, Kieri glanced around to see what his escort looked like in the daytime. Twenty massive gray warhorses, twenty plate-armored knights with spears and swords. Already the heavy horses were streaked with sweat; they were meant for power, not distance. Twenty mounted infantry, on gray horses much smaller than the warhorses; these carried short swords, with shields slung to the saddles. Ten mounted bowmen, on the same light horses, with the short, sharply curved bow of the northern nomad, to be used mounted or afoot: an excellent bow in the forest, as well. All these were in rose and silver or gray, the royal colors of Tsaia. His own tensquad, still in Phelani maroon and white, mounted on matched bays (how had Dorrin accomplished that, he wondered), with Vossik at their head. The king's squires from Lyonya, whom he hardly knew, but for Garris: they rode close around him, with the royal pennant of Lyonya displayed. And the two Marshals: High Marshal Seklis, and Marshal Sulinarrion, both in Gird's blue and white, with the crescent of Gird on chest and cloak. Behind came the pack train—servants, supplies, more than forty beasts extra, which the Tsaian Royal Guard insisted on.

Kieri looked around for the Royal Guard cohort commander. He had met the man the previous afternoon, before leaving the palace, but could not recognize him among the other knights. But the man caught his eye, reined his horse close, and bowed.

"My lord? You wish to rest?"

Kieri nearly laughed, but managed to hide it. "No, Sir Ammerlin. I'm used to longer rides than this. I wanted to ask, though, what your usual order of march would be."

Ammerlin frowned. "Well—it's rare that we travel far; we're the Royal Guard, after all, and we stay with the prince. We should breathe the horses soon, my lord. If they're to go far—"

"I suppose Lyonya is far," said Kieri. It seemed to him that the pace had been but a crawl—a man could have walked the distance as fast—but he knew better than to push another man's command beyond its limits. Ammerlin bowed in the saddle.

"I thank you, my lord." He returned to the head of the column, spoke to the cohort bugler, and a quick signal rang out. Kieri tossed a hand signal at Vossik that halted his own tensquad in their tracks while the Royal Guard straggled to a halt. High Marshal Seklis grinned at him.

"You did that on purpose."

"Marshal, my company doesn't know their signals."

Seklis laughed. "My lord, your company could probably keep an even interval without any signals at all—couldn't it now?"

"It might," said Kieri. Ammerlin had come back, on foot. "How long will we rest?" asked Kieri.

"A quarter glass or so, my lord. I need to check on the pack animals, and make sure everything is holding up well. And each rider checks his own animal."

"Then I'll walk around a bit." Kieri swung off his horse to find that Lieth was already down and holding his rein. "You're quick," he said, smiling. She looked down.

"My lord king, not quick enough."

He knew what she meant; the afternoon before, when they were all captured. He laid his hand on her arm. "Lieth, I will not ask you not to think of it—I think of it every moment. But I need my squires alert now—here—so I will ask that you think of it in the back of your head. Let you not reproach yourself for the past—for all of us have failed someone somewhere."

She met his eyes, her own full of tears, but nodded. "I will not speak of it again."

"We *will* speak of it again, Lieth—to the whole court of Lyonya—but first we will get there." At that she managed a smile, and he walked off the road to the snowy verge, stamping his feet. Suriya and Garris flanked him on either side; Vossik he found close behind him whenever he turned.

The pause lasted longer than a quarterglass, for some of the animals needed their packs reset. Kieri contained his annoyance, to Ammerlin's evident relief. High Marshal Seklis was less restrained.

"I've wondered, Ammerlin, how you could possibly get to the field in time for a battle, and now I see you couldn't."

Ammerlin reddened. "We could, close to Vérella, but—"

"Gird's shovel, man, you're not an honest four-hour ride from Vérella yet!"

"But we had to pack for a journey—"

"I daresay the expedition to Luap's stronghold had less baggage, and they meant to be gone a year," returned Seklis.

"High Marshal," said Kieri quietly, and shook his head. Seklis subsided; Ammerlin stalked off, still angry. "Don't bait him," said Kieri. "We will need his goodwill, when they attack us."

"You think they will?"

Kieri shrugged. "Why else would they have let me go? Paksenarrion said—and it makes sense—that two powerful evils do not want me on the throne of Lyonya. I'm not sure why they didn't kill me at once—but they must intend to do it, and this journey is the best time."

"Then why didn't you wait in Vérella for your Company?"

Kieri looked at him sideways. "Marshal, if I had brought down my whole Company—and the gods know what a comfort that would be to me now—do you think I'd have had leave to march it through Verrakai's lands? And what would the Lyonyans think, when I arrived declaring myself their ruler with my own personal troops around me? And what would have happened in the north, where my Company stands between Tsaia and the northern perils? No—that would never do." Seklis and Sulinarrion nodded. "As you know, I did ask—and get—permission to bring one cohort down; if the Royal Guard is slow enough, Dorrin may catch us up before the border."

"How fast can they travel?" asked Sulinarrion.

"They'll be in Vérella three days after they start," said Kieri, then grinned at their expressions. "Mounted, of course."

"Mounted on what?" asked Seklis when he got his breath back. "Flying horses?"

"No—and not warhorses, either. Good, solid nomad-bred beasts. Ugly as sin, and legs like stone."

"What do you use for supply?" asked Sulinarrion.

"For a cohort? A ten-mule string, usually, for a week's journey. Double that for speed. More if there's a lot of fighting, because I don't like to leave my wounded behind; I'll hire wagons, mule-drawn, if necessary."

"Umph." Sulinarrion seemed impressed. "So some of what I heard from Aarenis could be true."

"That depends on what you heard."

"That your Company marched from the upper Immer to Cortes Andres in less than twelve days, including fighting."

Kieri counted on his fingers. "Ten days, it was, from Ifoss to Cortes Andres. Yes. No wagons, though, until we captured some of Siniava's on the north border of Andressat. But that march wasn't bad—ask Vossik here." He smiled at the sergeant, and the Marshals turned to him. In answer to their questions he shook his head.

"No, Marshals, my lord's right. That was across high ground, mostly, and easy enough. I'd say that march through the forest, or across Cilwan, was worse."

"The weather was," said Kieri, "and we had walking wounded, too. And what about that last stretch in Fallo?"

Vossik grinned. "I was hoping to forget that, my lord. That damned mud—those Fallo roads haven't got no bottom to 'em at all, and the fields were wet as creeks. Seemed like we'd been marching forever by then."

Ammerlin came back and bowed stiffly to Kieri. "My lord, we are ready to ride when you please."

"Thank you, Sir Ammerlin," Kieri replied. "I would like to meet the other knights before we begin—it's easier to recognize those you've met in daylight, I find."

Ammerlin relaxed slightly. "Certainly, my lord." He led Kieri to the group of heavy knights waiting to mount. Kieri shook hands with each, noting their strength and apparent determination.

"It's been so long," he said, "since I have campaigned with heavy cavalry that I have forgotten much. Sir Ammerlin, you must be sure to tell me when the horses should rest, and what must be done. A mounted infantry company moves very differently."

Ammerlin thawed another fraction. "My lord, I am sorry that we cannot move faster; the prince said your journey was urgent, and must brook no delay. I know the Marshals think we are soft, but—" he patted his own horse, "these fellows were never meant for speed or distance. Yet in close combat, they are a powerful defense; we can ride down lighter cavalry without getting far away from you. We cannot, it's true, ride into a heavy polearm company, but—"

"If we run into that," said Kieri, "we'll have to go around. Believe me, I appreciate the prince's care in sending such an escort. But to make the best use of it, you must advise me."

Ammerlin appeared to give up his resentment completely. "Well, my lord, they can work all day—if it's slow—or a short time, if it's fast. That's the choice. I'd choose to go at their walking pace—a little slower than the light horses'—and rest them at least every two glasses. And a long break at noon, of course." Kieri, calculating this without moving a muscle, began to be sure that Dorrin would catch them before the border. "If we try to move out faster," Ammerlin went on, "we'll have a third of them lame in two days, and then what?" Leave them behind, Kieri thought, but did not say. He knew he would need them.

"Well," he said finally, "let's see how far we go. I would not ask haste, if it were not needed—I hope you understand that."

"Yes, my lord." Ammerlin looked much happier.

"About the order of march—" began Kieri.

"Yes, my lord?"

"What about sending some of the bowmen forward, as scouts?"

Ammerlin's expression was eloquent. "Well—my lord—if you like. But we're in Mahieran lands now—there's no real need."

"True, but then we'll be used to that—when we come to other lands."

Ammerlin chewed on this thought, and nodded. With a wave, Kieri returned to his own horse, and mounted. He watched as the bowmen got their orders and rode forward.

"That makes more sense," said Garris at his side.

"They're not used to maneuvering in hostile territory," said Kieri.

Where the road was wide enough, the heavy horses went five abreast, the four ranks in front of him and the squires. Then his own tensquad (for he had explained that since they had no officer in charge, he must be near them), then the mounted infantry. Now that the bowmen rode as scouts, the pack animals were directly behind the Guard light horse. Kieri fretted, unable to see over the four ranks of large horses in front of him; he had always led his own Company, or had trusted scouts in advance.

By the time they stopped that night, at Magen, Kieri knew it would take them a full ten days or more to reach Harway on the border. Ammerlin agreed, reminding them that he had escorted the prince's younger brother to the Verrakai hunting lodge, ten days on the road both ways. At the Marshal's invitation, Kieri, the king's squires, and the other Marshals stayed in Magen grange, and after supper they deplored the slow progress.

"My lord, they will have plenty of time to deploy a large force—"

"I know. That's why Paksenarrion wanted me to hurry. But they're going to attack—large force or not—and I need the troops."

"What about using yeomen from any grange nearby?"

Kieri shook his head. "Should I involve the yeomen of Tsaia in a battle to protect the King of Lyonya? No, if they choose to fight, I'll welcome them—but I have no right to call them out."

"Besides," said Marshal Hagin, "not all granges would be much help. Perhaps the High Marshal is not aware that some granges in the east have nearly withered away?"

"No—if I'd known, I'd have done something." Seklis scowled. "What's the problem?"

"I don't know. I hear things, from peddlers on the road, and that sort—and we all know about the troubles near Konhalt—and Verrakai."

"Duke Verrakai has never been one of my supporters," said Kieri mildly. Marshal Hagin snorted.

"I'd have put it somewhat stronger than that, my lord, begging your pardon. But he's not as bad as his brother. That one—!"

"But my point is, crawling around the country like this, on the one good road, they'll have time to set up an army—" Seklis bounced his fist on his chair.

"But not a very good one," said Kieri. "What can they do at most—let's look at the very worst."

"Three cohorts of Verrakaien household troops," said Seklis. "For a start."

"Your pardon, High Marshal, but they won't get more than two in the field this time of year," said Sulinarrion. "I've a cousin who married into a Verrakaien family." She held to that, and they considered what other forces might come: a half-cohort or so of Konhalts, ferried across the river, perhaps some local peasantry, ill trained but formidable in numbers.

"What about Pargunese?" asked Kieri. They froze, staring at him. He went on. "The Pargunese won't want me as King of Lyonya for several reasons. I defeated the Sagon of the west many years ago—using someone else's army, but I commanded. They know I will be a strong king, and they'll have no chance to gain ground anywhere. And they hate elves."

"But that would mean war between Pargun and Tsaia," said Hagin. "Would they risk that?"

"If they could raid, and get back—with, perhaps, Verrakai's connivance—perhaps not. And after all, it's not Tsaia's king they're after."

"Umm. You think Verrakai would let them through?"

"Yes—and blame the whole thing on them, as well."

"Would the Pargunese be stupid enough to fall for it?" asked Lieth suddenly.

"You mean, what would they gain? Well, they'd not have me to deal with—and they don't like me. And perhaps Verrakai has given or promised something else. A foothold on this side of the border? Gold? I don't know, but just how many Pargunese cohorts could the Sagon move if he wanted to?"

"Could he move through Lyonya?" asked Marshal Sulinarrion of the king's squires.

"Not without starting real trouble," said Garris. "We have garrisons all along the river—they've tried that before."

"The Sagon of the west has eight cohorts, they say," said Suriya. "But half of those are stationed along the northwest—"

Kieri laughed. "Yes—and I'm the reason. That leaves four—no more than two will be close enough to meet us, I daresay. So—a couple of Verrakai cohorts, a couple of Pargunese cohorts—and who will command those, I wonder? —and no more than one of Konhalt. What of Liart, Marshals? How many followers will they bring?"

High Marshal Seklis frowned. "I would have said there were no Liartians in Vérella, my lord. Yet there were. Gird knows how many are hiding in the forests."

Kieri shook his head. "They let the rabbits run, companions, knowing they had hounds. They did not know, perhaps, that these rabbits had teeth."

The others laughed. "Indeed, my lord," ventured Marshal Hagin, "you have the name of a fox, not a rabbit."

"Indeed, Marshal, I shall have a name worse than that before we are done." Kieri smiled. "But let's take heart: though they oppose our seventy or so with their four or five cohorts, they may not suspect my own marching behind. Two against four sounds better. Despite the slow progress of our escort, I judge those heavy horses will do their work well when it comes to battle."

"I hope so." High Marshal Seklis let out a long sigh. "If you will excuse me, my lord, I would like to pray in the grange—"

"And I will join my prayers to yours, Marshal, if they are sent as I think." For a moment everyone was silent, thinking of the captive by whom they were free and able to travel. This would be her second night of torment.

She woke cold and aching in a murky featureless light that made her doubt her senses. For some time she was not sure whether she was alive or dead: whatever she had expected was not this dim fog and cold. Fragments from a dream wandered through her mind: someone's hands, warm and kind, easing her cramped muscles. A gruff voice, gentled by time, soothing her fear. But this vanished. She felt space around her, as if she were outside in an open place, but she could not see anything but fog. She blinked several times. Then she tried to move. Strained muscles and joints protested; she caught her breath, then moved again. Something soft and warm cushioned her tender head; she managed to get a hand up and felt stubbly hairs growing back in, the shape of a hood covering them, tender lumps and cuts that made her wince. Her fingers explored, found a bundle supporting her head, the cloak that covered her nakedness. When she passed her hand before her face, she could see it; at least she was not blind.

She moved her legs again. Stiffness, whether from lying on cold ground or the torture, she could not tell. But she could straighten them, and when she ran her hands where the burning stones had been, no wounds remained. Her hands moved without pain, as if the bones had never been broken. She pushed herself up, running a swollen tongue over dry lips. Distant sounds: wagon wheels, a bawling cow. Thin snow patched the frozen ground. She found the bundle that had been under her head. It was clothing—her own, torn off her by the guards. Someone had mended it crudely, sewing wooden buttons in place of the horn ones, patching the torn pieces with bits of strange cloth. Underneath it was a small packet of bread and meat, and a flask. Paks pulled the stopper free, and tasted: water, and pure. She drank it down, wincing as the cold liquid hit her raw throat. Then she threw back the cloak, and struggled into the clothes, shivering, not bothering to look at herself and notice what had and hadn't healed. Wrapped once more in the cloak, she tried to think.

Alive, surely: she could not imagine any afterlife where she would find old clothes mended, some bruises still dark, and bad wounds gone entirely. Alive and free, outside the city by the sounds, and with someone's good will by the clothes and food. She chewed a bit of meat slowly, her jaws sore. Alive, free, clothed, fed—what more could she want? She thought of several things. Warm would be nice. Knowing what had happened. Knowing where she was, and what day it was, and where the king was—all that. She staggered to her feet. Her unknown benefactor had not provided shoes or boots—she remembered that her boots had been cut away. Socks she had, but she couldn't walk far in winter with socks alone.

Standing, she realized that she was lower than the surrounding ground, in a broad ditch or depression. The slope showed dimly in the fog. She took a couple of stiff steps toward it, glad to find she could walk at all. Something dark showed on the ground nearby. She stumbled that way, and nearly fell over the corpse.

It lay crumpled on the ground, already cold, the face like gray stone in that uncanny light. Paks stared, shaken out of her uncertain calm. Surely she should know that face. A light wind wandering through the depression, robbing her of the little warmth she'd made and stirring the dead woman's black hair. Barra. The corpse wore red, bright even in that light: a red cloak, red tunic, over black trousers and boots. The hand still held a sword. Gingerly, Paks turned the stiff body over, wincing at her own pain. A dagger hilt stood out in its chest, another in the neck. Frozen blood darkened the tunic. Paks swallowed a rock of ice in her throat. She looked at the ground. All around the snow was scuffed and torn, stained with dirt and blood both. She touched the dagger hilts, lightly, then the sides of her own cloak. She found the thin leather sheaths where those daggers would fit.

She shuddered. No memory returned to guide her: had she thrown those knives, and killed the one who had come to aid her? But she could not believe that Barra had had that intent. Had she fought Barra? But then where had the cloak come from, and the food? A trick of the wind brought her the sound of footsteps: she froze, crouching beside the corpse.

The footsteps came nearer, the steady stride of someone certain of the way and unafraid. Then a soft whistle, decorating a child's tune with little arabesques. Then the quick scramble down the slope, and she could see a shape looming in the fog. It moved to where she had been, and called softly.

"Paks? Hell's wits, she's gone. And she can't have gone far."

Paks tried to speak, but made a harsh croak instead. At that the shape came near: a tall man in black. He carried a couple of sacks.

"There you are. I daresay you don't remember me—Arvid Semminson?"

But Paks had already remembered the debonair swordsman in Brewersbridge who claimed to be on business for the Thieves' Guild. She nodded.

He came nearer. "Are you sure you should be walking around?" His voice was less assured than she remembered, almost tentative.

Paks shrugged. "I can stand. I can't lie there forever." It sounded harsh even to her, but she could not think what else to say. If she was alive, she had work to do.

Arvid nodded, but his eyes didn't quite meet hers, travelled down her arms toward her hands. "I am glad, Lady, to see you so well. But—" he held out a sack and jug. "I think you need more food and drink before you travel, if that is your intent."

Paks reached for the jug, and he flinched slightly as her hand touched his, almost dropping it into her hands. She glanced at his face; she felt no evil in him, but he was certainly nervous around her. Again his eyes slid away from hers, flicking from her brow to her hands to her feet in their rumpled gray socks. She uncorked the jug, and sipped: watered wine that eased her throat. Then, seeking a way to relax him, she nodded at Barra's corpse.

"Can you tell me what happened?"

"It's a long story, Lady, and you may not wish to hear all of it. But the short is that she bargained for you, to have the right to kill you, and they agreed. She would have done it, too, if I hadn't interfered. As it was, she broke my sword: she was good. So I had to use the daggers."

"You killed her?" Paks said. He nodded.

"I had no choice. She would not leave." He proffered the sack again. "Here's more food, Lady. Surely you should eat—"

Paks moved away from Barra's corpse and lowered herself to the ground carefully. Now she could feel some of the injuries still raw and painful under the clothes—but why not all? What had happened? Arvid stood over her, and when she gestured sat down more than an arm's-length away. She took a few moments to open the sack and take out a lidded pot of something hot, another loaf of bread. Arvid shook his head when she offered it to him, and handed her a spoon from his pocket. Paks ate the hot porridge, and tore off a hunk of bread.

"Arvid—" His head jerked up like a wild animal's, all wariness. Paks sighed, almost laughing to see him so, the man who had been so perfectly in control of himself, so offhand in every danger. "I don't bite, Arvid," she said crisply. "But I do need to know what's happened. Where are we? What happened at the end?" Clearly that was the wrong question; he turned white and his hands tightened on his knees. "Where is the Duke?"

"Lady—" His voice broke, and he started again. "Lady, I was not there. I would not attend such—" He paused, hunting for a word, and finding none went on. "That filth. It was in the Guild, yes, but not all of us. Thieves we may be, or friends of thieves, but not worshippers of that evil."

"I never thought so, Arvid," said Paks quietly. He met her eyes then, and relaxed a fraction.

"And so I do not know exactly what happened. I know what some said. I know—I saw—" Again he stopped short. Paks waited, head cocked. He looked down, then away, then back at her and finally told it. The way he'd heard it, Paks thought, sounded incredible, like something out of a storyteller's spiel, and it could not all be true. If Gird himself came down and scoured the Thieves' Hall, or drops of her blood turned into smoking acid and ate holes in the stone, surely she'd have been told about the possibility of such things in Fin Panir. She knew from her time in the Company how tales could grow in the telling, one enemy becoming two, and two, four, in the time between the battle and the alehouse. "I wasn't there," Arvid said again, his voice calmer now that most of the tale was out. "I had arrangements to make." For a moment he sounded like the old Arvid, doubled meanings packed into every phrase. "We—*I*—had no intention of having you murdered in the Thieves' Hall, though we couldn't do anything before. So certain persons were ready to carry you out to safety."

"Thank you," said Paks. He went on without acknowledging her words.

"You had a mark on your arm—a burn—when we were wrapping the cloak around you. I know nothing of the rest, Lady, but that—" He stopped, and looked her square in the eyes. "That mark, Lady, I saw change. *I* saw it. From a charred burn to red, then pink, then nothing. Slow enough to watch, and swifter than any mortal healing." His breath came fast, and she saw fear and eagerness both in his face. "Lady—what are you?"

Paks bit into the bread, and through the mouthful said, "A Paladin of Gird, Arvid. What did you think?"

"Then *why*? Why did Gird let you be hurt so? Was there no other way to save Phelan; is a paladin worth so much less than a king? It was no fakery: the wounds were real! I saw—" He stopped, blushed red then paled, caught for once in his lies. "I but glanced in, Lady, knowing I could do nothing, and having pity for you."

"I know you are not that sort, Arvid," said Paks, and set the bread down. "Yes, it was real." She grinned, suddenly and without reason lighthearted. "No one who saw it will doubt it was real, and that may be the reason." He looked at her now with less tension, really listening, and she wondered how far to lead him. "Arvid, there may have been another way to save Phelan: I don't know. Paladin's don't know everything; we only know where we must go. But think of this: was there any other way to save the Thieves' Guild?"

He stared at her, mouth open like any yokel's. "Thieves' Guild," he said finally. "What does Gird care about the Thieves' Guild?"

"I don't know," said Paks. "But he must care something, to spend a paladin's pain on it, and then scare the wits out of you into the bargain."

"Then is *that* what you—?"

Paks shrugged. "I don't know the gods' purposes, Arvid: I just do what I'm told. As you once told me, I'm very trusting."

His eyes widened, then he laughed, a slightly nervous laugh, and answered the rest of her questions about what had happened to Phelan while she was captive, and what Barra's bargain with the Liartians had been. Suddenly they heard hoofbeats coming closer.

"Damn!" muttered Arvid. "I didn't think anyone would—"

The unseen horse snorted. Paks saw a swirl in the fog, and then a big red horse scrambled down the bank. She stood stiffly, and he came to her, snorting again and bumping her with his nose.

"It's loose," said Arvid, surprised.

"It's not loose," said Paks, her eyes suddenly full of tears. "He's mine."

"Your horse? Are you sure?" Arvid peered at him. "I suppose you are." The horse was sniffing along her arms and legs now, nostrils wide. "I did think of trying to get your horse out of the royal stables, but that's a tall order even for a master thief."

"I can't believe it." Paks wrapped her arms around the red horse's neck and leaned on that warm body. Warmth and strength flowed into her. "He must have gotten away on his own—but he's saddled." The bridle she found neatly looped into the straps for the saddlebags. When she turned back to Arvid, he had wrestled Barra's boots off. He shook his head when he saw her face.

"I know you were in Phelan's company together—but she was going to kill you. Blind jealous, that one. You need boots, and she doesn't. You can try them."

Paks pulled on the boots unhappily; they would fit well enough for riding. Arvid meanwhile had freed the two daggers and sword, and cleaned them.

"I don't suppose you'll take my daggers—no? The sword? You can't travel unarmed—or can you?"

"I can get a sword at any grange," said Paks. "But let me thank you again for all your care. Without this cloak, these clothes, and your defense, I would have died here, of cold or enmity—"

He bowed. "Lady, you have done me a good service before, and in this you have served my companions. I count myself your friend; my friendships are limited, as all are, by the limits of my interest, but I will do you good and not harm as long as I can."

Paks grinned at him, hardly aware of the pain in her face. "Arvid, you have a way of speaking that I can hardly understand, but your deeds I have always understood. If you aren't careful, you'll end up a paladin yourself."

"Simyits forbid! I don't want to end up as you did."

Paks shrugged. "Well—it's over."

"Is anything ever over? Would you be here if you had not still a quest? I am honored to have served you, Lady Paksenarrion. Remember me."

"That I will." Paks let the stirrups down on the saddle, thought about bridling the red horse, and decided not to bother. She hoped she would be able to ride. Arvid offered a hand for mounting, and with his help she managed to gain the saddle. It hurt, but not as badly as she'd feared. That was probably the cold, numbing her still. She wondered suddenly how Cal Halveric had been able to ride out of Siniava's camp with his injuries.

"Good luck to you," said Arvid.

"Gird's grace on you," said Paks. He grinned and shook his head, and the red horse turned to climb the bank.

Chapter Twenty-nine

On the higher ground, Paks could see farther; from time to time the light strengthened as if the sun might break through. The red horse seemed to know the way—Paks had explained, as if he were a human companion, that they needed to find the grange at Westbells. She concentrated on riding. Now that she had time to think, she wondered that she was able to move about at all. Something or someone had worked healing on her: her own gift, Gird, the gods themselves. She was not sure why the healing was incomplete, but told herself to be glad she was whole of limb. Enough pains were left that she was glad when they came to Westbells near midday, with the winter fog still blurring distant vision. When she slid from the red horse's back, she staggered, leaning against him. Her feet felt like two lumps of fire.

Marshal Torin stared at her when he opened the door to her knock. "Is it—"

"Paksenarrion," she said. He caught her shoulder and steadied her.

"Gird's grace! I can't believe—we held a vigil for you. All the granges—" He led her inside. "We didn't really think you'd live, or be strong enough to travel."

Paks sank gratefully into the chair he gave her. "I wasn't sure myself." She felt as if all her strength had run away like water; she didn't want to think about moving again.

"Five days!" She wasn't sure if the emotion in his voice was surprise or elation or both. "This will show those—!"

He banged a kettle on the rack, and moved around the room, gathering dishes and food. "I won't ask *what* they did, Liart's bastards, but—I presume you need healing, eh? Rest, food, drink—we can do that—" He set a loaf down on his desk, and a basin of clean water, then came to her, easing the hood back from her head. His breath hissed at what he saw.

"Damn them," he said. His hands were warm and gentle. "Some of this needs cleaning." Paks winced as he worked at one cut and another with a clean rag. "What's this?" He touched a swollen lump on the back of her head.

"I don't remember—the stairs, maybe."

"Let's see the rest of the damage." He helped Paks out of her clothes. By the time the water boiled, he had cleaned all the festering wounds—not many—and she was wrapped in a soft robe.

"There isn't as much as I'd expected," he said, handing her a mug of sib. "Five days and nights—" Paks took a long swallow; the sudden attack of weakness had passed, and she was even hungry again.

"There was more." Paks sipped again. She did not want to say how much; the memory sickened her. "Broken bones, more burns. They're—gone—" she waved her hand, unable to explain.

"Your own gift healed some of it, no doubt. Perhaps Gird himself the rest—I've heard of that. And left just enough to witness what you'd suffered. As the Code says: scars prove the battle, as sweat proves effort. But with your permission, I would pray healing for the rest, and restore your strength. I daresay none will question your experience now."

Paks nodded. "Thank you, Marshal. I cannot—"

"No. *You* have done all you can; the gifts bring power but consume the user as well. That mark on your forehead—"

Paks grimaced. "Liart's brand. I know." She remembered too clearly the shape of that brand; they had shown her in a mirror the charred design.

"That's not what I see—have you looked? No, how could you—but here—" he handed her a polished mirror;

Paks took it gingerly. Her bald head patched with scrapes and cuts looked as ridiculous as she'd thought—bone white between the red and purple welts, smeared now with greenish ointment, and bristling with pale stubble where her hair was coming back. Beneath, her tanned face hardly seemed to belong to it. But the mark on her forehead was no longer the black horned circle of Liart. Instead a pale circle gleamed like silver. She nearly dropped the mirror, and stared at Marshal Torin.

"It can't—"

"Whatever happened, Paksenarrion, the High Lord and Gird approved; I have heard of such things. Such honors are not lightly won. It is no wonder you are still worn by your trials."

She told him then what Arvid had said: rumor, panic, wild tales told by thieves, and unreliable. But if the brand could change like that, and deep burns disappear, what might the truth be? Marshal Torin nodded, eyes alight.

"Yes!" he said when she stopped. "The gods always have more than one purpose. Certainly you were sent to save more than a king, and from that dark warren Gird will gain many a yeoman, many a one who knows that fear is not the only power. Well done, Paladin of Gird: well done."

After eating, Paks managed to stumble down the passage to one of the guest chambers. She was asleep almost before the Marshal covered her with blankets.

When she woke, she knew at once that her injuries were healed. She could breathe without pain. The lump on her head was gone, though she could feel uneven ridges of painless scar where cuts and burns had been. She scratched the bottom of one foot with the other; those burns were gone. She looked: scars to witness her ordeal, but nothing left of the weakness and pain. And a clear call to follow . . . she had not finished this quest yet. As she threw the covers aside and sat up, the Marshal tapped on her door.

"Paksenarrion?"

"Yes—I'm awake."

He looked in. "I would let you sleep longer, but that horse of yours is kicking the door."

"Gird's arm. I forgot him."

"He's all right—I fed him after you fell asleep. But he's decided he needs to see you, I suppose. I told him I don't eat paladins, but—"

"How long did I sleep?"

"It's still dark, but morning."

Paks had followed him along the passage, still in the robe she'd slept in; she could hear the steady thumps of the red horse's hoof. The Marshal opened the door, and the horse poked his head into the room.

"You," said Paks. The horse snorted. "I'm all right. I'm getting up. I'll eat before I ride, though." The horse snorted again. "And so should you," said Paks severely. "You could have let me sleep till daylight." The horse leaned into the room, and Paks held out her hand for a nuzzle. "Go on out, now; it's cold. I won't be long." The horse withdrew, and the Marshal closed the door.

"I thought I bolted the door to the stable," he said.

"I'm sure they bolted the stable door in Verella," said Paks. "That horse goes where he wills. I'd better get ready to ride."

Paks found that she had been left clean clothes as well as her mail and sword. Even boots that fit. Paks hurried into her clothes, then realized her helmet would not fit without her thick braid of hair coiled into it. Finally the Marshal found her an old knitted scarf that served well enough. Back in her own mail, with a sword at her side once more, she felt completely herself. By the time they finished eating, and she had fastened her saddlebags onto the saddle, the eastern sky was pale green with a flush of yellow near the horizon. She mounted, and turned the red horse toward the road. He stopped short, ears pricked at something west down the road. Paks glanced down at the Marshal, who had walked out with her.

"I don't know," he said. "But he thinks there's something—"

"I'd believe it," said Paks. She drew her sword, and settled herself in the saddle. She heard the Marshal's blade coming free from his scabbard. Now the red horse snorted, blowing rollers in the cold dawn wind. He tossed his head, and loosed a resonant whinny.

"That doesn't sound like trouble," said the Marshal. "And it's not spring yet."

Paks chuckled, thinking of the red horse with a herd of mares. "I don't think that's it." The horse whinnied again, and began prancing sideways. "What's got into you, you crazy horse! Settle down."

"Hush," said the Marshal. "I think I hear something—"

Paks strained her ears. A faint echo of the red horse's whinny? The wind died. Now she could hear it clearly: the drumming clatter of many hooves, the squeak and jingle of harness. She felt the hairs on her neck prickle up. She rode into the center of the road and peered west. Was that a dark mass moving in the distance? And who could it be?

"It might be the Guard," said the Marshal slowly, echoing her thought.

"Liart," said Paks. "They let me go, all right, and now they're after the king in force."

"Six—seven—days late?"

"It must be. What else?"

He shook his head, but said nothing for a moment. The early light, still faint, showed the front of the mass of riders moving steadily toward them.

"You won't try to hold them." It was half question. Paks estimated the size of the troop and shook her head.

"I couldn't, not here. I'll try to reach the king first, and then see what I can do."

"They won't catch you on that horse," said the Marshal. "But I'll see if I can delay them."

Paks nodded, and reined the red horse around. He shook his head, fighting the rein as he never had, and moved out stiffly when she nudged him. In a few lengths he tried to sidle back toward the Marshal. Paks bumped him harder with her heels, and wondered what he thought he was doing. Then a horn signal floated across the air, and she froze. It couldn't be. In a single motion, she reined the horse around yet again, and galloped toward the oncoming riders. She heard the Marshal yell her name as she rode by, but did not stop or reply.

Again the horn call: incredibly, the call she knew so

well. She rode on; the red horse slid to a stop just in front of the cohort's commander, who was already braced for an attack.

"You!" Dorrin's voice was hardly recognizable.

"I don't believe it," said Paks, believing it. The horn spoke again, and ninety swords slipped back into their scabbards.

Dorrin reached out to grip her arm. "It is really you? The Duke said—"

"It is. And this is you, and how—"

Dorrin pushed up her visor. "We," she said, "are not the Tsaian Royal Guard. It doesn't take my cohort two days to pack and ride."

"I thought he left that night."

"He did, but I nearly had to pack every Tir-damned mule myself. And a third of their heavy horses needed new shoes, and so on. It's a wonder I have a voice left."

"And?" Paks had turned the red horse, and they were jogging together at the head of the column.

"And as soon as he got back, he sent Selfer north, to pick up my cohort."

"All the way to the stronghold?"

"No-o. Not quite. In case of any difficulty, he'd stationed them along the southern line."

They were riding through Westbells now, and Paks waved to Marshal Torin, who stood watching with an uncertain expression. She pulled the red horse out of line, and went to him.

"It's Dorrin's cohort of Phelan's company," she said quickly. "They've come to help."

"I gathered it was his, from the pennant," he said. "By Gird, they move fast. When did they leave the north?"

"I don't have the whole story yet," said Paks. "Someday —" and she turned again and rode after them, for the column was past already. Again at the head of it, riding into the rising sun, Paks felt at home.

Dorrin reined her horse close to Paks's. "Paks, I never expected to see you again, let alone riding at my side this day. And you look—I have never seen you looking better. How did you get free of them? And that mark—"

"Gird's grace," said Paks. "I can't explain it all, but they kept their bargain, at least to leaving me alive. Then the gods gave healing: that mark began as Liart's brand. I presume," she said with a sidelong glance, "that they had more for me to do. Something is stirring the Thieves' Guild; they had a part in it."

Dorrin nodded. "The Duke—the king—blast, I must get that straight in my mind—anyway, he said something about the Thieves' Guild. They wouldn't let the Liartians kill him there, he said. But how did that help you?"

"Oh—a couple of years ago, after I left the Company, I met a thief in Brewersbridge." Dorrin grunted, and Paks went on. "A priest of Achrya had set up a band of robbers in a ruined keep near there, and the town hired me to find and take them. This thief—he said he was after the commander, because they hadn't been paying their dues to the Guild."

Dorrin shook her head. "I have a hard time imagining a Paladin of Gird with a thief for a friend."

Paks thought of Arvid. "Well—he's not a thief—exactly. Or my friend, exactly, either." Dorrin looked even more dubious; Paks went on. "So he says. Obviously he's high in the Guild, but he's never said exactly what he does do. He's not like any thief I ever heard of. But in this instance, he saved my life. He's the one who arranged to have me taken outside the city, alive or dead, when the time was up. And he killed someone who had bargained to kill me."

Dorrin turned to look at her. "A thief?"

"Yes." Paks wondered whether to tell Dorrin that Gird had as much interest in thieves as kings, but decided against it. A knight of Falk, born into a noble family, had certain limitations of vision, even after a lifelong career as a mercenary captain.

"Hmmph. I may have to change my mind about thieves." From Dorrin's tone, that wasn't likely. Paks laughed.

"You needn't. Arvid's uncommon."

"He's never robbed *your* pocket," said Dorrin shrewdly.

"No. That's true. Just the same, he took no advantage

when he might have, in Brewersbridge, and he served me here." She rode a moment in silence, squinting against the level rays of the rising sun. "What does the king expect, that he called your cohort in? And what did the Council think of it?"

Dorrin frowned. "He said they would never have released him if they hadn't thought they could take him before the coronation. That they thought, with you out of the way, to attack somewhere on the road. The crown prince would have given him a larger escort, but he refused it . . . said it might be needed even in Vérella."

"What does he have?"

"I suppose near seventy fighters altogether: a half-cohort of Royal Guards, the tensquad out of this cohort, those king's squires, the High Marshal and another Marshal. Plus supply and servants—an incredible amount, the Royal Guard insists on. It's easy to see they don't travel much."

"Umm. I wish we had the whole Company."

"So do I. But he said he couldn't strip the north bare, not after the other troubles this winter. And Pargun might move, knowing him so far away. He did tell Arcolin to move the two veteran cohorts to the east and south limits, just in case. Val's got the recruit cohort at the stronghold. He's afraid that the evil powers will move with all violence."

"And we have one cohort," said Paks quietly. Dorrin smiled at her.

"And a paladin they didn't expect us to have."

"And two Marshals—perhaps more, if we're near a grange. That is, if we can catch up to them."

"We will," said Dorrin. "Those heavy warhorses won't make a third the distance we're making. And I daresay that red horse of yours could go even faster. Will you go ahead, then, or stay with us?"

Paks thought about it. "For now, I'll stay with you. He has the Marshals with him; they will know, as I would know, if great evil is near. For all you are a knight of Falk, Captain, I might be useful to you."

"You know you are. I tell you, Paks, I was never so surprised—and relieved—as when you rode up. It harrowed all our hearts to go without trying to free you. But he said no one must do anything for five days."

Paks nodded. "That was necessary."

"But when I thought of it—" Dorrin shook her head. "Falk's oath in gold! For anyone to be in their hands five days—and you—"

"It was necessary." Paks looked over to Selfer, who had said nothing during all this. "How's your leg?"

"It's well enough," said Selfer. "The Marshal took care of it, before I rode north."

"How long did that take?"

"I left—let me think—well before midnight, and by dawn the third day I was with the cohort. We marched the next dawn—they were ready, but let me sleep until dark, and the Duke—the king—had said to march by day only, to Vérella."

"He didn't want the cohort too tired to fight," said Dorrin. "We needed to march out again at once. Selfer brought them in good shape—remarkable, considering the weather and all."

Selfer grinned and flushed. "At least we didn't get a thaw on that bad stretch," he said. "I was worried, when it turned foggy."

"You see, Selfer," said Dorrin, "all those things you must worry about if you're a captain? Do you still want it?"

He nodded, shyly. "Yes, Captain, I do. The more I do, the more I like it."

Dorrin grinned at Paks. "He's been acting as junior captain to Arcolin and me both this past year—and he's good." Selfer turned even redder; Paks remembered when she used to blush like that, and wondered how long it had been. She looked back along the cohort, at faces she knew almost as well as those in Arcolin's cohort. All at once she felt like racing the red horse along the road and singing.

They were six days behind the king's party. They asked word at every grange, and at each the news was good: they had passed without trouble. Curious eyes followed them; Phelan's colors had not marched that way before. Paks saw the worried glances. Dorrin carried a royal pass, which she showed in every town, but the local farmers were clearly uncertain. That night the cohort stayed in Blackhedge, sleeping a few hours in safety, but they were on the road again before daybreak. The towns rolled past. Now they said the king had passed only five days before. At Piery, they heard that his party had stayed over a day, because some of the Royal Guard mounts were lame. Dorrin muttered a curse, and Paks laughed, pointing out that they could catch them sooner. They had left three mornings ago.

That night they pressed on, passing the grange at Dorton in the falling dark, and camping in a rough pasture far from any village. Paks would have ridden on after only a few hours sleep, but felt she should stay with the cohort. She had spoken to most of them, uncomfortable only with Natzlin, who did not ask about Barranyi. Paks did not tell her.

The next day the red horse pulled away from the road; Paks thought she remembered that the Honnorgat made a wide bend. Paks urged Dorrin to leave the road. The captain's face creased in a frown.

"I'm worried about causing trouble," she said. "My pass is for the road to Harway, on the border—unless we're attacked, I can't justify leaving it."

"We won't be attacked," said Paks. "Not yet—but we can save several hours, at least, by cutting the bend."

"Can you tell if the king is in need?"

Paks shook her head. "I do not know if I could tell—and I feel nothing now but an urge to hurry. It may be that he will be in need."

"Paks—are the gods telling you to leave the road? Is it that sure?"

"If I were riding alone, Captain, I would go across country. If you cannot go that way, perhaps I should leave you now and go on. But I never expected to be here at all—and certainly not with a cohort behind me—so I cannot give you orders."

Dorrin gnawed her lip. Everyone waited for her decision. Selfer opened his mouth and closed it again, catching

Paks's eye. Then she sat back on her horse, easing her back, and sighed. "Well—wars aren't won by coming late to the battle." She grinned at Paks. "I hope, Gird's paladin, that your saint will cover us while we follow you. I would hate to raise new enemies for the king by this."

"Captain, the gods have led me into peril, but not without cause."

"So be it. We'll take your way."

Paks led them over fallow fields and through woods, the red horse moving as quickly on rough ground as on the road. No one challenged them; in fact, the country seemed empty under a cold sun. They met the road again at Swiftin. Here the yeoman-marshal said the king's party had passed only the day before. They paused to feed and rest the horses before they left. Again they rode most of the night, sleeping beside their horses for a few hours in turn. Dorrin seemed almost as anxious as Paks to catch the king's party. A thin cold drizzle began late in the night; Paks pulled her cloak over her mail when she mounted.

By dawn the drizzle had turned to sleet, and then fine snow. Sometime later, it ceased. The clouds blew away to the east, and the sun blazed on the fresh snowfall. Paks decided to scout ahead of the cohort. The red horse cantered steadily onward, flinging up sprays of glittering snow. She passed through one village too small for a grange, then came to a larger town. She barely remembered passing through it in a hurry on the way to Vérella. The Marshal stared at her when she gave her name, but said the king's party was only an hour or so ahead; they had stopped there overnight. They had had no trouble so far, he said. Paks explained about the cohort following her; his eyebrows shot up his forehead.

"You're bringing Phelan's soldiers through here? Through Verrakai lands?"

Paks had known that the Verrakaien held lands in the east end of Tsaia, but not precisely where. "His captain has a royal pass," she said slowly. "Signed by the crown prince himself—"

The Marshal snorted. "For all the good that'll do. Gird

grant they don't notice—though I don't suppose they'll miss a cohort of Phelan's troops. Why did he do something like that?"

Paks controlled her temper. "He expected trouble," she said crisply. "He wanted his own troops—trained as he knew—in case of it."

"Well, he'll get trouble enough, stirring an ant's nest with a stick. Why couldn't he ride peacefully to his kingdom without all this pomp?"

Paks looked at him. She knew that Marshals varied in ability and personality, but she did not like his sour, half-defeated expression.

"Sir Marshal," she said, "surely High Marshal Seklis told you that evil powers had already attacked the king—he had no chance to go peacefully."

"Seklis!" The Marshal spat. "It's easy for him—living in Verella, at court and all. He won't have to keep a broken grange together out here—who's going to help me, when half my yeomen are taken by something in the forest?"

"Gird," said Paks quietly, but with force enough to change his expression. "Tell me your problem, Marshal, and we'll see what can be done. Your yeomen have been taken?"

He glowered at her, but answered straightly enough. "They disappear. We search, and find nothing. I've told them back at Vérella, again and again. There's something out there, and I can't find it. But they don't listen."

Paks nodded, and he went on.

"Then they tell me to keep watch for Phelan—that he'll be coming through and may need help—that fox! And now I understand he's supposed to be a king, or something. In Lyonya, of all places: just what we need, a mercenary king next door, when it's all I can do to keep things quiet as it is."

"I think, Marshal, that you've kept things too quiet." Paks sat back in her saddle and watched him. He flushed, but still met her eye. "Gird did not value quietness over right."

"Gird is not here," muttered the Marshal. "No—I know

they say you're a paladin, but it's not the same as being here, year after year, with the yeomen more frightened, more reluctant—"

"Well," said Paks, "you don't have to stay here. Come along and see what we're talking about." He shook his head. Her voice sharpened. "Marshal, you can't hide forever. I suspect we're about to have as splendid a battle as you've ever seen—don't you think your yeomen will expect their Marshal to be in it?"

"They won't care."

"I do." Paks straightened, and called her light for the first time since Verella. He stepped back, startled. She saw faces turn towards her, in the town square, and reined the red horse into the middle of it. Children scurried in and out of doorways; faces appeared at windows. "What's this town?" she asked the Marshal, who had followed her slowly into the square.

"Darkon Edge," he said. "What—"

"I'll show you," said Paks. She drew her sword and laid it crossways on the saddle bow. "Yeomen of Gird!" Her yell brought heads around, and drew a flurry of movement. "Yeomen of Gird, hear me!" A few men hurried into the square: an obvious baker, dusting flour from his hands, a forester with his axe, several more. When perhaps a dozen had clustered around her, she pointed at the baker. "Is this all the yeomen in Darkon Edge?"

"No—why—what is it?"

"I am Paksenarrion," she said, "a Paladin of Gird, on quest. Do you know of it?" They shook their heads. "You know who stayed here last night?" One nodded; the others merely stared. "The rightful King of Lyonya," said Paks loudly. "The king who was stolen into slavery as a young child, and lost all memory of his family. He was taken, yeomen of Gird, to weaken Lyonya, to open a way for the powers of evil to assail both Lyonya and Tsaia."

"So?" asked one of the men.

"So in the end, the powers of Liart and Achrya failed, and he is going to his throne. If he gains it, peace and freedom will have a chance here. Do you think Liart and Achrya like that?"

"But he's a mercenary," yelled someone from a window across the square. Paks faced it and yelled back.

"He was a mercenary, yes—to earn his way, when he knew nothing of his birth. But he's more than a mercenary. Gird knows Lyonya needs a soldier on the throne, with those against her."

"It won't do any good," said the same voice. "Nothing does. Gird: that's an old tale. The real power's in the dark woods, where—"

"Come out here and say that," said Paks. "Is this light I carry an old tale? Will you face it and say that Gird has no power?"

"Not against Liart." The face at the window disappeared, and the yeomen muttered.

"Who is that?" asked Paks quickly.

"Joriam. He's an elder here," said the forester. "His son's gone, and his nephew's crippled by that there—" But a powerful gray-haired man had come out the door, and strode angrily across the square to Paks.

"You!" he yelled. "Paladin, are you? You come here and tell us to fight, and then you'll go away, and it will start again. What do you know about that, eh?" He looked her up and down. "Fancy armor, fancy horse, fancy sword. *You* never lay bound on Liart's altar! It's easy for you!"

In one swift gesture, Paks jerked off her helmet. Into the shocked silence that followed, with every eye rivetted on her scarred shaven head, she said quietly, "You're wrong. And this is the proof of it. I carried Liart's brand: look now, and see Gird's power."

The man's mouth opened and shut without a word. One of the foresters blushed, and looked away. Paks scanned the square, noting others who had crept in and peered from doorways. She raised her voice again.

"Yeomen of Gird, I have known what you fear. I have been captive—aye, by Liart's priests, as well as others. I have been unarmed, hungry, frightened, cold, naked—all that you have feared, I have known. If it were not a winter's day—" her voice warmed to the chuckle she felt "—you could see all my scars, and judge for yourself.

But let this—" she gestured at her head, "be enough proof for you. I know Liart and his altars, and Achrya and her webs, and I know the only cure for them. I call on you, yeomen of Gird. Follow Gird; come with me; together we will destroy the evils you fear, or die cleanly in battle. No more bloody altars of Liart, yeomen. Blood on our own blades now." She raised her sword; a shout followed. The faces watching her came alive.

"But—" the old man raised an arm and the shouts died.

Paks broke in. "No, elder Joriam. The time for 'but' and 'maybe' is long past. You have suffered evil; I am sorry for it. Now the yeomen of Gird must take heart and take weapons, and save themselves from more evil. Come!" The red horse danced sideways, clearing a space which filled with men, suddenly swarming from doorways and side streets.

"Is it true?" asked the baker, wiping his hands again. "Is it really true that you can find it, and we can fight?"

Paks grinned at them all. "Yeomen, we shall fight indeed." She watched them run to the grange, bringing back stored weapons, and form themselves into a ragged square before her. Then she heard the drumming hooves of Dorrin's cohort coming into the village, and turned to meet her.

Chapter Thirty

Dorrin looked at the small group of yeomen with distaste. She managed not to look at Paks's head. The rest of the cohort were not as careful.

"What's this?"

Paks met her eyes steadily. "This is the yeomanry of Darkon Edge; they will march with us to meet the enemy."

Dorrin's eyebrows rose. "This?" She said it quietly, but Paks saw one of the foresters redden. She wrapped the scarf around her head, stuffed the helmet back over it, and nodded.

"We will need them," she said. "Gird has called them."

"I see." Dorrin's eyes dropped to her hand on the reins. "Then I suppose—"

"That it's settled. Yes." Paks turned to the Marshal. "Sir Marshal, will you lead your yeomen, or shall I?"

A spark of interest had returned to his eyes; now it kindled into pride. "I will, Paladin of Gird. Do we go by the road?"

"For a time." Paks nodded to Dorrin. "Captain, I would recommend battle order, with forward scouts in sight of the cohort. For now I will ride with the yeomen." Dorrin's quick commands soon had the cohort moving at a brisk trot. Paks waited until the Marshal had brought out his own shaggy mount and they rode together at the head of the yeomen. Before he could say anything, she was asking about the road ahead, and the shape of the land around.

Just out of town, the road entered a section of broken,

rough land, more heavily forested than that on either side. Already some of the springs had broken; the road surface was a rough mass of frost-heave and mud. The red horse slowed, picking his way around the soggy places and slippery refrozen ice. The yeomen marched strongly, but in a loose, ungainly formation. Paks wondered how they would fight—but anything would be better than the blank apathy of Darkon Edge. The Marshal began to explain some of what had happened in the past several years. She realized that some powerful force had harried his grange and the next to the south, picking off the strongest and bravest of the yeomen. Only a few had been found, alive or dead. The old man's nephew had returned a cripple, and half-mad from torture. Another, terribly mutilated, had managed to kill himself. She shook her head as he fell silent.

"Indeed, Marshal, you have had hard times. You say you tried to find the source of this?"

"Of course I did!" Now he was angry again. "Gird's blood, paladin, when I came I was as full of flame as you are now. But year by year—one after another they died, and I could find nothing. How can they trust me, when I can't find a center of evil like that, eh? How can I trust myself?"

"And the other Marshals nearby, they did nothing?"

"Garin tried—until he got the lung fever so bad. His yeoman-marshal was taken, too, and that—well, it was bad to see, paladin. I know Berris, east of me, has had trouble too, but we neither of us had much time to meet—it's more than a day's journey across by the road. I've got six bartons outlying, as well as the grange, and always something gone wrong."

"And you quit hoping—"

"Hoping! Hoping for what? What's left? Half the yeomanry I had when I came—Gird's blood, I don't doubt this day will see the half of that half gone. But as you said, a clean death. I don't fear death itself—Gird knows I've tried these years, but—"

"Marshal, I swear to you, this coming battle will see your grange—and granges around—freed of great evil.

Some will die—yes, but die as Gird's yeomen should die. That man you call a mercenary will be Lyonya's king—as honest and just a ruler as any land could have—and if you and I live to see it, we will call it well bought, at whatever cost."

"I hope so." He chewed his lip. Then he lowered his voice and rode close to her. "It isn't what I thought of, when I was a young yeoman-marshal: I thought to be a Marshal whose grange increased, spreading justice all around. Instead—"

"You have fought a hard battle, in hard conditions, and held a position until help came. Think of it like that."

His face changed. "Is it?"

"Well," said Paks, grinning at him, "paladins are usually considered help. So is a cohort of Phelani infantry—you could have a worse broom to sweep your dirty corners."

He flushed, but finally smiled, straightening in his saddle with a new expression on his face. Paks looked back at the yeomen. They were settling to the march, beginning to look more like possible fighters.

They worked their way up and over one ridge, then another. The tracks of the king's party and the cohort were clear: massive broad hooves of the heavy war horses, the neater rounded hooves of the cohort's lighter mounts. Paks even recognized the slightly angled print of the off hind on Lieth's horse. Then she heard the swift clatter of a galloping horse and looked up to see Selfer riding toward her.

He pulled his mount to a halt. "Paks! Dorrin wants you—there's trouble ahead."

Paks looked at the Marshal. "Keep coming, but be careful. How far is it, Selfer?"

He looked at the yeomen. "Oh—a half-glass's walk, I suppose. Just over the far side of this ridge."

"Come up to the rear of Phelan's cohort," said Paks. "I'll have word for you there." The Marshal nodded, and she rode after Selfer, who had already wheeled his horse to ride back.

The red horse caught his in a few lengths; they rode

together out of sight of the yeomen. Over the ridge, Paks could see down the slope to a clearing at the bottom. The road angled down the slope into a narrow valley which widened to the left, then forded a broad but shallow stream, and climbed along the flank of the next ridge. Forest pressed on the right margin; to the left, a meadow opened from just above the ford downstream to the width of the valley. Fresh snow whitened the slopes between the trees, but the valley floor was churned to dark mud by hundreds of feet.

The clamor of battle carried clearly through the cold air. There were the rose-and-silver colors of Tsaia, a ring around the green knot of the Lyonyan king's squires. Kieri Phelan lived and fought; the elf-blade in its master's hand blazed with light that flashed with every stroke. But around them surged a mass of darker figures. A trail of horses and men lay dead on the road: the supply animals and servants, cut off from the others in the ambush. Paks did not recognize any standards, but the group of red-cloaked spike-helmed fighters at the edge of the conflict was obviously Liartian. They were unmounted: Paks suspected that they were using some arcane power that would frighten horses.

Clumped on the road only a few lengths ahead was Dorrin's cohort, still mounted but unmoving. Paks drew her sword and rode quickly to the head of the column, to find Dorrin bent over her saddle.

"Captain—what is it?"

Dorrin turned. Paks could see nothing but her eyes through the visor. "It's—can't you feel it? We can't move, Paks—he's being torn up down there, and we can't move!"

Paks reined the red horse forward; she could feel a pressure like blowing wind in her mind, but nothing worse. She looked back. "What does it feel like, Captain? Fear, or pain, or what?"

"Fear," said Dorrin shortly. "Don't you—?"

Paks threw back her head. "That I can deal with. Dismount then, and stay close behind me. Selfer, bring the yeomen down when they top the ridge—be sure they stay together." She called her light, and rode forward; she could feel the pressure veering away on either hand. She glanced back once, to find that they all followed, watching her with wide eyes.

She heard the yell when their advance was spotted; one block of enemy soldiers broke away and moved toward them in formation. Paks turned to Dorrin. "You know best how to maneuver here, Captain; I have a debt to pay those priests." She closed her legs; the red horse leaped forward, charging the Liartian priests. There were five she could see; her heightened senses told her that more fought elsewhere. She felt the pressure of their attack on the cohort lift; a crackling bolt of light shot past her head. Paks laughed, swinging her sword.

"Gird!" she yelled, as the red horse trampled one of them, breaking the cluster apart. Paks sliced deep into one neck; the priest crumpled. On the backswing, she caught another in the arm. He screamed, cursing her. The other two were already backing away, weapons ready, to join a mob of their followers. Paks laughed again, and her horse trumpeted. Again she charged, this time against a spear-carrier, who poked at her horse to hold her away. But she caught the barbs of the spear on her sword, and leaned from the saddle to grab the haft with her other hand. She reeled him in; he was too astonished to let go, until her sword sank in his throat. The fifth had escaped into the mob, and screamed curses at her from that safety.

Paks looked around quickly. Loosed from the spell, Dorrin's cohort was advancing steadily against the enemy, edging toward the main combat. The yeomen were starting down the ridge. The defenders around the king, harried as they were, had seen her; she heard the king's cry above them all, and raised her sword in answer.

Then she turned to the road. A ragged band of rabble—peasants or brigands—had broken from the forest to strike the yeomen, who faltered. Paks rode into them, the red horse rearing and trampling, and drove her sword into one neck after another. "Yeomen of Gird!" she yelled. "Follow me!" They cheered, then, and charged through the rest of the band. Their Marshal's eyes blazed, and he gave Paks an incredulous grin.

"They did it!" he cried. "They—"

"They're Girdsmen," said Paks loudly, so they could hear. "They're fighters, as Gird was. Come on, Girdsmen!" And she led them quickly to link with Dorrin's cohort. Together the two groups outnumbered the enemy cohort, and it withdrew and reformed. Paks looked for Dorrin; she had found what she thought was a weak point in the attacker's ring, and was shifting the cohort to strike there.

The attackers, finding themselves struck from behind, wavered and shifted. Dorrin's disciplined swordsmen sliced through the layers of fighters like a knife through an onion. Cheers met them, cheers cut off abruptly by renewed assaults on other flanks. Phelan's tensquad merged with the cohort instantly, as if they had never been apart. Even in the midst of battle, Paks saw that the Marshals noticed this. The yeomen, flanked now on either side by seasoned fighters, looked as solid as the others. The attackers wavered again, drawing back a little. Paks moved the red horse quickly to the king's side. His eyes gleamed through the visor of his helmet.

"Well met, Paladin of Gird. It lifts my heart to see you here."

"Sir king," Paks bowed in the saddle. "How do you find that blade in battle?"

"Eager," he said. "You schooled it well in your service."

Paks laughed. "Not I, sir king. From its forging it has waited its chance to serve you. What is your command?"

"Advance," he said, looking to be sure Ammerlin and Dorrin could both hear him. "We'll use Dorrin's cohort, and your yeomen, with the heavy horse ready to charge and break them."

"But—my lord—the supplies—" Ammerlin hesitated, looking back.

Paks remembered the king's gesture from her years in his Company, but his voice stayed calm. "Ammerlin, we know they have reserves. All that we had behind us is now with us. Our hopes lie before us—and only there. If we can fight through—"

"But—" Paks saw the indecision in his face, and rode

toward him. His face turned to her. She realized he had never met her before her ordeal, and had no idea who or what she was. "And—and is that—"

"Paksenarrion," said the king quietly. "A Paladin of Gird."

"Ammerlin," said Paks, "take courage. Gird is with us." Ammerlin nodded, his eyes bright. She turned to the king. "My lord king—"

"To Lyonya," he said. And with a few quick commands to Dorrin and the Marshals, the defenders were ready to move.

At first it seemed they might break through to the higher ground along the east road. The priests of Liart commanded a motley crowd of ill-armed peasantry; these could not stand against disciplined troops. The enemy cohorts—Pargunese by their speech, though they showed no standard—put up more resistance, but gave way step by step. Paks could see something back in the trees—brigands, or perhaps orcs—waiting for a chance, but unwilling to fight in close formation.

The Tsaian heavy horse charged again and again, breaking open the enemy formation and letting the foot soldiers advance a few strides with ease. But once on the slope up the next ridge, they could not break through; the enemy still had the higher ground, and outnumbered the defenders two to one. Paks looked around for more of Liart's priests; she was sure more were nearby, but they kept out of sight, only occasionally showing themselves in the midst of their fighters.

They had gained perhaps half the upward slope when Paks heard a battle-horn's cry above the clamor. At once the enemy attacked in full force, slamming into the defenders' lines and forcing them back down the hill. It was all they could do to keep their formation in this retreat; one after another staggered and fell, to be trampled underfoot. Paks sent the red horse directly at the enemy; those in front of her melted away, but on either side they drove on. When she looked up again, the eastward road was full of men: two full cohorts of heavy infantry, in

Verrakai blue and silver that gleamed in the afternoon sun. A half-cohort of archers in rose and dark green halted above them and shot down the hill into the defenders. As the Verrakaien infantry charged downhill, the enemy opened to let them through, the force of their charge undamped.

But the king had seen all this as soon as Paks; in moments Dorrin had swung her cohort and the yeomen off the road just enough that the Verrakaien charge slid along the flank of the defenders rather than hitting it squarely. Now they scrambled downhill to level ground as best they could, losing in seconds ground it had cost hours to gain. By the time they were reorganized in the valley, more than a dozen yeomen, and eight of Dorrin's veterans, lay dead.

Shadow already streaked the little valley. They had been fighting for hours; Paks herself felt little fatigue, but she saw in the drawn faces around her that they could not keep going without a respite. Meanwhile the Verrakaien, finding stiff resistance, had slowed. As the day turned on toward evening, they eased their attack and disengaged. Paks could see their supply train coming down the road; Liart's followers were scavenging in the king's, pulling packs off the dead horses and mules. The defenders rested as best they could, locked in a tight square with the king in the center.

When the attackers pulled back, all three Marshals began healing the wounded they could find. By unspoken agreement, Paks stayed alert for any arcane attack of evil. She knew that the Liartian priests were not finished; they would have something else planned. Enemy campfires began to flicker in the fading light. Soon the smell of cooking would come along the wind, tantalizing the defenders. Dorrin edged over to her.

"Paks, my troops have some food—trail bread—and we still have four of our mules. That's enough for one meal, perhaps."

"What about the yeomen?" Paks remembered seeing them stuff food into pockets and sacks.

"I didn't think they'd have any—I'll ask."

In the end, only the Tsaian Royal Guard had nothing; when the rest was shared out, all had an almost normal ration: cold, but strengthening. Water was a harder problem, but one of the yeomen solved it for them. They had been driven back nearly to the ford, but one unit of enemy troops had cut them off from the water. The yeoman, however, knew this stream, and said that its water came near the surface some distance from the stream itself. So it proved: a hole scarcely knee-deep filled with fresh water. They widened the hole until several could fill their helmets at once; the water sufficed for both men and horses. Before full dark, all had drunk their fill, and had eaten enough to feel refreshed.

Yet they were surrounded now by a force three times or more their size. With the Marshal's healing aid, their losses that afternoon were not as severe as might have been expected, but even so too many defenders lay stiffening on the hill. In the center of the square, Paks urged the king to rest while he could. They made an inner square of the horses, and knights, leaving an open space where it was possible to lie, out of sight of archers (though not, of course, out of range).

With dark came new troubles. First was the Verrakai commander, who came forward under a parley flag lit by torches. He accused Phelan of invading Verrakai lands, and refused to accept the royal pass Dorrin carried.

"That princeling has no right to give passes—only the Council can. These are Verrakai lands, and Verrakai's road, and you have no right to invade on behalf of that northern bastard."

"Hold your tongue!" bellowed High Marshal Seklis. "He's the rightful King of Lyonya, and no bastard."

"And who are you?" asked the commander.

"High Marshal Seklis, of the court at Tsaia, and you'll have the Fellowship of Gird on you for this cowardly attack, sir."

The commander laughed. "The Fellowship of Gird is far away, Marshal; if you insist on sharing this dukeling's fate, it will never know what happened."

"Share his fate—Gird's blood, sir, I'd rather share his fate than yours."

"Besides," the commander went on, raising his voice, "I've heard he sacrificed a Gird's paladin to save his own skin. What kind of a king is that? What kind of commander, for that matter? If you had any honor at all, you'd turn on him now."

Paks called her light and stood forward. "Sir, you know not what you speak of. This king never sacrificed a paladin—I am the paladin involved, and I know."

In her light, the commander's eyes were wide, white-rimmed. "You! But I heard—"

"You heard lies, Commander." She saw a ripple of alarm pass through the commander's escort, and her light extended in response. "Would you risk your life—and more than your life, your soul—against a paladin as well as these Marshals and Lyonya's king?"

"It is my command."

"Indeed. Despite the commands of *your* rightful liege lord, the crown prince—"

"He hasn't been crowned yet—not until Summereve—"

Paks laughed. "Sir, you argue like a judicar, not like a soldier. Unless some treachery falls on him, as this has fallen on the King of Lyonya, he will be your ruler, and acts now as such. You must know that the Council and prince together gave Lyonya's king not only passage but also royal escort—have you never seen the Tsaian Royal Guard before?"

"He might have hired them," said the man sulkily. At that even the Royal Guard laughed scornfully.

"He did not—and you know it. You know it is the Council's will that he pass safely into Lyonya and be crowned there; it is the prince's wish as well."

"Not Lord Verrakai's," said the man. "And he's my lord, and gives my orders."

"Then he's rebelling against the House of Mahieran?" asked Paks. Again that uneasy movement. "Forming alliance with Pargun?"

"No—not that—but he takes no orders from a stripling boy—"

"Who is his king. That sounds like rebellion to me," said the High Marshal, "and I shall report it so when I return."

"You are not like to return," answered the commander tartly, "unless you agree to disown this so-called king. We've heard enough of him, we have—a bloody mercenary, that's all he is, whatever lies he tells of his birth."

"And is this a lie?" The king had come close behind Paks and the High Marshal. He drew the elven blade; its brilliant light outshone even Paks's for a moment. "This blade is like none you have seen, and no other hand can hold it. It was made for Lyonya's prince, and lost, and when I first drew it, proclaimed me its master. Could that be a lie, Commander?"

The man bit his lip, looking from one to another. But finally he shook his head. "It doesn't matter. You're Phelan, I suppose. My orders are that you must not pass; you and all your soldiers' lives are forfeit for treason and trespass. As for these others, if they forswear your cause, they will be spared as our prisoners. If they fight on, all will be slain."

Bitter amusement edged the king's voice. "Your terms offer little gain, Commander."

"Your situation offers less." The commander's voice sharpened in turn. "You are outnumbered, on bad ground, without food or water or shelter for your wounded—"

"Whom you plan to kill anyway," the king pointed out. "By the gods, Commander, if we are to die, we need no supplies, and I think you care little what happens to our wounded. Since you say I and my soldiers must die anyway, we shall see how many of yours we can take with us."

"And you?" asked the commander of the Marshals and Ammerlin.

"It is my pleasure and honor," said Ammerlin stiffly, "to serve the King of Lyonya as I have served my prince. You will find the Royal Guard a worthy opponent, Verrakaien scum."

"And you will find Gird's Marshals a hard mouthful to swallow," said High Marshal Seklis grimly. "Since you claim to have the stomach for it, you may gnaw our steel before our flesh."

The Verrakai commander stared at them a long moment, as if waiting for another answer. Then he made a stiff bow and turned away. They heard a flurry of sound as he returned to his own men, and a rough cry in a strange tongue from another enemy unit.

The king's head turned sharply. "That's Pargunese. Something about the Sagon's orders. As we thought, Verrakai and the Sagon have moved together. I dare say, Marshals, they intend none to tell the tale later."

"So I would judge," said Seklis, still angry.

"I would hope for no mercy from them," added Ammerlin. Then he turned to the king. "My lord, I am sorry—I should have foundered every horse in the troop before landing you in this trap."

The king touched his shoulder. "The trap was planned, Ammerlin, before we left Vérella. Without your knights, this afternoon, we could never have come so close to breaking free—nor would we still be standing here, I think. Don't waste your strength regretting it now."

"You do not blame—"

The king laughed. "Blame? Who should I blame but the Verrakai and Pargunese, and Liart and Achrya, who planned all this? By the gods, Ammerlin, if we come out of this, you will hear such praise of the Guard as will redden your ears for the next fifty years. Do you believe me now?"

"Yes, my lord." Ammerlin's eyes glittered in Paks's light. "We will ward you, my lord, until the end."

"Hmmph. I admit, Ammerlin, I see no easy way out of this, but the end I intend is my own throne in Lyonya, and not death in this valley." The king turned to Paks. "You, I know, have seen worse than this, and come out alive and whole—do you despair?"

"No, sir king." Paks smiled at him. "The wolves must come within reach before the spear can touch them. We are in peril, yes—but if we withstand despair, the gods will aid us."

"As they already have, with your return," said the king. "Ah, Paks—I had feared greatly for you."

Paks smiled. "And I for you, as well. Now—in the hours

of darkness, they will try what evil they can, sir king. I feel it near—"

"I also," said Seklis. "We have healed what we can of the wounded, my lord. For this night, we Marshals and Paksenarrion must ward your defenders."

The priests of Liart began their assault with loud jeers from their followers: they had brought the bodies of slain defenders down the hill to mutilate them in front of the rest. It was all Paks and the Marshals could do to keep the yeomen in line when they saw their friends' bodies hacked in pieces; the seasoned troops glared, but knew better than to move. That display was followed by others. These ended when the king authorized a single volley from the Royal Guard archers; Paks extended her light, and the front rank of capering Liartians was abruptly cut down.

After that, and a single thrust of fear from the Liartian priests, the enemy camp settled down as if for sleep. Everything was quiet for a time. Then shouts and bellows rang out in the forest to the east.

"What—?"

Paks could hear shouts in the enemy's camp; the turmoil of troops roused from sleep.

"Whatever it is, they didn't expect it either."

"Trouble for them—good for us?" Seklis stretched; he'd napped briefly.

"We can hope." The king, too, had rested, but Paks could hear the fatigue in his voice. He pushed himself upright, and made his way across the square. Paks extended her light again. They could see dimly as far as the forest edge. Something moved between the trees.

"Whatever it is, it's *big*," muttered Dorrin.

"And not alone." The king sighed. "I was hoping for a cohort of Lyonyans, perhaps—just to make things interesting."

In a sudden flurry, a tumbling mass of creatures burst from the edge of the woods. Paks recognized several of them as the same monster that had lived in the robber's lair near Brewersbridge: huge, hairy, man-like shapes.

"Falk's oath in gold," muttered Garris, "that's a gibba."

"I thought they were hools," said Paks.

"No—hools live in water, and aren't so hairy, nor so broad. These are gibbas. And those others—"

Orcs she had seen before, but not the high-shouldered dark beasts that ran with them, like hounds with a hunting party.

"Folokai," said Lieth quietly. "Fast, strong, and mean."

"I'll believe that," said Paks. "Any weaknesses?"

"Not gibbas. The folokai are night-hunters; they don't like fire or bright light. But they're smart, as smart as wolves at least. The best sword stroke is for the heart, from in front, or the base of the neck."

In moments the dire creatures were charging across the open space. Paks called in her light and rolled onto the red horse's back, where she could see. The enemy ranks seemed as concerned as their own; she heard shouts in Pargunese and Tsaian both, and screeches from the orcs, who hesitated for a moment between the defenders and one of the Verrakai cohorts. A priest of Liart strode into the Verrakai torchlight, and snapped an order to the orcs. Paks saw heads turn toward them, saw one of the folokai crouch for a spring. She urged the red horse forward, to the lines.

The orcs swung their short spears around, and ran at the defenders. The folokai jumped high, soaring over the first rank to fall ravening on the secondary. But Paks was there, the red horse neatly avoiding the defenders. She plunged her sword into a heavy muscled neck; the folokai's head swung up, quick as light, and long fangs raked her mail. The red horse pivotted, catching the beast with one foreleg and tossing it away. It reared, threatening the horse with long claws on its forefeet. Paks swung the horse sideways, and thrust deep between foreleg and breast. For a moment the heavy jaws gnashed around her helmet, then its dead weight almost pulled her from the saddle. She wrestled her sword free. Two gibbas had hit the defending line together, and driven a wedge into it. At the point, Lieth and Marshal Sulinarrion fought almost as one, their swords swinging in long strokes that hardly seemed to slow the gibbas at all. Remembering Mal, Paks looked around for someone with an axe. A hefty yeoman in the secondary stood nearby, bellowing encouragement to the front rank, but otherwise free. She tapped his shoulder with her sword, and he swung round, axe ready.

"Come on! Follow me!" She waited for his nod, then forced the red horse through the fight to a point just behind the gibbas. "Get the backbone!" she yelled at the forester, sinking her own sword into the angle of neck and shoulder—a level stroke, she noted, for a mounted fighter. But this maneuver had put her outside the square, and the yeoman as well. She covered his retreat back into the line, then whirled the red horse in a flat spin, sweeping her sword at the orcs who tried to take advantage of the gibbas' position. Dorrin's cohort snapped back into position, straightening the line, and Paks was back inside with the king.

The king, meanwhile, was fighting another folokai that had jumped the lines. Garris had fallen behind him; High Marshal Seklis tried to flank the beast, but it was too fast, whirling and snapping at him, then returning to the king. The king's sword blazed, its color shifting from blue to white with each change of direction. Before Paks could intervene, the king sank his blade into the folokai's heart, and it fell, still snapping.

More orcs poured out of the forest, this time attacking without hesitation. Now the east flank of the defender's block was fully engaged. In the darkness beyond the Verrakai front ranks, Paks saw torches moving.

"The Pargunese," said the king quietly, beside her. "They'll attack now too."

"In the dark?" asked Ammerlin.

"Yes—they've got torchbearers."

"How long—?" began Ammerlin.

"Paks," the king interrupted. "Can you sustain your light for long?"

"I don't know," said Paks. "I haven't tried to hold it and fight both."

"We'll fight," he said grimly. "Give us light, and we'll fight."

Even before she asked, her light came, brighter than before. For an instant, she remembered the golden light that hung above Sibili the night they took the wall. Now her own light, unshadowed, lit the narrow valley. The Pargunese cohorts stopped abruptly, then wheeled into position. Verrakaien shaded their eyes, then looked down. She saw the orcs pause at the wood's edge, throw up their shields, and keep coming: a dark wave. Her light flashed from shifting eyes, from the edges of swords and the tips of spears. She saw a folokai's teeth glint, then it turned and loped away to the west and north. The red horse wheeled beneath her as her eyes swept the scene. The enemy pressed close, compressing the square into a tight mass. The remaining cavalry mounts shifted nervously, ears back and tails clamped down.

Then the enemy cohorts attacked. Paks ignored the screams, the arrows that flashed by her head, the clangor of arms. With all her might she prayed, holding light above them.

Chapter Thirty-one

How long she might have sustained the light, Paks never knew. All at once the piercing sweet call of an elvenhorn lifted her heart, the sound she had heard in Kolobia and never forgotten. She looked east. A wave of silver light rolled down the forested slope, as if the starlight had taken form. Out of the trees rode what none there had ever seen. Tall, fair, mounted on horses as pale as starlit foam, they cried aloud in ringing voices that made music of battle. Rank after rank they came, bringing with them the scent of spring, and the light of elvenhome kingdoms that is neither sun nor star.

The orcs nearest them faltered, looked back, and broke. Before the orcs could run, the first rank of elven knights was on them, trampling them. The flank of the Verrakaien cohort on that side panicked and scattered. One group of elves peeled away, harrying the fugitives; the others advanced in order. At their center rode one not in armor. Paks stared, hardly believing her eyes. She looked away, to see that the Pargunese, deserted by the Verrakaien, were withdrawing in order. Another group of elven knights rode by the far side of the square. The light enclosed the defenders, walling them off from their enemies.

The sounds of flight came clearly through the air—the quick thunder of the elven knights' horses, the cries, the distant skirmishes. But all around the king a pool of silence widened, broken less and less by voices and movement, and coming at last to completion. Without a word, the front ranks of the square, Dorrin's cohort, opened a lane for the elven riders. Without a word, the king came forward to greet them.

With the great elven sword still glowing in his hand, he looked a king out of legend. And the Lady on her horse bowed to him. He slipped off his helmet and handed it to Lieth, who had followed him that far. Then he set the sword point down before him, and bent his knee to her.

"Lady," he said, in a voice Paks had not heard him use. "You honor us."

"Sir king," she said, and Paks had to believe now who she was. "You honor us, both our kindred and our land."

He lifted his head. "You consent to this?"

"Rise, sir king." She gestured to the sword. "I have seen my daughter's son defend his own with his own sword. I have heard and seen how that sword answers his need. We came here to greet you in all joy, and we rejoice to greet you in time."

He had climbed to his feet; now he brought the sword to her side. She leaned from her tall mount to touch his head: one light touch, with a hand that glowed like silver fire. Her voice chimed with amusement.

"Were I minded differently, son of my daughter, the enemies you make would be good witnesses for you. No wicked man could contrive to have all these assault him at once; he would ally with one or another of them."

The king laughed. "Lady, I thank you for your faith. Surely a stupid man might blunder into this?"

"I think not. Stupid men are too cautious. But, sir king, I have drawn you from a battle unfinished. Perhaps you would be free to finish it? My knights are at your disposal."

The king glanced back at the defenders. "With your permission, Lady, we will cleanse this valley of such perils for the future." She bowed, and he returned to them.

Suddenly Paks realized that she was not sustaining her own light. Whether it failed from weakness or surprise she did not know; they stood under the elflight alone. But the king, coming back into the square, commanded her attention. Still bareheaded, his face conveyed a majesty that even Paks had not imagined.

"We will not harry the Pargunese," he said. "I suspect they were lured here, and the Verrakaien intended to blame them for the massacre. But the priests of Liart, the orcs, and the Verrakaien—these must be accounted for."

"And you, my lord?" asked Dorrin.

"I will stay, and speak with the Lady, if she will."

That night the enemy found themselves penned by the forest taig, which would not let them pass, while a line of elven knights swept the valley from side to side. Elflight lay over them, leaving no place to hide. The three Marshals and Paks rode with them, hunting the priests of Liart. By dawn, which added a golden glow to the radiance around, Paks had killed two more of them; the Marshals each had killed one, and the elves found one dead of wounds. A score of gibbas lay dead, and more than a hundred orcs, and a score of folokai. The Pargunese cohorts stood in a sullen lump at the far end of the valley, where trees closed off the escape. The Verrakaien had broken into several groups, all now under guard. The Konhalt archers, having lost more than half their number, huddled together not far from the king's company. As for the followers of Liart, they had fled pell-mell, and most had been ridden down in the last of the fighting.

Paks rode back toward the king's company through the blended light of dawn and elven power, still musing over the Lady's arrival. She joined the Marshals in praying healing for the wounded. When the last one lay resting quietly, she felt a presence and turned.

Behind her stood the Lady, now watching Paks as closely as she had watched the king before.

"Paladin of Gird, I would speak with you. Come." Paks followed her a little way from the line of wounded. New grass carpeted the ground; every blade seemed to glow with its own light. The Lady led her near the stream, now edged with yellow flowers. Here the Lady spread her cloak on the bank, and gestured to Paks to sit with her. Gingerly Paks folded her legs and sat. For a moment, as it seemed, they listened to the singing water, now released from winter.

"We did not come for battle," said the Lady finally. "I wished to meet Falkieri myself, first, before he came to Chaya."

"I remember," said Paks.

"I do not mean to injure your honor when I say that it seemed better to attend to that myself. We had heard you were taken, that you had asked a Kuakgan to rouse the taig in his behalf." Her gaze sharpened a moment. "If it is a matter of the taigin, Paksenarrion, it is a matter for elves."

Paks shook her head. "I am sorry, Lady—I only knew it must be aware for him, and the Kuakkganni came to mind."

"We forgive you. After all, you were healed by one; we knew you meant no insult. But even so, it seemed wise to us to come and greet him. It is true that we knew he might find trouble, but it has been so long since I traveled in these lands that I did not know how bad it was. The Tree grieves, paladin, to harbor such in its shade, and the Singer is mute." For a moment she was silent, running her hands over the grass as a man might fondle his dog. "Yet the Singer and the Tree joined together in praise, and we came when the time was accomplished. I am well pleased, Paksenarrion, with my daughter's son; you spoke truly when you said he would be a worthy king."

Paks said nothing; reft of argument, she could do nothing but stare at the Lady.

"And I am well pleased with Gird's paladin," she went on. "We have heard how you entered captivity for the king, in Vérella; we grieved, thinking you surely doomed, and yet you are here, defending him still. Will you tell that tale, Paladin of Gird, that it may be sung rightly in our kingdoms?"

Paks looked away, watching the swift water tumble and swirl between smooth rocks. She thought she saw the quick metallic flash of a fish. "Lady," she said. "I would not dwell on those days—they are better forgotten than sung. Nor can any human tell a whole tale: only the gods know all of it."

"Would you truly forget your torments? We owe you much, Paksenarrion, Paladin of Gird. If you wish we can fill your mind with joy, and erase every scar that reminds you of that pain."

Paks shook her head, meeting the Lady's eyes once more. "No. I thank you for the thought of that gift. But what I am now—what I can do—comes from that. The things that were so bad, that hurt so. If I forget them, if I forget such things still happen, how can I help others? My scars prove that I know myself what others suffer."

"Wisely said," she replied. "Though an elf need see no scar to know what you are and what you have done. But we must make some song of you, for your service to our king."

"Let it be imagined from what you know of the Master of Torments: it is much the same, I daresay, wherever and whenever men desire power and the use of power on others."

"You can tell at least how you escaped, and how you came to be here."

Paks laughed, suddenly and unaccountably eased. "I could if I knew." She related, briefly, Arvid's confused and incredible tale, adding, "Thieves lie, as everyone knows, and tales of wonder grow quickly: but Liart's brand changed to this—" she touched the circle on her brow.

"But you arrived with a cohort of the king's own mercenaries, and a band of yeomen—how was that?"

Paks explained about meeting Dorrin in Westbells, and the journey east, and finding the apathetic Marshal in Darkon Edge. When she had finished, the Lady nodded.

"So the servants of evil forged in their own fires a weapon to defeat them—that makes a well-rounded song.

Falkieri through all his years took whatever came to him of good and used it well, learning kingship without a kingdom. You did the same, learning what good you could of all you met—even a Kuakgan." Her smile took the sting out of that. "Truly, the high gods will be pleased with this day's work, Paksenarrion. The forest taig is clean, from here to Lyonya—"

"What?" asked Paks, startled.

"You saw what happened before we came—all the unclean things that ran from the forest?" Paks thought of the folokai and gibbas, and nodded. "Those cannot abide the touch of our kingdoms, so when I rode there, and brought as I must the elvenhome light with me, they fled."

"They were fleeing you?" Paks asked.

"Even so—but they are dangerous in their fear."

"And beyond, the forest barrier—was that you?"

"No. You asked the Kuakkganni to rouse the taigin for you; the Kuakgan who holds the barrier west of this valley will speak to you when you wish."

Paks could feel the blood leaving her face. "The Kuakgan —who—"

The Lady laughed gently. "And what did you think would happen if you roused the taig?"

Paks fought her muddled head. "I thought—I suppose—that it would—would let him know if evil neared—would protect him."

"And so it has. But you asked a Kuakgan; he has done this in his way. I do not interfere with the Shepherds of Trees." She looked past Paks, toward the western side of the valley. Then she smiled again. "But you, Paladin of Gird—what can we do for you? Are you beyond any wish we could grant?"

Paks shook her head. "I don't know, Lady. It's enough that it's over: the king is alive, and you accept him—" She said nothing about Gird's other purposes: they would mean nothing to elves.

"Gird is well served in you, Paksenarrion, as the king was. The Singer of Names has sung well. We will see you again; for now, I must return to Lyonya, and prepare for the king's journey. The knights remain, though I think none will trouble him now. Take off your helmet, will you?"

Without thinking, Paks slipped it off, and the knitted scarf slid down, exposing her head; she unwound it slowly. The Lady smiled, and touched her head with one hand. It felt cool and warm at once.

"It is little enough," said the Lady, "But I enjoyed your yellow hair in the sunlight, in Aliam Halveric's garden: I would see it again at court, when my daughter's son takes his throne." And all at once Paks felt the long strands warm and heavy on her head, brushing her neck, slipping past her shoulders, a golden tide that flowed to its former length and lay still, ready for braiding. "The Kuakkganni are not the only ones with healing gifts," said the Lady, her eyes bright.

Before Paks could frame an answer, the Lady withdrew, moving lightly to her horse and drawing in the elflight around her until Paks could see nothing but that brilliance. Then it was gone. Only the springing grass, still green, and the flowered border of the stream, were left to show her power. These did not wither in the sunlight of a late winter morning, for the air was still warmer than it had been. Paks sat motionless for a time that might have been only a moment, or an hour. Then she took the long heavy hair in her hands, and braided it quickly, her eyes burning with unshed tears. When it was done, she wrapped the braid around her head and put her helmet on, then looked around.

There, a few lengths away, the king stood talking to several of the elven knights, with his squires beside him. High Marshal Seklis stood near, and Ammerlin of the Royal Guard. Beyond, yeomen of Darkon Edge and soldiers of Dorrin's cohort sat around two cookfires; already Paks could smell roasting meat. Others were busy gathering and stacking arms and supplies from the enemy's camps and the supply train. A tall man in a cowled robe bent over one of the Royal Guard horses, running his hands down its leg. Paks walked that way. Closer, she could see the deep gash between stifle and hock. The man hummed, touching the wound gently; it closed over, leaving a dry scar.

"That should do," he said to the knight who held the bridle. "See that he gets extra grain, and fresh greens when you can find them." He turned his head and saw Paks watching. "Ah—Paksenarrion. I had word you could not come to the Grove, yet needed me."

"Sir, I—" Paks saw the glint of humor in his eyes. "I could not, at that time," she said at last.

"So—and you are here now. From what I saw last night, you also are healed of all the wounds you once bore. Is that true?"

"Yes," said Paks steadily. "By the High Lord's power, that is true."

"And so the gods declare they will not be bound in human patterns," said the Kuakgan. "Which both we and the elves know, who live apart from men." He smiled at her. "If I thought, Paksenarrion, that you were my creation, I would be proud. But you are like all of us a branch of the tree, or a song of the singer, as the elves prefer. I am glad for you, that you have come to your powers. And as always, you are welcome in my Grove."

"Sir, I thank you—and you should know how much I have to thank you for."

He waved his hand. "I but freed the trapped wilding, to grow as it could. Your skill is with steel, and mine with living things."

Paks grinned at him. "Yes—and with frightened ones. I have not forgotten, sir, and will not."

"And when did you eat last?" he asked tartly—but it was teasing.

"When I needed it," said Paks, laughing. "Will you come with me now, and share our meal?"

"I think not. I would not strain the patience of the knights—and the forest hereabouts is unsettled, and needs calming."

"Master Oakhallow," said Paks, and he turned back, silently. "If Gird sends me elsewhere than your Grove, then take my thanks, and know that I remember. I have nothing this time to give you that is mine to give, but this."

He nodded shortly. "Paladin of Gird, Paksenarrion, you have given all you could give to my grove and the taigin before now. Go free of all gifts and returns, and come as you please and as you may. You are in my heart, and in the forest taig, and in the elfane taig; the First Tree knows what fruit it bears." With that he was gone, walking swiftly into the trees where no path was.

Paks found that the king's squires had already pitched the king's tent; he was sitting under the flap of it, at a table with an elven knight, Sir Ammerlin, and the three Marshals. An empty place was set opposite him; as soon as he caught sight of Paks, he rose and called her over.

"Lady, we are about to eat—come, join us."

She took her seat at the empty place, and almost at once the squires handed around platters of roast meat and bread. She thought it strange to be eating like this with Pargunese and Verrakai troops under guard down the valley, but said nothing. The king seemed completely at ease. Some old hurt was gone, some bitterness had fled; his face showed his kinship to the elf beside him. Paks ate slowly, watching him. She could not define the difference, except that he seemed, if anything, younger than before.

For some time little was said. Beyond the clinking of knives at their own table, Paks could hear the others eating: Dorrin's cohort squad by squad, in order, the yeomen of Gird in a happy, disorderly crowd. Then the king spoke.

"Well, companions, we have seen another day come to birth: more than we thought last night, eh?"

Sir Ammerlin turned to him. "Sir king, I remember that you did not seem certain of death and defeat."

"Of death I am as certain as any mortal, Ammerlin, but defeat is certain only in despair. And I have been well taught that in the worst of times despair is still the work of evil." He looked at Paks, a look that said a great deal. "But we are alive, this fine morning, by the aid of the elven knights you command, sir," and he turned to the elf beside him. "You have our thanks for your timely arrival."

"And you have our regrets that we sent before us unworthy messengers of our coming," said the elf, laughing lightly. "By all the gods, I would not have landed those foul things on you!"

"The contrast," said the king drily, "was all the greater when you came. I did not quite despair, last night, knowing my companions to be who and what they were, but I little thought to be eating such a meal in such comfort as this, with so many of them spared to enjoy it." High Marshal Seklis laughed with the others, then set his elbows firmly on the table.

"That's all very well, my lord, but what about the Pargunese and the Verrakai troops? The Pargunese won't fight elves, but I doubt they'll march in your procession. As for the Verrakai—rotten root and branch, that family—"

"Not so," said the king quietly. "Captain Dorrin, of my Company, is Verrakai by birth. She has never been less than loyal to me, and just and honest to all. She's even crossed my will, where she thought me less."

"I didn't know—" muttered Seklis.

"No. You wouldn't. High Marshal, I am one to prune—severely, if necessary—and not one to root up the tree. I have known other honest Verrakai in my life; it's probably kept me from quarreling more with the Duke and his brother."

"But this can't be ignored," Seklis said angrily. "By Gird's arm, they defied the prince's power, attacked a traveller under royal protection, threatened to massacre us all—"

"I don't ignore it. They did all that—and for that they should face justice. But not my justice, High Marshal: this is not my kingdom. Were I to hold court here, and rule on this, I would myself be usurping the prince's powers. To him I am either a vassal or the king of a neighboring realm. I can make complaint in either sense, but in neither sense do I have a right to judge or sentence."

"Hmmph." Seklis settled back, disgruntled. The elf leaned forward.

"Then what do you plan, sir king?"

The king looked around the table. "I plan to let Tsaia rule itself, as it should. The prince must know this—the Council must know this—but they also need to know that the King of Lyonya did not exceed his authority. Seklis, you're the High Marshal in Tsaia—on the Council itself. You can bring what charges need be brought. Ammerlin, you're a commander in the Royal Guard, the prince's direct military representative. His authority flows through you; you can take what military action need be taken to ensure peace here until the Council and prince decide what to do. By Tsaian law, you Marshals have court-right over some things—such as the followers of Liart."

"And what will you do, sir king?"

"I will go to my kingdom," he replied mildly. "I have heard that they have need of me."

"Are you taking your cohort with you?" asked Ammerlin.

"I planned to, yes. I would not expect a single cohort to alarm Lyonya—would you think, sir elf?"

"Not at all," said the elf, smiling.

"Then you could stay here, Ammerlin, with the Royal Guard—"

"But we're your escort—"

"You were, yes. But now I have my cohort, and these elves, and you have no need to come farther."

They were interrupted just then by a shout from Dorrin, who had ridden east up the slope. Her cohort leaped back into formation; Paks found the red horse beside her as she stepped beyond the tent flap, and mounted. Then she saw what was coming down the road from the east, and nearly laughed in relief. Gird's crescent on a pennant, and the rose and silver bells and harp of Tsaia on another, two Gird's Marshals, and several hundred yeomen.

"Late," commented Suriya, after a quick look, "but welcome."

When the Marshals arrived, Paks recognized Marshal Pelyan; he introduced Berris, whose grange was the next to the east. He grinned at Paks, and nodded to the other Marshals.

"One of my yeomen came in the other day," he said, "with word of a strange cohort sneaking through the woods between Berris and me. From what he said, I thought it might be Pargunese; we looked and found boats hidden along the river. So I remembered what Paksenarrion had said, and rousted out my grange—"

"And then came storming into mine," said Berris. "I told him I didn't have many fit to fight, but I came along—"

"And we've come too late, I see," said Pelyan, looking around.

"Not so," said the king. "We cannot stay and deal with the Pargunese—"

"I told you!" Pelyan thumped Berris on the shoulder. "I knew those Tir-damned scum would be in this."

"—or the Verrakai," the king went on. "We must be on the road to Lyonya; your arrival gives High Marshal Seklis and Sir Ammerlin enough troops to take care of this."

Pelyan scratched his ear. "Well, sir—sir king—it's good to know we didn't have this long march for nothing. But I should tell you that some of these are Lyonyans, who left Lyonya for fear of war."

The king smiled. "And so you showed them that trouble follows those who flee it? Well done, Marshal; when you have them schooled to your liking, then send them home if they wish to go."

"You don't want to take them with you?"

The king let his eyes rove along the ranks, then pursed his lips. "No—I don't think so. Those in my party are proven fighters. Those who awaited events in Lyonya have shown steadfastness. These—these I leave to your care; you know best what they need."

* * *

For the rest of that day, the king's party rested before traveling. Those who had been killed were laid to rest with due ceremony; the enemy's dead was piled and burned. Under the Marshal's directions, the yeomen took control of the Pargunese and Verrakai prisoners, containing them at a distance from the king's encampment. The horses of Dorrin's cohort were found still waiting at the ridgetop to the east, penned, as Paks explained it, by the taig. Dorrin looked at her oddly, but said nothing more about it.

In the morning, they set out for Lyonya again. Paks rode beside the king, at his request. With no pack train to slow them down, they made good time and rode into Harway just at dark, where the Lyonyan Guard waited in formation to greet him. Bonfires flared as the king came into his own land; candles burned at every window, and torchbearers lined the streets. Both Marshal and Captain came to bow before him. Paks saw distant fires spring to life, carrying the news across the darkness.

The king said little: courteous words for those who greeted him, but nothing more. Paks saw tears glisten on his cheeks in the firelight. They stayed that night in Harway, the king at the royal armory, and Paks at the grange, to ease the Marshal's memory of her earlier visit.

By the time the king's party reached Chaya, the last snow had melted away, filling the rivers with laughing water.

"An early spring," said the king, looking at the first flowering trees glimmering through the wood. "I feel the forest rejoicing."

"Do you?" Amrothlin, who had come to meet him, smiled. "That is well. Both the rejoicing of the forest, and your feeling it. Your elven senses wake: you feel the taig singing you home, and your response calls forth more song. So the season answers your desire."

The king looked across green meadows to the towering trees that made the palace seem small, a child's toy. Tears glittered in his eyes. "So beautiful—they almost break the heart."

"This is the heartknot of the joining of elvenkind and

man," said Amrothlin. "We put what we could of our elvenhome kingdom in it. Be welcome, sir king, in your kingdom."

Between them and the city a crowd was gathering, pouring out of the city in bright chips of color like pebbles from a sack. The king's party rode through a broad lane, past those who cheered, and those who stood silently, watching with wide eyes the return of their lost prince. Paks felt her own heart swell almost to bursting when the music began, the harps that elves delight in, horns both bright and mellow in tone, all singing the king home.

That music followed into the palace itself, where the lords of Lyonya, the Siers and their families, waited to welcome the king. One by one they knelt to him, then stepped back. When old Hammarrin came forward, he peered into the king's face a moment, as if looking for the boy he had known, then reached to touch his hand.

"Sir king—you do your father justice."

"You knew him?" asked the king gently.

"Aye—and you as a tiny lad. Thank the gods you've returned, Falki—let me call you that just this once, as I used to do." Then he stepped back, nodding, for his old knees were too stiff to kneel.

When all had acknowledged him, the king turned to Paksenarrion.

"Lady, your quest brought me to this court: is it discharged?"

"Not yet, sir king." Paks turned to the assembly. "You, in Council here, bid me find your lost prince and bring him. I have brought him now, and his sword proves him. Are you content?"

"We are content," they answered.

And of all the deeds of the paladin Paksenarrion, it is this for which she is best known in the middle lands of the Eight Kingdoms, for restoring the lost king to his throne, and thereby saving Lyonya from the perils of misrule and confusion. Which of her deeds most honored the gods she served, only the High Lord knows, who judges rightly of all deeds, whatever tales men tell or elves sing.

In the chronicles of that court, it is said that the coronation of Falkieri Amrothlin Artfielan Phelan (for he kept the name he had used so long) was outdone in joy and ceremony only by his marriage some time later. Falkieri ruled long and faithfully, and in his time the bond of elf and man was strengthened. Peace and prosperity brought honor to his reign. And after him the crown passed to his eldest, and to her son and her son's sons after.

As for Paksenarrion, she was named King's Friend, with leave to go or stay as she would, and when Gird's call came, she departed for another land.

POUL ANDERSON

Poul Anderson is one of the most honored authors of our time. He has won seven Hugo Awards, three Nebula Awards, and the Gandalf Award for Achievement in Fantasy, among others. His most popular series include the Polesotechnic League/Terran Empire tales and the Time Patrol series. Here are fine books by Poul Anderson available through Baen Books: